STARBIRTH ASSIGNMENT

SHIFTER

J M JOHNSON

This book is a work of fiction. Names, characters, places and incidents are either a product of the author's imagination or are used fictitiously. Any resemblance to actual people, living or dead, is entirely coincidental. Where real locations have been used, the settings and characters within them are entirely fictional.

ISBN-13: 978-1535187404

ISBN-10: 1535187409

Dedication

This book is dedicated to the Armed Services and Special Forces of the United Kingdom and their allies, who are engaged in battles far removed from the public eye. They face dangers and horrors on a daily basis that most people in the West will never experience during a whole lifetime. Special Forces are particularly at the 'cutting edge' of warfare and their courage, professionalism and commitment is astounding. These people are the true heroes compared to any fictional counterpart.

Acknowledgements

There are many people I would like to thank for their input regarding the Starbirth series of books: firstly my family and dear friends for their love and support. Theresa F gave me valuable guidance and inspiration in the early days.

Without the unwavering enthusiasm, encouragement and support of Paul M, and Rosemary and Bob E, I would have given up long ago. They have been instrumental in keeping me writing.

I would also like to thank the ex-Special Forces veterans and also Mark and Avril, for answering a multitude of questions about military life, terminology, attitudes and all the rest, with considerable patience.

Many thanks go to my editor, who provided valuable insights and whose suggestions have been brilliant. She worked hard and conscientiously on the books and improved their readability. I will be forever grateful for her efforts and highly recommend her services to any other author.

Andy King, whose amazing cover art turned the books into something special.

Lastly there are two people, who wish to remain anonymous, who made invaluable contributions regarding the content of the book.

My thanks to all of the above whose input, in whatever form, was essential.

Contents

CHAPTER 1

The Special Air Service Officer Commanding put down his Satphone.

'Mr Lock, we've just lost the last air cover. Search and Rescue teams are returning to base. Conditions are too dangerous for going out, especially alone.'

Lock Harford reclined in his seat at a switched-off computer console and smiled at the patronising tone and the mistake over his name.

'I can look after myself, Captain Bilton. I got here on my own. Show me where Dagger Four's bike was found and where he was seen afterwards.'

Outside the blacked-out windows of the British Army communications truck a heavy Sea King helicopter flew overhead, so close it sent shivers down the truck's reinforced framework and blew a blizzard of snow against the roof. Lights flickered on a built-in wall of electronics, radar, screens and radio equipment before settling. A girl soldier monitoring radio frequencies of the search teams waited for the noise to reduce back to howling wind before resuming a radio conversation. A bulky soldier at a separate workstation studied virtual terrain maps.

Lock made eye contact with the OC, a stocky, pallid man with prematurely thinning hair. Bilton's mouth twitched in an impatient grimace, but he broke eye contact, got up and bent over Lock's shoulder, switching on the computer. Lock saw his own reflection in a panel of shiny plastic next to the monitor. A pair of dark eyes stared at him, their normal open good nature narrowed by grim determination. His dark hair was messy judged by the military standards of his companions. Four-day-old stubble covered the lower third of his face disguising a square-set jaw line with a full mouth. It made his straight nose more of a feature than it would be without the beginnings of a beard. Well-developed muscles in his neck hinted at a sturdy framework underneath, his five-foot-eleven build kept in shape more by genetic predisposition than hours spent in the gym.

'The teams are fully stretched,' Bilton said, returning to his seat and synchronising the computers to share the screen page. 'The only reason you're here is because I've been asked to co-operate with you. If you get into trouble there's no help. I won't endanger anybody else for your sake.'

'Noted. The locations,' Lock repeated, suppressing his irritation. He unzipped his outer layer of mountaineering shell suit, delved into a chest pocket in his jacket and took out his ruggedised computer. Using a secure password he connected it wirelessly to the mainframe in readiness. Bilton would normally have comprehensive reports about everybody of interest to the Special Air Service, but didn't know who Lock was beyond his recent role as a winter survival instructor. Lock considered telling Bilton the truth about his abilities and his unique relationship with the SAS, but something more than Bilton's terse manner prevented him. Gut instinct, not mere dislike, warned him not to say anything. He couldn't put his finger on what was wrong, but Bilton's eyes conveyed something deeper and darker than the common military suspicion regarding interfering men who held a civilian rank.

Bilton's cursor indicated a triangular red marker on the computer screen. 'We found the bike near the Linn of Dee where the road turns. As for the sightings, two of the three are not confirmed. Here at Devil's Point, and at Angel's Peak.' The cursor pointed at more markers on the computer map. 'Twice the helicopter picked up body heat and a man's outline, but when the teams arrived there was no sign of him.'

'A fault with the thermal imaging equipment?' Lock asked, studying the map.

'That's what we suspected, but ten kilometres away at Derry Cairngorm the helo picked up a heat signature two hours ago. The team there thought it was Dagger Four but when they shouted, he ran off and disappeared in the blizzard. That's our best sighting so far.'

'They definitely saw a person?'

'They wouldn't have called it in if they hadn't.'

Lock ignored the sarcasm. He tapped in the coordinates of the last known position of the missing man and returned his ruggedised computer to its waterproof pouch in his pocket, leaving a length of cable exposed. The computer had wireless connectivity to his helmet and visor via electrode implants on both sides of Lock's head, but he liked to have a cable back-up.

'Okay, that's where I'll start my search.'

'It's a waste of time. I don't see how you can get there and it's already been searched. Angel's Peak is closer.' Bilton switched off the monitor and returned to his own computer screen, ignoring Lock.

'No harm in looking again,' Lock said to Bilton's back. He picked up his bergen, a heavy military rucksack, with one hand and slung it over his broad shoulders. His actions were automatic as he pulled on his helmet. The visor received a signal from Lock's computer and updated all its computer graphics displaying altimeter settings, a virtual map of the terrain with cursor marks, and compass bearings. Lock connected the helmet to the computer cable sticking out of his pocket and went through a series of radio checks with one of the computer operators.

He tugged on close-fitting thermal gloves before speaking to Bilton.

'I'll report at thirty-minute intervals. My call sign is Ghost.'

Bilton acknowledged with a curt nod. Lock turned for the door, paused and looked back as if struck by an afterthought.

'If you get stuck up here, mate, give me a shout. I'll be happy to help.' He smiled at Bilton's glare, zipped up his jacket to cover his neck and mouth, and left.

A gust of freezing wind nearly ripped the door from his grasp when he stepped outside. He slammed it shut and faced the steep sides of the valley. Swirling air filled with icy particles whipped at his shell suit, flattening the thin outer layer of Goretex against his body. He trudged uphill, using a snow-covered wall as a guide to show him where a path would have been. Derry Cairngorm lay ten kilometres to the north of the Linn of Dee, over terrain known to be difficult by day, and feared as treacherous at night in an approaching hurricane.

Normal drugs didn't account for Mackenzie's ability to trek across the Grampians at the speed indicated by the markers. It could be a long night of cat and mouse. Lock didn't want to dwell on the other possibility. Given his state of mind and his misfortune of being lost during the worst winter conditions in mid-December for decades, Jimmy Mackenzie, code named Dagger Four, might be lying dead in the snow.

Lock's boots sank into drifts with every step. He glanced back. Even though he had only gone nine metres up the bare hillside he couldn't make out the radio antenna or globe satellite dish on top of the truck. A few steps further and he couldn't see either the truck or the farm buildings further down the road. He had walked far enough. Using voice command he switched the radio receiver to an encrypted signal similar to the one his satellite phone used and focused his mind. If anybody looked his way they would see nothing but blizzard. Lock stood in a cleared area where snow slowed and drifted as though caught in outer space. He lifted out of the snow and teleported, fading in a second.

At a height of three thousand metres, the winds subsided to the point where Lock could levitate above the clouds, hovering steadily to attempt a clear satellite link and update the GPS settings and extra information needed for his virtual reality visor. The connection faltered as the visor indicated a fault with satellite coverage. Lock cursed at the time lost in reconnecting to a different system and the effort expended in hovering. In his mind's special sense, the gravitational pull of Earth was weaker and he couldn't rise any further otherwise his connection to the ground would break. If the mental link broke he would plummet towards solid ground. It had happened before. On three occasions he lost concentration and fought to regain control on the way down. After so many years of levitation-flying – or levi-flying as the scientists named it – he was a good judge of the strength or weakness of the levitation bond anchoring him to Earth when he was in the air.

Years earlier, when he was full of questions about how he managed to levitate and teleport, he gained an insight. A research scientist, a young woman, thought she had an answer.

'It's to do with quantum technology, but it's based in nature. Have you seen lizards sticking upside down on ceilings? They have a way of using a force that attracts objects and glues them together. It allows them to climb upside down against the laws of gravity. We call it the Casimir force. During levi-flying and teleportation – or Shifting as you call it – you use a reverse Casimir force. It repels objects, rather than attracting them. We think that's the mechanism that allows you to levitate and Shift. We've been able to reproduce the reverse Casimir force in the laboratory, but only on a cellular level. We've managed to get microscopic objects to levitate.'

The satellite link reconnected. Using thought command Lock rushed to the menu settings on his visor, eager to download the updates he needed to resume the search for Mackenzie over the whole of Scotland. The connection was slow, and his thoughts drifted back to his discussion about levitation hovering.

'You mean it's like positive and negative matter, working the same way as magnetic fields?'

'It's more complicated than that. The reverse Casimir force is like turning the key in a car ignition. It's only the start.'

'And that enables me to Shift?'

'Not exactly. We've done a lot of research on Shifting, but we still don't know what's involved. All I can tell you is that there's something like another dimension all around us, called dark matter. We can't see it, or touch it, but there's five times more of it than what we call our world. It isn't made of atoms in the way that we are. It's at the edge of our understanding of the universe. It's like black holes – you can't view them, you only know they're there because of the way things act in this universe when they're in close proximity to one. It's the same with dark matter. We think teleportation involves a dimensional shift. You move through another dimension.'

Lock had left the research facility in shock. It took him three weeks and more questions to digest the information and accept the possibility of the existence of another dimension, despite knowing that he could see things that other people couldn't. He never thought of his other world as another dimension. It gave him more respect for what he was doing. He had taken teleportation for granted because he could do it so easily.

Lock's thoughts ended when his visor informed him he had an incoming phone call. The name, Steven Stringer, flashed up on the transparent menu panel. He ignored the call. Stringer didn't know about the Starbirth poisoning in Scotland and Lock wanted to get on with the search. The advent of Starbirth, an illegal mind-enhancing drug, meant many more people could teleport, but they didn't have Lock's knowledge or respect for what they were doing and they made some terrible mistakes. Jimmy Mackenzie, the missing man, was in danger, possibly teleporting against his conscious will. He could be anywhere in the world, but in all likelihood his confusion meant he wouldn't have the skill to stray very far from Scotland. All his known contacts in Scotland had been traced and checked, with no sign of him, and Military Command put two soldiers on guard at his parents' home near Fort William in case he showed up there.

Lock went over large areas of the virtual map, trying to second-guess Mackenzie's movements and where he might find shelter from the bitter weather. Stringer was still trying to get through on the phone. While Lock pored over the maps he accepted the encrypted call.

'There's been an incident in Scotland,' Stringer said, against a background of helicopter engine noise.

'I know. I'm at the place now.'

'Oh. Right.'

Lock heard the unspoken question in Stringer's voice, the disquiet over how Lock knew about the missing person problem before Stringer told him. In Stringer's sphere of influence regarding Lock's deployments he prided himself on being the first to know any reliable intelligence and the first to pass it on. Lock answered the question before Stringer asked.

'I was here already. They were my patrol. I'd just finished teaching them a survival skills refresher course.'

'Right. Wait one second.'

Lock pictured him looking through his computerised diary for notes headed Lock's Movements. Lock accessed the menu on his visor. The GPS setting flashed green and changed the virtual map to show a coordinate fix and compass bearing for Derry Cairngorm, thirty kilometres distant from the mobile Forward Operating Base Lock had just left.

'Any news on what was taken?' Stringer asked.

'Nothing confirmed but it looks like Starbirth.' Lock turned east, levi-flying towards the place where the obscured Cairngorm mountain peaks would be.

'How the hell did it happen?'

What Stringer meant was; how could a patrol of sharp lads from the Special Air Service Regiment do something as stupid as take an illegal drug, let alone take it in public?

'I don't know. I left them in the pub at Braemar. I was getting ready to leave Scotland when I heard about it.'

'How many are missing?'

'Just one. If the others are anything to go by, he's hallucinating. He could be teleporting. I have to go, I'm looking for him. We'll talk about this later.'

'Okay, I'll be at Braemar in two hours.'

'Hang on, my map's showing a change. The wind speed at ground level is registering in excess of one hundred and forty kilometres per hour. Looks like the hurricane has altered course. You're heading directly into it.'

'I'll pass that on to the pilot.'

Lock broke the connection and teleported to half a kilometre above Derry Cairngorm, where he arrived seconds later. Apart from the usual hissing in his ears, the travel was too short to experience much beyond the grey shapes that he flashed past and through. Teleporting exhilarated him. He felt alive after it. Wiping snow from his visor, he descended unsteadily in the gale force wind, slipping into mental awareness of the mountain as he drew close to it.

The frozen landscape transformed into a bleak panorama as though the snow had been washed away. Blurry black masses rose in front of him, the darkest areas indicating dense rock. The landscape moved with a life of its own, parted by grey lines that wriggled in and out of view like snakes caught by their tails. Years of experience told him he sensed peaks and ridges of a mountain beneath the snow, its lower levels furrowed by streams plunging down the sides. The mountain lay naked before him. The fingers of his mind crept over it like the caress of a lover, exploring the secret places; a soft curve here, a harder ridge there giving way to a rise that swept upwards before it dived and turned in an arc taking it past another dense, black mound.

He found what he wanted and landed in a sheltered place on the lee side of the mountain ridge. Staying in his grey world he searched for signs of life among the dark barriers of dense rock. He read the ground as if thumbing through a dog-eared book, touching and recognising, dismissing and moving on. Enfolded within the greyness he found a few small animals hidden in holes beneath the snow. He knew them by their colour. Their life signals – what he called auras – appeared in his mind's eye as tiny, wispy clouds that twisted and turned, always changing shape. Soft tendrils curled, dissolved and flicked out again. Passing over one animal, a visceral connection existed and he bonded with the mauve aura for a fraction of a second.

He pushed his senses further until the mental input from all directions became an overload and his mind disengaged from the widening circle. If Mackenzie was anywhere within it Lock would have found him. Lifting off the ground, he moved two hundred metres east down the mountain and tried again, with the same result. Working methodically, he boxed the area with overlapping circles until he covered several kilometres within twenty minutes. All he found near the foot of another mountain were the blue human auras of one of the search teams, toiling back to base. He covered craggy terrain until his energy ran out, which it did quickly when using both levi-flying and sensory probing together, so he stopped to make a satellite radio call.

'Ghost to Zero, come in.'

Bilton took his time answering.

'Zero to Ghost, go ahead.'

'No luck at Derry Cairngorm.'

'Are you sure you are at Derry Cairngorm? Over.'

'I'm going west of it. No sign of our man over fifty square kilometres. Switching to Angel's Peak and Devil's Point.'

'This is not the time to play games, Mr Lock. I suggest you get into shelter and stop arsing around as though you're–' the radio call tailed off.

'Ghost to Zero, repeat please. Over.'

'Zero to Ghost, just get back here. Over.'

Lock thought wryly that the penny must have dropped as he headed for Angel's Peak. Turning his attention back to the search, he was on his own and would have to re-think his strategy, because when he finished covering an area and moved on Mackenzie might teleport back to it. That could go on all night. He had to think like Mackenzie and try to figure out where instinct would lead him. Apart from pubs, nowhere nearby had significance for him as far as Lock knew. He had a strong hunch he would find Mackenzie in the mountains. The Scot loved them because they were remote, but if Mackenzie stayed in the open, hypothermia would kill him. Time was running out.

The thought spurred Lock on and he switched to Devil's Point in the Cairngorms, then Angel's Peak, battling against the hurricane to stay aloft. Gusts of wind blew him out of alignment and he fought to complete his searches methodically. The minutes ticked by and he pushed harder. Half an hour passed. He stopped levi-flying and squatted in snow by the shelter of a rocky outcrop, taking time to rest and eat a muesli bar to restore his energy levels. Thoughts drifted to his latest compulsory interview with the Ministry of Defence psychiatrist. Lock hated these sessions and he attended because his contract with the MoD required his compliance.

The new psychiatrist introduced himself as Porter. A fifty-something in a crumpled suit, he was not up to speed on Lock's history. He shuffled the papers in his hands as though looking for an ace in a deck of cards and only came up with a six, in pointing out that Lock spent a long time in South America. With morbid curiosity Lock focused on a large wart on Porter's bald head as he bent over his folder. He told Porter that his time in South America wasn't that long; in fact it was only from the age of seven to thirteen, which could hardly be considered a long time.

If his words had any impact, Porter showed no sign of it, lapsing into silence while he flicked through the folder. He picked out a page and read it. Lock suggested returning later after his file had been read, and got up from his seat. Porter pushed his glasses back up on his nose with his index finger with the triumphant air of having found a knave in his pack of cards.

'I see that at the age of four, your aunt cared for you after school when you were in North London. Exactly how was your aunt abusive?'

'Not in the way you're thinking. She didn't do anything sexually. She was just a nutcase whose idea of after school care was to lock me in her cellar when she thought I'd been naughty.'

'I see,' Porter said, in the meaningful manner reserved for psychiatrists who can see a whole world of trauma in one sentence. 'Did you tell your parents?'

'Not for a long time. I thought it was normal. Part of the after school routine.'

Porter had changed tack and interrupted with a blunt question about why Lock experienced problems with rocks, buildings and caves. Lock was exasperated. He could see the connection Porter made between the cellar and being underground, but the man latched on to the wrong reason. Lock said he'd always had problems with them, it was nothing new. Porter wasn't going to let him off the hook. He wanted to know exactly how Lock had problems.

Lock gestured at the notes.

'It's all in there, isn't it?'

'I'd like to hear it in your own words.'

Lock resigned himself to repeating something he had said many times before.

'I can sense creatures, humans and objects in a way that nobody else can. I see living beings as colours. Things like bricks and rock are shades of grey and black. In open countryside it's very clear, up to a radius of four hundred metres – but substances like thick walls and outcrops of stone deflect my senses. If I go in a cave, for example, where I'm surrounded by stone, I'm pretty much blind.'

With a shiver of excitement Lock jolted back from the meeting in London to his icy surroundings in the Cairngorms. Caves. A couple of days before, Mackenzie said something about exploring newly discovered cave formations by the River Nethy and how he wanted to go back there. The place lay more than twenty-five kilometres north from where his bike was found, but for a man flying high on Starbirth, the distance posed no obstacle. Lock scanned his virtual map, obtained a GPS fix halfway along the river and headed further north above the Cairngorms. He regretted not paying more attention to what Mackenzie said. The name Bynack Beg was familiar, and he recalled Mackenzie's description of his caving team being forced to abseil to the entrance as there was no other way of reaching it.

That implied a cave in a cliff face.

Levi-flying blind, he switched to using his senses and descended towards a gully between mountains. He went into a hover to explore the cliff, buffeted by fierce winds. In the physical world, he could only see six metres in any direction. Thick rock stood proud of the snow in sheer black sheets, criss-crossed by small lines of white ice on narrow horizontal ridges. In sensory mode, the sharp-edged surface dropped below his feet at least thirty metres. Folds and clefts imitated cave entrances.

Several times he thought he found the entrance, only to discover another jagged fracture in the rocks, and then the southern end of the cliff face ran out. He turned away, pushed from behind by gusts that threatened to knock him into the rocks. Passing his start point, he rounded a ragged outcrop and stopped, probing with his special sense. His excitement rose when he saw deeper into the mountain. He could not detect any aura within and the sharp fissure entrance gave no sign that a cave lay beyond, but Lock sensed a lengthy gap piercing the rock. He had found a tunnel.

He teleported a short distance into it and crouched on dry, sharp rocks while behind him air ripped in a hollow moan across the front of the tunnel, like a giant blowing across the end of a tube. Attaching a small LED torch onto the side of his helmet he crawled forward a couple of metres in the narrow tunnel and peered at a rounded passageway on his left.

'Jimmy?' he called, scanning floor ridges and jutting rock shelves. He listened for another voice or the sounds of human presence, willing a reply that never came. The inescapable task of carrying on hung over his head more oppressively than the slanted roof.

'Bloody caves,' he muttered. 'Why did it have to be a cave?'

Every time he entered a cave formation, something bad happened. Above ground, mountains were his guides. He played teleporter bagatelle with their icy peaks, zipping from one to another along remote mountain ranges. Below ground it was a different matter. They tried to crush him with rock falls or sent cascades of water leaping through their dried up channels, attempting to flush him out like an infestation of vermin. He had explored many caves and underground passages during military exercises, but he never enjoyed the experience. All he felt was relief and a sense of achievement when the training ended.

He took off his bergen and pushed into the tunnel. The channel didn't extend far before it became cramped and several side passages led from it into the depths. Lock reversed, picked up his bergen and pulled out a container the size of a tub of butter. Accessing the menu setting on his visor by voice control, he opened the box and activated four small flying drones. The nano-aerial vehicles lifted off and followed his computer instructions to navigate the main channel and three smaller tunnels. Radio contact was lost as they went deeper into the mountain.

While he waited for them to return, he scrambled to the tunnel mouth and made a call to Bilton with information about his plans.

'What you're doing is bloody crazy. And how the hell did you get there?' Bilton replied.

'I'm going. Over.' Lock cut the connection.

Three flying drones returned. One didn't come back. Looking at footage from the survivors on his visor, it seemed two of the drones turned back when they hit dead ends. Only one meandered on until low battery power forced it to return, but they provided valuable updates of the underground terrain. End footage of the cramped longer channel showed it was blocked by rock falls, though he might be able to Shift past the obstruction to see if anything lay beyond it.

He replaced the batteries in the drones, put them back in their container and pulled out equipment from his bergen. He needed to reduce his girth. Taking off his shell suit he donned a belt kit, a piece of military clothing resembling a mesh waistcoat with pouches attached, and reorganised the pouches. Dumping most of his supplies by the entrance, he kept essentials such as a couple of first aid pouches, emergency rations and water, a spare LED torch, Leatherman multi-tool, batteries for his computer and torches, a survival sheet, strong ropes and thin nylon marker rope to act as a navigation aid. He tied one end of the marker rope round a boulder and took a couple of deep breaths. The cold tunnel resembled an empty artery with smooth sides. Looking at it his special sense told him no more than the torchlight, except that it was claustrophobic.

Small stones crunched and scattered under his feet when he moved forward and wriggled inside. After a short distance he emerged, like a wet worm, into a higher space where he could stand. A hard left face bulged over his head before meeting the right in a sharp peak like a crooked church steeple. Going forward he levitated where he could. Teleportation in the side channels was impossible, as he found out when he was bounced back out, sliding on slopes covered by fine grit. He cursed Mackenzie as he forced himself to go back along the main passageway the hard way, and slithered along seventy metres of shrinking tunnel that plucked at his clothes, squeezed his chest, and captured his boots.

Forty minutes later he clambered along a ledge past an overhanging boulder and fell as he leaned at an awkward angle. It happened too fast for him to go into a hover. He dropped into a crevice with his hips wedged between the sides, unable to move up or down.

'Damn it,' he yelled in frustration, scrabbling with his fingers and boots at the hard surfaces. Somewhere in the distance he thought he heard a sound that wasn't an echo of his own voice.

Holding his breath, he listened. He heard his boots scraping on stone as he tried to regain his footing, but a faint sound reached his ears and he turned his head towards it. Somebody was singing. It sounded like a rough, guttural chant. Elated, he found a toehold, prised himself up and levitated out of the crevice, landing in a crouch on the tunnel floor. Singing implied reasonably good health. His visor located the direction of Mackenzie's voice. Lock crawled downwards along cold stone, zeroing in on the source of the alternated chanting and swearing, until a rolling, thick noise of heavy rock hitting rock reverberated along the tunnel. He stopped and listened in alarm.

'Jimmy.' His voice charged along the tunnel. He regretted shouting. It might drive Mackenzie away, just as he had run from his rescuers earlier. He cursed and quickened his crawl, reaching a place where the tunnel widened and allowed him room to stand hunched in front of the obstruction. His visor indicated the voice came from his right. He sent a drone into a tiny opening. Two minutes later it returned with evidence of a wider tunnel beyond. He teleported into it and pushed on. The tunnel turned right, then left, and as he ducked under a limestone arch it opened unexpectedly into a large expanse of cavern.

The view took his breath away. Rows of stalactites hung from the roof like folds of curtains. Water dripped from them onto rippled stalagmites, whose chunky bases emerged from pools of water like stunted plant stems that rose and petrified into hard columns. In two places stalactites met stalagmites to form a calcified dragon's tooth grin. Slippery rock walls curled in and out of view. On the left-hand side of the cavern there was a stony pedestal a metre and a half high, a giant's porridge pot with sticky limestone ripples overflowing wetly down its sides as they had done for thousands of years. Loose round boulders littered the cavern floor.

'Jimmy,' he called, but there was no reply. Taking out two more drones, he activated their thermal imaging settings and sent them into the cavern. One of them picked up the heat signature of what appeared to be a cooling body lying among the boulders.

'No,' Lock whispered, and he lifted from the ground to land next to Mackenzie. He raised his visor to see clearly, only to find a bundle of clothes with the sole of one boot lying sideways under a trouser leg. A faint noise distracted him and the light from his torch swung wildly as he turned his head. A naked figure hurtled towards him out of the shadows at a speed that took him by surprise. He saw Mackenzie's heavy-browed face twisted into a grimace of venom and caught the vicious glint of a knife in the man's right hand.

Instinct sent Lock hurtling upwards. The knife bit empty air and missed his raised feet by inches, but his head slammed into stalactites. He felt a sharp pain in his neck. Dazed despite his helmet, he plummeted. His right ankle twisted on slippery boulders and he fell in a heap letting out a grunt of agony, an animal sound that bounded back as though it came from somebody else. His head reeled like the shadows dancing over cavern walls. In the swinging torchlight he caught sight of Jimmy turning, sure-footed on the rocks with the knife in his hand.

'Fuckin' thief. Get out ma hoose!' Mackenzie roared, his face contorted into a ghoulish mask. His voice thundered around the cavern. The heavily-muscled man dived forward with his knife gripped in a meaty fist. Sweat glistened on his naked chest. Lock twisted, but he wasn't fast enough to deflect the slashing swing. The knife sliced across his cheek, a half-inch under his left eye socket. The tip of the blade caught the side of his nose.

Mackenzie overbalanced and fell like a tree across Lock's chest, grappling with the helmet with one hand and trying to stab Lock with the knife in his other hand. Lock grabbed the knife arm and panicked when he lost his grip on wet flesh. He wrestled for a hold, fastened both hands on Mackenzie's solid wrist and struggled to keep the point of the knife from puncturing his neck. Mackenzie ripped off Lock's helmet and while Lock grappled with the knife arm Mackenzie hit him on the top of his head with a rock. The glancing blow rattled Lock's brain and his eyes lost focus. Mackenzie overbalanced again, a mistake he would not normally have made. It allowed Lock to recover enough to jerk his left knee up and push Mackenzie sideways onto slippery rocks by the porridge pot, following it up with a kick to Mackenzie's thigh that toppled the other man into a roll, freeing Lock's right leg.

Lock levitated and flew outwards by four metres to avoid a backward slashing swing. The helmet torch light flickered and went out. Blood trickled down Lock's forehead. It mingled with the sweat in his left eyebrow, flowed over his top eyelid and made its way to the outer corner of his eye. He dared not raise a gloved hand to brush the fluid away. Mackenzie was close, but Lock couldn't see him in the impenetrable darkness of the towering cavern. He closed his eyes and switched to aura vision, searching for a small cobalt cloud among dense, lifeless rock folds that blurred into a mess of blackness. No aura. The cavern provided plenty of places in which somebody could hide and evade detection, and Mackenzie, though driven mad by hallucinations, was using his Special Forces skills and training instinctively.

Lock worked hard to control his pounding heart and ragged breathing, taking quiet, shallow breaths through his open mouth. He strained to hear Mackenzie, and froze. He heard two sounds together. A rasping intake of air and the rounded, wet chunk of small boulders rolling under bare feet. Lock held his breath and switched to aura detection. The cobalt aura was alongside, too close. Lock levitated higher, shocked that he had missed Mackenzie's presence.

Mackenzie changed direction. The drug had sharpened his senses. He moved fast to block the way. The only thing Lock saw was the bright blue aura in front of him. He couldn't see which hand held the knife and couldn't see the knife itself, or even a hand. He levitated in the opposite direction, his pulse rate accelerating. The breath he held escaped in a quiet hiss, smothered too late. The aura lunged.

Lock shouted at Mackenzie, kicked out with his undamaged leg and flew sideways. He heard him fall and didn't feel the bite of the knife. The torch flickered into life. Mackenzie must have knocked the helmet. The fluttering, weak beam illuminate both of them. Lock saw he had some leeway under a rock shelf and sped upwards in an attempt to roll over Mackenzie and come at him from behind. Mackenzie sprang up faster and higher than any normal man and caught Lock's injured foot.

Lock yelled and lashed out with his free foot, but missed. Mackenzie fell back towards the boulders, pulled Lock down with him and tried to stab his thigh. Lock kicked and made a lucky connection with Mackenzie's wrist. The knife flew out of his grasp and clattered among the boulders, but his strong left hand still gripped Lock's right ankle. The Scot slipped, pulling Lock down, and fell with him against the porridge pot. Lock howled as his injured ankle hit the cavern floor, and his fear turned to fury.

Mackenzie's bulky form twisted, silhouetted against the flickering light, his laboured breathing rasped and curdled like a rabid animal. Before Lock could move, Mackenzie gripped his belt kit. The Scot's other arm drew back for a chopping killer punch to the throat, but it landed on Lock's raised forearm. Lock brought his knee up hard.

The first effort missed and hit the inside of Mackenzie's thigh, but the second one hurt. Lock heard a grunt of pain and Mackenzie folded over by Lock's side, clutching his balls. Lock rolled to his knees, clasped his hands together and brought a two-fisted blow down on the back of Mackenzie's neck, though his awkward position meant his punch had less power than he wanted. Mackenzie's head jarred as he hit the side of the porridge pot and he wobbled, but didn't fall. Lock put all his strength behind a second blow. Mackenzie fell on his side and lay still.

Gasping curses, Lock levitated to avoid putting weight on his right leg and aimed a tentative kick at Mackenzie's arm to see if he was faking loss of consciousness. His boot hit fleshy bicep, sending a shudder through Mackenzie's chest, but he made no sound or movement. Lock's anger turned to anxiety and he lowered himself to the cavern floor and checked for a pulse. His trembling fingers detected a surge in the carotid artery. At least he hadn't killed the man. He inspected the side of Mackenzie's head where it hit the porridge pot, feeling for a softness that indicated a skull fracture, but it felt normal.

Still shaking, he took out the spare LED torch from where he had stashed it in a pouch on his belt kit, found the nylon rope and cut off two lengths with the Leatherman multi-tool. Pain in his ankle made him shiver as the adrenaline wore off. He shoved the limp body over stones into a position where it could be trussed up and tried to rouse Mackenzie, but there was no response. Lock collapsed onto a boulder, retrieved the drones and patched up the cut on his head to stop blood interfering with his vision. He eyed Mackenzie and thought he would like to beat the shit out of him, unwilling to check him further. He'd been lucky. Mackenzie was taller, at least a stone heavier, much stronger, and more skilled in close quarter combat. Lock's escape reinforced his determination to shut down Starbirth production.

He didn't want to leave the knife lying around when Mackenzie regained consciousness. He had a healthy regard for his opponent's ability to escape, despite the circumstances. While he stowed the knife inside a pouch, he expected to hear a groan or furious roaring from Mackenzie but his captive made no sound. He discovered how sick Mackenzie was when he checked him with a medical sensor. A fine mist of steam rose from Mackenzie's skin and rivers of perspiration ran off his face and neck. The internal fire and the strain on his heart would kill him unless Lock could get him to a hospital soon, and there might not be time to get out of the mountain.

The casualty's veins bulged over his skin like gnarled tree roots. Lock had no trouble finding a place for the saline feed needle and he taped the pump-action bag to Mackenzie's hairy chest. He pictured Mackenzie's enraged face when it came to pulling the tape off again. Fumbling in his haste to get started, he laid out a silver survival blanket on the rocky floor by the tunnel, placed the wet, dirty jacket over that and levitated the unconscious man onto it. He had just finished tying Mackenzie up like a package, when the Scot made waking up noises, slurring incoherently.

Lock pulled his helmet over his head wound and levitated them into the tunnel. He knew the route into the mountain. Using the tunnel as a guide, he could teleport out through the fissures. It took seconds to reach the tunnel mouth. Mackenzie's head lolled and he opened his eyes. He thrashed his bound legs and screamed.

'Let me go. Let me out, you bastards!'

Lock let go of the jacket and put his hands on Mackenzie's head.

'Jimmy. Listen to me, Jimmy. It's Lock. You're okay.'

He stopped as everything in his peripheral vision blurred. They were back in the cavern at the exact spot where the fight took place. Mackenzie was a pain in the arse. He struggled to free his arms and chest from the nylon rope, oblivious to what he had just done. Lock shuffled to face him and knelt on his legs, gripping his shoulders. He was in no mood to play teleporter hide and seek with a sick man.

'Jimmy, look at me. It's Lock. Remember me?'

Mackenzie tried to head-butt him.

'For fuck's sake, mate, I'm trying to get you to hospital. Jimmy, look at me.'

But Mackenzie was having none of it. He shouted curses, stopped abruptly, stared up at the stalactite roof with eyes like round saucers – and screamed.

Lock couldn't deal with Mackenzie's irrational fear as well as his own, and the need to get Mackenzie out of there was urgent. Remembering his training in close-quarter combat techniques that disabled rather than killed, he slugged Mackenzie unconscious with a right hook and resumed his Shift with his unwilling patient. When Mackenzie came round he didn't counter-teleport again. His attempts to throw Lock off became weaker and that worried Lock. Kneeling by the mouth of the giant's hollow tube he rummaged in his bergen for a small air mix bottle and fixed the mask over Mackenzie's face before making a satellite phone call to Bilton.

'Zero to Ghost, come in.' Bilton sounded as though Lock was interrupting something important.

'Ghost to Zero, I've got Dagger Four. Condition critical. Which hospital is receiving casevac? Over.'

When Bilton spoke he sounded more alert.

'Acknowledged. What are your coordinates for casevac?'

'I don't need a rescue team. Just tell me which hospital.'

'Negative, hold on where you are. We're sending assistance. Relay casevac coordinates.'

Lock gritted his teeth but kept a cool voice on the radio.

'Casualty's condition is deteriorating rapidly. He needs urgent medical attention. I can get to the hospital a damn sight faster than anybody else. I'm taking him to A&E in Edinburgh.' He repeated the last part of the message.

It wasn't a bluff. Lock knew the police and other services would have set up security at a designated hospital where they could keep a lid on the incident using the Official Secrets Act. Bilton wouldn't want to upset that arrangement, and sure enough Lock received a grudging reply.

'Zero to Ghost, Ninewells Hospital, Dundee.' Bilton gave him GPS coordinates. Lock told Bilton to inform the authorities he would be arriving imminently, gathered his kit and Shifted with the sick man away from the mountain range.

Less than five minutes later he hovered over the hospital, swaying in the air and looking for a landing spot that wouldn't spook any of the numerous blue auras milling around the brightly-lit entrance. He found it in shadow near the entrance of the Accident and Emergency department, next to a closed service door. Behind it a group of four auras clustered within the building itself, probably ambulance drivers on their tea break sheltering from the force of the hurricane. He lowered his burden, crouching on one knee to check the comatose man. He would have to levitate inside. Mackenzie was too heavy to drag.

He glimpsed movement on his right. A black shape, less than two metres away, moved from the opened door, followed by another. A gun barrel pointed at the side of Lock's head.

'Don't fucking move,' a harsh voice shouted, as other black shapes ran from the darkened service door. The man shouted at him to get down on the ground. Lock did as he was told. He couldn't dodge bullets, even without exhaustion.

CHAPTER 2

The hurricane roared up the valleys, blasted trees aside as though they were nothing more than matchsticks, ran out of fury and dissolved. It left the rugged Scottish countryside folk stoically shaking off the latest onslaught, working at night to dig roads out from under drifts of snow, patch up power lines and move fallen trees from highways. Lock discovered this gradually as most of his time was occupied by saying as little as possible to suspicious police. Still irritated by the welcome committee, he wondered if Bilton had set him up.

In the small side ward reserved for Lock's patrol everybody was on the move. Porters pushed beds out and dragged in other beds with sedated figures on them. Drip bags and plastic tube lines swayed. Shoes scuffled and squeaked along the linoleum floor. Voices filled the air, too loud for the early morning. At the nurses' station by the door telephones buzzed without being answered while nurses shushed and placated two delusional and aggressive men. The porters left.

One of the sick men raised a dirty blond head, smiled at Lock as if in recognition, raised bandaged hands, threw his head back and laughed manically. Lock recognised him as Pete, the joker of the patrol, Mackenzie's friend. Pete thrashed about on the bed, swearing, with restraints on his forearms and legs holding him back. Lock levered himself up on crutches and hobbled from his straight-backed easy chair towards the bed.

'Pete, settle down, mate.'

Pete roared and shouted curses that could be heard all over the ward. A male nurse barged in front of Lock.

'We'll deal with this. Sit down, please.' He called a second nurse and they pulled curtains round the bed. Lock turned and nearly collided with a young female doctor. Her eyes had heavy rings underneath, the sort he witnessed on exhausted soldiers. She smiled, and side-stepped around him, entering the closed-off area. Lock loitered outside, mid-way between Pete's bed and the chair. After a couple of minutes the furious yelling subsided into silence and the curtains swished back. Pete lay peacefully on his bed with his eyes closed. He looked dead.

'Is he going to be okay?'

'He's sedated. You were with him, weren't you?'

'No. Not last night.'

'So you don't know how they got hold of the drug?'

'They didn't get hold of it. They wouldn't have taken it deliberately.'

'Sit down, I'll see to those cuts.' She walked out of the ward, returning with a trolley of dressings, antiseptic wipes and instruments. Pulling out some latex gloves she said,

'This is the first time I've seen anybody with this type of poisoning. I wasn't expecting eight casualties all at once.'

'Congratulations. You'll be famous for having the first epidemic in the UK.'

'The police said we're not to talk about it to anybody.' She paused, opening a pack of sterile wipes. 'One of them said this is a new type of cocaine. I've seen cocaine addicts and cocaine abuse, and this is definitely not just cocaine. Cocaine doesn't make people fly around a ward or hang in the air near the ceiling, or suddenly disappear from one cubicle and end up in another one. It's obvious, it's Starbirth, isn't it?'

'I can't say.'

'That's a pity.' She swabbed the cuts on his cheek and nose with a force that indicated her displeasure. 'I can guess this is Starbirth. It's the same kind of thing on the news from America. Did you see the news this morning?'

'No, I didn't.'

She rushed on.

'They've declared a state of emergency. They had over two hundred incidents in one night. People were looting and burning buildings, killing, women were raped and God knows what else. Some of the druggies are flying around and the police can't catch them. There are others who change shapc just by willpower. They say some of them can read minds. It scares me to death. I knew we'd see it eventually, but I didn't expect the first time to be in my hospital, or on my shift.' She put the wipes down. 'Hold still, I'll use medical glue to seal the cut on your cheek. You'll need a few stitches in the scalp wound.'

Her hands shook as she held the tube and she fumbled with the top. Lock reached up and held her hands still.

'Take a deep breath, you're doing fine. You have everything under control. Nobody is going to attack you.'

Her hand steadied. She glanced at Lock's ring finger.

'Married, eh? Shame.'

They laughed and the tension eased.

'Is there anything you can tell me about the drug that isn't covered by the Official Secrets Act?' she asked.

Lock was silent for a few seconds while she applied the stinging glue and pressed the sides of the cut together, and when he spoke he considered his words carefully. He couldn't tell her about Starbirth's secret ingredient, the catalyst drug AH-4 that produced Starbirth when mixed with cocaine.

'The drug you're dealing with stimulates the brain. It creates new neural pathways allowing people to develop these extraordinary powers. I can tell you it came from South America first. It was expensive, so only gangsters or rich people could afford it. That's why you're seeing the worst coming out, because it's mostly criminals who got it first. That's all I can say. In terms of treatment, you're dealing with the unknown.'

The doctor finished by applying butterfly plasters on Lock's cheek. She inclined her head in the direction of the beds.

'Are these men criminals?'

'What? No way. They're soldiers, not idiots who risk their lives by taking a designer drug. They're brave guys. I hope they'll get through this okay.'

'You know them well, then?'

'Not really, but I know enough. I've worked with them for the past week.'

She opened more packs of gauze, to prepare for stitching.

'Just because they're soldiers it doesn't put them above experimenting.'

'Believe me, if they'd taken the drug I would know. You must have noticed how fit these guys are. They have too much respect for their bodies and they wouldn't jeopardise their position in the armed forces by dabbling with a drug like this.'

Even as he said the words, Lock hoped he was right. The fact that Starbirth hit the Special Forces patrol he had been working with unnerved him. It was too close to home and he didn't like the new future dawning on his previously secure world, where he had been one of only two teleporters.

'This will hurt a bit. I can give you some local anaesthetic if you want.'

'No, carry on.'

Lock kept still and lapsed into tired silence, gazing at the sedated men on the ward while she worked He had not met this group of troopers from A Squadron of 22 SAS before, apart from a brief meeting with Mackenzie months ago. They had no hint from him about his undercover role working alongside troopers from D Squadron as a teleporter taxi and reconnaissance scout during covert operations. He could have trusted them to keep his secret, but he found that revealing it to troopers outside D Squadron changed attitudes towards him.

Troopers from other Squadrons still included him in their banter and black humour, especially when they relaxed in the pub, but the watchfulness that underscored their lives on or off the battlefield extended to watching him as well, as though they feared their secrets being uncovered, or some kind of compromise to their personal lives. The last time he was required to inform some B Squadron troopers about his role, a few expressed cynical doubts in private about how he used his abilities. News of it filtered back to

Lock, who was forced into a defensive explanation that he was not a telepath and could not read their minds. For that reason, and many others, he knew he would always be considered an outsider.

'All done. Eight stitches.'

'I know. I counted them. Thanks.'

The doctor finished bandaging the wound and cleared up. A floor cleaning machine started up in the corridor. Lock turned his head at the sound and caught sight of Bilton talking to a nurse. Bilton met Lock's gaze, looked away and stood rigid until the nurse finished speaking. Lock didn't want to speak to Bilton, but he had to in order to get the latest news. Bilton looked as though he didn't want to speak to Lock, either, but he marched over anyway.

'A chopper will be here in fifteen minutes to take you and the boys back to Birmingham for specialist treatment.'

'How's Mackenzie?'

Still on edge, Bilton replied as though using the time to prepare for something else.

'He's off the critical list and they're taking him out of intensive care.' He paused then continued in a low voice, 'You should have told me who you are.'

'You should have read your brief, then you'd have known.'

'Things would've been easier if you'd said. It would have made a great deal of difference.'

'You wouldn't have tried to have me manhandled out of the truck when I arrived at the Forward Operating Base?'

'I didn't know who you were. If I had, I would have acted accordingly.'

'You mean you wouldn't have acted like a complete prick.' Lock grinned. Bilton didn't. He looked about ready to thump Lock, but he didn't pursue the argument, perhaps moderating his obvious hostility with the knowledge that Lock's civilian Ministry of Defence status, the equivalent of an Army Major, outstripped his own rank of Captain.

'There's a message for you. Somebody will be here with the evac chopper. He wants a word in private. Name of Steven. He asked me to let you know. I've let you know.'

Bilton stalked away, leaving Lock wide awake. He picked up the crutches issued to him and limped to the toilets to have a look at his injuries. A thoughtful face gazed at him from the metal mirror, a pleasant face when he wasn't under pressure. He touched the swollen sides of the red slash on his cheek and tipped his head down to peer at his crown. He could see the edge of a shaved patch underneath the bandage.

Inspection over, he hobbled to the ward and sat down. Tired nurses gathered by the ward station to brief fresh colleagues before the change of shift. After thirty minutes, his eyes closed. In a half-asleep state, his mind drifted to his discussion with the Ministry of Defence psychiatrist, Porter, who asked him when he had first taken Starbirth. Lock insisted he wouldn't take Starbirth, which was illegal as well as highly addictive, and the notes were wrong.

Porter studied his file. Lock regarded the intervention of psychiatrists as intrusive and manipulative. Their notes were opinions and the targeted person didn't have access to what was written. Until the shrinks came up with a definition of normal, which nobody had been able to do as far as he was aware, he would remain distrustful of whatever conclusions they came up with. He suppressed an urge to seize the file and rip it to shreds.

Porter's face cleared as he picked out one sheet, held it up and confirmed that yes, there had been a misprint. An unknown substance had given Lock his abilities, not Starbirth. He put the paper down, made a steeple with his fingertips in the curious way that academics often do, and gazed at Lock over the top of his spectacles.

'Why did you take the drug?'

'Long story,' Lock said, in a tone of voice that indicated he didn't want to talk about it.

Porter persisted. 'What happened to you?'

'It was a childhood accident. I was about thirteen when we lived on the border between Colombia and Brazil. Kids do stupid things.' Porter nodded sympathetically, which irritated Lock. He continued, 'Me and my friend Mike, who was about sixteen, we got lost one day. To cut a long story short, we ended up drinking some kind of sweet juice that made us sick. We nearly died. Afterwards we developed abilities nobody had seen before. An unknown substance affected our brains.'

Lock stopped. Porter waited for him to go on and when Lock didn't he prompted,

'In what way?'

'When people learn something intricate, like juggling, their brains increase in size, by a tiny amount. New message pathways are created. Essentially, the brain rewires itself and grows new cells. Scientists think the substance in Starbirth speeds up that process in people who are genetically programmed to react to it. Their brains alter and they develop abilities like teleportation, telekinesis, telepathy, transmutation and a few other things that haven't even got names yet. They think that's what happened to us. We were exposed to the substance early on, before it was used in Starbirth.'

Porter leaned his elbow on the armrest and peered at the papers in Lock's file.

'Tell me about the accident when you were eighteen years old.'

Lock stiffened. 'No.'

The psychiatrist brightened up. He stared at Lock with an expression akin to triumph at finding the ace in his deck of cards.

'It played a key part in your life,' he said quietly, making a pen mark on the relevant sheet. Lock's mouth set in a determined silence. He could see Porter returning to that time and again, like an over-enthusiastic dentist worrying at a painful tooth. In the distance he heard the distinctive whup-whup of a Chinook helicopter, getting louder.

'Lock?' Porter said. His voice lowered and sounded younger. 'Lock?'

Lock jolted awake, focusing on Steven Stringer, officer in Her Majesty's Secret Intelligence Service – an institution known as MI6, a nod to its military origins.

Stringer did not give an immediate impression of being anything other than a well-heeled thirty-two year old, as stylish in expensive, casual winter clothing as he was in a city business suit. Dark haired, tall and thin with a hooked nose broken in his teens, his lean face had a smile that was both engaging and strangely empty. Lock always had the feeling Stringer looked out through a shell, and was never quite there, as if he viewed the world from somewhere set back. The real Steven Stringer stayed well hidden behind an outer show of charm, his shrewd intellect calculating, appraising and evaluating, before any thoughts left his lips in carefully placed words.

'How are you doing?' Stringer asked, putting a holdall down by Lock's chair. They shook hands formally, neither one willing to betray in public how well they knew each other.

'I'm okay.'

'Good. We have to go. I would've been here earlier but we were grounded at Edinburgh airport because of the hurricane.' He surveyed Lock's face before passing on to the dressing on his head and the bootcast on Lock's ankle. 'Not a good night out, then?'

'I've had better,' Lock said, smiling. The smile pulled on his sore cheek and he added, 'I'm going to have some interesting scars.'

'The hospital in Birmingham should sort that out.'

'Yeah,' Lock said, with some regret. He liked the idea of battle scars although he knew the fewer distinguishing marks he had, the better his chances of going unrecognised by hostiles. His attention strayed to several men who followed Stringer into the ward and busied themselves removing clothes belonging to the patrol, stuffing them into black bin liners. Stringer followed Lock's gaze.

'We'll need your clothes and equipment too. They'll be returned to you later.' He picked up the holdall and handed it to Lock. The words conveyed more than their casual delivery suggested, and Lock understood. Standard operating procedures required examination of everything in case there had been a compromise, or a breach of security. Nobody knew why the patrol had fallen victim to an overdose of Starbirth. There might be micro-trackers hidden in their clothes or bergens and possibly in Lock's clothes as well. It was unlikely but it paid to be sure.

Lock opened the holdall and pulled out some baggy tracksuit bottoms which had zips at the ankles, allowing for looseness over the lower leg and the bootcast. He took off his shirt, pulling on an old fleecy jacket Stringer handed him. Stringer gestured at Lock's ankle.

'Is it broken?'

'It's a hairline fracture with ligament damage.'

'Good.'

'Good? What kind of response is that?'

'I didn't mean that. You know me.'

'What would you have said if I'd broken both legs – excellent?'

'Okay, okay.'

A smile twitched at the corners of Lock's mouth as he changed pants. The only time Stringer's less guarded moments were revealed was when he used phrases or words like good inappropriately. It meant he was thinking of two, perhaps three things at the same time, and plotting ahead. Lock stuffed his clothes, phone, glasses and handheld computer into the holdall. Stringer passed it to one of the men, who left the ward.

'We need to speak in private. Are you okay to walk?'

Lock nodded. He picked up the crutches and hobbled after Stringer towards an empty reception area near the A&E entrance. Lock spoke first as they walked along the corridor. He watched Stringer's reaction as he said in a low voice,

'I suppose now wouldn't be a good time to tell you Lianne found a bug earlier today.'

'She actually found one?' Stringer stopped walking. 'Where?'

Lock couldn't be sure if Stringer was shocked by the security breach, or was surprised by his wife finding a bug he already knew about.

'The central light socket in our bedroom,' Lock said. 'Actually it was the electrician who noticed something odd after Lianne called him in because the light wasn't working properly. It kept making strange noises.'

'You're sure it's a bug?'

Lock nodded.

'Yeah, Mike P's team did a sweep and confirmed it. It's faulty, that's why it was making sounds. It's definitely an eavesdropping device.'

'Did you call it in on the emergency number?'

'It wasn't necessary. Mike P's team were close by and they've got the place sorted.'

Stringer's face rarely showed emotion, but Lock knew him well enough to see beyond the mask and catch the change in facial language that indicated vexation.

'The security services made special arrangements to protect your family. It's best to let them deal with this kind of thing. They have the latest equipment and the most highly skilled operatives.' Stringer added a conciliatory shrug. 'It's up to you, of course. Your choice, but if I were in your position I'd want to know how anybody could circumvent the security measures we installed, to make sure it didn't happen again. I'd call people I could trust.'

'I trust Mike P.'

'Are you saying you don't trust us? You think the security services are bugging your house?'

'It wouldn't be the first time.'

Stringer exhaled impatiently.

'We've been over this before. If you're referring to that time two years ago, that wasn't us. We cleared them out for you, not the other way round. As I said before....' He trailed off, glancing over Lock's shoulder. Lock turned his head and saw porters wheeling out a trolley accompanied by an armed guard he recognised as an SAS soldier he had worked with previously.

'In here,' Stringer said. He opened a pair of sliding doors by stepping towards them, and led the way inside. Lock followed him into a large, empty waiting room. Rows of scratched metal seats bolted to the floor sat in front of a couple of vending machines, one containing drinks and the other packets of crisps and sweets. The doors slid shut behind them and Stringer said,

'We wouldn't do that to you. We drew up guidelines for your sake, five years ago, if you recall. Not only is it a clear breach of those guidelines, it would be counter-productive. Why would we want to alienate somebody who is helping us?'

Lock leaned against the wall by a vending machine.

'Okay, but we both know that if powerful people in the intelligence services want to listen in on my conversations, no set of guidelines will prevent transcripts being delivered to the appropriate desk.' Through the glass partition, he caught a glimpse of Mackenzie being wheeled out to the waiting Chinook helicopter, and changed the subject, unwilling to get drawn into an argument that had no hope of being resolved. 'Is there any new intel on who was responsible for that?' he asked, nodding towards Mackenzie.

Stringer relaxed, a gesture that indicated he was relieved to be talking about something else.

'Nothing definite. There's a lot of confusion but I've been told the police are questioning one of the barmen. A simple case of jealousy, though we're looking into that. He didn't like your patrol chatting up his girlfriend. She worked at the pub as a barmaid and they were hitting on her.'

'They were kidding around with all of them. I didn't see one being singled out.'

Stringer shrugged.

'Obviously the barman thought differently.'

'Do you think anyone else could be behind it?' Lock asked, watching the porters return at a run to get the next batch of casualties.

'Like who?'

'The Decons are the obvious bet.'

'We thought of them, but it's unlikely. They're busy in the States, if they exist at all. Why would they bother with one Regiment patrol in Scotland? No, it appears to be local, a one-off. Though where the drug came from might be related to our unofficial American friends in the unofficial base not far from here.'

'Seriously?'

'Seriously.'

Lock knew what Stringer referred to – the disused RAF airfield which had a small number of British personnel and a large detachment of US military visiting forces, coupled with a discreet cache of anti-missile ordnance in silos. The thought of that lot connected to the madness produced by Starbirth was not good.

Stringer's computer watch beeped. He glanced at it.

'I have to take this call. See you in a minute.'

'No problem.'

Lock watched Stringer's retreating back and thought he might be looking for the culprits in the wrong place. Judging by what he had heard about the Decons, the shadowy and secret group of powerful, rich people, they had global influence. Nobody knew much about them and their existence was limited to Press speculation. Lock didn't believe in conspiracy theories, but this one didn't seem so far-fetched. A group of billionaires and people from different backgrounds, including military, banded together as anti-teleporter vigilantes to do what they considered was beyond the capabilities of their respective governments.

Such an alliance would be impressive had it not included the wholesale slaughter of Starbirth addicts. The Decons took it upon themselves to cleanse the world of all teleporters and people with extraordinary skills brought about by Starbirth use. They made no distinction between criminals, murderers and the curious. Somebody coined the term 'Decontaminators' and the Press shortened it to Decons. Any unnatural or violent death of Starbirth addicts was attributed to the Decons, and if they didn't exist, their reputation did, whispered among drug users and people dealing in Starbirth.

Lock eyed the contents of the vending machine then remembered he had no cash in his borrowed clothes. The sliding doors opened and Stringer returned.

'The Special Investigation Branch is looking into any connection with the unofficial base but the barman's not being cooperative. Even if he does say anything useful, the Yanks will deny any knowledge of it.'

'I could always take the barman on a little trip above a loch and threaten to drop him in it. That might make him cooperate.'

Stringer looked sharply at Lock.

'That wouldn't be a good idea.'

'It was a joke. I have guidelines regulating my behaviour as well, right?' Lock smiled, but Stringer got the point about being ruled by regulations.

'If we want the notion of an enhanced-ability team to get off the ground, you've got to keep your nose clean. The PM's dithering as it is. There's only one way to counteract Starbirth crime and that's to fight like with like. The US has got their team. We must have one too, and soon.'

Lock wasn't sure that he wanted to head up an enhanced-ability team, but it wasn't the right time to say so. He was too tired to think about it rationally. He stared through the glass partition at another of the SAS patrol being taken out on a trolley and listened to Stringer.

'We've got to find out where the supplies of AH-4 and Starbirth are coming from. The Yanks aren't going to tell us where they get their AH-4 and they aren't going to give us any, either.'

He passed a smartphone to Lock. The screen displayed a map of Colombia.

'We need you to go back ASAP on the Starbirth assignment and we're particularly interested in what you can find out about that area.' He nodded at the screen then paused. 'Something wrong? You look as though the cat just pissed on your dinner. You don't have to go back until the accelerated-healing factor has done its job.' He put the phone in his pocket.

'It's not that.'

'What's the problem?'

'Personal stuff. I've been away a lot. I thought I could take some time off before being away for months again. I have a wife and child, remember?'

'It won't be months, just a couple of weeks. You'll be back long before Christmas. Patuazon trusts you.'

'Patuazon doesn't trust anybody. He's paranoid,' Lock scoffed.

'Well, let's say you're the only outsider who's got close to him.'

'Yeah, there are times I think saving his granddaughter from drowning was a bad idea.'

'Well, work on the fact he still thinks the sun shines out of your arse. I'll send you details by secure link.'

A few minutes later Stringer stood in the downdraft of the Chinook helicopter and watched it depart with Lock and the SAS patrol on board. He turned and walked briskly to the car park, taking out his smartphone to make a call. It beat him to it, vibrating in his hand.

'Yes,' he said, and listened. 'He's on his way to Birmingham.' He paused, shivering in the icy wind. 'No, he doesn't know about that. I thought it unwise to tell him, it'll jeopardise the Colombian operation. I've arranged for our contract men to keep an eye on his family, just to be sure.' He paused and listened. 'Okay,' he said, and cut the connection to make his own call.

'Hanslope, Ghost's wife found a bug in the central light socket. Find out if it was one of ours.'

He touched the screen and pocketed the smartphone. Unmoved by the admission about bugging Lock's house, he walked to the car and settled in the back seat.

'Let's go,' he said to the burly driver. The car sped away in the ethereal light preceding a troubled dawn.

~~~~~~~~

Seven days after therapy with an enhanced healing drug, a substance based on the chemical manipulation of nanoparticles, the bootcast was removed at the Birmingham hospital by medics who expressed surprise at how quickly his injury had healed, even by the standards of drug-induced speed. Lock Shifted home, elated.

'No more daily trips to Birmingham, then,' Lianne commented, standing by Lock's side in the driveway of their home in Harpenden in Hertfordshire. A flurry of winter wind caught her long, dark hair and blew it over her face. She brushed it back behind her ears. He stopped tinkering with his classic motorbike, a Triumph Bonneville, and stood up, wiping his hands on a dirty rag.

'I have one more trip tomorrow.'

'Couldn't you break the other ankle and stay home for Christmas?' An impish smile played around the corners of her mouth and her blue eyes sparkled.

'Cheeky sod.' Lock threw the rag at her. She dodged it and laughed. Their three-year-old son, Thomas, stopped prodding the front lawn with a stick and ran to them.

'Can I go on the bike?'

'I'll take you on it when you're older.' Picking up his fair-haired son, he swung him round by his wrists. Thomas yelled in delight. Lock plonked him back on the driveway.

'You're not going out on that thing, are you?' Lianne wrinkled her nose at the Bonneville. Thomas answered first.

'No, Daddy's going on this one.' He ran into the open garage and tried to clamber onto the seat of a sleek Triumph Tiger Explorer adventure motorcycle.

'Good guess, Tom, but what did we say about climbing on the bikes?' Lock led Thomas away. 'Li, do you want to change your mind and see
~~~~~~~~

everyone? The security guys can look after Tom. I might be passed as combat ready tomorrow. We can have some fun before I leave.'

'I'll give it a miss, thanks. It's too cold to stand and watch you lot going round the course.'

'Chicken.'

Lianne fixed him with the kind of look she reserved for Thomas when he had been naughty.

'If you want double servings at dinner tonight, you'd better watch your step.'

'I'll eat out.'

'I bet you will. We're nearly out of food again. You scoffed all the biscuits while I was asleep – and the leftovers, and the rest of the cereal.'

'It's that enhanced healing stuff, it makes me ravenous. You know that.'

'No, I don't believe you. You just want an excuse to pig out. I wouldn't be surprised if you break the bike when you sit on it.'

'No way. It can take my weight, but the tyres will pop if you get on the back.' Lock gave Lianne's slender frame an appraisal worthy of a sergeant-major, and chuckled when she retaliated with a playful swipe at his arm. He captured Lianne in an embrace while Thomas clamoured for attention and tried to push in between them. Lock gave up, knowing he stood no chance when it came to Thomas, and left.

The sky stayed clear of clouds, perfect for a proposed off-road race on a dirt track that looped over steep inclines and sharp bends, tipping over hills and launching the bikes in the air. The group at the pub car park knew him as Dan Lewis, an alias and persona constructed with meticulous attention to detail by the SIS and various units employed by them who forged a passport and drew up false background papers. The club knew nothing about his real life. Col, one of the older members, called Lock into a small group who greeted him with high fives and friendly banter.

'You missed a good race last weekend. Where've you been?' Col asked, taking Lock's entry fee.

'Oh, you know, flying around Scotland in a hurricane, saving someone from getting frozen to death. That sort of thing.'

'Yeah, right. Mark, did you bring your breathalyser kit? Dan's been on the piss before he got here.'

'I left it at home, mate. See if you can smell anything on his breath. We'll get him barred from the race.'

'Like hell you will,' Lock said. Squealing tyres drew their attention to the end of the car park, where a youngster on a Honda did a wheelie. Lock and his friends moved aside fast as the bike roared towards them. The driver braked hard and stopped short, met by a chorus of jeers from the more experienced men and shouts of 'Dickhead,' and 'Wanker.'

Lock basked in the warmth and good humour. His competitive streak took over in the race but at the last lap common sense prevailed. He couldn't risk stirring up the injury so close to being designated as fit, and he came in third after Mark and fellow competitor Al. The meeting broke up and Lock checked the time. He had a couple of hours before early nightfall, and he wasn't tired. Leaving the pub in a convoy with his mates, as soon as he turned off the main road and lost sight of them, he Shifted with his bike to the lower Alps in Switzerland. For another hour, he relished the joy of opening up the throttle and blasting along roads at two hundred kilometres per hour.

~~~~~~~~

Two days later Lock teleported to Mocoa in Colombia. Trips to South America evoked many bitter-sweet memories of the six years he spent there with his biologist parents. Their search for a new antibiotic yielded a promising result at first, but later experiments could not replicate the early success. They didn't give up. Lock's father, Richard, decided to dedicate his life to research in South America. Uprooting his family from a comfortable existence in Berkshire, he led them to Brazil, first to the city of Rio de Janeiro and then to the rainforest, moving further away from European-influenced civilisation every few months until Lock's mother, Cathy, put her foot down in a conversation Lock overheard.

'We should stay here. There's a little school where Lock can go three days a week to learn Spanish and the basics, and the rest of the time we'll home school him as usual. That way I can concentrate on my research and you'll have more time to do yours.'

'I'm not so sure it's a good thing, sending him to a mission school. They'll fill his head with all sorts of religious rubbish.'

'They're good people, Richard. They mean well and they're kind. I think it would be good for him.'

'I think we should stick to home schooling.'

Squinting through a crack by the kitchen door hinges Lock saw his mother sit down at the table opposite his father.

'Home schooling is fine to a point, but we need the extra time to work,' she said. 'Besides, the Northwoods are here. He gets on with their boy, Mike.'

Lock's father looked up from his laptop.

'That boy is trouble.'

Lock's mother folded her arms, exasperated.

'They're boys, Richard. They're always trouble. Lock doesn't have any other friends the same age as him, they're all younger. I like the Northwoods. Don't you like them?'
~~~~~~~~

'They're okay.' Lock's father shrugged. 'I just don't like their approach. Shamanism is unscientific.'

'You'll get used to it. Won't he, Lock?' She turned her head and stared at the kitchen door. Lock pelted up the stone stairs to his tiny bedroom, shocked that his mother knew about his eavesdropping. She seemed to have a sixth sense about things like that. Later developments, connected to the drug both boys drank, proved his father right about Mike Northwood's persuasive powers over his much younger friend.

CHAPTER 3

Two days after Lock's arrival, he renewed his link with Pablo Patuazon, a billionaire ex-drug lord. The Colombian had never been tried or convicted as a drug lord, though his status was an open secret. Having bribed his way to respectability he appeared to have 'retired' as a criminal and put his money into legitimate businesses instead. He had an extensive portfolio of property, most of it in and around Cali where he ran his empire from a favourite villa and estate.

Lock's brief required him to locate the source of AH-4, the catalyst element of Starbirth and the essential ingredient of the cocaine mixture. It sounded like a simple task for a teleporter but Lock was up against other teleporters eager to stop him. Even the Americans, with all their resources, had not discovered where AH-4 came from. They dismissed Patuazon as a spent force and concentrated their efforts elsewhere, but Lock's gut instinct told him Patuazon was important.

Nine months earlier something happened to Patuazon. The loss of two of his close family, including one of his sons, caused an unforeseen and astonishing transformation, if taken at face value. He became a convert to the Church. Lock's cynicism led him to think that Patuazon's epiphany had less to do with seeing the light than seeing drug lords meeting bloody ends, and the fact the angel of death had come too close to his own family. Regardless of his scepticism he had to play along with Patuazon's amended outlook in which dealing in cocaine was a bad thing, and dealing in Starbirth even worse. Patuazon took it upon himself to eradicate Starbirth with the religious zeal of the evangelist.

Despite his new-found enthusiasm, Patuazon wouldn't cooperate with the American authorities. Lock heard that he blamed the CIA for the death of his son in a Starbirth deal that went wrong. If, as Lock suspected, Patuazon dealt in both AH-4 and Starbirth, he did so on the sly. Nothing could be traced back to him directly. In the meantime Patuazon required training for his private army. He insisted on the best, so the British sent a few of the SAS under the guise of members of the Parachute Regiment.

Four days after his arrival, Lock received an encrypted message telling him to make contact with London. Sending and receiving messages while in Patuazon's compound carried risk of detection by Patuazon's state-of-the-art electronic devices, so Lock knew the contact must be important. Using the excuse of getting supplies, Lock travelled out of the compound with a trooper and when out of sight of Patuazon's covert surveillance men, he teleported to a safe area where he could speak freely.

'New orders. We're switching your reconnaissance tonight from Patuazon to a known drug lord, Antonio Mosquera,' Stringer told him. 'We think he's the supplier. We want you to take a closer look at the new villa complex he's building and plant eavesdropping equipment around it. I'm sending details now. We want you to keep a closer eye on him from now on.'

'I thought we agreed Patuazon is more important. We could lose any breakthrough if I have to divert my attention to Mosquera.'

'Your concerns are noted, but the intel we have is solid.'

'What intel?'

'A consignment of Starbirth was intercepted. It came through men known to have links with some of Mosquera's gang.'

'No firm evidence, then.'

'Find the evidence. Have you received the details?

Lock looked at the map and instructions on his computer screen.

'Confirmed.'

'Get there by midnight local time. Contact us when you are on target.'

'Acknowledged.'

Lock cut the connection and teleported back to the depot to help the trooper load up the last of the supplies. The knowledge that Stringer relied on him as much as he relied on Stringer gave him some leeway to put questions that would not have been tolerated from anybody else, but he was frustrated at being left guessing about aspects of the decision to switch critical surveillance from Patuazon to Mosquera. The armed forces and intelligence services disseminated information according to rank, security clearance, need to know and the expectation that people contracted to the SIS, like him, would follow orders without disagreement.

The structure did not allow the lower ranks to query decisions made by those higher up: they did as they were told or they were booted out. Lock felt his level of security clearance should have allowed him access to more intelligence than he was given. The only way he could change the situation for the better involved patience, cooperation and constant demonstration by his actions that he had matured since his headstrong teenage years.

Involvement with the army and the SIS gave structure to a life that could otherwise fragment due to his abilities. He reined in dark desires to behave recklessly, weighing it against the stability he craved and the feeling of being useful to society. He could do anything he wanted, and had done a lot of things that thrilled him at the time, but they brought no feeling of lasting satisfaction. Instead, they generated an internal anguish over wasting his talents, a dread of slipping into a moral void where he was of no use to anybody and perhaps even harmful. Married life, responsibilities and his work gave him boundaries.

Late at night he set off to do the reconnaissance. He hovered in darkness twenty-five metres off the ground near the top of the jungle canopy amid the noise of millions of insects. Specially-designed combat clothes cooled his body heat and prevented detection by thermal imaging systems. The task of assessing the strengths and weaknesses of Mosquera's defences took over, consuming every conscious thought. He scanned the villa through the night vision setting on his visor and sent images to a satellite which relayed them in real time back to Control and Command at SIS headquarters in London.

The villa fitted the description of a work in progress. Spanish style villas, with their rectangular inner courtyards, all looked very similar to him, but instead of rows of low, terraced buildings around a courtyard this one was only three-quarters built in a U-shape. The remaining section had foundations and some walls with building supplies stacked at one end. Part of it had a temporary roof of steel beams and tarpaulins.

Through the greenish light of night vision Lock watched two men swaggering up a grand stone staircase to the main entrance, between fake Grecian-style columns. They didn't look at the armed guards on the door, which implied high status. One of the men turned, and as Lock looked at him, the grid overlaid on the visor automatically followed Lock's eye movements and zoomed in on a pudgy profile.

'X-Ray in view,' Lock said, using the military phonetic alphabet designation for a hostile. The SIS identified the man who ambled up steps to a circular building as the eldest of Mosquera's three sons. He disappeared inside. Lock resumed mapping the buildings and followed the columns up two storeys to a huge bell dome, the largest of three on the front section of the complex but the only one that had real bells.

'Close up on that,' Control ordered. Maximum zoom revealed three figures and the outline of heavy calibre weapons – mounted General Purpose Machine Guns and a larger .50 calibre gun.

Once Control had enough images from that angle Lock moved on around the courtyard buildings and found another four small domes, which stuck up above pitched roofs like gun turrets on a battleship. Armed men in the domes had a clear view of both the front of the villa and the courtyard behind it and that made the domes priority targets if an assault was required in the future. One at the back hadn't been completed.

'Changing position,' Lock said, teleporting to another tree to get a closer look at the sides and back of the villa. Mosquera liked circular buildings with columns because two of them bisected one-storey and two-storey family houses, but the domes on top of those looked different to the gun turrets. Lock moved, making it easier for him to see glass panels. They allowed light to filter through each dome to balconies on the first floor and a small ornamental garden feature on the ground floor. The buildings acted as a connecting area between the family houses on either side. Lock moved on.

He couldn't be certain Mosquera had taken measures to deter teleporters, but he spotted four tall, thin structures that resembled high flagpoles placed around the villa. They looked like an electronic deterrent, and the SIS lingered over them like vultures excited by the prospect of picking over a fresh carcase. The villa complex was well-defended. In the grounds below, armed guards with dogs patrolled the compound. The perimeter razor wire fence extended eighteen hundred metres, interrupted by four metal watchtowers at strategic places. Lock's surveillance took him past the mirrored surface of a swimming pool. Hastily constructed outbuildings lay further down the slope near a boathouse by the riverside, patrolled by more armed men. Forty minutes later the SIS had all the information that could be gleaned from short-term surveillance. Lock retrieved his radio transmitter, sealed it inside a waterproof container with the helmet, visor and other equipment and teleported back towards the training camp.

For all of Patuazon's famed craftiness, he overlooked the river as a method of teleporter entry into his training grounds. Lock plunged into it and levitated fast underwater along its length to a lake Patuazon had created, emerging near huts occupied by the SAS. A quick sensory check told him that besides the dull blue auras occupying bunks within the old stone huts the only other blue aura was a short distance away between the huts and the lake side, unmoving.

Lock removed his helmet from the waterproof container and put it on. The visor zoomed in on a familiar, bulky figure sitting amid the foliage, weapon at the ready, staring in Lock's direction through a night vision scope on his weapon. Lock used a narrow-beam laser pointer to send three quick flashes of infra-red light followed a second later by one, flashes that could be seen only with night vision equipment. The figure reacted by getting up. He sauntered over to one of the huts and disappeared inside. Lock waited until the figure emerged, the signal that the SAS anti-teleporter device had been coded to recognise him, and he levitated to the hut.

~~~~~~~~

While Lock sweated in South America, back in Birmingham Jimmy Mackenzie, the trooper he saved from an icy death in Scotland, wanted to get out of hospital, although going home was the last thing on his mind. The long spell in a hospital rehabilitation ward chafed him into raging
~~~~~~~~

anxiety at the thought that he would miss out on being sent back to a war zone. He wouldn't be there if his mates went into action and he wouldn't be part of the team, watching each other's backs. Jimmy set out to prove he was fit to go.

'If the guys out there hear much more of your heavy breathing they're going to get the wrong idea about us,' his patrol mate Pete Andrews said, adding, 'and I'm still waiting.'

Jimmy ignored him and carried on. He counted silently and willed his arm muscles to break his own record for push-ups. Perspiration ran through short, reddish-brown hair creating saw-tooth clumps that stuck to his forehead. Drops of sweat glistened in arched eyebrows, crept past dark brown eyes and trickled to the end of a straight nose before dripping off onto the linoleum floor. Powerful muscles in his neck and shoulders tautened, bulged and relaxed. His biceps hardened like rocks as he lowered himself slowly then straightened up. The air pulsated with strong body odour. Jimmy collapsed on his front, panting, got to his knees and sat back on his haunches.

'So stand outside the curtain where they can see you.'

'Half of this is my cubicle you're stinking out, and you're so bloody busy being an exercise junkie you still haven't given me an answer.'

'You should get some exercise too, pal. Then you could wipe your own arse.'

'Sod off. I'd like to see you doing push-ups on two broken hands.'

Jimmy grinned. His pleasure at stoking his friend's anger lit up steely features where natural smiles were rare visitors.

'So what's the plan, Einstein?'

'We do a recce first, see what we can find.'

'You talked that nurse into it, then.'

Jimmy stood up, straight-backed at his height of six-foot-two, and jogged on the spot, pacing his breathing into his second wind. A damp T-shirt over his combat trousers defined bulky muscles on his upper torso, the result not just of exercise and weight training but also carrying heavy bergens for long distances. It gave him a top-heavy appearance. Pete scratched his untidy blond hair with a bandaged hand.

'Piece of cake,' he said smugly. 'It's all set for tonight.'

'Oh, Pete,' Jimmy sang in falsetto, 'you're so wonderful, Pete, come and shag me in the broom cupboard.'

Pete grabbed a pillow from a chair and threw it at Jimmy, who fended it off and laughed. He kicked the pillow under the bed and sat down, still panting.

Girls liked Pete, and for other reasons besides his good looks and well-balanced physique. Men of the Special Forces radiated a contradictory but heady mix of cheerfulness, confidence, threat and secrecy, guaranteed to arouse the interest of women drawn to soldiers. SAS men often referred to themselves as Blades. It was said that Blades could last longer in the bedroom and were more sexually athletic due to their supreme fitness, though some women whispered it didn't make much difference if the whole event was over in less than two minutes. Jimmy and Pete had no such problems and no shortage of female admirers. The air of menace Jimmy radiated enticed and aroused girls, but they were less than impressed by being dumped afterwards. Pete knew how to look after his girlfriends as well as giving them a good time sexually. He had an abundance of openness that welcomed people into his world to the opposite extent that Jimmy closed them out of his.

Jimmy didn't much care that girls gravitated towards Pete. He found cheap pleasures less thrilling than they had been and he sought something that lasted longer than a few nights, no matter how much fun those nights were at the time. When he thought about his feelings he put it down to simple boredom, not with a girl's body but with what he saw as an absence of mind accompanying it. He didn't know what he wanted, but he knew what he didn't want.

'What're we looking for on this recce?' he asked, getting his breath back.

'How about stuff from the kitchens?'

'Sounds good to me. It'll give these poor bastards in the ward something to laugh about, anyway.'

Getting up, he separated beds and slid the cubicle curtains back, glancing down the long military ward partitioned into smaller spaces to provide cubicles for injured soldiers. Although comfortable, the Victorian hospital was not a hotel even though the décor gave it the appearance of aspiring to be one. The ward looked as though somebody designed it to create a feeling of optimism for children, long ago. Marks and scratches marred pink walls. Brown paper curtains with star-shaped flowers hung from railings around the cubicles. As far as Jimmy was concerned, by the end of ten days the ward had the ambience of a cheerful prison and he knew every square inch of the curtain pattern in intimate detail. If he stared at it much longer he'd have permanent brain damage. The place needed some life. Thinking of their plan, he gazed at the bright wintry sunshine outside the window with a feeling of glee that warmed him like a shot of good whisky.

He picked up a newspaper he'd read three days earlier, scouring the pages for something interesting that he might have missed. The main story covered several pages and grabbed everybody's attention, regarding the famous actress and her husband who woke to find three teleporters in their bedroom. Jimmy thought it was funny. Among the other soldiers, it sparked debate over whether the actress lied to gain publicity for a flagging career, since no-one boasted of being responsible and the police hadn't found evidence of other people entering the house. The actress declared, 'Of course they won't find any evidence. The guys teleported in, so looking for evidence of entry is nonsense.'

On the following pages he read items about deaths in strange circumstances. The murder rate in New York shot up, and every suspicious, lonely death at home assumed the proportions of murder according to the media, who were on a roll with the universal panic over teleporter criminals. Jimmy regarded the news with a sceptical eye, keeping in mind scaremongering tactics and newspaper circulation rates, but there was no denying the scale of the problem, nor the fact that eventually the SAS would be called in to help. He could hardly wait.

Pete interrupted him.

'Watch out, mate, the vampire's back.' Pete nodded at a very overweight, masculine-looking staff nurse at the end of the ward who pushed a trolley towards them. 'I think she's after your neck this time, mate.'

'She won't get far with those teeth.'

They both laughed, but watching her march towards their beds, Jimmy's training as a medic told him the level of interest in both of them verged on excessive. The rest of the patrol had already left the hospital. He and Pete were kept behind, the only occupants in a four-bed cubicle. Nobody would tell them what they had been dosed with, though it didn't take a genius to work out which drug was involved. From the way the doctors scrutinised every move, they seemed to think he and Pete would fly out of the windows any minute.

'Quick, get the garlic out,' Pete said loudly, making the sign of the cross at the staff nurse.

'You boys, you'd better behave yourselves,' she scolded. 'As for you, Sergeant Mackenzie, get a shower when we're done. You smell like you've just run a marathon. Seeing as you're here for a change, Sergeant Andrews, I'll see to you first, before you disappear.' She pulled the curtains round the bed with the swift, sure touch of somebody who did the same thing thousands of times every day.

'How much blood are you taking?' Pete's voice from behind the curtain sounded worried, though Jimmy knew he feigned indignation.

'You've got plenty more to spare,' the staff nurse replied.

Left alone, Jimmy thought about the events in the Cairngorms. He remembered feeling hot and had a hazy impression of being caught inside a giant television set in a whirl of white noise. He recalled sounds of voices: so close they made him jump then so far away the sound seemed to be coming from the wrong end of a megaphone. The memory of hair-raising movement gripped his mind most of all, the sensation of being off the ground and going forwards and backwards at the same time. It excited and frustrated him in equal measure, with its hint of something unnatural. It could have been a hallucination, but if not, it meant Starbirth caused a stronger reaction in his body compared to other members of the patrol. He tingled at the possibility of exploring just how far he could go by taking more Starbirth. The prospect tempted him although he liked his body honed, not drugged-up. He liked being strong and physically capable of enduring trials that most men, even the healthiest of ordinary soldiers, could not complete.

A couple of minutes later the staff nurse brought the instrument tray to Jimmy's bed.

'You'd better lie down for this, Sergeant Mackenzie. We don't want you passing out again, do we?'

'Yeah, I'm not picking you up off the floor again,' Pete said from outside the curtain.

'It was only the once when I was feeling ill. You never picked me up, you bastard, you just stepped over me.'

'Language,' the staff nurse scolded.

Jimmy grinned as she pushed the needle into the cannula in his arm.

'All right, Pete?' a Cockney voice asked. Jimmy glimpsed the hook-nosed face of one of their colleagues through a gap in the curtains. At the same time, he saw the fifth phial on the cannula, filling up with blood, and looked away quickly. When it came to anybody else's blood he was fine. Seeing his own made him feel queasy.

'Stick around, mate, you're just in time to see Jimmy faint again,' Pete said loudly. The new trooper leaned cheekily round the curtain.

'Wait outside, please,' the staff nurse said severely.

'Yeah, that's right, no dogs allowed in here,' Jimmy agreed. Pete laughed. The staff nurse eyed the man's bag as she replaced the lost blood with saline injected through the cannula.

'If they want more blood tomorrow, it'd better not be full of beer,' she warned, without looking at anybody in particular. The three men waited until the staff nurse left. The newcomer put the bag on the floor and Pete made a grab for it.

'Hey, hey, deal first,' his friend said, pulling it out of his reach.

'You're a mean bastard. Okay, fifteen when we get out of here.'

'Seventy-five.'

'For a few cans of beer and some second-hand clothes? You are fucking joking.'

Jimmy left them to haggle over the price. He had more interesting things to think about, like how Lock Harford managed to get him all the way from the mountains to a hospital in Dundee without using a rescue helicopter. Staff told him he arrived at the hospital in a helicopter. Jimmy's canny research exposed that as a lie. No rescue aircraft arrived at Dundee at the time stated. It always amused him that people thought they could pull the wool over his eyes, but sometimes that had its advantages. If people thought he was a stupid grunt who couldn't work things out for himself, they missed his capacity for being sneaky.

His probing confirmed his suspicion of there being more to Harford than appearances suggested. Harford had a greater connection to the Regiment than simply being a survival skills tutor, or an admin officer at Credenhill, his job when Jimmy first met him. Jimmy noted Bilton's cagey reaction when the subject of Harford came up, as though Harford's name shouldn't be mentioned. Jimmy's discerning nose smelled a secret and he guessed Harford might be able to tell him more about what happened that night, if he could only get hold of him. At the very least, he could apologise to the guy for injuring him in a fight he couldn't remember.

Jimmy spotted Bilton stalking up the ward, his dour face an echo of the pallid late December morning.

'X-Ray nine o'clock,' Jimmy warned the other two. Pete's friend looked up, hastily hid cans of beer in the bag and said a temporary goodbye, nodding to Bilton on the way out. Jimmy thought grimly that if Bilton told him one more time how lucky they were to be in the military ward, he'd shove the man's head down the bloody toilet.

'Are we being discharged today, Boss?' Pete asked with exaggerated cheerfulness. Every time they saw Bilton they asked the same question and they guessed the answer.

'If you were, I'd have informed you by now.'

'For fuck's sake.' Jimmy caught the look on Bilton's face, but he was past caring. He continued, 'We're both fit enough to get out of here.'

'It's not for either of you to decide when you're fit. You'll leave when you receive your orders, and not before.'

Jimmy clamped his lips shut. He scrubbed a hand over his short hair and looked away.

'Has there been any change in your memory?' Bilton's tone of voice softened when he wanted something.

'No.' Jimmy shook his head, thinking he wouldn't tell Bilton even if he could remember anything more than he told the medical staff. Bilton gave him a filthy look as if he knew Jimmy was holding back and turned to Pete.

'How about you?'

'Like I said, boss, I don't remember anything except beating the shit out of a wall,' Pete replied, raising his bandaged hands and their broken fingers.

While Bilton questioned Pete, Jimmy picked up the newspaper but didn't read it. He amused himself by imagining Bilton's forehead in the crosshairs of a sniper rifle. Over the top of the page, he scrutinised Bilton's head as if studying the face of a high-value target. Bilton's preference for brushing back thinning fair hair revealed premature widow's peaks. Jimmy moved on to liquid blue eyes below eyebrows so light they were hardly noticeable. Bilton had smooth, pallid skin, a small nose with a flattened bridge, a long area from the nose to thin lips and barely any stubble on a soft-jawed chin. Bilton asked a few more questions and took his leave. Jimmy watched him disappear out of the cubicle.

'Aye, we're both doing nicely, thanks for asking,' he muttered, adding, 'wanker,' when Bilton was safely out of earshot.

Pete's friend returned.

'We're off in a few hours, mate. That's why I can't bring in any more booze.'

'What's that? What d'you mean, you're off?' Jimmy said.

The trooper looked round, leaned forward and lowered his voice, determined to spin out the superior feeling of being in the know over something the other two hadn't been told.

'The whole Squadron. We're out of here.'

Jimmy and Pete exchanged a glance and Jimmy fumed. Bilton was going into action with the lads and leaving him behind. Pete's hands needed time to heal but Jimmy was fit enough to go and Bilton knew it. He stared down the ward at the doors, a cauldron of conflicting emotions concentrated into loathing of Bilton, a misplaced focus for feelings Jimmy could barely recognise, let alone put into words.

His feelings related to the ward. Within each partitioned cubicle lay damaged men. Some had facial injuries, one was paralysed, others had legs or arms missing, one had been blinded, and most were wounded psychologically. Cheerful Pete wanted to entertain, lift spirits and crack jokes with the lads. Jimmy was afraid of them. Their courage humbled him but at the same time, the faces and the shattered bodies reminded him that he wasn't invincible. It could be him in one of the beds instead of them. He entertained them too, but didn't want to be near them, and found it easier to explain his desire to be out of the ward as wanting to be at the cutting edge of life rather than the fear of being tainted or weakened by the suffering of other soldiers.

Later the same day, Jimmy waited in the television lounge while Pete chatted up the young nurse, their reluctant assistant who needed some further persuasion, as Pete put it, although he had something else on his mind besides verbal persuasion. Jimmy yawned at the news on the screen, getting up to pump life back into his flagging muscles. The heat and lack of fresh air made him feel geriatric. He glanced at three young amputees watching the news on TV, sprawled in easy chairs with metal crutches at their sides. The sight of them made him feel uncomfortable and he turned to leave.

'Some breaking news just in,' the newsreader said. Jimmy stopped. The Prime Minister's visit to the US had been thrown into disarray by a fight in the skies over Washington. Jimmy stared at blurry images captured by somebody's mobile phone and wished he'd been in the thick of it, even though he knew he was no match for what he saw. The soldiers in the chairs bucked into life, leaning forward to stare at the television.

'How does that fat bastard manage to fly?' Jimmy said, though nobody answered. They were too busy chatting excitedly to each other. The footage switched to pictures from a news helicopter, much clearer.

'Bloody hell,' Jimmy exclaimed. He caught Pete's attention with a whistle and an urgent hand gesture. Pete loped towards him. Jimmy laughed in disbelief at the scenes on TV.

'Look at that. That's those US guys.'

'The Yank team – Eagles,' Pete provided.

'Yeah, Eagles. Look at those bloody clowns, poncing around in stupid costumes.'

'Doing the business, though, aren't they?'

'Why don't they just shoot him?' one soldier asked.

'Nanotechnology,' Pete and Jimmy responded together, and chuckled.

'Material with new, improved versatility incorporating nanotechnology,' Pete said in a salesman voice. 'Stops just about any kind of shit and includes a visor, as you can see from the demonstration. Obviously MP7s do fuck all against that stuff.'

'Whoa. Did you see that?' the soldier gasped, as a concentrated beam of energy hit the fat bank robber and threw him back in a mid-air blur of light. The beam disappeared and the Eagles team piled into him, to shouts of encouragement and some jeers from the soldiers in the lounge.

'That's five against one,' somebody pointed out as the fat robber crashed to the ground and lay still.

'So? He's bigger than three of them put together,' another voice said.

'Why haven't we got a team like that?'

'Because we've got the SAS,' somebody else said, to knowing nods.

'They could beat the shit out of the SAS,' one man said, to more jeers and denials. He persisted, 'Look, they can fly and everything.'

Jimmy and Pete exchanged a glance. Jimmy nodded towards the doorway. Without saying anything they moved away from the group.

'The SAS have probably already got a team. It's got to be covert. They're not going to tell the whole bloody world they've got one, are they?'

Jimmy and Pete left them arguing the merits of the Eagles versus the SAS and walked back down the ward. They'd heard it all before. Jimmy wished he could be confident about the capabilities of the SAS in dealing with teleporters, but the truth was they didn't have a team, officially or unofficially, as far as he knew. Not only that, the training to fight Shifters was slow and mostly ineffective. It would only be a matter of time before the small number of Starbirth-related crimes in the UK became an all-out war with Shifters robbing banks, looting stores and stealing secrets from sensitive buildings that hadn't been electronically protected against teleporters.

That problem would have to be faced, but in the meantime they had another task. Pete looked at his watch then peered round the side of the cubicle.

'It's time. Ready?'

Jimmy nodded. They opened their bedside cabinets and pulled out loose trousers and white coats provided by Pete's friend and put them on. Posing as junior doctors they headed for the ward doors past an empty nurses' station. The security guard based outside the ward didn't even turn to look at them. He must have thought it was his lucky week as the young nurse paid him particular attention for the second time in as many days.

Pete stuck his bandaged hands in his pockets and they sauntered down the corridor past a cleaner. Jimmy kept his fingers wrapped around the handle of a small knife they had liberated from the kitchen the previous evening, concealing the blade up his sleeve. They strolled down a long corridor to the next ward to visit a Warrant Officer being treated for a broken leg. The man had a reputation as a bully and had reduced a nurse to tears two days previously. Pete heard all about it from the nurse's friend, who worked on their ward.

Pete gave him a cheery, innocent greeting.

'How are you?'

The Warrant Officer gave him a murderous look.

'It's about time you showed up. I've been waiting for days. The standard of care in this place – I wouldn't treat my dog the way I've been treated. I'm putting in a complaint about the incompetence here. Most of the staff don't know what they're doing.'

The Warrant Officer moaned on while Jimmy inspected the suspended foot. He shook his head at what he saw, motioned Pete to have a look and they huddled over the foot, muttering. The patient watched them with growing nervousness. Jimmy interrupted the man's rant, his face sombre.

'It's very unfortunate.'

'What is?'

'Your toes.'

'What about them?' the patient said, craning his thick, bristly neck to look at his toes.

'They're not the right colour.'

'What colour are they?'

Jimmy didn't answer. He looked at Pete and moved the big toe. Pete leaned over it.

'See that?' Jimmy said. Pete nodded, his face deadpan.

'Very bad. Shouldn't be that colour.'

'What colour?' The Warrant Officer tried to sit up to get a better look but Pete blocked his view.

'Have they been hurting?' Jimmy asked. The Warrant Officer frowned.

'No. I mean, the leg's been hurting, but – no.'

Jimmy nodded sagely.

'That's why it's so deceptive, it never hurts.'

'Never hurts,' Pete agreed, adding, 'until it's too late.'

Jimmy drew himself up straight, and patted the man's hand.

'Never mind, we'll sort it out for you,' he said. The man pulled his hand away, giving Jimmy a filthy look.

'What the hell are you talking about?'

'All your toes are gangrenous and will have to be amputated immediately.'

'What? Don't be ridiculous. You can't do that.'

'Yes, we can. We have to do it right away. That's what 'immediately' means. Otherwise the infection will spread up your leg under the plaster. We won't be able to save your balls if it goes to your groin.'

The man swallowed hard. Before he could say anything more, Jimmy produced the knife.

'Unfortunately the operating theatres are all full right now,' he said, and turned to Pete. 'Dr Smith, draw the curtains round the bed.'

'What the hell do you think you're doing?' the man said. He stared at the knife in horror. Pete turned away to hide his grin and pulled the curtains.

Jimmy continued, 'We don't need the operating theatre. We can do this here.'

'You're not a doctor, you're crazy. Get off me! Nurse!' yelled the man.

'No good yelling for the nurse. Don't worry, this won't hurt a bit. Gangrene kills all the nerves so we can cut your toes off and you won't even feel it.'

He leaned over the foot, blocking the Warrant Officer's view of it, placed the blunt side of the knife against the toes and started sawing.

The Warrant Officer swore and kicked out with his free leg, but didn't connect. He thrashed on the bed, grabbed the water jug from his bedside cabinet and threw it at Jimmy, hurling a torrent of expletives at the same time. Judging by laughter coming from the other beds in the ward Jimmy knew nobody would respond very soon. Pete doubled over, holding his belly from laughing so much.

'You want me to stop?' Jimmy said. The answer that came back was another volley of spirited abuse, but basically the man said yes. Jimmy put the knife back up his sleeve with a flourish.

'Okay, pal, but remember the staff are doing the best they can. If I hear of you getting nasty with the nurses again we'll be back. Next time it won't be the blunt side I'll use.'

The following morning Pete roused Jimmy from his newspaper.

'Our ray of sunshine is coming.'

'I thought he'd gone with the lads.'

'Well, it's not his frigging ghost.'

Jimmy peeked at Bilton from behind Pete's waist. 'He looks like something just crawled up his arse.' He pulled his head back and opened the newspaper again. 'Bet you a tenner he lets us go.'

'You're on. He's going to keep us here till Christmas.'

Bilton's opening words heralded the storm to come.

'You two, you don't deserve the treatment you're getting.' Jimmy stared at the wall and hardly listened while Bilton denounced their childish behaviour. He mused over whether Bilton had been born a wanker, or had taken a course in wankership later. He knew they were going to get their medical discharge because the staff nurse hadn't been round to take blood samples. She removed the cannulas from their arms instead. They had already packed their bags and stashed them behind their bedside cabinets. Jimmy waited for the time when Bilton would have to give in and acknowledge they could leave. He wasn't disappointed.

'The CO has decided it's time for you to get your kit.'

Jimmy's heart leapt but he kept his face deadpan.

Bilton continued, 'Andrews, you're to return home until further notice. You're not much use if you can't fire your weapon.' Jimmy put his hand up to his mouth to hide a smile and turned the gesture into rubbing his chin. Pete wanted some leave with his wife and baby, and he'd got it.

'Mackenzie, get your things together. Meet me downstairs in ten minutes.' Bilton turned on his heel and marched down the ward. Jimmy and Pete grabbed their bags and nearly ran to follow him. They shouted exaggerated goodbyes to the other lads and received a chorus of jeers and one-fingered salutes in return. Pete took time to kiss the nurses. At the main entrance Jimmy revelled in fresh air and sunshine.

'Catch up with you in the Stan,' Pete said in a low voice.

'Don't forget you owe me a tenner.'

They parted company. Jimmy strode down the steps to Bilton, who gazed at him sourly.

'You'll need jungle supplies. Get them from the base in Birmingham, they're expecting you. And a set of civvies for city wear. A smart suit, room enough for getting tooled up. English supporter's football kit, too, for the plane out.'

'English?' Jimmy couldn't see himself in the kit of Scotland's worst enemies.

'Yes, English. You're here all day. Plenty of time to get something from the shops. Meet me outside the Departures terminal at Birmingham airport at seventeen hundred hours.' Jimmy frowned. He knew he shouldn't ask, but he did.

'Jungle supplies, not desert, Boss?'

'You heard me.' Bilton opened the back door of the car he had arrived in. The military driver stared ahead. Jimmy stiffened. Surely Bilton must have made a mistake.

'No jungles in the Middle East, boss.'

'Who said anything about the Middle East?'

Bilton slammed the car door shut after him and gave Jimmy a withering glance before the car sped away. A little way from the entrance Pete put his bag into the boot of a taxicab, trying to avoid weight on his hands.

'Hey, Pete. Wait up, mate,' Jimmy bellowed.

'Miss me already?' Pete grinned when Jimmy reached him.

'Pain in the arse like you? 'Bout as much as last night's dinner. Listen, mate, you're going straight back home on the train, yeah?'

The cab driver slammed the boot down and went back to the driver's seat.

'Yeah. What's up?'

Jimmy rummaged around in his bag, pulling out a set of door keys. He handed them to Pete.

'Make a detour by my pad. In the wardrobe in the bedroom you'll find a black holdall. Send it by courier to the base here, ASAP. I'll forget that tenner you owe me. And don't bloody poke around, either. I'll know if you have.'

'What d'you mean, don't poke around? I wouldn't do anything like that to a mate.'

'Piss off, Saint Peter, your halo's blinding me.' Jimmy raised his hand to shade his eyes. 'And send the keys back, too.'

'Okay. You want a lift to New Street?'

The cab driver gave Pete a filthy look and made much out of being asked to take another passenger and open the car boot again for another bag. Jimmy settled on the back seat and thought he would have to buy another lock for his front door after Pete returned the keys otherwise he might arrive home to find all his kitchen stuff piled up in the front room, again.

~~~~~~~~

Patuazon deployed electronic devices everywhere on his estate near Cali, especially around the training ground used by the SAS troopers. He made sure his visitors kept within their boundaries and behaved themselves. That included Lock, despite Lock's rescue of Patuazon's granddaughter. Patuazon made a show of being grateful yet his bodyguards always remained close at hand whenever the pair had any conversations.

Imagining himself under an electronic microscope, Lock took extra care
~~~~~~~~

over exiting the training ground in the middle of the night to send a report by radio burst transmission to London. He stood motionless below the ridge line of an Andean mountain, concealed in deep shadow, waiting for Stringer to reply. The jutting peaks of the Andes rode a sea of silvery jungle breath like fossilised galleons in full sail. Above them cirrus clouds parted in patches allowing soft light to fall on tumbled mounds of dark jungle canopy poking up above the rainforest mist.

When his dealings with Patuazon and Mosquera finished, he should bring Lianne and Thomas to see the beauty of the rainforest and this rare view of South America. Thomas would love it. They hadn't shared much holiday time lately. He shook the thoughts out of his mind and concentrated on the job in hand.

A soft yellow glow below the clouds marked the distant location of Cali. Lingering so high above Colombia gave him a sense of detachment and profound relief at being absent from Cali's nightly battles. Less than four days earlier he intervened in the aftermath of a road traffic accident, taking the injured to hospital. Years ago he would have been tormented by guilt at not being down there, knowing he possessed the ability to help people in trouble in Cali and wasn't making any effort to do so.

He rationalised the dilemma on the basis that he couldn't go to the aid of everybody, he had limits to his physical capabilities. He needed to sleep, rest, eat and make love, like normal folk, and the odds against stumbling on a situation where he could intervene were a million to one. Given prior knowledge, he could be there like a superhero, but generally the knowledge came after emergency services responded. On the occasions he did turn up, he spooked them by trying to explain how he could help. Reactions varied from outright disbelief to fear that he was mad and the threat of arrest if he didn't go away. Though, he thought, that might have changed in the months since Starbirth hit the streets.

London acknowledged receipt of the report and Stringer answered Lock's call, sounding morning-cheery. Lock felt hung over by comparison as he gave an update.

'There's been an increase in activity here at Patuazon's estate. We've seen twelve heavily guarded truck shipments arrive throughout the day. It looks like crates of ammo and weapons. If Patuazon is re-supplying his private army, he's getting in enough kit to start a war. Sending details now.'

Stringer acknowledged receipt of the covert photos.

'Keep an eye on developments. Let me know about any further shipments.'

'Acknowledged. Next item. Comms will be down for a couple of days. Patuazon's engineers worked on the river all day installing underwater anti-teleporter defences. It's in the main report but I'm sending images taken later in the day.' He pressed a button on his satellite phone to transmit digital photos and video footage obtained by the SAS men.

'Received.'

'I'll look for another way to leave without electronics picking up on the movement. There may be an opportunity soon. Patuazon heard I'd taught jungle skills to his men and wants me to do the same for his nephew. The boy doesn't seem interested, but if he is I may be able to get out of the estate.'

'Acknowledged.'

'Next item. I need a delivery date for my package.'

'We're working on it. I'll let you know.'

'Okay. Next item. Mosquera's new villa near Mocoa. Surveillance drones haven't seen anything except normal construction work. I get the impression they're in a hurry to finish it. From the chatter we've picked up, it seems they're expecting a visit from Mosquera soon. It sounds like he intends moving in.'

'Acknowledged. Anything else?'

Lock paused.

'Is there anything going on with Patuazon that I should know about?'

'Like what?' Stringer's voice was guarded.

'Mosquera.'

There was a short silence on the other end of the line.

'That's a separate issue. You don't need to be concerned. What made you ask?'

'The weapons shipments to Patuazon's estate. I hope we're not helping Patuazon hit Mosquera.'

'We wouldn't. Whatever's going on, it's nothing to do with us. The intel on Mosquera is for the Colombians at their request. If there is a hit going down, it's likely they'll do it with help from our American friends. The sooner you find out the information about Patuazon the sooner we can kiss him goodbye. Report in when you can.'

Lock felt that Stringer was on the level. He'd had plenty of practice over the years in judging Stringer's words by the tone of his voice. He turned to pack up the radio equipment. A movement about eighty metres away caught his eye. He froze and went into sensory mode, expecting to see an animal aura, but he saw blue. Nobody could be up the mountain at that height since his last sensory sweep unless the person had teleported. Using thought he ordered his visor to switch to sensitive thermal imaging and zoom in. The aura vanished. Through the visor Lock caught a telltale short heat streak indicating the teleporter's direction.

He gauged the Shifter's speed by the length of the trail and teleported after him. On the next jump the distance closed to forty metres but the man Shifted straight into the centre of Cali. Lock lost him among the hotels and thousands of people still asleep in their homes. Worried, he weighed up the possibility of compromise and after some minutes of deliberation decided that he had seen one of the many Shifters in Colombia out for a night stroll. He still felt uneasy when he returned to the river and Patuazon's estate, and the team raised the threat alert level at the training camp.

CHAPTER 4

When Jimmy met Bilton outside the Departures terminal at Birmingham Airport he didn't expect the offer of a covert assignment. He put on an act of being blasé, as if the intelligence community dished out black operations every day of the week, but his excitement jumped several levels at the thought of an adventure, especially one in Colombia, the South American heartland of Starbirth. Bilton gave him a disdainful look then checked the rear view mirror of the rental car for the tenth time in a minute. He employed counter-surveillance techniques en route to a hotel they could have reached easily on foot. It indicated that either the op was extremely sensitive, or Bilton was twitchy.

'It will only be for a day, two at the most,' Bilton said. 'The offer is a grand for the duration and after that you're back on normal payroll. Don't screw this up. The only reason you're here is because you've been to Bogota twice before. D'you want it or not?'

'Yes.'

Jimmy wondered how much Bilton knew about his trips to Colombia. One of his visits to Bogota ended after three days, but if Bilton didn't know that, Jimmy wasn't going to tell him.

'After the op you'll be replacing a man from D squadron who's been injured and casevac'd out,' Bilton said. Jimmy could hardly believe his luck – an extended stay in Colombia and the prospect of some action. He itched to get into a fight with a Shifter or two. The other lads would be so jealous. They'd give their eye teeth to be in his seat.

The black, rectangular shape of the hotel loomed up like a domino standing on its end. Dark clouds scudded past the flat roof and gave the impression it was about to topple forwards and squash them. Bilton phoned ahead then led the way to a room on the first floor. He rapped a series of coded knocks on the door. A burly, middle-aged man opened it. The newcomer's receding sandy hair, surly eyes and a nose that had been broken more than once gave the impression of somebody who had seen a lot of life and didn't take a great deal of pleasure from it. He let them into a large, bland room dominated by twin beds and a dark blue carpet with black stains just inside the door. A smell of stale coffee hung in the air as Jimmy passed plastic cups on the dressing table.

'Put your bergen there,' Bilton said, waving to the left. Jimmy took off the bulging Army rucksack, leaned it against a wall and Bilton introduced him to the rest of the black ops crew. Ken, the burly man, nodded at Jimmy and returned to scrutinising a map. Jimmy recognised the one keeping watch at the window, though he had forgotten his nickname until Snapper gave him a grin and firm handshake. Snapper stood out in the Regiment as not just one of the few mixed-race Blades but also because he was a fine Rugby player.

'Chris,' Bilton said, indicating a balding man in his early forties with a large waistline. Chris walked from the bathroom and stuck his hand out. Jimmy recognised him as another ex-Blade.

The dark haired fifth man, conspicuous in stylish clothes, introduced himself as Steven, following standard procedures for black ops by omitting his surname. Though Steven's surname would not have meant anything to Jimmy, he thought he had seen the man before, but couldn't place him. He puzzled over it for a few seconds then let it go. Even though he couldn't recall who Steven was, he knew what he was, having come into contact with plenty of similar people at briefings. It gave him a discerning nose when it came to the Secret Intelligence Service. Regiment men labelled them 'the Slime', a reference to what they regarded as their slippery nature and general inability to see backstabbing of colleagues as an antisocial trend. Jimmy didn't like them much.

'Now we're all here, let's get on,' Steven said. Bilton took over guard from Snapper at the window overlooking the car park and closed the blinds, leaving an 'accidentally' damaged area for powerful binoculars to look through. Jimmy settled on the edge of one of the beds. Steven unzipped a jacket pocket and took out a pen. 'The lights, please,' he said, pulling out a base for the pen to stand on. He put a closed laptop on a chair, balanced the pen and base on it and twisted the top of the pen. A light projected a photo onto the wall above the dressing table. Steven said the paunchy man getting into a limousine was Antonio Mosquera, long suspected of dealing in cocaine and now suspected of supplying Starbirth. Mosquera claimed he could supply the Brits with the essential ingredient of Starbirth, the drug AH-4. The job of the black ops crew would be to ensure smooth progress of a proposed deal with Mosquera.

When Steven turned his head, the half-light fell on his face at a different angle and Jimmy remembered where he had seen him before. It was in a corridor at Credenhill, the headquarters of the SAS. Steven had been huddled over a smartphone with Lock Harford and he had shielded the phone when Jimmy walked past. Jimmy thought that was odd, a gesture that bestowed importance on what the two men were talking about. At the time he thought they might have been viewing a raunchy bit of porn, but now he knew more about both men Jimmy doubted that theory. It increased his curiosity about Harford and his role with the SAS.

Steven looked at the group and said,

'The venue for the deal won't be known until the last few minutes so you'll have to wing it, no time for an in-depth recce.' He nodded at Bilton. 'As soon as Fred has the location we'll provide satellite images of the area.'

Jimmy stifled a snort of laughter at Bilton's first name. He'd owned a dog called Fred. Bilton gave him an icy glare. Steven continued,

'You'll be carrying lightweight drones with you so you should have decent overhead coverage.'

He turned back and the picture on the wall altered to a rough-looking bunch of swarthy men. 'The opposition. Lanceros employed by Mosquera. We know he has at least twelve of them besides his ordinary foot soldiers. Memorise their faces and know your enemy, in case anything should go wrong.' Steven paused as he inserted a memory stick in the side of his laptop.

Jimmy had heard of Colombian Lanceros from an American who completed their harsh training course. The US Ranger told him how he was kept in a state of exhaustion while undertaking gruelling tasks over seventy-three days. Instructors inflicted a regime of brutality aimed at imitating combat and capture conditions. Jimmy chipped in that it sounded similar to British Special Forces training, but the Ranger shook his head. It was nothing like it. Most armies wouldn't train their Special Forces that way, it was too dangerous. Jimmy had laughed and said the Ranger should try SAS training, but the Ranger was irritated.

'You know the Magdalena?' he asked. 'It's the biggest river in Colombia. They blindfolded us and took us to the deepest part. A test of confidence, they said. They shoved us blindfolded along an iron footbridge. We couldn't see nothin' but you could hear it, water thrashing and roaring underneath. They push you up against the side, shove a rope in your hands and scream at you to abseil over the edge. If you hesitate, you fail and there's only seconds to get down. We didn't know until later, we were over a forty-metre drop. So you go down fast, but the rope stops fifteen metres short. You can't go back, so you drop and hit the water like a sack of cement. You rip off the blindfold and have to catch a cord stretched across fifty metres downriver. Miss that and you get swept away.'

Jimmy recalled similar events jumping from planes and helicopters during his own training, but he didn't say anything. Later that day in military exercises he had great satisfaction when the SAS unit completed every task ahead of the Rangers.

His reminiscences about the skills of Lanceros were interrupted when Steven found the computer file he was looking for and resumed the briefing.

'As you would expect in that area, there are Starbirth addicts and we know Mosquera has at least one teleporter – this man. He seems to be a straightforward Shifter and acts as a courier.' The face on the wall was a young Creole, somebody with a mix of Spanish and native Indian ancestry. He looked barely out of his teens. 'Any questions at this point?'

'What can we expect from the Starbirth freaks if any turn up?' Chris asked.

'Your guess is as good as mine, given the variety of abilities, but it's similar to what we've seen on the news. People who are airborne, but we believe the way they are affected by the drug means their physical control is reduced.' Steven smiled. 'Basically, they might be able to fly, but they can't shoot straight at the same time. They're worse than a pack of kids taking pot shots with fairground rifles.'

Everybody laughed at Steven's attempt to lighten the atmosphere, but Jimmy had a nasty foreboding and was apprehensive about the venture. It didn't pay to underestimate the opposition. Steven described other hostiles in the area, types of weaponry the group might encounter, the terrain, and handed out photos of Mosquera's henchmen. He ended by saying,

'Your cover is that you're football fans travelling to Bogota to see England play the Colombian national team in two days' time. Jimmy, in your case, you'll have to adopt an English accent or keep your mouth shut.'

While Steven packed up his equipment, Bilton gave Jimmy a swipe card.

'Keycard to your room. You're sharing with Snapper.'

That suited Jimmy, who didn't fancy sharing a room with Bilton or Ken. Steven said goodbye to Bilton and left the hotel.

'Courier's here,' Snapper said without turning his head.

'Ken, Chris, Jimmy, collect the bags from downstairs,' Bilton ordered. Snapper stayed on stag, guard duty, in Bilton's room.

Afterwards, alone in the shared bedroom, Jimmy unpacked the holdall he had asked Pete to send. In the zip-up section was the pale grey suit he would be wearing in Colombia. The good quality material wouldn't show any sweat marks or the bulge of a shoulder holster underneath, and the jacket allowed for lightweight body armour. The shirt had ultraviolet proofing to keep him cool in direct sunlight, which would serve him well in the heat of Bogota. He put the outfit back into the holdall and picked through the rest of the garments, including the England football supporter's kit and casual clothes that would allow him to blend in with an airport crowd and conceal a weapon. The moment he put on the clothes, Jimmy the off-duty soldier became Jimmy the professional, like donning a new skin. The person he had been was folded up and put away in a spare bag to be stored with the rest of his kit at the Birmingham base until his return.

Back at the briefing room the team selected weapons from a range laid out on the bed. Bilton handed Jimmy a shoulder holster containing a 9mm Sig Sauer pistol, extra magazines, and an English flag to go in his holdall alongside an England supporter's baseball cap.

'Do we pick up extra weapons in Bogota?' Jimmy asked.

'No, they go out with us by diplomatic bag.'

'In that case I want an ankle holster with a Walther PPK.' Jimmy looked at the standard holster for the Sig Sauer pistol. 'And a shoulder holster that holds the Sig butt down.'

Bilton gave him an irritated look, but Jimmy's unwavering gaze – a direct challenge demanding Bilton prove he knew more about weapons than an experienced trooper – forced the officer to silently give ground and get on the phone. Although the battle of wills was over in a second, it marked a point where Bilton's dislike of Jimmy turned into something more. Jimmy didn't care what Bilton thought, his only thought was about maximising his chances of survival. The standard rig was fine for a cooler zone, but there was a lot wrong with it in a hot city and a sub-tropical climate. Sweat made the felt lining of the holster stick to the metal of the weapon, which meant he needed two hands to draw it. That wouldn't be helpful when every fraction of a second counted.

He looked over the rest of the arsenal, mostly weapons they would use once they were in Colombia. They had a wide choice, encompassing metre-long M-16 Colt Commando semi-automatic rifles of the older type used mostly in South American countries, and MP7 sub-machine guns, a snub-nosed weapon used by US Navy SEALs. They had long AK 47 semi-automatic rifles that had larger calibre rounds and packed a greater punch than the M-16s, plus extra personal weapons, mostly pistols, to be kept in the hire cars they would pick up in Bogota. Jimmy selected an MP7 and an M-16 to go with his Sig Sauer pistol and checked the weapons thoroughly. Bilton raised his voice above the sound of oiled machinery sliding and clicking into place.

'Okay, listen up. The pipe range. Snapper, Chris, with me. Jimmy, you go last with Ken, after the courier returns with your extras, and make sure you clean up. Let's go.'

The door swung shut behind them leaving Jimmy alone with Ken, whose idea of conversation extended no further than grunts, or saying nothing at all. Jimmy guessed Ken was South African but didn't know for sure until they drove to the disused factory a short distance from the airport. Ken surprised him by stringing together enough words to make a couple of sentences.

'I don't know what the SAS is coming to when they allow so many blacks and coloureds in. I don't trust them.' It confirmed Jimmy's guess.

'Really? That's a pity. The SAS isn't exclusive when it comes to colour. We take people according to how effective they are as soldiers, nothing else, and not because of some piss-poor reason like the way they look. Snapper's a good bloke, as good as any I've worked with – are you?'

The snide references to Snapper and the Regiment irritated Jimmy and he took an instant dislike to Ken. Blades moaning to each other about the Regiment was acceptable, but he didn't want to listen to an outsider making disparaging remarks. Ken should have known better. They hardly spoke to each other for the rest of the evening.

At the disused, dirty factory they met Chris, who had stayed behind to guard the entrance and keep watch on the empty streets. Jimmy settled down in front of a thirty metre length of metre-wide drainage pipes laid end to end. He flicked the toggle on his M-16 to single shot and fired along the length of pipe. Five rounds smacked into a pile of sand at the end. A smell of cordite overpowered the musty, damp sand odour of the factory. He made adjustments to small screws by the rear sight of the M-16 to trim the weapon to his personal requirements – a process known as zeroing. The drainage pipes masked the sound of gunfire but didn't hide the noise completely.

Jimmy put down the M-16 keeping it close by his side, picked up the MP7 and kept a wary eye on Ken. Stranger things than accidents had been known to happen with touchy men who felt slighted, but the time passed without incident and Ken was calm. They dismantled the pipes, picked up spent cartridge cases and cleared away sand containing the rounds. The three of them drove back to the hotel in silence, except for Chris blowing his nose as though he had a cold. Jimmy decided to keep away from him as much as possible, to avoid catching it. Infection slowed reflexes.

The next rehearsal involved tiny in-the-mouth radio receivers, which fitted over the back teeth like small dentures and relayed signals to the inner ear, using bone conduction. The team fixed miniscule microphones behind their ears, went through a radio check to make sure everything worked and Bilton gave them radio call signs using the universal military phonetic alphabet. He designated himself as Zero, the commander. He pointed at each man in turn.

'Ken, you're Delta One. Snapper, Delta Two. Chris, Delta Three. Jimmy, Delta Four. Hostiles are X-Rays. Stay in comms reach and wait for my orders.'

Jimmy went to his shared room to clean his weapons. He picked up the MP7 and ran his fingertips over the metal. The slick, cold steel flowed past his hand. The mechanism unlocked in a smooth, precise action. He smeared the working parts with gun oil, lovingly, intuitively aware of the sexual metaphor in his love of weapons, though it wasn't defined in his conscious thoughts as such. If a semi-naked, erotic girl had appeared before him, pleasure with her would have to wait unless he could squeeze in a bit of down time. She would not figure in the compartment containing a persona that was as cold as the steel in his hands. He inhabited a mental world devoid of emotional distractions, his mind narrowed into a single line of thought encompassing nothing more than the task for which he needed to be armed.

He moved bolts and cylinders expertly, slotting them into place, constructing a lethal jigsaw. The finished product sat in his grip with easy familiarity, not just an extension of his arm, but the covering for his nakedness. It completed him. Weapons had been a part of his life for as long as he could remember, since childhood outings when he accompanied his father in his work as a gamekeeper. His dad had been in the Army so entering the armed forces was a natural progression, following in the footsteps of not just his father, but his grandfather and elder brother. He inherited their love of weapons.

He picked up the M-16 and stripped it down, contrasting his confidence with rifles and sub-machine pistols against the way Lock Harford held them. Harford didn't have full Special Forces training and wasn't as comfortable with weapons, and it was obvious the first time Jimmy saw him carrying one. He wondered how much weapons training Harford had undergone. Picking up a lint free cloth from the cleaning kit he pulled a trace of oil along the bore of the barrel, stopped, and frowned at his oily fingertips. The strange tingling he experienced in hospital returned. He rubbed the oil between his fingers, wondering what caused the sensation and if it was linked to the overdose of Starbirth.

A series of coded raps on the door were an unwelcome distraction. Snapper barged into the room and searched for something on the dressing table.

'Where's the TV remote?'

'Over there.' Jimmy pointed to a bedside cabinet and carried on cleaning the M-16. The tingling altered to something he hadn't experienced before, waves of vibrations flowing through his fingers down to the knuckle joints. It made the hairs on the back of his neck stand on end.

'Boss is going apeshit,' Snapper said, pressing buttons on the remote control to switch the wall-mounted television to a news channel.

'Yeah?' Jimmy wasn't interested in what Bilton did. He slotted the sections back into place, ignored the heightened sensitivity in the palms of his hands and looked along the rifle sights while the television stuttered into life.

'This is it,' Snapper said.

Jimmy watched views of a large glass building and the words 'Breaking News: Manchester Airport Attack' on a tickertape section at the bottom of the screen. Snapper turned up the volume.

'–confirmed a number of thefts at the airport but refused to comment further, saying investigations are ongoing,' the journalist said. The scene switched to fuzzy footage from a mobile phone, showing scared people streaming out of the airport to a fleet of waiting ambulances before clearer camerawork focused on a flustered woman.

'We thought it was a terrorist attack. People were being sick all over the place.' The journalist asked a couple more questions that were blindingly silly in Jimmy's view then said,

'Police have confirmed this isn't a chemical or biological attack, but the airport terminal remains sealed off and there are extensive delays to flights in and out of Manchester.'

Snapper said excitedly,

'That's weird. What would make people throw up like that?'

'Dunno, mate.' Jimmy stuck a piece of coloured tape on the butt of the M-16 to identify the weapon as his and wiped his hands to see if the weirdness stopped when he removed the oil. It didn't. He hardly noticed another coded knock on the door.

'Boss wants everybody in his room,' Chris said. Jimmy sighed. Nobody would be getting much sleep, he was sure of that. Besides poring over maps and computer visuals to sort out the actions-on plan for Bogota, they would have to spend more time than was necessary going over details for Birmingham Airport, just to satisfy Bilton's paranoia over the attack at Manchester.

The warm fingers of dawn hadn't touched the silvery glass of Birmingham Airport's Departures hall at six-thirty in the morning, yet the terminal was full, due to delayed and cancelled flights the previous evening. Passengers had been diverted from Manchester to Birmingham. Tired, irritable adults wandered around as if drugged, barely coping with screaming toddlers and hyperactive children who skidded about on the black and white marble effect floor. Shrill voices echoed in the fifteen metre high space, drowning out announcements over the speaker system. A mouth-watering smell of freshly cooked bacon wafted from the restaurant on the open-deck upper floor. Jimmy ran his tongue over the radio receiver in his mouth, poking it like a sore tooth. The crew were all armed in case anything happened.

Snapper did a reconnaissance of the upper floor, and stayed there in an overhead position. Ken joined the check-in queue, covering the front of the terminal. As the commander at the centre of an imaginary clock face, Bilton positioned himself midway between Ken at twelve o'clock and Jimmy at seven o'clock. Chris took care of the rear and right flank by standing near a trolley park at the five o'clock position. Since Jimmy's arc of responsibility covered the rear and left flank, he stood near a cookie shop watching for anybody who didn't fit in, whose body language gave out the wrong signals. Bilton carried important documents that he didn't want to entrust to diplomatic bags.

'Delta Three to Zero, ten metres two o'clock, escalator, possible three X-Rays,' Snapper muttered. Jimmy glanced towards his right. Three youths in loose fleece jackets with their hoods up made their presence felt as they bundled down an escalator.

Jimmy sensed they would be a problem and his adrenaline pitched in. Everything about them, including their loud voices, over-emphatic gestures and the way they elbowed other people aside, was provocative and attention-seeking. Jimmy's nose for trouble told him something else, that lads like those didn't make a fuss unless they had another game-plan. He swept his gaze over everybody behind him. Keeping a thin, sallow-faced youth in view, he dropped his chin, folded his newspaper, spoke softly and broke into the radio communication on the common channel.

'Delta Four to Zero, four metres seven o'clock, possible X-Ray Four. Checking.'

X-Ray Four was up to no good. The three noisy hoodies attracted the attention of the airport police, leaving their accomplice free to do some opportunistic thieving. He sidled forward with his hands in his pockets and his neck and shoulders rigid with tension, his eyes darting around to keep others in view. Jimmy looked away before he could make eye contact, but kept the lad in his peripheral vision. The target was a woman three passengers in front of Jimmy. She made the mistake of putting an open shopping bag on the floor with a small handbag poking out of the top and had walked a few steps away to deal with her noisy child.

Jimmy watched the way the thin youth held his hand in his pocket. The unnatural angle of his arm indicated a weapon – probably a knife. He couldn't let that go.

'Delta Four to Zero, X-Ray Four has possible weapon. Intercepting now.'

As the potential thief came alongside, Jimmy reached down for his holdall, straightened up and twisted as though he'd decided to wander off. He swung his holdall into the youth's legs and cannoned into him sideways. His weight and a surreptitious shove sent the lad sprawling. Jimmy pretended to stumble and fell on top of him, ending up with his knee on the weapon pocket and his hand on the lad's right arm. The waxy face in front of him, blotched and scoured by drug abuse, contorted into a grimace of fury.

'What the fuck you doing, man?' the lad yelled in an American accent, his eyes widened with battle fever. Jimmy leaned forward and whispered,

'You go for that knife, pal, and I'll break your arm.'

The youth's lips parted in a sneer. Jimmy's head swirled. He felt as though he'd consumed every piece of rotting food in the airport and he felt faint and threw up. Thin arms pushed him away as though he weighed nothing more than a feather pillow. He vomited all over the tidy black and white floor, to the vocal disgust of the people closest to him. They moved away swiftly to a safe distance. He heard the lad say, 'Fuck you, man,' but was too busy getting rid of his early breakfast, and some of the previous night's dinner, to think of acting beyond putting his hand on his pistol to make sure it was still there. Bilton's orders over the radio were drowned out by a crescendo of shouts.

The nausea and projectile vomiting stopped as suddenly as it had begun. Jimmy felt a hand on his shoulder.

'Okay, mate?' Chris asked, his voice tense.

'Yeah.' Jimmy nodded, wiping his mouth on the back of his hand. He wobbled to his feet and was nearly bowled over by panicky people stampeding for the exit. He wasn't alone in being sick. A line of people leading to the exit, including a couple of police officers, had either fallen or staggered, vomiting violently. The queues parted like the Red Sea to get away from them.

'Where'd he go?' Jimmy asked.

'Buggered off out the front,' Snapper came in breathlessly on the radio. 'Bloody hell, he was fast. I've never seen anything like it. Must've gone in two seconds, flat.'

The airport authorities evacuated the terminal. Bilton was livid. He didn't give credence to the notion of a chemical attack and he worried the delay would jeopardise the deal in Bogota. He made a lot of phone calls and liaised with the police who were alarmed at finding armed men in the airport, but once they knew who they were dealing with, they gave Bilton access to the airport's closed-circuit television footage. It showed the situation was due to one man whom MI5 identified as Brad Paulson, an American Starbirth addict responsible for a string of robberies in the UK, including the one at Manchester Airport the previous evening. Snapper dubbed him 'Barfing Brad' and ribbed Jimmy mercilessly about being beaten in close quarter combat by a wimp with arms like bits of string.

The team handed their weapons to a courier to send them out via diplomatic bags after all. Bilton used Credenhill's influence to get preferential treatment for himself and his team. The plane to Bogota left two hours late but with only a third of its passengers on board and Bilton's team had the whole of Business Class. They made themselves at home and settled down. Jimmy broke the silence with a guffaw.

'What's so funny?' Snapper asked.

'I was just thinking. There's this guy, he's taken Starbirth to get some kind of superpower like flying or Shifting. And what does he get? The power to make people puke. He's going to be right bloody popular. Can you imagine him at a party? How would he ever get laid? They'd be too busy chucking carrots at him.'

'Maybe he takes a supply of plastic bags,' Chris said.

'Or a few condoms to hold the sick. He should get a job as a trolley-dolly, they're used to people throwing up and he'd have an endless supply of sick bags to give out like party favours.' Jimmy laughed, with Chris and Snapper joining in. 'Poor bastard. His social life's screwed, isn't it? I think I'd turn to thieving. What would you tell your mates if they ask what power you got? 'Yeah, man, I can make you sick.' I'd like to see him at home. I wonder if he makes the dog sick, too.'

~~~~~~~~

In Bogota's main airport Jimmy stared at a sign translated from Spanish to English, which said offering bribes to customs officials would be followed by a long visit to jail. It was his first indication of how Bogota had changed since his last tour. The doors of the air-conditioned airport slid apart, a symbol of privilege opening to an onslaught of fierce heat, strident car horns and those who couldn't afford to fly anywhere. Jimmy sniffed the air and discovered some things hadn't changed. A pungent perfume of orange blossom caught him with easy familiarity like an exotic mistress welcoming him back to her room. He put on his sunglasses and smiled at pleasant memories.

During the ride to their hotel, Jimmy realised Steven's briefing on Bogota was out of date. The Colombian capital, safer for tourists, extended a less enthusiastic welcome to well-muscled men in football gear in a couple of white four-wheel-drive Explorers. Shortly after heading through an older part of town on the outskirts of Bogota, a patrol of suspicious army and police stopped them, a random check though nobody in Bilton's group believed that. The new Explorers were an obvious target for a shakedown. Jimmy stood with his hands on the roof of the hire car as he was frisked by a policeman. He stared over a blue painted wall at American-style skyscrapers in the city centre. People jostled past on the other side of the road, merengue music blared from a house nearby, and Creole children gathered to stare at the gringos. One called out in Spanish and the rest laughed until a woman shouted at them and they ran off. Jimmy exchanged a glance with Chris, being frisked on the other side of the car, a silent communication of relief that they hadn't yet picked up the weapons they were due to collect.

The group's accompanying contact, a European-looking Colombian, had good teeth and a smart suit, and that influenced the way the police dealt with him. He rattled off a non-stop barrage of indignant Spanish at a bored police officer, who checked their papers and let them go having found nothing except a discreetly offered wad of US dollars, which he pocketed.

'Why the hell weren't we warned about the stop-and-search patrols?' Chris asked Jimmy and Ken as they followed the lead car containing Bilton, Snapper and the contact. Since nobody bothered to answer, Chris shook his head and twitched restlessly on the seat all the way to the hotel, unnerved
~~~~~~~~

by the incident.

The hotel was similar to thousands the world over: an ordinary-looking tower block about fifteen storeys high with a plush lobby, a reasonably clean, nondescript interior, pleasant pictures of boats and marinas on the walls, and fresh sheets on the beds. The room Jimmy shared with Chris on the sixth floor smelled musty and had a tired air as though hung over between wild nights of partying. Bilton warned them to expect a visitor, a Mr Lewis, he said, passing round a smartphone photo of a man Jimmy recognised as Lock Harford. He didn't say anything as he passed the phone to Snapper.

Jimmy was smarting about coming off badly in his first encounter with a Starbirth user. On the flight, and at Bogota, he watched civilians for signs of people doing extraordinary things and was disappointed at not having the opportunity to prove he could handle anybody drugged-up on Starbirth. Not one person appeared like a ghost, vanished into thin air, or suddenly started flying. Everything had been boring and ordinary, just the usual city mix of the poor rubbing shoulders with the rich. Harford's visit excited him. Now that he knew the truth about the man, he didn't want to miss a chance of seeing him do something odd like suddenly appearing in the car park. When Bilton informed them the weapons had been delivered downstairs, Jimmy took the opportunity to go outside the hotel and collect them with Ken and Chris. He looked at the sky, afraid he might miss the moment of Harford's arrival.

At the rear of the hotel two undercover security men from the British Embassy had parked a white Explorer next to one belonging to the group. Any casual observer would assume Jimmy and Ken were walking to their own car, not the duplicate. Ken opened the boot, took out the bags of weapons and ignored Chris, who moaned about having to do the first guard duty in Bilton's room. Jimmy saw a tremble in Chris's hand as the other man reached into the boot for a heavy bag containing disassembled parts of small drones – the spies in the sky that would give the crew aerial surveillance capability.

During the plane journey Chris paid several visits to the toilet, which was not significant in itself but he didn't look as healthy as he should. He carried more weight than was ideal for his age and build considering his high-risk occupation. Nevertheless, Jimmy assumed it would not affect his performance. If Chris was ill, he wouldn't have been allowed to take part. Jimmy, Chris and Ken took the bags inside the hotel and Jimmy saw no sign of Harford. He turned to Chris as they walked to their rooms.

'I'll do your stag, mate,' he said. Chris's mournful expression lifted at the prospect of Jimmy taking the bait.

'Sure?'

'I'm not tired,' Jimmy lied, concealing his real motive of being in Bilton's room when Harford turned up.

He felt safer once he donned the semi-automatic MP7. The swivel harness allowed the weapon to hang vertically between his arm and body. The weight of extra magazines held by the harness counterbalanced the weight of the MP7, so when he looked in the full length mirror his jacket showed no sign of a hidden weapon. The MP7 packed a heavier punch than any pistol and was what he needed for the rough parts of Colombia. He swept his right arm back, a fluid movement that pushed aside his jacket and took his hand straight to the grip and trigger of the weapon. In one second any opponent would go from looking at a man in a suit, to staring down the menacing barrel of a sub-machine gun. Years of practice drawing weapons gave him confidence and an edge over any bad guy he came across.

He strapped the Walther PPK pistol to his ankle. The light weapon could be a life-saver in a tight spot. He put aside the Sig Sauer pistol and shoulder holster. They would be stored in one of three vehicles the group would be using, the two Explorer cars and a van lined up for them by Ken's contact. They inspected the M-16 Colt Commando semi-automatic rifles and AK47s and put them back into bags with spare magazines of ammunition, to be stored in the vehicles. Jimmy picked up a new mobile phone supplied by the Embassy, switched it to vibrate mode and put it in his inside pocket. He was fully tooled up and ready.

Following another radio comms check, Ken went downstairs to stand guard in the lobby and return the keys of the duplicate car to the Embassy men, who picked up the documents carried by Bilton. Chris and Snapper decided to distress the Explorers to make them less attractive to the Colombian security services while they waited for Harford's arrival and the phone call telling them the time and location of the meeting.

Back in Bilton's room, Jimmy regretted offering to do Chris's stint of guard duty. Bilton ripped into him for intercepting Brad Paulson at the airport and drawing unwanted attention. Jimmy took the flak. Bilton finished his rant and sat on one of the beds. He opened the last holdall and spread out packs of US dollars, counting what looked like two hundred thousand before putting them back. Jimmy ignored him and stood guard where he could cover both the door to the corridor and the patio door leading to a balcony overlooking the sweltering city, since any attack might just as easily be airborne.

He liked to think he was a good judge of character. He had seen many Ruperts – as British Army soldiers called their officers – to discern those who knew soldiering from those he regarded as tossers who didn't have a clue. Bilton, as a Rupert in the SAS, could not be defined as a clueless officer since SAS officers had to pass the same rigorous Selection process as the troopers under their command, and undergo the same year-long Continuation training programme afterwards. On operations they shared quarters with the men and were referred to as Boss rather than Sir, distinctions that marked the relationship as special compared to regular army discipline.

Bosses were supposed to get on with troopers and at the very least give the men under their command some credit for being more cunning and more self-sufficient than regular army grunts. Bilton didn't do that, at least in his interactions with Jimmy. He was neither civil nor tolerant and tended to treat Jimmy as an imbecile, unlike the consideration Snapper, Ken and Chris received. Jimmy wondered why HQ, the Head Shed, allowed Bilton to get past the psychological vetting that formed part of Selection. In his view, Bilton showed none of the attributes expected of a Boss.

Bilton received a brief phone call.

'Lewis is here. Let him in,' he ordered.

Jimmy opened the door, his weapon ready to fire straight through the wood if necessary. Harford's face was a picture of shock when he saw Jimmy, though he said nothing to give any hint of recognition. He simply nodded a greeting and turned to Bilton.

'I've come to pick up a package.'

'Yes, it's here.'

Bilton handed him a slim briefcase. Harford said,

'I may as well test the kit here. If it's faulty it can go straight back.'

'Make it quick.'

Bilton returned to his laptop. Jimmy resumed his position by the window and watched as Harford took a pair of wraparound sunglasses from the briefcase and put them on. Harford startled him by walking in his direction, as if he sensed Jimmy covertly peering at him.

'Okay to open the blinds?' Harford asked. Jimmy moved back into a shadow and nodded.

'Aye, go ahead,' he said, slipping into his Scottish accent as he did when rattled.

Harford turned sideways on to Jimmy and opened the blinds. His spectacle lenses darkened. Strong sunlight lit a thin red line on his left cheek, the legacy of the knife fight in Scotland. Jimmy glanced away, embarrassed, but his curiosity got the better of him. Keeping the city outside in view, he watched Harford in his peripheral vision. Harford took off the glasses and fiddled with them, an indication they were more than ordinary sunglasses.

Jimmy guessed, wrongly, that Harford was a lot younger than himself. The guy looked like hundreds of others, with an open face that invited trust, conveying a sense of inner calm tinged by tension around the eyes. His face spoke of having been touched by the furnace of powerful emotions, something Jimmy had seen countless times among soldiers before a battle and after a harrowing experience. He wondered why he didn't notice all that during the survival training course. Maybe he missed it because Harford smiled and laughed then. Having a good time with his mates distracted Harford. Jimmy had dismissed him as a lightweight who knew some survival tricks, and chided himself for not looking deeper than the quiet surface. It struck him that Harford might be telepathic. Alarmed, he tried to shield his thoughts.

Harford put the glasses back on and stared outside, occasionally touching the sidebar. He took them off.

'I'm done,' he said. Jimmy nodded and closed the blinds, resuming his watch. Nothing about Harford's movements indicated anything extraordinary, though Jimmy wasn't sure what he expected to see. He didn't want to think about it too much in case Harford had telepathic powers. He scanned the hazy sky. The computer chip in his binoculars picked out the shape of an aircraft in the distance and recognition patterns identified it as a Bell helicopter, of the type favoured by the Colombian military. He touched a central control button. The binoculars zoomed in and Jimmy saw the Spanish word 'Policia' on the side of the Bell. The chopper arced in the sky, away from the hotel.

Jimmy's sensitive ears picked out a faint, alien noise among the background hotel sounds he had become accustomed to. Something buzzed. He looked round sharply for the source, finding it near Harford. Bilton heard it as well. A small object hovered in the air. It shot across the room towards Jimmy. He ducked automatically and swore, staring at an insect hovering near his head. Harford strolled over and plucked it out of the air.

'I need some more practice,' he said, but the sly smile twitching the corners of his mouth reminded Jimmy of antics on the last day of the survival course.

'An insect drone, right?'

'Get back on watch,' Bilton said, peering at the object in Harford's hand. Harford glanced at Bilton as though tolerating a petulant child and moved to show the fake insect to Bilton in a way that Jimmy could see it as well.

'It's the latest design, nothing secret. Goes places where the bigger drones can't reach, right into any building you want to monitor.'

Jimmy scrutinised the silky yellow and black body of a bee. It looked real.

'It's biomimetic, a mix of metals and plastics,' Harford said. 'It has a composite bee shell with part biological machinery inside. The wings contain silicone chips. They're as small as specks of dust, which is why the boffins call them smart dust. You've probably heard of it. That's what allows the wings to mimic insect flight.' He made the wings flutter without touching the drone. 'It can move in any direction, just like an ordinary bee. On-board sensors have been updated to monitor sound, temperature, the chemical composition of air, and so on. Improved radio comms means we won't lose contact with the insects after they've entered a building. The controls have been improved. The power supply is the same, something called synthetic chemical muscles.' He smiled. 'Don't ask me to explain that, I don't understand the techie shit.'

Jimmy saw Bilton seethe, which amused him, especially when Harford offered the bee to himself and not Bilton.

'Here, take it. I'll keep watch. Pick it up by the body.'

Bilton's mouth tightened in frustration when Jimmy handed over the binoculars and picked up the insect, but he didn't argue.

Spiky legs made small indentations on the palm of Jimmy's hand, but other than that, he found nothing to arouse suspicion that the insect was false. With the tip of his index finger he touched the shiny, micro-thin, delicate wings.

'Careful of those,' Harford said.

Jimmy gave the bee back to Harford, who turned to show it to Bilton, but Bilton was at his laptop as though he had no interest in the insect drone. Harford put the bee in a small plastic box and Jimmy glimpsed more tiny drones lined up inside bubbles of plastic. Harford closed the lid and shoved the box in his rucksack.

'Need an extra body?'

'No. We have everything we need,' Bilton said.

Jimmy frowned. Bilton was a dickhead. Of course they could do with somebody else, especially given whatever talents the man had, but it wasn't his place to argue with the officer in command. Harford left using the door, as any ordinary person would.

Chapter 5

An hour after leaving Bogota, Lock had a dilemma on his hands.

'Tell me, Senor Lewis, do you like to go fishing?' Patuazon asked.

Taken unawares Lock paused for a second before replying. Patuazon would interpret that second as being meaningful, but Lock needed it. If he lied and said yes, he would spend most of the afternoon with Patuazon out on the fishing lake in a speedboat listening to his host expounding his theories on God, and Patuazon would detect a lie. If he told the truth and said no, he risked disappointing his host, and Patuazon had agreed to provide extra equipment for the SAS troopers.

'It's a relaxing sport but I'm not good at it.'

He glanced at the swarthy, fit man standing beside him at the lakeside amid the sizzling sound of billions of sub-tropical insects. A breath of steamy wind flowed across the fishing lake and ruffled Patuazon's dyed black hair. A smile of veneered white teeth, provided by the best dentistry in the world, gave Patuazon the appearance of a genial crocodile. No amount of plastic surgery on the bulky, solid face had been able to smooth his pockmarked skin, though it had made Patuazon look much younger than his sixty-two years. Hooded, glittery eyes studied Lock from under bushy eyebrows.

'Typical British tact. Something I learned when I studied in London as a young man. You mean no, but didn't want to offend me, correct?'

Patuazon enjoyed seeing people squirm, and Lock hated him for it. He smiled and inclined his head as if acknowledging the older man's insight, hoping Patuazon wasn't already making plans for his guest's early death. Rumour said Patuazon reserved human prey for special occasions when he entertained his right-wing colleagues such as the judges and military he had on his payroll. The judges earmarked political prisoners and sympathisers to act as prey and sanctioned a jail move at the appropriate time. The prisoners left the compound in a prison van and disappeared.

'Join me in hunting, then.' Patuazon gestured to a bodyguard, who handed him a towel. 'My pilot will take you there and wait while you change clothes. Meet me by the stables in one hour. We'll talk after the hunt.' He wiped sweat from his face, slung the towel over his shoulder and strolled back to his personal gym followed by his guards.

An hour later Lock climbed aboard the Huey helicopter, a small three-seater. It banked away from the seven thousand acre estate lying against the foothills of the Andes, south-west of Cali. Bright terracotta roofs and a razor wire fence marked the boundaries of human intrusion into sub-tropical forest previously inhabited by thousands of animal, bird and insect species. Below the sculpted villa, Patuazon kept a private zoo, set among high trees he had left in place with some regard for what had been bulldozed. Patuazon often released exotic animals into an enclosed section of jungle for the purpose of hunting them down.

Lock didn't feel inclined to shoot anything, but the hunt would give him an opportunity to use the drone bee and find out what Patuazon hid in the villa's locked eastern wing. The drone might be able to penetrate the anti-teleporter neural net that extended over the villa and its outbuildings. Neural nets had been developed in response to threats posed by teleporters. The name reflected their effects on the brain and ranged from paralysis and loss of consciousness, to death. Patuazon's invisible net acted as a lethal deterrent. Lock heard that several Cali teleporters, perhaps as many as a dozen, had been killed attempting to land inside the villa grounds.

The helicopter flew ten kilometres west of Patuazon's estate to the training camp set in raw terrain among the valleys of the lower Andes. It landed in a clearing cut from rampant jungle growth, near a huge lake created when Patuazon built a dam across the river. He ignored the wishes of local people. Intelligence suggested that anybody who objected was relocated. They disappeared in a similar manner to the political prisoners.

Lock left the helicopter to change clothes. Giant ferns towered over him on either side of a raised stone track as he sped towards a well-trodden path by the lake. On the far side of the water gunfire jolted his momentum. He glimpsed some of the SAS troopers at a cluster of rough buildings by the dam, teaching house assault techniques to Patuazon's mercenaries. He only had a short time to retrieve the insect drones from their hiding place and he headed past a boathouse where one of the Blades, speaking to a group of men in small dinghies, glanced up and nodded in recognition.

Lock rushed on towards a small deforested yard and the stone hut housing the SAS men. Inside the hut he changed his casual suit for combat kit in Multi Terrain Pattern material. He picked up a machete and checked there were no other auras nearby. Making sure the pilot hadn't moved, he dashed across the yard to a track partly obscured by the waiting green arms of creepers and ferns.

Teleporting or levitating higher than tree tops risked detection, not by human eyes but by Patuazon's electronic devices. Lock slashed at the impenetrable undergrowth and his chest heaved in the humid air. Aside from gunfire, the only noises were from the ever-present insects and occasional whoops and whistles from birds flying away from the canopy more than thirty metres above his head. Stopping to wipe sweat from his eyes, he peered at the direction finder on his smartwatch and reached a massive, buttressed tree, only metres from the track. It had taken him eight minutes to get there. Circling the trunk in the gloom he climbed hand over hand on a carefully placed creeper to a hole in the bark and fished out his stash. Panting, he put the box and control sunglasses in a pocket, went back down the creeper the same way and ran through the cleared foliage to the stone track. Just before he reached it he stopped dead. The pilot was striding across the yard towards the hut.

At the moment Lock thought he would have to risk teleporting into the hut to avoid arousing suspicion, a voice halted the pilot, who swivelled on his heels. The trooper who had been by the boathouse loped up, alerted by the signal from the SAS's own electronic sensor ring set around their quarters.

'Can I help you, mate?'

Lock didn't hear the pilot's gruff reply. While the pilot's back was turned, he signalled his presence to the trooper, dashed across the yard and slipped into the hut. He fumbled his way into another dry shirt, grabbed a bottle of water, slowed his breathing and heart rate to normal and stepped out of the hut, putting on the sunglasses. The pilot gave him a sour look, frisked him for weapons and chivvied him with insincere politeness towards the helicopter.

Once they were in the air Lock pressed a button concealed as a raised section on the sidebar of the sunglasses. It switched on a solar power supply which activated a microchip, though nothing altered on the lenses. He gave a mental command, entered a pin number and a navigation grid appeared on the left lens, with a small pop-up menu box in the lower section. He hadn't told Jimmy and Bilton about controlling the insect drones by thought relayed through the sunglasses. That information was need to know, and they didn't need to know it. Using his mind to signal, he checked through the functions including Volume, Recording Mode, Image and Sensory Input, and stopped at one that said Speed. From a list of one to ten he chose the fifth setting and closed the menu. He opened his bottle of water and took a long swig, pleased that he would be ready when they landed.

He expected to be met by more of Patuazon's bodyguards at the helipad but his escort turned out to be a raven-haired, slender young woman in a skimpy white top. The plunging neckline revealed a cleavage guaranteed to raise any man's blood pressure. Below her breasts soft, downy skin on a bare midriff stretched over toned muscles to a gold bellybutton ring and skinny, pastel blue jeans that only just covered her crotch. He recognised her from intelligence reports and identified her as one of Patuazon's mistresses. She walked forward from the side of a silver four-wheel-drive car, greeted him with a warm smile, lifted her sunglasses onto her head and stretched out a delicate hand for a formal but firm handshake. Caramel eyes fixed Lock with a serene gaze, but the smile on her brown, oval face was mischievous and warm.

'My name is Maria. Senor Patuazon asked me to take you to the stables.'

Lock stumbled out a reply, flinching at his inability to get past her mesmerising sexuality.

He got in on the passenger side and peeked a sideways look at her breasts as she drove at a leisurely speed towards the villa and the stables beyond. She held the steering wheel with her left hand while the right rested on a shapely thigh. For half a minute they drove in silence, Maria confident and impassive, Lock struggling to keep his eyes on the road. He had rarely felt such strong sexual arousal.

'Do you like to ride horses, Senor Lewis?' she asked, and her hand slid suggestively towards her lap between her thighs. Electrified, Lock caught a flirty smile on her lips and looked away.

'Yes, I go riding occasionally.' Flustered, he turned his head to look out of the window.

'Senor Patuazon is the best rider in Colombia.' There was no doubting the mischief in her sultry voice as she emphasised the word rider. Lock didn't dare look at her. He had a hard-on.

She continued, 'He has good taste, he likes thoroughbreds. Do you like thoroughbreds, Senor Lewis?'

Lock cleared his throat and muttered something about not knowing much about horses. He stayed stiff-necked, staring ahead as they ambled past the villa towards the stable block. Unscrewing his bottle of water he took a gulp, trying to subdue the swelling in his lap. Maria continued,

'I've been told thoroughbreds are like good women, strong as well as elegant. They outlast all the others. I can guarantee, once you've been on a thoroughbred and had the time of your life, you won't be happy with anything less.'

Lock nearly choked. He shuffled on his seat and put the bottle strategically across his pants as Maria laughed openly. The car came to a slithering halt on gravel by the stables.

'Come, let me show you a mount worth millions of dollars,' she teased as Lock exited the car and shut the door with a trembling hand. A quick check showed only one aura in three stables. Lock recognised the purple hue as belonging to a horse. He glanced at Maria's curvaceous behind. The temptation to stray from his marriage vows plagued his thoughts. She walked to an exercise yard and leaned on a rail to watch one of Patuazon's stable hands putting a mare through her paces. She ignored the effects of her prick-teasing as though nothing had happened, rambling on about racehorses and the magnificent Andes backdrop. Lock moved away from her and his erection slumped.

While she twisted her dark hair round in her fingers with a preoccupied air, Lock removed one of the bees from the box. Hiding it in his cupped palm he stretched his hand out from his side and activated the insect drone by thought. The tiny bee wings stirred into life, moving so fast their outlines dissolved into a shimmering blur. He selected a point on a virtual grid on his sunglasses and the bee rose from his hand. It buzzed and hovered a metre from his head. Lock switched on the bee's own lenses and what the bee saw overlaid the sunglasses with a transparent image.

He looked up at the villa perched on a plateau carved out of the lower part of a mountain. It took a few seconds to orientate the bee on the navigation grid in relation to the villa and send it on its way. All he had to do was think about flying towards the villa and the bee responded. He adjusted the focus in the bee's lenses for a wider view and held his breath as it zipped towards the neural net. He breathed out as it passed the net and flew on to manicured terraces, ornamental trees and swimming pools. It hadn't been attacked.

'Beautiful,' Maria said, sidling up to him so close her arm brushed his. 'Don't you think so, Senor Lewis?'

Lock started at the touch, halted the bee and moved his arm. He wondered how much life he would have left when Patuazon showed up and took exception to a guest making moves on one of his mistresses. He doubted saving Patuazon's spoilt granddaughter from drowning in a jet ski accident would count for much if the older man considered Lock's actions insulting.

'Yes, very elegant,' he said politely, and concentrated on helping the bee find a way in. Maria smiled, and leaned her back on the fence rail, an action which accentuated her breasts. Lock sensed the animal magnetism and found it hard to keep his eyes on the villa. He drained his bottle of water.

He manoeuvred the bee under overhanging eaves along the two-storey main building, searching arched balconies for an opening. Mosquito netting covered all of the small slatted windows of the eastern wing so he sent the bee over the terracotta roof tiles to the massive stone courtyard within the villa complex. In the centre of the courtyard, women from the household sat on stone steps at the base of a large fountain, looking after children who splashed around in the biggest plastic paddling pool Lock had ever seen. He directed the bee to the central wing and found what he was looking for – an open balcony door upstairs. Through the bee's eyes Lock entered the bedroom, headed for a carved mahogany door which had been left ajar and turned right to an ornate metal staircase.

At the bottom he slipped into a large, dark living room where one of Patuazon's grandsons lay on a cream sofa, fast asleep with the remains of what looked like a cocaine stash on the mahogany table next to him.

Patuazon wouldn't be happy about the cocaine use when he found out. He idolised his grandson. Lock turned the bee towards the window and realised he was heading in the wrong direction. He spun the bee round to a closed door leading to the eastern wing and the view caught an open marble fireplace with antique vases on the mantelpiece.

Maria's hand made him jump as she brushed the back of his neck. The bee's vision twisted and swirled as he turned. He lost his balance, gripped the yard rail and swayed, trying to bring his focus back on the door before halting the bee in mid-air.

'There was an insect on your collar. Are you all right?' She moved her hand away.

'Yes.' Lock straightened up. 'I'm dizzy. It must be the sun.' Maria gave him a strange look, as if she'd seen through him.

'I'll get you some more water.' She sauntered towards the car, hips swaying.

Lock reconnected with the bee and looked for a way in at the bottom of the door, anxious for his insect spy to get inside the eastern wing. The bee would have to crawl in. Lock hadn't done that before. Time was running out. He heard Patuazon's car coming down the road. Settling the bee on the floor, he opened the sunglasses computer menu box and went through it so fast he nearly missed the Walk option. From the corner of his eye he saw Maria returning with a bottle of water, and Patuazon's convoy kicking up a cloud of dust on the road as they closed fast on the stables. The bee took a few steps and veered sideways when Lock hurried. He straightened it and made it go full speed under the door just as Patuazon's car stopped.

Lock's world exploded. A lightning bolt of pain pierced his eyes and a high-pitched sound screeched in both ears, jarring his head so hard it made his teeth hurt. He pulled off the sunglasses and doubled over in agony, his hand over his eyes.

'What's wrong?' Maria asked, more irritated than concerned.

'I'm okay.' He straightened up, feeling sick and dizzy. He looked at Maria, or at the spot where Maria's voice came from, and blinked twice. The darkness didn't go away. He was blind.

~~~~~~~~

Bilton snapped his phone shut, tapped once on his laptop screen to switch pages to a map and glanced at Jimmy.

'The deal's on. Call the others in,' he ordered. Dour Ken and cheerful Snapper showed up promptly in response to Jimmy's radio message, but Chris was missing. Bilton looked up impatiently.

'Jimmy, find out what's going on. Snapper, on stag.'

Chris didn't reply to coded knocks on the door or to Jimmy's voice.
~~~~~~~~

Jimmy heard lift machinery start up at the end of the corridor. The whine of an electric motor rose in pitch, quietened, dwindled and stopped. Jimmy dropped his hand by his waist, ready to draw the MP7. He knocked on the room door with his other hand without using the code, to warn Chris not to open the door yet, and moved to an angle that covered the whole corridor. He watched as a red light lit up over the lift accompanied by the sound of a soft ping. The doors swished open and a man and woman walked out of the lift, chatting animatedly in Spanish. Jimmy scrutinised their hands and clothing for a weapon. They spotted him and lowered their voices. They didn't pose a threat, so he knocked again and kept his eyes on them as they passed through a set of glass-topped doors, disappearing from view. He rapped out the code again, louder, and then a second time.

The door unlocked with a click and swung open. Chris was heavy-eyed and puffy-faced, with only his trousers on and no shirt, shoes or socks. He lowered his pistol and dropped his arm loosely by his side. Retreating into the room he sat down heavily on a bed, wiped his nose on the back of his hand and avoided eye contact. Perspiration glistened over his hairy chest, and a small paunch hung wetly over the belt of his trousers. Jimmy slammed the door shut.

'What the fuck're you doing, man? We're ready to rock 'n' roll and you're sitting there not even tooled up. Why didn't you open the door when I gave the signal?'

Chris grunted, rubbed a hand over the stubble on his shaved head and tugged a sock onto his damp foot.

'I was being extra careful.' He gave up on the sock, yanked it off and shoved his bare feet into a pair of old shoes.

'You didn't recognise my voice?'

'Yeah, but you know, someone could have used a recording of your voice to trick me. They'd wait until I opened the door, and then take me out.'

'You're fucking kidding, right? If anybody wanted to take you out it's more likely to be an RPG through the window.'

Chris threw his head back and laughed manically.

'You should see your face, man.'

Jimmy didn't see the funny side of it at all and stalked towards the door. Chris struggled to put his shirt on, peering out of the window as if expecting to see a Rocket Propelled Grenade streaking towards him. Jimmy fumed all the way to Bilton's room. Chris was delaying the operation when every wasted minute could make the difference between success and a life-threatening rout. Worse, it ate into psychological preparation time he regarded as sacrosanct. He needed to set the mental scenario his mind would be travelling through. They all needed to get psyched up, not distracted.

Jimmy told Bilton that Chris was on his way. He expected a blast of fury for conveying the message, but Bilton didn't respond with anything more than a grunt, engrossed in his task of projecting satellite feed from his laptop onto one of the walls. Jimmy and the others used the time to fine-tune one another's appearance, making sure the straps of weapon harnesses were flat over their shoulders and backs. Bilton, Ken and Jimmy wore suits for their role as the team who would meet Mosquera's men. Snapper, as undercover back-up man if anything went wrong, wore scruffy clothes more appropriate for the barrios, the poorer areas nestled against the edges of the city.

Chris breezed in, oblivious to a wall of unspoken hostility.

'So glad you could join us,' Bilton said, but he left it at that and began the briefing, unwilling to add bad temper to a tense atmosphere. He used a cursor to indicate areas on a projected satellite view of Bogota, overlaid with a map of the city.

'We're heading north. Ken, you know the roads best round here so you're driving the lead car taking me and Snapper. Jimmy, you're driving the second car taking Chris.' He pointed at a crossroads on the virtual map. 'Before we leave Bogota, we pick up the van at a junction four clicks from here. The Embassy mechanic is on his way with it.' He threw a set of keys to Snapper. 'Snapper, he'll park it on the right-hand side of the road. The vehicle looks like shit but it has a powerful engine. When you give the signal, he'll leave the van, you walk up and head out on this road. We'll cover you.'

Snapper acknowledged with a thumbs up. Bilton changed the satellite view and continued, 'When we reach this point, eight clicks out, we phone for further instructions.'

Chris interrupted with stifled sneezes that came three times in quick succession. Bilton gave him a trademark sour look. Chris pulled out a handkerchief that looked as though it doubled as an oil rag and mumbled, 'Just an allergy.' Jimmy doubted an allergy. Given Chris's unprofessional behaviour he suspected something else.

Bilton continued, 'Okay, moving on. When we reach a good spot we stop. Ken, you release the drones to scout ahead. I'll monitor surveillance. Snapper, Jimmy, Chris, you kit out the cars with weapons, then Chris will take the second car and set up a sniper position. Snapper will take the van and act as back-up. We keep the same call signs as before – Ken, Delta One; Snapper, Delta Two; Chris, Delta Three; Jimmy, Delta Four. Any questions? Good. Chris, Jimmy, Snapper, check out the cars for any tampering.'

Down in the car park the three men used sensors, mirrors and expertise to covertly check the vehicles for magnet bombs and tracking devices. Jimmy knew it was unnecessary since they had kept the cars under constant surveillance, but checking could make the difference between success and disaster. Snapper went into the hotel to help carry down weapons and equipment. Jimmy took the opportunity to collar Chris and ask about the allergy.

'I'm fine,' Chris grunted, wiping sweat from his face.

'You don't look fine. I'm a trained medic, I can check you over.'

'I said I'm fine, and my health is my business.'

'It's my business if you jeopardise the op.'

Chris turned his back on Jimmy.

'I won't jeopardise the bloody op. I said, I'm okay. It's just an allergy, it's under control. The Boss knows about it.'

'Yeah? So if I ask him, it's not going to be news to him?'

'Do what the fuck you want.'

Jimmy left it at that but he managed to get Ken on his own and asked his opinion as Ken and Chris knew each other.

'He's okay. Mind your own business and don't make trouble. I'm not missing out on a wad of dosh just because you're getting sweaty,' Ken said with a degree of menace.

They set off at speed, jumping red lights as they started out from the city centre. The urban landscape altered. Seen from the air, Bogota looked pretty. It sprawled from the mountains into the plains as a vast, complex grid of terracotta and white buildings that housed seven and a half million people. Unlike most major cities, Bogota had a few modern skyscrapers complemented by a scattering of tower blocks that rose no more than thirty or forty storeys. Most tower blocks were divided by patches of green, or by wide plazas, terracotta pavements and American-style four-lane highways.

On the ground, away from the vibrant, youthful centre, residential houses resembled the best of middle-range American homes complete with basketball hoops on driveways, neatly-kept gardens and clean brick walls. The difference lay in the details. Sturdy steel bars overlaid every window and door as if the houses were under siege, waiting for the nightly scrum of burglars, muggers and crazy drug addicts wielding guns and knives. Further on elegant houses with pitched terracotta roofs turned into flat-topped, squat homes huddled side by side. Residents barely had room to walk in a back yard before they bumped into several neighbours in theirs. Tall, spiky fences topped by rolls of barbed wire dominated the streets. The atmosphere altered to resigned, beaten-down watchfulness by day and night. Jimmy felt the hungry eyes of that part of the city following their every move as Ken sped on, leading the way to the van pick-up point.

Ken eased the first Explorer into place on a road near a new supermarket, short of the junction. In the second Explorer Jimmy kept Ken's sandy-haired head in view and stopped further back on the other side of the road with the engine idling. The embassy contact chose a good spot.

The blue van was visible in front of Ken's car. The supermarket, shops and cafes gave everybody a good reason for being there. A tantalising smell of tamales and soup wafted into the car from an open-air café and next door a bakery displayed a tempting range of salty and sweet pastries.

None of the people wandering on the dirt pavement looked threatening. Young street sellers, joined by child beggars, ran across the road towards Jimmy's side of the car and jostled for attention by the open window, some holding trays of sticky things that must have resembled food hours earlier. He waved them all away, saying, 'Gracias,' and scanned his arc of responsibility on the street beyond the front of the car, which included bored policemen frisking shoppers going into the supermarket. Chris kept watch behind.

Jimmy stared at a young kid lounging by a shop doorway five metres down the road, at the ten o'clock position. He seemed very interested in the group and his body language gave out the wrong signals. It didn't pay to dismiss kids barely into their teens. Colombian law regarded anybody under age eighteen as a child. Drug gangs and paramilitary groups made use of that by training children as young as twelve to become sicarios, assassins, in the knowledge that if the child was caught he – or she – wouldn't be dealt with in an adult court, nor given a harsh sentence. Weapons were available in the country and it looked as though the kid carried a concealed weapon. Jimmy pressed a button on his radio and cut in on the common channel for everybody to hear.

'Dicker, my ten o'clock.'

Bilton acknowledged. Jimmy kept his eyes on the lad as the Embassy mechanic left the van and walked away.

'Soldiers behind us,' Chris's voice broke into Jimmy's concentration.

'I see them,' Jimmy replied, glancing in the rear view mirror. A military truck rumbled to a stop, two cars' lengths behind them. The young kid slunk down an alley between shops and Jimmy informed Bilton they were clear. Snapper got out of the lead car and strolled towards the van, his dark head and shabby clothes blending in with the locals. Checking the rear view mirror, Jimmy's heart rate quickened as four soldiers got out of the truck.

'Delta Three to Zero, four possible hostiles approaching,' Chris said. Bilton acknowledged and told Snapper to get moving. Jimmy was reassured when the soldiers paid them no attention. They seemed more interested in the café and he guessed they were after a free drink. He was much less reassured when one of them took more than a passing interest in their vehicle, trying to see in through the tinted back windows.

'Fuck, let's go,' Chris said. His jitteriness annoyed Jimmy, who checked the situation. Snapper was getting into the van. Ken and Bilton were parked in the first car. A delivery truck rumbled up, taking up most of the room on the road.

'No, we stay put.'

The soldier sauntered towards their car, bringing his Galil assault rifle round from his shoulder to his front. He said something to his mates and all three of them eyed the Explorer and followed him. Snapper still hadn't moved off, blocked by the delivery truck in front and people crossing the road behind. Chris took his Browning pistol out. His breathing slowed, a deliberate tactic for staying calm, which meant he was getting twitchy. Jimmy took a fraction of a second to take everything in and decide on bluff. He got on the radio.

'Delta Four, intercepting.' He turned to Chris. 'Cover me and don't fire unless I say.'

He pulled a nearly full pack of cigarettes from his jacket pocket with a lighter and grabbed a map of Bogota. Getting out of the car, he kept the door open and walked towards the soldier, unfolding the map.

'Hi.' He smiled and pointed at the map, making sure his attempt at translation was terrible. 'Las Saltires, por favor?' he asked, putting a cigarette in his mouth. The expression on the soldier's face changed from wary to a broken-toothed smile and his eyes glittered as he looked at the pack of American cigarettes. Jimmy had him.

'Ah, gringo. Tourist.'

Jimmy nodded. 'Tourist.' He stood facing the supermarket, offered the pack of cigarettes and weighed up whether the soldier might accept a few dollars or collar them for bribery.

'American?' The soldier took a cigarette, an action that relaxed his grip on his assault rifle.

'Si, senor.' Jimmy nodded again and spread the map on the bonnet of the car. Most Colombians couldn't distinguish between British and Americans, assuming everybody who looked foreign and spoke English must be an American.

Jimmy heard noises that sounded like trouble. He looked up in time to see one of the store staff calling out to the policemen, gesturing at the supermarket. A dark-haired man appeared out of nowhere, at the entrance to the supermarket. The man raised a weapon and two bursts of automatic fire felled the policemen who were frisking customers. Jimmy and the soldiers reacted by taking cover. The map fell off the bonnet, joining the cigarettes on the ground. Stunned by the unexpected sight of a Shifter, it took Jimmy longer than usual to draw his weapon.

'Contact nine o'clock,' he shouted.

In another fraction of a second, a young boy around eight years old zoomed out of the supermarket. He ran faster than anybody Jimmy had ever seen, man or boy. Jimmy cursed but didn't fire. The lad thrust a bag at the armed man, who fired a burst of bullets into the supermarket, scattering people coming out. Civilians ran into Jimmy's line of fire. The man gestured towards the store and the boy ran back in. Jimmy moved to get a clear shot. The man turned, spotted the soldiers and disappeared just as a hail of bullets hit the spot where he had been.

The soldier crouching by Jimmy stopped firing and looked wildly in all directions. Ken moved the lead car further down the road. Bilton wanted to know what was going on.

'Store robbery,' Jimmy said.

On the street civilians ran. Women screamed at their kids, heading towards anything that gave some shelter. The soldier nearby moved into better cover. In Jimmy's ear Bilton gave the order,

'All stations, move out, move out.'

Jimmy grabbed the map and bundled into the car. The young lad appeared at the supermarket entrance and stopped, bewildered to discover the man had left him. Jimmy slammed the car into gear. He heard a sustained burst of automatic fire from the soldiers and the boy fell. Cursing, Jimmy floored the accelerator, kept his hand on the horn and drove the car up over the pavement and past the delivery truck while Chris leaned over the back of the passenger seat, keeping the soldiers covered. Nobody fired after them but Jimmy glimpsed the older lad from the alleyway, the spotter, standing by the side of a shop, staring at them.

'Dicker on left,' he informed everybody.

'What the fuck was all that about?' Chris said, too loudly, his voice an octave higher.

'Shifters.'

'Shifters? I didn't see any Shifters. How many?'

Jimmy didn't answer and wouldn't be drawn. All he could think of was the expression on the young boy's face when he discovered his partner had left him in the shit. He avoided further talk by giving a brief account of what had happened, and then fell silent, thinking. He'd never seen anybody teleport. At Birmingham airport Brad Paulson used super-normal speed – not teleportation. The speed of Shifting shocked Jimmy, forcing a rapid re-evaluation of how effective he might be going up against them.

Shortly after they left the area, Bilton gave instructions to turn north-east, then east, then south, then east. Twenty minutes later, brightly painted houses gave way to grey-grim barrios, shanty towns that reeked of open latrines and sprawled across the land, swallowing up hills like an infestation of ants. The barrios petered out and Ken stopped fifty metres before an intersection with a freeway, parking behind scrubby trees that provided some cover. Bilton argued with somebody on the phone, buying the crew some time by refusing to be messed about with bogus directions.

The group guessed Mosquera had a drone in the air, watching their movements. On Bilton's orders, Ken activated a hand-held signal jammer. The jammer would render Mosquera's drone blind. Ken kept watch for hostiles and the boy spotter in the area near the cars. The spotter was probably another Shifter. Bilton sat in the lead Explorer scrutinising his laptop.

The rest of the crew worked on tasks they couldn't have done in the hotel car park without attracting attention. Jimmy pulled some polystyrene from a holdall and prised off interior door panels from the two front doors of the Explorer. He lined the bottom of the door wells with the polystyrene and slid a Browning pistol into the driver's door and his Sig Sauer into the front passenger door, making sure the weapons would not rattle around and the windows above had clearance to wind all the way down. All the time he listened to one side of Bilton's phone conversation, above the throb of traffic on the freeway. No, Bilton said, they weren't going to drive three kilometres west, and if they wanted the deal to go ahead they had to meet in the next half-hour.

There was a long pause in which Jimmy worked then Bilton said the name of a small town with a gas station at the perimeter. He agreed they could meet there and no, they weren't going to walk in, if anybody thought they'd be stupid enough to do that they could piss off and would have to go home with no deal and no cash, and did they really want to tell the boss they'd screwed up and lost out on a quarter million dollars. Jimmy put the door panels back, still listening. For the first time since meeting Bilton the Boss's assertiveness in taking control over the deal impressed him.

He stowed other weapons, including his M-16 and spare ammunition, on the back seat under a coat. Snapper finished the same routine with the second car and Chris worked in the dilapidated blue van, stashing his sniper kit inside. Bilton finished his phone call and called everybody over to see live feed from the group's drone, sent up to hover eight hundred metres above their heads. Jimmy felt calm, but his damp shirt stuck to his back despite the material's cooling properties. Bilton pointed to the laptop screen as it alternated between thermal images and terrain mapping.

'Okay, the town has a couple of thousand houses, lots of connecting roads, so it's good if the shit hits the fan, we can duck around the area.' Bilton broke off. 'Where's Chris? Jimmy, get him here.'

Jimmy sprinted past the cars to the van. What he saw as he looked round the open back door sent a chill through him. Chris was sitting on the floor of the van, his legs dangling outside, hastily putting away a small bag of white powder and rubbing his nose. He made a move to get out, but Jimmy blocked his path.

'All right, mate?' Chris said. It was more of a challenge than a query.

'You put us in any danger and I'll drop you. Understood?'

'Don't know what you're on about, mate.'

'Don't mess with me. You know what I'm talking about. That wasn't fucking icing sugar.'

Jimmy felt like dropping Chris where he stood. Chris just shrugged. 'Don't worry about it. I won't compromise anybody.'

'You're wanted,' Jimmy snarled. He didn't trust himself to say anything else to Chris, but Bilton would have to be told regardless of Ken's warning to Jimmy to mind his own business.

Chris got out of the van as if he had all day. Jimmy took the opportunity to call Bilton on the radio and pass on what he had seen.

'I know about it. I've seen him in action, it doesn't impair his ability. Leave him alone, and concentrate on your orders,' Bilton said.

Jimmy took a deep breath and loped to Bilton's car with Chris trailing after him. He found it hard to take in what he had seen and burned with fury, but he had to put it aside, reasoning that neither Ken nor Bilton would put their lives in extra danger for the sake of somebody else's presence on the operation.

'The meeting's at the gas station.' Bilton pointed at the overview on screen. The place looked typical of many gas stations in South America. When built it would have been isolated from the rest of the town on the wide main road until traders moved in, attracted by customers drawn to the gas station, and an outer settlement grew up with the station as the central focus. Buildings of various shapes and sizes surrounded it at a distance that supposedly allowed a safety zone in case the station caught fire, though in reality they were too close.

Bilton indicated a range of hills facing the station. 'Chris, take up the sniper position here.' He pointed at the right-hand side of the station and swept his finger round to the front. 'Jimmy, you cover Green.' He indicated the left side of the gas station. 'Ken, take care of Red. Snapper, stay with the reserve car on the slip road at the back. There's Emergency Rendezvous One, just by the junction of the slip road with the main road.' He pointed at another junction two streets away. 'ERV Two, in case the shit really hits the fan. We're approaching from the south, along this road here, which takes us in at an angle to the gas station. Open comms from here on. Snapper, Chris, move out now. Jimmy, take care of the cash. Ken, you're driving.'

Jimmy memorised the Emergency Rendezvous points, got in the front passenger seat of the Explorer and took a swig of water. He watched Chris's van leave, followed by Snapper kicking up a trail of dust along the road, and put the money holdall by his feet. Ken sat in the driver's seat and Bilton got in the back. Jimmy cursed at missing signs of Chris's cocaine habit, though he had suspected it – excessive sweating in the air-conditioned hotel, restlessness, paranoia and the nonsense over not opening the door. He glared at Ken, who must have known about the risk posed by Chris. In a short while Bilton would transfer control of the overhead drone to Chris so he could keep them aware of threats ahead: it was a big responsibility. Jimmy hoped Chris was up to it.

~~~~~~~~

Lock struggled to keep his panic hidden from Patuazon and Maria. The blindness might be permanent, a thought that filled him with horror. He couldn't make out anything unless he used sensory mode and it didn't come anywhere near replacing normal vision. Within his dark world, the cobalt auras of Patuazon, his men and Maria stood out clearly in the greyed landscape, but auras only revealed the position of living beings, not their physical outlines. Patuazon's aura exuded tendrils that arose like long, wispy fingers and evaporated as quickly as they appeared. He stood next to Lock. The game would be over if he suspected Lock's illness was more than a bit of dizziness.

Lock's head throbbed on both sides above his ears where the electrode contacts in the sidebars had fried his skin. He fumbled with the sunglasses, switched the power off and kept them on to cover his watery eyes and the sores over his ears. The electrodes that read his brainwaves and relayed his mental commands to the fake bee had backfired after being zapped by Patuazon's electronic counter-measures.

'Perhaps you should see one of my medical team,' Patuazon said.

'No, I'll be okay. Just give me a couple of minutes.' Lock squatted on the ground on one knee and wondered how long he could keep up the charade before admitting the seriousness of his situation. He stared in the direction of the cars, sensing them as dense objects more compressed than the air around them, with dimmed blue auras inside. Trying to find a path to a car would expose his blindness.

A human aura detached itself from the car zone and hastened towards them. The person spoke to Patuazon in a low voice and they moved away from Lock and Maria. Patuazon sounded angry. Lock couldn't hear another voice and he realised Patuazon was using a phone.

'Don't you want any water?' Maria asked, bringing Lock's attention back to her. Lock still couldn't see anything. He guessed she held the bottle, waiting for him to take it.

'No, thank you.'

More auras drifted towards Patuazon and the atmosphere changed to one that Lock had experienced before, people dealing with an emergency. Two auras stayed in the car zone while one hurried towards him and Maria. Lock thought it was Patuazon, but a new man said,

'Senor Patuazon's apologies, but he has urgent business. He says you will hunt another day. Miss Zamora will drive you to his doctor.'

'No, it's just a migraine, I'm okay–' Lock trailed off, squatting helplessly by the fence while the aura receded. He wondered what kind of emergency would galvanise Patuazon into abandoning a hunt. He heard the convoy leaving much faster than they had arrived.
~~~~~~~~

'Senor Lewis?'

'I'm not going to see a doctor.'

Lock stood up. Maria laughed, and for the first time Lock noticed the brittleness in her voice and how unattractive it sounded.

'Of course you are.' She linked her arm through his and pulled him away from the fence. He stumbled and stopped walking.

'I'm not seeing any damn doctor.'

Patuazon employed the best medic in Cali, somebody who might ask awkward questions about the cause of two identical sores above Lock's ears and their relationship to sudden blindness. Lock needed to get back to the SAS training ground and get one of the lads to take a look at his eyes.

'Okay.' Maria rubbed his arm, which irritated him.

He searched for her car then remembered she parked it behind the stables. He couldn't see the smaller mass of the car beyond a large fuzzy block on his right.

'If you don't want to see the doctor, my quarters are not far away. You can lie down there until you feel better, stay as long as you like. I've got no plans for the rest of the day. It would be nice to have company.'

Her perfume, the touch of her fingers and the electrifying warmth of her body next to his sent sexual shockwaves through his system. He could have her so easily. The opportunity offered itself. He shuddered at the thought. Maria reminded him of a snake luring prey before striking. She invaded his personal space, as though it was hers and he had no will of his own. She took for granted her ability to use her body to get what she wanted, but his loss of sight concerned him more than screwing some hyper-sexed chick who could blackmail him afterwards. He yanked his arm away.

'I have to get back to the training camp. Take me back to the chopper that brought me.'

'As you wish.' She led the way to the car.

He stumbled after her aura, watched where she went and heard a car door open as she got in the driver's side of the thickened shape. He heard her slam the door and most of her aura lost its lustre behind the metal. Lock used her position to navigate the back of the blurry form as she started the engine. He fumbled when finding the door handle on the other side, and sat down, relieved. She didn't move straight away. He jumped as her hand stroked his thigh.

'Are you sure you won't change your mind?' she purred, as though unwilling to believe he rejected her advances. Lock brushed her hand away.

'I'm sure.' He looked out of where the window should be.

Lock heard Patuazon's helicopters in full-throated roar and as the car drew closer to the villa, auras sped across the grounds and disappeared. The problem must be serious to require sending out a chopper. The loud thudding of rotor blades ahead drowned out the car engine. The black form of a helicopter rose from behind one of the outbuildings, followed by a second. Two choppers – definitely serious. Maybe Patuazon had a gang war on his hands.

'What's going on?' Lock asked as the noise receded. Either Maria didn't answer or her reply was non-verbal, perhaps a shrug.

Lock guessed she was still annoyed. He didn't care. He stared out of the window blinking and switching between aura and normal vision until they reached the helipad. Patuazon's helicopter waited. The rotors turned and the passenger door opened. Lock saw it open. He nearly let out a shout of joy when he realised he could just make out the chopper at close quarters. He could see a blurry shape with his normal vision. He could even see the thick white stripe on the side of the blue door. Ripping off the sunglasses he stared at it until his eyes streamed. He had never been so happy to see such an ordinary machine as a chopper. Everything else took second place to the elation of regaining some sight.

CHAPTER 6

Bilton's group kept up constant radio communication about threats they detected on their way into town.

'Two X-Rays in the store,' Chris said over the radio common channel from his vantage point on the hill overlooking the gas station. He added, 'Possible X-Ray at Two-Three, open window. Checking.'

Jimmy glanced up at the location identified by Chris, without moving his head. He stared at the second floor, third window along, in the general store. From his vantage point in the front passenger seat of the Explorer, he couldn't see anybody at the third window but Chris had the benefit of a state-of-the-art sniper helmet. It picked up images from a hovering drone and projected them onto his visor in a transparent virtual display. The central area of the viewing screen had the capability of zooming in with pinpoint accuracy.

The general store stood out from the rest of the dirt-poor buildings as the only one with three floors. Every other house nearby had two floors and simple shacks further out had no extra floors. The shop made an ideal place for an armed scout, but it was obvious and not a place Jimmy would have chosen. Although Mosquera and his men had a massive advantage in getting to the location first, he would use trusted people from his extended family to make the deal. They wouldn't be as skilled as Bilton's crew in surveillance or handling weapons.

'Delta Three, confirmed X-Ray at Two-Three. I have eyeball,' Chris said. So far they had identified four of Mosquera's men, which meant there were bound to be some they hadn't spotted, out of sight in buildings and alleyways, brought in by Mosquera's Shifter.

A steady flow of cars passed through the town from the south. The Explorer containing Ken, Bilton and Jimmy passed a couple of women laden down with shopping in their mochilas, brightly coloured Colombian shoulder bags used in many rural areas. A group of six children got off a school bus and dispersed noisily. A workman strode along the pavement, carrying a half sack of cement on his shoulder. A Creole lounged in a doorway, guarding the approach to the gas station. Jimmy recognised him as one of Mosquera's men. The Creole's head barely moved as he watched them coming towards him.

'X-Ray fifty metres doorway left,' Jimmy said.

Two petrol pumps sat on their own in a loop of road between the main street on one side and a terrace of dumpy, flat concrete houses on the other. The pumps squatted on a raised dirt bed covered by a pyramid-shaped panelled canopy with sunken centres. The canopy looked as though a number of drunks had jumped up and down on it, and they probably had during wild nights. Ken covered a shabby bar on the left of the gas station. Jimmy's area of responsibility covered the right side of the gas station including the general store crammed with supplies that spilled out onto the pavement.

The count of Mosquera's men had risen to seven. Jimmy and Ken watched what they could see of the sky. Jimmy was nervous as well as fired up by the volatile situation. Having seen what happened at the supermarket he knew people could spring on them from anywhere. Ken pulled up on the side of the road just beyond the petrol station, opposite a piece of scrubland that had been turned into a car park for the bar next door. He kept the engine running. The car pointed up the road away from the gas station, ready for a quick exit.

At the front of the station a couple of dark-skinned Creoles, more of Mosquera's men, lounged against a wall drinking beer. One faced up the road, the other one down it, and they were both twitchy. Jimmy looked out of the car window and waited for the next few seconds while Bilton made a call. He listened to Bilton's conversation and his gaze flicked from the Creoles to movement at windows of houses nearby, then to the road as other vehicles and pedestrians passed. The count rose to eleven.

'Yes, we see you,' Bilton said as a silver saloon car with blacked out windows appeared on the road approaching the right-hand side of the station, accompanied by a cream four-wheel drive Nissan behind it. The cars stopped on the opposite side of the road. Three swarthy men in suits got out of the Nissan, heavy-set bodyguards with a professional demeanour. They scanned the road but their attention fell on the white Explorer where Jimmy and the others waited. Jimmy felt calm. If anything went wrong he knew exactly where to aim – the Lanceros who got out of the Nissan, because they posed a greater threat than the amateurish lookouts he had already spotted.

Two more men exited the silver saloon and walked towards the gas station. Jimmy recognised them. As expected, Mosquera was not with them. He had sent his top family lieutenants to make the deal.

'Let's go,' Bilton said. Bilton and Jimmy left their car, making no sudden movements. Ken stayed in the driver's seat. Bilton and Jimmy walked at a leisurely pace, keeping their hands in view as they stepped up from the main street towards the petrol pumps. It gave them a psychological advantage to appear relaxed and confident. Bilton sauntered across the loop road and

Jimmy followed two steps behind with the holdall full of cash. Bilton passed the petrol pumps. Jimmy eyed the men in his arc of fire on his left. He was two steps away from the pumps when the men he was watching froze in a familiar pose of pre-combat shock. Chris yelled over the radio.

'Incoming from Red.'

Jimmy barely had time to turn his head or draw his weapon. Something slammed into his right side, sending him sprawling. He hit the dirt on the loop road so hard his teeth rattled. The side of his face scraped the road and he came to a halt lying at an angle on his front. He felt pressure on his legs. Dazed, he thought he'd been hit by a truck, but as though in a dream reasoned that whatever ploughed into him had emerged too fast to be a truck. A missile or an RPG, then, but he wasn't dead. He would be dead if he didn't move, though.

His head cleared with that last thought. People screamed, shouted and ran, taking cover in buildings. Rounds bit around him. He lay in the middle of the loop road, exposed. He needed to roll out of the way, get up and run for cover, but he couldn't. Something pinned him down. He turned his head and looked up. Silhouetted against the sun, an obese man dressed from head to toe in grey fatigues, body armour, helmet and visor stood with one enormous foot on Jimmy's thighs. The man resembled an oversized maggot. He didn't look at Jimmy. A line of something bright and hot seared from the man's weapon, hitting the Nissan with a ball of crackling energy that enveloped the car. Men screamed and fell and others ran for their lives.

Jimmy couldn't tell if Maggot fired at Mosquera's men or Bilton and Ken. He heard Bilton yelling at Chris to fire at the target.

'I am,' Chris said. 'It's not stopping him.'

Jimmy swung his right arm under his jacket, a movement that would have been smooth had it not been for a sharp, knife-like pain in his arm and shoulder. He brought his MP7 round, finger on the trigger, and fired into Maggot's leg at point blank range. Rounds hit the trousers. He expected them to rip the leg to shreds, making Maggot fall. The rounds hardly made a dent. It was as if they had hit thick gel. The leg twitched and spent bullets fell from it. Jimmy fired at the helmet. It had no effect other than the bullets ricocheting off. Worse still, he had Maggot's full attention.

Jimmy's eyes widened as he stared up a gun barrel which had the diameter of a tennis ball. His last thought at the imminent ending of his life was simply, 'Shit.' Maggot didn't fire. Jimmy wondered why not; then it dawned on him that firing the large weapon so close to the ground would create a fiery backwash. It could kill both of them. Maggot reached forward with his free arm, grabbed Jimmy's weapon with a huge paw, twisted it and pulled Jimmy's top half off the road by the harness. Jimmy yelped as pain shot through his shoulder.

Maggot lowered his weapon, letting it dangle on a chest sling while he reached forward. Jimmy saw what he was going for – the holdall of money Jimmy lay on. That was why he hadn't fired. He didn't want to burn the money. It occurred to Jimmy his foe was not the sharpest crayon in the box, as it was impossible for Maggot to prise the holdall out. Jimmy's lower half covered most of it and Maggot stood on Jimmy's legs, tugging at the bag and trying to pull it from under the weight of both of them. Jimmy struggled to get free, looking for a weak spot to use as a lever, but it was like tussling with an elephant.

Over the radio Bilton called for Ken to come in. Ken didn't answer. They were a man down. Just when Jimmy thought it couldn't get any worse Chris cut in.

'Delta Three to all stations, two choppers closing in from Red.'

The swivel harness slipped and tangled in Jimmy's jacket, pulling it off his shoulder and twisting his body. Jimmy fell sideways on his left arm. Rounds whistled past but Maggot was oblivious to them and wasn't giving up, even with helicopters arriving. He let go of Jimmy's weapon, which dangled in a tangle of broken straps and material. The weight lifted from Jimmy's legs but before he could move he felt a powerful blow on the middle of his back. Maggot tried to kick him away from the holdall. One more kick like that and Jimmy could say goodbye to kidney function – assuming he lived. He scrambled to his feet and ran for his life towards the main road. He wasn't going to be killed over a bag of money.

Over the radio he heard Bilton say something but the noise of helicopters coming in for the kill drowned out the words. Heavier rounds raked the ground behind Jimmy, pummelling the area where Maggot lumbered to his feet. A missile streaked over his head down the road and the silver saloon car exploded, sending a shock wave surging up the road. He dived for cover behind a low wall. The chopper passed overhead as debris rained down. Looking back towards the gas station, he saw the lumbering grey form take off away from the helicopter. Maggot looked wobbly. He'd met his match against the choppers.

Jimmy struggled with the swivel harness, tugged his weapon free and ran for better cover, but the first chopper, a Huey, swept back along the road. He realised they weren't on his side when the door gunner lined him up in his sights and fired. Rounds whistled past Jimmy's head, peppered the road and threw up grit shrapnel. Jimmy moved fast. He squatted on one knee, took aim at the gunner and pressed the trigger. Nothing happened. Glancing at the weapon he saw why. The area above the magazine had been crushed by Maggot's grip. He dropped the weapon and hurtled away, expecting to be hit any second, but the firing stopped abruptly and over the radio Chris said,

'Gotcha.'

'Who are the guys in the choppers?' Jimmy yelled, but in the chaos and noise he didn't hear a reply. He scooted to an alleyway, threw off his jacket and harness to make himself a less obvious target and pulled out his Walther PPK from its ankle holster. It was little more than a pea shooter against the heavy weaponry outside, but better than nothing. He had no idea who the newcomers were, but they seemed to be shooting at anything that moved and were doing a lot of damage. Small arms fire eased temporarily. He peeked out of the alley to take stock. The main road was deserted. Everybody had fled. Drivers who couldn't turn or reverse away from danger abandoned their vehicles and ran. One of the choppers circled overhead. He couldn't see the other one.

Smoke billowed from the burning wreckage of Mosquera's cars and he couldn't see beyond it, but it would give him some cover. The gas station was opposite; empty as far as he could make out. The Explorer he arrived in was about ten metres away with the driver's door open. He couldn't see Ken, or a body nearby. The Explorer had the extra weapons, and was a tempting prospect. Jimmy wondered why nobody had driven away in it and then he spotted something else. The holdall full of money lay on the road near the Explorer. Maggot must have dropped it while tangling with the choppers. Perhaps their heavier weapons wounded him.

'Delta Four, Zero, package is in the open.'

'Zero, Delta Four, can you get it?' Bilton replied.

'Negative. Need covering fire, repeat, need cover.'

'Where are you?'

'Green. I have no effective firepower.'

'Delta Four, stay firm.'

Bilton tried to make sense of the confusion with help from Chris and overhead views from the drone. Chris said the choppers had brought in about twenty assailants. Small groups of armed men were popping up all over the place. He couldn't tell which was which and it wasn't the military or police, and Bilton couldn't leave by the back because X-Rays were pouring down the spur road. Snapper was forced to move out of range to another junction. Bilton called for Ken to come in, but there was still no response. Jimmy heard gunfire close on his left. Chris said armed men were approaching Jimmy from behind the smoke. Bilton ordered Snapper to stay put and said,

'Zero, Delta Four, I'm opposite. Get the bag. I'll cover. Go, go go.'

Jimmy shot out of the alleyway and turned right, keeping low, heading towards the Explorer and the junction beyond it where Snapper waited with the van. He saw Bilton zip out of a house and cover him. Chris relayed commentary about hostiles, confirming the road ahead of them looked clear except for women and kids. Jimmy scooped up the holdall, slung the long strap over his head and around his left shoulder, and reached the Explorer. The engine was switched off and there were no keys in the ignition.

Bilton warned him about hostiles at the end of the road, and Jimmy heard him firing. Wrenching open the back door, Jimmy re-holstered his Walther, pulled the M-16 and spare magazines from the back seat, unzipped the holdall and stuffed the magazines inside. A frightened woman dragging two crying children with her stopped by his side and pleaded something in Spanish. She saw the weapon. Fear swept across her face and she shrank back, turned and ran. Jimmy ripped off the interior panel from the front passenger door, took out the Sig Sauer pistol and stuffed that in the holdall as well.

'Jimmy, the chopper has locked on. Get the fuck out of there!' Chris yelled.

Jimmy charged along the road. He didn't catch up with Bilton. An explosion knocked him off his feet. Something hit his back and for the second time in a few minutes he tumbled over the tarmac. He was on his back, his head towards the gas station. Around him Mosquera's men picked themselves up off the road, their mouths moving, though he couldn't hear anything. One didn't get up. Jimmy grabbed the M-16, kept the weapon aimed down the road at the smoke and took cover by a house wall near the dead man. He looked for Bilton. The Explorer was wrecked, a twisted heap of burning metal. A stench of burning fuel clogged the air.

His back hurt and his right shoulder was stiffening from the injury inflicted by Maggot. The radio receiver in his mouth fell loose and he pushed it back in place. He looked at the dead man, who was familiar. The briefcase near the guy looked too expensive for the clothes he wore. Jimmy recognised him: one of Mosquera's Shifters, and the briefcase probably contained something important. He ducked forward, grabbed it and ran to search for Bilton. Stopping in cover by a house he stuffed the briefcase inside the holdall below the Sig Sauer.

In between clouds of smoke, the chopper appeared and disappeared around forty metres away, but without warning an arc of white light, like lightning, seared up from the roof of the general store and hit the chopper. Jimmy looked through the scope on the M-16. On the other end of the white beam, the grey bulk of Maggot stood on the roof and next to him squatted a smaller figure with sandy hair. Jimmy's heart sank when he recognised Ken. For an instant the chopper froze and hung in the air, enveloped by fiery lines scudding and crackling over its surface. The beam shut off and the chopper burned and fell like a stone.

Bilton appeared from a doorway, signalling a retreat. He staggered, bleeding from a wound on his head. The chopper hit the ground out of sight and a plume of smoke rose behind houses in their wake. Jimmy asked Bilton if he was okay. Bilton nodded. Jimmy told Bilton breathlessly,

'Ken's double-crossed us. He's with the X-Ray, the big bugger that looks like a maggot.'

Bilton stared at him in disbelief.

'Acknowledged. Satphone. All stations, cut comms.' Bilton's action excluded Ken from the group's radio communications. Jimmy thought about Chris being involved with Ken, but Chris had warned him about the chopper. He wouldn't have done that if he'd been one of the hostiles.

They pepper-potted down the road. Bilton crouched ready to fire while Jimmy ran ahead, then Jimmy stopped to cover Bilton. Jimmy passed the woman with the two kids. When he turned to cover Bilton, he gestured at her to get out the way and out of danger, but she was in shock and didn't respond. Bilton hand-signalled Jimmy to stop by a house. They crouched behind some railings and Jimmy kept watch while Bilton sent text messages of one number to Snapper and Chris, telling them to switch radio channels to number six. He and Jimmy did the same. The process took less than a minute and they were up and moving without Ken listening in.

Chris gave them directions.

'Alleyway four metres on your right, it curves and takes you close to the van.'

An armed man appeared from the smoke behind them, close to the houses with his weapon at his shoulder. He spotted Jimmy at the same time that Jimmy fired. The man fell. Bilton flew down the alleyway and Jimmy raced after him with bullets chasing his heels.

'I've lost the bird. Repeat, lost the bird,' Chris informed them. That was bad news. They had lost drone surveillance and it would take Chris too long to get the second drone in the air.

'Zero, Delta Three, acknowledged. Move out, go to ERV Two. Delta Two, status.'

'All clear,' Snapper replied.

Bilton and Jimmy paused at the end of the alleyway. It opened at a pavement two metres above the road, with a wall in front, a long ramp to the road and a set of steps. Snapper had positioned the van, their lifeline, by the bottom of the steps, keeping the engine running and the side door open. Snapper glanced in their direction while keeping watch ahead of him. Jimmy covered the alleyway behind them. Bilton leapt down the steps. He had only gone halfway when rounds smashed through the windscreen of the van. Jimmy turned his head in time to see Snapper slump over the steering wheel, rounds still hitting his lifeless body. Jimmy spotted muzzle flash from his right and saw Ken on a house roof with Maggot.

'Contact two o'clock!' Jimmy fired as Bilton sped back to the alleyway.

Maggot and Ken flew diagonally behind some houses. Jimmy fired down the alleyway to discourage their other pursuers. Loss of input from the drone meant they were at a severe disadvantage. He thought it unlikely they would get out alive. He didn't panic but felt an intense state of composure, as if everything was right in the world. Leading the way along the road, he kicked at a rickety wooden yard door, shattering a rusty lock. The door flew inwards, half off its hinges.

'This way.' He headed for the back of a house despatching the back door in the same way. They moved tactically through the house to the front door, ignored a frightened couple and exited along a dirt track with Bilton taking the lead, following the map downloaded onto his phone.

Weaving through a maze of dwellings they tried to shake off the pursuit, but their foes were hard on their heels. They headed south, then doubled back towards the main road and turned east. Aiming for the cover of smoke, they sped across the street and headed north, intending to turn east again for a track that would take them to safety and the second Emergency Rendezvous point. Everywhere they went they seemed to be heading into trouble and firefights, either with Ken and Maggot or with whoever had been brought in by the helicopters.

They stopped in a house after they thought they had shaken off their enemy. A terrified family of four cowered in a corner. A paunchy man in a dirty T-shirt raised his hands as if in prayer and shook his head in silent pleading. Jimmy gestured at him to stay quiet and stay down.

'I'm out of ammo,' Bilton panted, putting his MP7 on the floor. Jimmy took off the holdall and passed it to Bilton.

'The Sig's inside.' He resumed his watch on the road. When Bilton unzipped the holdall he pulled out the briefcase.

'What's this?'

It dawned on Jimmy what the problem was.

'It's the fucking bag!'

'What?' Bilton said, stuffing magazines into his pockets.

'The bag. We have to ditch it. Ken must've put a tracker in it. That's how they know where we are.'

'Okay, we take the money out. What's in the case?'

'No. The tracker could be hidden in the bundles. No time.' Jimmy looked at the briefcase. 'There's probably one in the case, too.'

'What's in it?'

'I don't know. Mosquera's Shifter had it.'

'It could be a bomb. Did you think of that?'

'He wouldn't carry a bomb around if he was trying to get out of trouble.'

'But you don't know.'

Jimmy turned the M-16 and used the butt to hit the lock on the briefcase, breaking it open. Bilton stopped wincing when Jimmy opened the case, revealing packs of what looked like cocaine. Bilton picked up one of the plastic-covered packs and put it in his pocket.

'We leave the bags here.' He stood up.

'That's a death sentence for them.' Jimmy nodded at the family. The man's wife wept silently and two girls, about ten and twelve, clung to each other and stared at Jimmy with wide, frightened eyes.

'What do you care?'

'We throw the shit out in the road, go out the back. With any luck those fuckers out there will fight each other for it.' Jimmy picked up the case and thrust it back in the holdall. He glanced out of the window. 'We have to move, they're onto us again.'

Bilton paused then nodded.

'Okay, let's do it. Check the way is clear.'

Jimmy motioned at the family to get up. He wanted them out at the back of the house and away from any fighting at the front. They were too terrified to move.

'Leave them – that's an order,' Bilton said.

Jimmy wasn't going to give up. He pointed his M-16 at the family and motioned them towards the back of the house. They fled like terrified sheep. Jimmy followed them into the kitchen, checked the back was clear and returned to the front room. Bilton was pissed off.

'Hose the window,' he said. Jimmy fired at the glass, shattering it. Bilton hurled the holdall as far as he could into the road. It hit the dirt and broke open, spilling packs of drugs and bundles of dollars on the ground. Jimmy and Bilton pelted for the back while rounds whistled into the front of the house.

Hurdling garden pots they flung themselves over a fence. Jimmy turned to cover the house they had just left. Sounds of gunfire and shouts rose from the road. Bilton fell, picked himself up and ran, turning east along a muddy track fringed by tall weeds. Jimmy didn't move. He was transfixed by the sight of Ken, in cover on a roof, looking at the road, his weapon trained on something below. He hadn't seen Jimmy. Balancing himself on one knee, Jimmy brought his weapon up, switched it from automatic to single shot, took careful aim at Ken's head, breathed out and fired. Ken slumped on the roof and slid out of sight.

'Gotcha, you bastard.'

Elated, Jimmy raced after Bilton. The sounds of battle receded. The track twisted, dipped and opened onto a road, and the front of the Explorer jutted from an intersection. Chris had come through for them; Chris the junkie whom Jimmy had thought was the least reliable of the crew. Jimmy could have kissed him. Bilton jumped into the front passenger seat. Jimmy ran to the back door, threw himself inside and Chris floored the accelerator before Jimmy closed the door.

Jimmy covered the rear, expecting to see a chopper in pursuit, but with Maggot around maybe the pilot had decided not to risk being a target. He was on fire, euphoric that he had faced death and cheated it again despite overwhelming opposition. They had escaped and he had avenged Snapper's death. He felt like laughing, an adrenaline reaction to a close call.

'I got Ken,' he gasped.

'When I give you an order, you fucking do it,' Bilton panted. Jimmy frowned, the exhilaration slipping away. Bilton looked over his shoulder. 'You do what you're told. No arguments. No fucking around, like back there in the house. Chain of command. Understood? I want no more shit from you.'

Jimmy resisted the urge to put a round in Bilton. The rest of the journey continued in silence except for Chris humming all the way to Bogota.

~~~~~~~~

Steven Stringer used an early morning start as an excuse to drive his beloved Porsche to Whitehall on empty roads. He stopped at the vehicle entrance of the Ministry of Defence. An armed guard inspected his pass, lowered an electronic road barrier and waved him down a ramp to a large perspex capsule guarding an underground car park. A variety of sensors scrutinised him and his car for nuclear, biological and chemical substances as well as explosives. Security personnel on the other side gave him the all clear and allowed him through another set of clear perspex doors into the car park.

The bleak, uncompromising walls resembled a concrete bunker. Stringer drove past unloading bays, stopped in front of a set of shiny steel doors and wound down his window. He swiped his security card through the laser-guarded checkpoint terminal and entered his six-figure pin number. The doors slid open with a whisper, revealing an industrial lift that descended to a level deeper than the foundations of the smart buildings of Whitehall above him. He drove out of the lift on a subterranean road that veered southwest to take advantage of a disused, converted Underground railway tunnel. The road dived under the Thames following the path of Westminster Bridge and curved to the right below the hub of Waterloo rail station.

Stringer usually enjoyed the privilege of using a secret run from Whitehall to Vauxhall, but recent setbacks filled his mind and he barely registered the drive as pleasurable. The black operation in Bogota had turned into a fiasco. His superiors laid responsibility for the loss of a large sum of money at the door of his department. He had to make good the damage.

The tunnel led to a sharp right-hand bend and an exit in the underground car park of Vauxhall Cross, the Secret Intelligence Service's headquarters building. Stringer drummed his bony fingers on the steering wheel while being processed through another perspex capsule set-up identical to the one at the MoD before being allowed through. His parking space in the car park didn't have his name on the sign denoting it as his,
~~~~~~~~

only a number. Everybody working at Vauxhall Cross knew his or her spot and never dared pinch anybody else's place no matter how fierce the competition for a coveted parking bay below ground.

He eased the Porsche into a narrow space, locked it and proceeded on foot past more steel doors, heading down a long hallway for the lifts. A few night staff in a basement office manned the phones, ready to call people in if required. Only outsiders would be deceived by the slumbering, benign air of empty corridors. Cameras recognised his face, computers accessed details and decided on friend or foe. Even when they designated him as an employee, they marked his arrival, watched every step and logged every move. Under their scrutiny, he got out at the sixth floor and padded down the plush grey carpet, the square patterns reminding him of airport terminals. The white-walled corridor looked the same as every other corridor, lacking not just bright pictures to break up pristine surfaces, but any floor plan.

The label on his department door could have given the full title of 'Global Tasks 2A' but SIS loved its acronyms and a few mysterious letters like GT2A provided something that spies could hide behind. Stringer headed for his office, swiped his card, tapped in another pin number and entered. He turned on the light, strode to triple-glazed bombproof windows and closed the blinds, excluding the darkness outside and the silent river that wended its way through the centre of the city like blood from an open vein.

He turned back to his minimalist office. Compared to the one occupied by Allan Defford, Lock's nominal boss at the MoD, it was sparsely furnished. He had an ivory leather chair and two soft-seat swivel chairs for visitors, an organically curved, white oak veneer desk with its computer console and three monitor screens next to a sleek, locked filing cabinet and a white oak bookcase housing sets of maps and historical texts about intelligence agencies. Cream walls enhanced an impression of space in a large work area. A panel of bullet-proof glass, looking into the open plan office, appeared to be an ordinary window but it was one-way, allowing him to observe his staff without being seen by them. At the far end of his personal office a huge television screen, flanked by four smaller screens for video conferencing, took up most of the wall. The functional, tidy office accurately reflected Stringer's preferred method of working – efficiency with a minimum of fuss.

He put his briefcase down on the desk and switched on the computer. Without waiting for details to appear on the screen, he unlocked his filing cabinet and took out a file. A diagonal red cross marked the top cover from corner to corner and on the right side the words 'Top Secret, GT2 Eyes Only' were typed in large letters. Besides himself, only his superiors had clearance to read it. He flipped it open. Stapled inside the cover was a photograph of Lock. Taking the folder to his desk Stringer sat in his pallid swivel chair and typed a cryptic report on the computer.

'As of current date Ghost is unaware of the attempt on his life in Scotland, believing it to be an unpremeditated attack on his patrol. His family are still under 24-hour protection. To avoid compromise it is deemed necessary to keep information about the attempt from him until he returns from Colombia. Ghost is also unaware of our dealings with Mosquera -see file XGT2SO12.'

Stringer hit the print button on the computer and checked his emails, zeroing in on a laboratory report from the British Embassy in Bogota. His face darkened with anger and he reached for the phone, dialling an encrypted direct line to the residence of the SIS station chief. He glanced at the clock. Bogota time lagged five hours after London time. He was waking the station chief at one forty-five in the morning.

'I know it's the early hours, Max, but this is important. The results of the tests came in half an hour ago.'

'Tests?'

'The substance our boys got from the deal.'

'I'm guessing it wasn't what we wanted.'

'That's right. It's not the same as the sample Nightingale gave us. What Mosquera has isn't AH-4, but it isn't Starbirth either. It's the reverse mix, the stuff we've already obtained by reverse-catalysing Starbirth. It's useless. My guess is, the sample was all Mosquera had. He couldn't get any more so he tried to trick us.'

Stringer heard sounds of his colleague getting out of bed. Max sounded more alert.

'How do you want to play this?'

'We have a problem. Nightingale. Even though he's Mosquera's brother and deputy, Mosquera doesn't trust him. Nightingale is kept out of the loop regarding important activity. He wasn't informed about the deal.'

'So he's not very useful.'

'It's more than not being useful.'

Stringer stared at computer screens showing a report from Lock about the departure of two Huey helicopters from Patuazon's estate, and Bilton's corresponding report about the attack by two Hueys during the botched deal.

'Nightingale found out about the deal. Our equipment picked up a coded call from Mosquera's estate to Patuazon just before our team was hit. It doesn't take a genius to work out who sent the call. I bet when voice analysis comes back it will be Nightingale's. He's playing us. Nightingale is Patuazon's man and he's been double-crossing us as well as his brother. He has blood on his hands, our blood. Cut him loose. I want you to put a hint down the line, let Mosquera find out who the traitor is.'

'Nightingale could still be of some use to us, Sir. He's already given us info that's been of interest to our friends across the pond.'

'My order stands.'

'Noted. And Mosquera?'

'Leave Mosquera for the time being. In due course he'll find out that it's unwise taking us for fools.'

CHAPTER 7

Despite taking accelerated-healing factor Lock's vision remained blurry, more so when he was tired, and his eyes watered in strong sunlight. He was concerned the condition might be permanent. Stringer conferred with the boffins and assured him the accident had been a fluke, a million-to-one chance in which Patuazon's electronic defences caused neural shock resulting in temporary blindness. Stringer wanted the burned-out control sunglasses back to find out what had happened. Lock returned them to the Embassy in Bogota to be sent out by diplomatic bag and exchanged them for a replacement pair from London.

In Bogota he caught up with the news, which was full of the helicopter fight that took place two days earlier in a small town. The media blamed it on super-powered beings, with wild stories that eclipsed the notorious one of three Shifters who broke into Bogota's central bank on a thieving spree and caused havoc until one got too greedy. He stayed around long enough for armed police to turn up and they shot him dead.

It took Lock two days before he healed enough to risk any practice sessions with the thought-controlled insect drones. He stood by the lake and watched sunlight rippling over the surface of the water through a fly's eyes, escaping for a precious moment from the steamy green oven enveloping him with its sticky heat. He had to put up with the annoying presence of Bilton, who arrived at the training camp thirty minutes earlier. Bilton wasn't the only distraction. Jimmy Mackenzie crept around the edge of the lake, out of sight if Lock used normal vision. Lock made the insect drone hover close to Mackenzie's right ear. Mackenzie raised a hand to swat it away, but stopped. He turned his eyes first, then his head, and stared at the fly. Lock laughed aloud at the sequence of expressions on Mackenzie's face: first suspicion as he removed his sunglasses to scrutinise the fly, then chagrin as he guessed what it was and finally a sheepish look. Through the fly's eyes Lock watched him push his way back to the track as if he had just been taking an innocent stroll. Lock smiled.

'You find what I'm asking funny? Because I don't,' Bilton growled. Lock re-focused away from the navigation grid on the sunglasses and back to Bilton's angry blue eyes peering at him from under a camouflage jungle hat.

'I wasn't laughing at you, Bilton. Everybody asks how that guy can fly when he's so fat.'

A shaft of sunlight pierced the gloom a few inches away. It caught the vine encircling a huge tree trunk and lit the leaves, creating an emerald glow, and it lit up something else. Lock moved away from a leech on a vine leaf.

Bilton stared across the lake and continued, 'What's Maggot's real name? Where does he come from?'

'Offhand I don't recall his real name. I do know from intel reports that he's a Southern states hick with a mental age of about fifteen. The reason I remembered him is because he's nicknamed Bloater. Like the fish.'

'The one that puffs up?'

'Yeah. He doesn't like the name.' Lock grinned. 'He was called that at school.'

Bilton interrupted.

'So how can he fly? How does it work?'

Lock recalled the fake insect from following Mackenzie and sent it over the lake.

'It's levi-flying, a slowed down version of teleportation. It doesn't matter how big a guy is, they can be the size of an elephant and still levitate. Bloater can pig out on ice cream as much as he wants. Don't let that flab fool you, either. He's immensely strong.'

'Could you handle somebody like Bloater if you went up against him?'

Lock swiped at a real insect biting his neck.

'It's difficult to say. I'd give him a run for his money, but I can't predict the outcome. From what I've heard he's not a Starbirth addict, he's taken AH-4. That makes a difference.'

'In what way?'

'It makes him more dangerous because he has better control of his abilities. Starbirth contains cocaine and AH-4 doesn't, so he's not under the mind-altering influence of cocaine. And I heard he's updated his outfit, so he's stronger. He gave the Eagles a hard time before escaping.'

Lock decided it was time to be blunt.

'What's this all about? Two days ago Patuazon acted as if he had the devil on his tail. Two of his helicopters left with some of the best men from his army, and only one returned, with casualties. Obviously they got in a fight. It doesn't take a genius to work out that it was connected to the town that got trashed. Since then the guard here has been doubled and people are scanning the sky as though it's about to fall. Everybody's twitchy. Then two days later, you arrive with Mackenzie and you both look as though you've been in a fight, too. Now you're asking me about Bloater as if he's going to be an uninvited houseguest. If you had a fight with him and you're worried he's going to attack here, I need to know.'

Lock waited then nudged, 'Did you tangle with Bloater?'

Bilton didn't answer. Lock was impatient.

'I have to go. Patuazon's boy, Diego , will be contacting me soon.'

'London has ordered us to assist Patuazon in an assault on Mosquera. They want you in on it in case Bloater turns up.'

Lock nearly lost the fly to the lake. He put it in a hover, took off the sunglasses and stared at Bilton.

'You're shitting me.'

'No.'

'Fuck.' Lock stared across the lake at birds wheeling and dipping near the surface as they caught insects, recalling how Stringer had assured him such a thing wouldn't happen. He exploded.

'That's a fucking stupid plan. Don't you realise what you're doing? You're helping a murderer.'

'Those are my orders. If you don't like it, take it up with London.'

Bilton was right; it should be Stringer feeling the brunt of Lock's wrath.

~~~~~~~~

Jimmy sweated on his bunk under a mosquito net and scratched at the scabs on his face where skin had been scraped off during his encounter with the road in Bogota. The accelerated-healing factor, a drug based on nanoparticles that speeded up the body's normal healing rhythm, made him feel lightheaded. Not unlike being pleasantly tipsy, he thought, ignoring the side effect that interfered with his rest.

Every time he was on the verge of drifting off, something in his brain gave out the equivalent of an alarm siren and woke him up, trying to warn him about a body-wide attack from an army of multi-millions. When Jimmy woke, the anxiety receded and the incessant chirring of night-time insects outside made him feel dozy and the process repeated. He tried to shrug off the experience, but couldn't understand it. He'd taken healing factor before without any trouble. The battle three days earlier at the gas station might have jiggered things up and made him jumpy.

His back hurt. He couldn't lie on his right side where he'd been kicked. Moving cautiously to avoid pulling on the bandage covering the shrapnel wound, he turned to his left to ease the pressure and stared at a yellow and green lizard in the shadows. It clung motionless to the wall by the doorway two metres in front of him. Splayed toes held it at a ninety-degree angle to an oil lamp hanging from a hook in the wall. Moths battered the lamp, occasionally straying close enough to the wall for the lizard to strike with its sticky tongue. Jimmy watched the lizard's hunting efforts with interest. The lizard regarded Jimmy with arrogant disdain, as though he had no right to be there. It was an expression Jimmy found very familiar, and not just from the new Regimental mascot. He noticed the resemblance as soon as he saw
~~~~~~~~

the lizard after he and Bilton arrived at the training camp. Jimmy named the gecko Fred, though never when Bilton was around. Jimmy felt more fondness for Fred than he did for his namesake.

He rested his hand on the new Diemaco Special Forces Weapon assault rifle next to him, and felt frustrated. There was never a chance to talk to Harford in private and set things straight. Jimmy wanted to clear the air about the knife fight in Scotland and find out more information about that night, and about Starbirth and Shifters in general. Patuazon kept Harford busy and the hut was never left empty.

The hut accommodated twelve men, though the eight Brits had sole occupation. They liked to keep a distance between themselves and the men they were training, so the Colombians stayed in two larger barrack buildings near the mess hut. Jimmy and Bilton joined the six men already camped in the SAS hut – Ginge, Mick, PC, Nails, Vicar and Harford. Jimmy put himself as far away from Bilton as possible but made the mistake of choosing the bottom bunk underneath lanky Nails, the youngest man in the group whose smelly feet stuck out of the end of the bunk. That explained why Nails had the bunk by the door. After some hours catching whiffs of the ripe stench, Jimmy moved himself and his kit and slept the rest of the night under PC's bunk, something that didn't go unnoticed by the lads. It became the subject of leg-pulling the next day.

Jimmy dozed off until the electronic sensors pinged a 'friend approaching' signal. The hut door wrenched open.

'Wakey-wakey, Jimmy.'

Something reptilian flew through the air, hit the side of Jimmy's mosquito net and flopped on the floor. Fred ran for the safety of a crack between the roof and the wall.

'Shit. What the fuck?'

Wide awake, Jimmy pulled his legs away to howls of laughter from the doorway. The tail end of a snake slithered under his bunk. He pushed himself away, peered over the other side of the bed and saw the snake disappear under the next bed. Throwing the mosquito net up, he leapt off the bunk with his Diemaco and made a fast exit from the hut. Nails, Vicar and Ginge were creased up outside.

'Bastards.' That made them laugh even louder.

'What d'you reckon, lads? Five out of ten?' Nails grinned.

'Nah, he was too slow. Three out of ten. Poor reaction time,' Ginge said.

'It's okay, it's not a poisonous one,' Vicar said.

'In that case you get in there and catch the fucker.' Jimmy pushed him into the hut.

The excitement grew as a hunt got underway in the shadows but eventually a very pissed-off snake escaped into the night, leaving the men resting on bunks or sitting at a rickety metal table where perimeter defence equipment monitored the area outside the hut using a system of sensors.

Jimmy knew he wouldn't get any more sleep when PC and Mick joined them. The event had to be re-lived, with embellishments and Jimmy's indignant denials. He enjoyed being with a good bunch of lads, even if they were from D Squadron. He liked Staff Sergeant PC, a Yorkshireman of thirty with gappy teeth. On arrival at the camp Bilton designated PC as his second in command, or 2ic. Like many men in the Regiment who lived life at full throttle, PC was prematurely bald, but he made up for it with a heavy, dark moustache. Jimmy chuckled at his dirty laugh when the conversation turned to women, and wondered if PC was a real policeman before joining the army.

PC's conversation piece about a prostitute who could do the splits was interrupted by Mick, a wiry, strong Tyneside lad of twenty-five, who was shorter than any of the other men. Jimmy noticed the short guys felt that they had more to prove, in every aspect of life. They were often the fittest men in the Regiment, and the fiercest. Mick fancied himself as a ladies' man, but his boasting about sex sessions with a female mud wrestler came unstuck when he revealed she was a Manchester United fan, like himself. That didn't go down well with Nails and Ginge, both Londoners who supported Arsenal. Nails said the mud wrestler would fit right in with Man U considering they all played like women. And looked like them, Ginge added. Mick retorted that Arsenal would never win the League unless every pitch widened the goalmouth for them, and even then they'd miss. Wrangling that started as good-natured banter got heated.

Jimmy was bored. In his opinion, English football clubs were a walkover compared to Celtic, his beloved Scottish club. He changed the subject.

'What's all this about your own Shifter, then?'

The conversation stopped dead. Ginge and Nails glanced at PC, who lay on his bunk with one arm across his eyes. PC didn't move, either asleep or pretending to be. Without input from the most senior trooper present, Ginge resumed reading his book, wiped a hand over the sandy stubble on his head and flicked a moth away from one of his radar-dish ears. Nails found a bit of fingernail to bite, living up to his nickname. Mick glanced at Jimmy, mumbled something about his kit and retired to his bunk next to Vicar.

Jimmy looked at Vicar as a fellow trooper from A squadron, although they didn't know each other well. He was a stocky man of twenty-nine and solemn-faced. Vicar was a Scot like Jimmy, though not from the Highlands. He came from the meaner side of Glasgow. Despite what should have been a natural affinity, Vicar wasn't going to say anything either. Jimmy knew better than to pursue the subject. He went back to his bunk and rummaged for his weapon cleaning kit to pass the time. Vicar and Mick had a whispered conversation then Mick said, loud enough for Jimmy to hear,

'We should tell him. He needs to know. He's going to find out anyway. Best to be warned.'

'Warn me about what?'

'Have you heard of the Ghost?' Vicar asked.

'Shut it,' PC said sharply.

'He's going to know anyway, possibly tonight,' Vicar remonstrated. PC reluctantly agreed they could go ahead.

Jimmy suspected he was being wound up, but he wanted to know. He moved closer to Vicar, sitting on Ginge's empty bunk.

'Go on.'

Vicar hesitated. 'Is this place secure?'

Jimmy nodded, looking at the defensive sensor kit on the table. LED lights glowed a steady green, normal.

'Of course it's fucking secure. I checked it fifteen minutes ago. There's no bugs in here.'

'What about outside?'

'Leave it out, will you? All the equipment's working fine. If a beetle farted out there we'd know.' Jimmy waited.

'I'm surprised you haven't heard of the Regiment Ghost,' Vicar teased.

'Get on with it before Sunshine comes back.'

They were all listening, though they pretended not to.

'About ten years ago – was it ten?' Vicar paused theatrically, looking up at the corrugated iron roof just to wind Jimmy up, before continuing. 'Anyway, there was an operation based on a young lad attached to the Regiment. He was wet behind the ears, barely out of school, and about seventeen or so. Nobody knew much about him. It was all very secret. Rumour had it he could move soldiers and equipment from one place to another in seconds. He was the Regiment's first Shifter, but nobody knew about that stuff back then. He wasn't around long. There was an incident.'

'What kind of incident?'

'I don't know exactly, but six of our guys died, around here I believe, up in the Andes. The MoD passed it off as training deaths. The young lad disappeared. Four years ago, we got–'

'How do you know all this?' Jimmy interrupted. Vicar looked smug.

'From a spook in MI5. He's retired now.'

'So, what, you slipped him a few whiskies and he spun you a load of bullshit?'

'If you don't want to believe me, that's up to you, tosser.' He lay back on his bunk and picked up a ragged magazine that he couldn't read because it was in Spanish. Jimmy waited then said,

'Okay, go on.'

Vicar ignored him until Jimmy got up from the bunk and headed for the door, saying he was going for a piss. He sat up, his face lit in the glow from the oil lamp.

'So four years ago, the Regiment suddenly has its own man again.' Vicar bent closer to Jimmy, who had come back, and lowered his voice. 'Four years is long before…' he paused again, emphasising the word by saying it twice, '…before all these guys show up with weird powers, able to fly around, move stuff and all that shit. This Ghost guy was the only one around back then. Rumour has it he was the first in the world.'

'So it's the same guy. So what?'

'You don't understand.'

'Yeah, I do. The Regiment has its own Shifter. I could have told you that.'

'No, no, look. According to intel, when he Shifts with other people it's touch and go. When guys get to the other end, some are misshapen. They're lumps of flesh with bones sticking out instead of arms, and heads missing, that sort of thing. Proper horror stuff.'

'Yeah, right, good one, Vic.'

'I'm not kidding. The MoD covers it up. Guys they said died in combat, or road accidents – they didn't. Not all of them. It's only about one a year maybe, but it happens. The MoD don't say anything because he's too useful.'

'So who is this guy?' Jimmy said. Vicar was spooking him.

Bilton's arrival cut the conversation short.

'Vicar, Mick, Nails, Jimmy, get your kit together for a spot of training. Belt kit only, survival, rations, light weapons and spare ammo. Briefing at twenty-one fifty in here. Be ready to leave immediately after. PC, Ginge, you'll be on stag here.'

Vicar winked behind Bilton's back. Jimmy convinced himself he had nothing to worry about, but he couldn't dismiss what Vicar said. He didn't want to pass judgement on Harford if he really was the Regiment's Shifter. After all, he'd been wrong about Chris, something Chris emphasised to Jimmy when they reached Bogota. He told Jimmy he had been taking Starbirth, but it wasn't working. Teleportation carried risks, but Harford had got Jimmy down from the Cairngorms without any harm being done. Jimmy stopped repacking his kit as a new thought struck him. Maybe it wasn't the drug overdose that had made him ill. He'd been unconscious on the Cairngorms. Anything could have happened during teleportation and he wouldn't know about it. He considered it, then shut the fears out and put on his camouflage face paint.

~~~~~~~~

Twenty-five minutes later Lock teleported higher than the Andes peaks to send the nightly report to London. Levi-flying had its uses, but sometimes
~~~~~~~~

he found it best to teleport to avoid hitting millions of insects and the occasional bat on the way up. Despite a lack of oxygen at an altitude of six thousand metres, cold air on Lock's face made a welcome change to the heat of the jungle. Down there the humidity, swarms of insects and constant stench of rotting vegetation made him feel as though he lived in a compost heap.

He sent off the signal 'packet' by burst transmission and waited for a reply. Looking upwards, away from the half-moon and clouds, he was a small speck adrift in the universe. Layers of stars, each one representing a galaxy, drew him onwards into infinity. The Milky Way stretched like a crinkly ribbon across his field of view. It contained a swathe of suns and unreachable worlds, some of them already gone, a legacy of light trailing out from a centre that evolved into something else millions of years ago. He recognised a bright star on his right as Vega. Somebody told him it sat in the Lyra constellation. The memory was an intrusion. Lock hadn't wanted to know then, and didn't want to think on those lines now. Categorising and plotting constellations reduced the magnificence and mystery of the sight; it diminished the universe to a human foible. He preferred to marvel at it.

A shiver sent a warning signal into his consciousness alerting him that he was floating higher. The altimeter on his computer watch showed a height of six thousand and eight hundred metres. The satphone blinked a green light twice to indicate a reply of further orders for him and the SAS team. Ten seconds later the LED display confirmed receipt of the burst transmission. Lock drifted down to six thousand metres, sent a standard message of acknowledgement, and read the orders with growing anger. He glanced at the satphone screen. It showed London time as one forty-five in the morning. He dialled Stringer's number and waited, feeling a twinge of belligerence.

The Secret Intelligence Service, an institution at the apex of power in the UK, did not take kindly to being crossed. Most UK citizens had no idea how much power the intelligence services wielded. Spies garnered secrets, and knowledge gave them power in covert ways regarding the uninformed public. It was impossible for an individual, even a teleporter, to go up against the resources of a nation state. Lock knew the dangerous side of the SIS, and other intelligence services, and he recognised how difficult, lonely and frightening his circumstances could be if they judged him as not being on side. He felt his vulnerabilities keenly because of his family. Lianne didn't want to live anywhere other than England, and he had his son's future to consider. His relationship with Stringer was complicated. He felt an obligation towards him, not just on a professional level, but because Stringer had acted as his guide and mentor for several years, before and after Lock's disappearance from the UK. They had a relationship of mutual benefit. Nevertheless, he had to do what he thought was right, and the way Stringer was acting with regard to Patuazon verged on recklessness.

Stringer answered the phone. He sounded emergency-alert, then irritated when Lock asked why there had been a U-turn on the issue of helping Patuazon hit Mosquera.

'The situation has changed. We have to respond accordingly.'

'You gave your word.'

'No, I didn't. I made no promises. Look, I'm well aware of your opposition to us giving aid to Patuazon, and I don't like it either, but if a change in circumstances dictates a course of action, you know we have to follow up.'

'What change?'

'For reasons of operational secrecy–'

'Fuck that. Operational secrecy. You saw the photos from yesterday's report?'

'Of course.'

'That's not the first time Patuazon's tortured somebody. We couldn't intervene because of blowing our cover. What you saw is the kind of thing he does every week.'

'I read the report.'

'No, you just read the sanitised version. That man took twelve hours to die. Twelve hours of him screaming for them to shoot him, begging them to stop. He wasn't into dope, he was just a dirt-poor farmer. Patuazon had him killed, for no other reason than the guy wouldn't turn his scrap of land over to him. That's the sort of bastard Patuazon is, and we're helping him.'

'You don't have to be involved in the hit on Mosquera.' Before Lock had time to consider the implications, Stringer continued, 'The patrol can do it on their own, with the boys they've been training.'

'Bilton said I'm needed in case Bloater turns up.'

'Your presence is optional.'

'Optional? That's ridiculous. They can't fight Bloater on their own. That's the guy who fought the Eagles to a standstill on the White House lawn – I can't fight him alone.'

'No, we know that. We don't expect you to fight him. We want you to evacuate the guys if he shows up, but that can be done the normal way instead. Intel says he won't turn up. He has no beef with us and there's no cash at stake. We can manage with the resources we have.'

'Okay, that's good. It will give me time to have another go at Patuazon's locked wing with the insect drones.'

He felt lightheaded. Talking used up oxygen. Having an argument at that height was not a good idea especially when he played a game of bluff and double-bluff. He wanted to see how far Stringer would go, and find out if Stringer was serious about not having to rely on him for the assault. He had forced Stringer to re-think his position.

'I agree, it's a good idea,' Stringer said. 'Patuazon may be distracted long enough to be unwary. Inform Bilton of my decision. And another thing – next time you want to discuss something like this, make an arrangement at a reasonable time, or put it in a report. I don't appreciate being woken up for an argument.'

Lock felt dizzy with anger. If three Bloaters showed up he would fight the lot. He hadn't expected Stringer to call his counter-bluff, but Stringer knew about his worries of being replaced. He had just used it. Lock's anger rose at the realisation he had been played, not for the first time – and probably not for the last time, either. That was why he hated the sessions with psychiatrists. Their reports gave spies like Stringer a huge advantage, another weapon to add to an arsenal of manipulation that already overflowed with information used to control and bind.

He thought about it as he drifted towards land. Stringer saw fit to deny his usefulness, when Lock knew damn well he was very useful. It followed that Stringer's dismissal was pretence. He knew that telling Lock he wasn't needed would produce an angry reaction. Lock would set out to prove he was needed, thereby fulfilling what Stringer wanted. He was being played by basic reverse psychology. He took comfort from unravelling the bluff. Maybe he would piss Stringer off by really concentrating on the insect drones and Patuazon's eastern wing. He still had two drone flies and two bees. But Stringer might be pulling a double-bluff and did want Lock to be out of the assault, and playing around with the drones instead. Whatever Stringer wanted him to do, Lock determined to do the opposite.

He remembered he'd left a fly hovering over the training lake. Cursing his carelessness he put the satphone away in his belt kit and teleported back to his start point, near the perimeter fence. He levitated in the air a metre off the ground, hemmed in by the deafening whirring of billions of cicadas sounding like an orchestra of electric drills. The sound was punctuated by bursts of unearthly wailing from a group of howler monkeys, further out than his aura sense could detect. A pungent odour, different to the background stench of rot and wet wood, marked the passage of wild boar, not long ago.

He sensed an abundance of wildlife, none of it human and none of the larger mammals that could be a threat to him. Auras could not be classified in primary colours because there were too many hues. Insects, for example. Their presence lit up the jungle. Swift, acid yellow rivers of ants, slower creamy beetles and centipedes, and sickly custard seas of cicadas, so many shades of bright yellow bugs they sometimes outshone the cooler mauve-rose auras of the small mammals feasting on them. Insects were prettier in the aura spectrum than in ordinary colours.

He looked up and recognised the biscuit-brown speck of a toucan among an oatmeal flock of smaller birds. Birds varied from cream to tangerine to burnt umber, through to almost black. Humans were mid-range blue – cobalt. Apes and monkeys varied from the darkest navy to ice blue and some were even aquamarine. Other mammals glowed deep purple to light jade green according to which species they belonged to, like the light mauve coloured tree rats scuttling up the trunk of a fruit tree on his right.

Lock turned his attention to the tunnel under the fence. Days spent teaching survival tricks to Patuazon's nephew had been complemented by nights evading the boy's minders to dig a short tunnel under the perimeter fence, circumventing Patuazon's electronic anti-teleporter sentries attached to the highest trees in his estate, and beyond it. Lock knew where the electronic sentries were, courtesy of portable detection equipment given to him by the SIS, but he couldn't switch off the invisible net covering the villa, its grounds and the training camp without the risk of detection. Sometimes simple methods were best, like the tunnel.

He wondered if other Shifters had the same in-built memory of the location of a teleportation departure point. It never lasted long, maybe a couple of hours, a half day at most, like a subconscious computer memory. It baffled scientists, years after they first examined Lock's abilities. Nobody had come up with an answer for that ability and Lock was also unaware of how he did it. It simply existed, like his other skills. The tunnel existed, too, though that had taken strenuous hours of digging in the darkness, and he had to find it by torchlight.

He touched down amid a foaming mass of insects. Keeping a wary eye on yellow ochre signatures he had learned to recognise as small, poisonous spiders, he angled his body in alignment with the tunnel. He didn't crawl through it. He took the easy way and teleported into the narrow gap. It avoided the danger of being snagged. He had no worry about being merged into anything else because dense matter didn't like Shifters trying to occupy the same space as it and simply pushed them away.

Lock materialised on the other side of the fence and struggled through the undergrowth towards the lake. Turning on the night vision setting and navigation grid on the control glasses, he wobbled as he accessed the fly. Its erratic path zoomed back and forth as well as dipping up and down in a stomach-lurching manner. Its eyes transmitted a blank screen. Over the receiver an odd swishing, gurgling noise steadied into regular beats. He visualised the fly returning to him, but it didn't respond to commands. It took Lock two minutes to work out that the fly was inside a bat's stomach.

~~~~~~~~

Stringer's mobile phone rang for the second time in the early hours of the
~~~~~~~~

morning. It seemed like five minutes after Lock's call but when he squinted at the clock, he saw forty-five minutes had passed. The blonde woman in his king-size bed sighed to register annoyance and rolled away from him. The number on the caller display belonged to Hanslope, one of the intelligence officers working in his department.

'Sorry to wake you, Sir. There's a situation in Australia.'

'Australia? Why the hell are you waking me in the middle of the night about Australia?'

'You said to call you if there was any serious incident concerning teleporters, and this one is serious.'

'Okay, tell me.'

'Someone hit the High Commission in Canberra. An explosion. It's all over the news. It looks pretty bad.'

Stringer threw the covers off and got out of bed. The woman put an arm out and yanked the bedclothes back over her bare shoulder. He bent over to the varnished wood floor and picked up a pair of trousers. Aside from assorted clothes strewn carelessly on the floor, everything about Stringer's bedroom mirrored the neatness of his office. He thrust his legs into his trousers, balancing the phone between his jaw and shoulder, while Hanslope described the scene.

'Most of the building has been destroyed. Ten people dead and lots missing. It happened in the afternoon, so the High Commission was busy.'

Stringer padded barefoot to the lounge and picked up the TV remote, still listening to the phone.

'People were getting documents to visit the UK for Christmas. The Commissioner was meeting a trade delegation. He's listed missing. So is our station chief. His office is just underneath.'

'I know where his office is, Hanslope.'

The loop of pictures on the television screen showed a damaged building with a fire raging in the background. Rescue people clambered over rubble looking for survivors. Medical personnel led a woman covered in dust to an ambulance which sped out of sight, and grim-faced police waved journalists away while they set up a cordon. The breaking news tape at the bottom of the screen said ten dead, many missing, and eleven wounded.

'Any early intel on who did it?' Stringer asked.

'No, nobody's claimed responsibility.'

'So how do we know a teleporter is involved?'

'There's an eyewitness report. An injured woman said she saw a man appear out of nowhere and disappear, and then there was an explosion.'

'One bomber couldn't have done this much damage.'

'There are no reports of any more, not so far.'

Stringer's phone buzzed to let him know somebody was trying to get through on the encrypted priority line.

'Okay, good work, Hanslope. Keep on it; see what you can find out.' Stringer didn't wait for a reply. He took the second call, from his boss, Palmer.

'You've heard the news?' Palmer asked.

'Five minutes ago. I'm looking at it now.'

'Paul's dead.'

Stringer inhaled through his teeth. 'I'm sorry to hear that. He was a good man.'

Paul, the Canberra station chief, had been one of Stringer's line managers a few years previously, though Stringer hadn't known him well. Nevertheless, he respected him as a capable intelligence officer.

'Yes, indeed he was a good man.' Palmer's tone implied that Stringer wasn't. 'There's a Cobra meeting in forty-five minutes. Your attendance is required. Bring the Ghost file. You're doing the briefing due to your close connection with the subject.'

'Understood.'

Stringer put the phone down with growing excitement. If he was right, the Prime Minister had been spooked into agreeing the creation of the UK's own team of enhanced-ability operatives, and it looked as though Palmer's objections to Stringer's involvement had been thrown out by somebody higher up.

Palmer didn't like Stringer. He regarded him as a red-brick university upstart, inferior to Oxbridge graduates. Palmer's notion of suitable SIS officers was mired in old-school conservatism. He would refer to the military origins of SIS, and its more popular name of MI6, with nostalgia for a time when the name meant Military Intelligence Six. Palmer served in the army, unlike Stringer, and he lamented the lack of discipline among intelligence staff. He moaned that the Service could do with restoring some military-style structure, or at least restrict its intake to graduates of Oxford and Cambridge universities. The SIS grapevine relayed his view and Stringer knew about it. He saw Palmer as out of step with current thinking. In modern times, the Service offered employment to civilians and service personnel alike. Most recruits had university backgrounds, but they were not restricted to Oxbridge. To Palmer's disgust, some came from ethnic minority backgrounds.

Stringer went to his study, turned on his laptop and accessed Lock Harford's file. Leaving the printer chattering, he returned to the bedroom, shook his guest awake and informed her she had to leave.

'Right now?'

'I've got work to do.'

She looked at the clock and sat up.

'What kind of bank needs you to work at this hour?'

Stringer didn't reply. The woman threw off the bedclothes as though they smelled of dung instead of sex. She pulled and pushed and shoved her clothes back on, thrust her feet into high heels and marched out to the hallway. Stringer followed her. The printer finished and it waited for further instructions, green-eyed and silent. He closed the study door.

'You must think I'm an idiot if you expect me to believe that was the bank. I'm not that easily fooled. Give my regards to your wife. I hope she had a good trip.'

Her heels clicked down the hallway. Stringer shook his head, declining to argue the point that he wasn't married, and after she slammed the front door shut he went to his study to update the files. He needed to be well-prepared for the Cobra meeting in Cabinet Office Briefing Room A, the room that gave Cobra its name.

CHAPTER 8

During a late evening briefing, Jimmy listened as Harford told the group they would be teleporting. Harford's briefing didn't extend beyond saying the men might experience nausea, mild dizziness and garbled sounds, and he couldn't tell them more because each person's experience of teleportation was unique. The news of teleporter training excited Jimmy. At last he would find out what it was like, though the recent conversation with Vicar played on his mind. Jimmy wanted the answer to the one question that nagged him. In the end, he didn't ask how many men died during teleportation. Even if some had died, he reasoned, Harford would not tell him. The risk had to be accepted as one more in a job that involved plenty of life-threatening scenarios. Jimmy had a gut feeling nothing would go wrong. Though maybe something could happen to Bilton, he thought mischievously. Looking at Bilton's face, Jimmy guessed he hadn't teleported before, either.

The six men donned night vision visors, trekked to a hidden boat and paddled to the other side of the lake, hiding the boat behind long ferns. Harford led the way, as he had done since they left the hut. He seemed sure when giving the all-clear, alerting them to the presence of animals as they entered the jungle. Harford's certainty about animal positions puzzled Jimmy. Bilton didn't question what Harford said, but Jimmy preferred to double-check the information visually where he could. After twenty minutes he acknowledged Harford was right, every time. They reached the start of a path marked by laser sensors. Although only a short distance from the perimeter fence the cleared path was narrow. Harford spotted and pointed out poisonous snakes and spiders that Jimmy barely saw even with the help of his visor and a green low-light torch.

To round off the oxygen-consuming slog, they crawled through a disgusting tunnel under the perimeter fence. Jimmy emerged covered in slime, and insects which bit into his hands and face. They wriggled into his clothes and tried to make him their new home. He brushed off insects near his eyes but his training in being alert at all times meant he closed his senses to the pain and itching, allowing the insects to go on munching. The skin had closed over his wound from the fight with Bloater otherwise some of the insects might have found a home they really liked.

Harford stopped and looked at coordinates on a computer map.

'Close up. We're travelling for eight minutes. Get ready,' he said, turning off his green low light headband torch. Jimmy's mouth dried. He moved closer to Harford. Everybody faced outwards in combat-ready stance, with Harford in the centre.

'Ready?' Harford said. A low chorus of affirmative grunts came out of the darkness.

Jimmy hoped the teleportation would kill off the bugs. Harford hadn't mentioned that.

'On my mark. Three – two – one – go.'

Jimmy clutched his weapon in a clammy fist. An icy breath drove right through his sticky, damp shirt, and his hot breath exhaled in a white cloud as though somebody had pushed him into a freezer. His feet felt as though they were sinking in quicksand. Before he had time to get used to it his stomach plummeted and pressed against his bowels as if he was in a lift that shot up too fast. He gasped. Despite his mental preparation, he was frozen by fear. The lift stopped as suddenly as it had started and a loud hissing noise filled his ears, like the sound of steam escaping from several valves, and his nose stung. He felt disorientated, unable to tell if he was going backwards, forwards or sideways.

Dark shapes zipped towards him from all directions and fell away again. He raised a hand to ward them off before he realised they were passing by. Lowering his hand, he tried not to flinch as they brushed his body. Some felt as though they licked him, sucking his energy in a split second before spitting it back into him as they departed. Others gave him their energy, infusing him with a heady rush of adrenaline and making the hairs on his neck stand on end. Euphoria washed over him, a familiar feeling. Jimmy recognised it from his dreams after his brush with death in Scotland.

The hissing died. He had just got used to the dark shapes and the weird sensation of opposites, the push and pull, when they disappeared. An explosion, unearthly and terrifying, enveloped him. It vanished, replaced by the hissing. A blurred light beneath his legs widened into points then into glowing yellow lines. A spider's web of city street lights fanned out below, a comforting sight of something familiar until he remembered he was floating hundreds of metres in the night sky with nothing beneath his feet. Without warning his stomach tried to force its way through his mouth as the group lurched and fell. Jimmy automatically bent his knees as if landing from a parachute drop. More blurry shapes crackled past before they stopped. Harford held the group in the air, in a pitch black hole, and then lowered them slowly to solid ground. Jimmy stumbled and threw up.

He trembled with a mix of terror, excitement, relief and exhilaration that he had done it. The ground was solid and normal under his feet as he straightened. He felt around his body and over his face. Everything seemed okay, all in the right place. He tuned in to his new environment. The glow on his left came from the city on the horizon. He heard the throb of traffic behind the ever-present sizzling of cicadas. A shimmering sea of waist-high plants lit by moonlight stretched away over a long field. Jimmy recognised them as a crop, which meant there was a farmhouse nearby. Harford said,

'We're in a field outside Cali. There's nobody around for three hundred metres except four people inside a farmhouse two hundred metres, at ten o'clock.'

Harford's knowledge about the people inside the farmhouse confirmed that he possessed a sense way beyond anything familiar to Jimmy. Harford turned on his headband lowlight torch and asked each man if they were okay. When he got to Mick he had no response other than the sound of plants being crushed as Mick keeled over.

~~~~~~~~

The day after the aborted training session, Jimmy regarded Harford with a mixture of fascination and frustration. Going over the sequence of events, Jimmy recalled how Harford had leapt to Mick's side, thinking he was unconscious. A few seconds later, Mick sat up, laughing, and the men sniggered. Jimmy had never seen or heard Harford really livid until that moment. He called Mick every name he could think of, which amounted to quite a few. Was Mick some kind of imbecile, Harford wanted to know, to pull a stunt like that, what was he, a stupid street kid who thought it was clever to arse around? Was he the type of idiot who'd sit at the back of class pulling faces while everybody else was learning? If Mick was typical of the next wave of troopers in the Regiment, God help the Regiment, because they'd got a useless tosser who couldn't tell when it was time to be serious. If it's a joke you want, Harford said, how about I take you to the top of Mount Everest and leave you there for a week, let's see how good your survival skills are. Then you might appreciate when it's not a good time to fuck around.

Harford's rant ran out of steam, but not until he'd told Mick if it was up to him, he'd be Returned To Unit, the one thing that every SAS soldier dreaded – being returned to their original army regiment in disgrace. Bilton didn't intervene; he let him get on with it. Everybody kept their heads down after they got back to the hut. Harford had proved that he wasn't to be messed with. The lads chatted among themselves, some light banter to ease the tension. They knew when it was time to leave an angry man alone. Bilton, true to his usual tactless form, blustered on about some reconnaissance Harford was supposed to do according to new orders. He wanted Harford to leave straight away so he'd be back by first light to take the lads to set up an Observation Post at Mosquera's villa. Harford said no,
~~~~~~~~

there was plenty of time and he had to deal with the insect drones first. Bilton didn't like it. Harford said he needed the drones for the recce, and Bilton backed down and informed everybody else about putting in an OP at Mosquera's villa. He said they couldn't rely on drones alone and needed eyeball, even if it was just for a few days.

Jimmy wasn't surprised when Bilton picked him for the OP as well as Mick, Nails and Vicar. Bilton liked giving them the shitty jobs as punishment for Mick's horsing around. Usually Jimmy didn't mind doing OPs, but a jungle stint would put a strain on his healing wounds. He didn't say anything because it was bad form to complain to a boss. The lads sorted out their supplies and kit. Jimmy had the bunk nearest the table and while he repacked his bergen, out of curiosity he kept an eye on what Harford did. So did Bilton. Jimmy wasn't sure if Bilton crowded in on Harford's personal space unknowingly or deliberately, but either way Harford didn't like it. Nor did he like Bilton's questions about teleportation, though Jimmy had a keen interest in the answers.

Harford picked up one of the drone flies and held it steady.

'It looks like an owl's eye,' Bilton commented, peering at spots Harford had precision painted on the fly's wings.

Harford adjusted the sweat bandanna on his head and held the fly in front of him, inspecting it in the dim glow from an oil lamp.

'That's the whole idea. Insects with fake eyes on their wings fool birds into thinking they're a predator, so the birds leave them alone. I can't do anything about the bats, unfortunately.' Harford put the fly down beside the other two he had finished. 'Stand back. I need to see if they can still get airborne.' He put on the glasses. The fly lifted off the table and hovered a metre and a half above the floor. Fred the lizard eyed it greedily.

'It's a bit sluggish, but it'll do.' Harford landed the fly and took off the glasses.

Bilton turned the subject back to teleportation.

'You said people don't dematerialise in Shifting, right?'

'Right.'

'So how can Shifters get through walls into buildings if it's not on a cellular basis?'

The fly descended to the table and Harford took off the control glasses. Jimmy stuffed the contents of some twenty-four-hour ration packs into his bergen and listened.

'Nobody knows for sure. I haven't kept up with recent research, so I can't tell you.' Bilton knew he was being fobbed off. Harford put the drones away.

'I need to test these outside.' He grabbed a low-light torch and left.

Jimmy waited a couple of minutes after the hut door closed. Bilton was talking to PC. Jimmy seized the moment to get Harford alone. He grabbed his Diemaco rifle and slipped out of the hut with his visor, saying he was going for a dump. The humid night air carried with it the fluttering of moths and bats, and the oppressive feeling of being slow-cooked. He guessed Harford headed for the lake. He put the visor on and switched the setting to high-definition thermal imaging rather than the usual passive setting which picked up on ambient light. He caught a human shape not far away, partially hidden by a tree trunk. Turning on the low-light torch on the end of his Diemaco he switched the visor back to passive and picked his way past spiders' webs towards Harford, who didn't move. Jimmy took that as a sign that his presence would be tolerated even if it wasn't welcome.

Harford stood by the lakeside, staring over black water through the control glasses. Jimmy couldn't see a drone by the light of his torch, only thousands of clicking, whirring insects.

'Nice night for fishing.'

'Thought it was you.'

'Yeah? You could smell me from a hundred paces?'

Harford chuckled.

'You looked like somebody with something on his mind.'

'Yeah. Yes, I have.' Jimmy made a mental note to be more careful not to let his troubles register on his face. An awkward gap ensued, an acute awareness of the other person without real communication. Jimmy broke the silence. 'You're right, I wanted to speak to you.'

'Okay. What about?'

'About that time in Scotland. I owe you for getting me off that mountain.' He hesitated and added, 'And I'm sorry about the fight.'

'No problem.'

Jimmy's embarrassment was so strong he felt Harford could have reached out and touched it.

'That wasn't all you came to say, was it?'

Jimmy hesitated. He had the opportunity to ask his questions but he wasn't sure he wanted to know the answers.

'It's about Scotland. I think I might have teleported.'

'You did. Didn't they tell you that?'

The confidence in Harford's voice was a relief. Here, at last, Jimmy had somebody who might know enough to help.

'No, they didn't. They didn't tell us anything. But that wasn't it. Not everything I want to know about. That overdose of Starbirth. I think it's had some effect on me.'

'What kind of effect?'

'Can this be off the record?'

'That depends on whether it affects your ability as a trooper,' Harford replied.

'No, it doesn't.' Jimmy hoped the unease he felt didn't come across in his voice.

'In that case it's off the record. It won't go in any report.'

'It's just…' He faltered. He didn't know how to put it into words and wished he'd rehearsed what to say. He started again. 'When I touch things…' He looked at his hands as if they could speak for him.

'Go on.'

'There's this weird sensation, more than tingling, I can feel what I'm touching, as if I know it.' He trailed off, embarrassed that what he said had been rushed and came nowhere near the experiences he'd had. 'It's weird, as though I'm absorbing things.' Jimmy stopped again. It sounded crazy, even to his own ears. He regretted starting the conversation.

'That's it?'

'Yeah.'

'Does it make you feel anxious when it happens?'

'No. Well, yeah, I suppose it does. It's like I get drawn into the sensation somehow, becoming one with it.'

'Getting drawn into enhancements is typical of Starbirth, but I've never heard of that particular effect related to it.'

Disappointed, Jimmy needed more.

'Do you think it's permanent?'

'That's something you'd be better off discussing with the medics.'

'They don't know shit. They were learning from observing me and my mate Pete. I just thought you might know a bit more, seeing as you're a Shifter.'

'Look, mate, I'm not dismissing what you're saying. The drug hasn't been around long enough. Nobody knows exactly what the effects are so I don't know if it might be permanent or not. People are still doing research. They're the ones best placed to answer your question. Contact the hospital when you get back.'

'I'll be their favourite guinea pig.'

'They have to learn from somebody, why not you? You can learn from them at the same time.'

'If it gets to be a problem, I'll go.'

'Okay. I suggest you keep a record. When, how long – that sort of thing.' Harford paused. 'Is there anything else you want to know?'

Jimmy didn't need to be asked twice.

'Yeah, there is. How come me and Pete had a different reaction than the other guys? They got hallucinations and a high. We were the only ones who developed abilities.'

'That, I can tell you. Researchers think it's down to genetic predisposition.'

'What, you mean it alters your genes?'

'No, not exactly. Well, possibly. We don't have enough long-term studies to say for sure. It means that if some people have the right genetic makeup, they react to Starbirth by developing abilities. If they don't, the drug doesn't affect them in that way. Like your mates in Scotland. They got high but they didn't do much more than hallucinate.'

'You're saying me and Pete have the right genetic makeup.'

'Yeah. You teleported, he developed amazing strength. I heard it took eight men to hold him down long enough for the medics to sedate him.'

Harford held out his hand for a drone to land on. Jimmy pondered over the information and frowned.

'I don't understand. Why are we looking for this AH-4 stuff if we can use Starbirth?'

'We can't. Starbirth kills people and sends them mad. It's too unpredictable and dangerous. As far as we know, with prolonged use, the mortality rate is one hundred per cent. You had a massive overdose and you were all lucky, you survived. If it was going to kill you, you'd be dead by now. It's not the same as prolonged use.'

Harford put the insect drone back in the box and took out another one, releasing it into the swarms of night insects buzzing over the lake. He continued,

'We can't get AH-4 from Starbirth, either. When AH-4 is mixed with cocaine it produces a catalytic reaction, like mixing wood filler paste with hardener. It can't be reverse-catalysed. People have tried and it doesn't work. They ended up with a toxic substance instead of AH-4. When they try to refine the compound it becomes inert.'

Jimmy felt an unpleasant tickling sensation on his left leg. Looking down he saw a large spider making its way up his trousers. He bent down and flicked it off with the barrel of his Diemaco. Something wasn't right with the scene lit up dimly by the low-light torch on the end of his weapon. Harford's feet weren't in the right place, somehow. Then he realised. Harford wasn't standing on a rock or piece of tree, as he'd assumed – Harford wasn't standing on anything.

'Shit,' Jimmy chuckled as he straightened up. 'Nice trick. There's me acting like a handy vertical runway for the wildlife and you're just fucking hovering. Nice one.'

The tree nearest them slid down several inches, as did the surface of the lake, and the solidity under Jimmy's boots vanished. His curse at finding himself inches off the ground was met by a grin from Harford, who didn't look round, but smiled over the lake enjoying his moment. He held out his hand to retrieve the drone.

'That's the last test. Let's go.'

There might not be another chance to ask the question that would be awkward, but Jimmy had to ask.

'How many people have died in teleportation?'

He went down with a bump, squashing hundreds of beetles, centipedes, spiders and ants.

'None during mine.'

Jimmy kicked himself for touching what was obviously a raw nerve. Harford put the box in his pocket and said,

'I know the rumours. They're rubbish. Nobody has ever died, or even been injured by Shifting. I've seen some minor injuries caused by landing on boats in gales, or guys caught on slippery surfaces, that's all. If anybody here is worried, they're free to stay behind.'

Jimmy thought it best to keep his mouth shut as they turned from the water's edge. Ahead of him Harford seemed to glide, still hovering. Jimmy felt he crashed around by comparison, though his progress was, as always, silent. Harford slowed and spoke over his shoulder.

'There's nobody around except the guys in the huts. You can relax.'

He paused, not moving. Jimmy wanted to know, but thought it prudent not to ask, exactly how Harford knew that, whether he used a special sense, a piece of sophisticated kit or perhaps an implant.

Harford sighed, and when he spoke there was heaviness in his voice Jimmy hadn't heard before.

'Okay, here's the truth. Years ago there was an accident. I was with some Blades up in the Andes north of Bogota, doing some caving. I was up top at base camp, resting, and the guys had gone off exploring deep inside the cave system. They got caught in a flash flood. I couldn't get to them in time. Four of them died. Not six, the number being bandied about.' He paused and looked away, and Jimmy understood why he had gone off the deep end with Mick's prank. Harford felt responsible for the safety of whoever he had in his group.

'Shit. Tough deal.'

'Yeah. You can tell the lads that. I doubt they'll believe you, because rumours are more interesting. As far as I'm concerned, that's all I'm saying.'

~~~~~~~~

Lock was glad he delayed the reconnaissance of Mosquera's villa until after ten at night. He might have missed the valuable intelligence being gathered. He straddled a branch of a tree overlooking the estate, concealed by foliage and absorbed by what he saw through the eyes of an insect drone fly. It squatted on a bookshelf in Mosquera's study, looking diagonally over Mosquera's shoulder, with a perfect view of everything on the heavily sculpted hardwood desk. The drug lord, an overweight forty-eight-year-old who looked closer to sixty, stared at his computer with his phone in his hand.
~~~~~~~~

The room looked like a cheap copy of the Oval Office, from the gold and red circular rug to gold-cushioned chairs set around it and low marble-topped tables in between the chairs. Vulgar paintings of nubile women and a trashy Cupid sculpture, that looked as though it ought to be the centrepiece of a fountain, spoiled the effect. At the other end of the room, a swarthy bodyguard armed with an AK47 semi-automatic rifle stood by a heavy, reinforced door that incorporated a panel of what Lock assumed was one-way bulletproof glass.

He slipped into an easy translation of Spanish, learned during his years in Brazil as a child, and recorded everything. Over the previous hour Mosquera spoke to a lot of people. Judging by the deference in Mosquera's voice, they seemed to be people in high places; politicians, government workers and perhaps high-ranking police. Lock heard Mosquera refer to one as councilman and another as Colonel. Mosquera dished out party invitations like handing out sweets, with promises of a good time. The delights started with basic attractions of 'Happiness by the truckload,' which Lock thought referred to cocaine, and a supply of the most beautiful girls his guest was ever likely to see, to assurances that his guest's valuable services had not been overlooked and they would hear something very attractive to them if they turned up.

Then there were the people whom Mosquera ordered to turn up. It excited Lock because they were talking in code. The party would be either a front for a business meeting, or combined with it. Mosquera flicked screens between sets of numbers, peering at them over the top of his glasses. Lock saw and recorded every number. He didn't know what the figures meant, but London would be able to unscramble it and use voice recognition software to identify some of Mosquera's contacts.

A buzzer drew the guard's attention to the door. He glanced at somebody who appeared at the glass panel and turned to Mosquera, saying a name that Lock didn't catch. Mosquera nodded. The guard opened the door to allow in a dark-haired man in his thirties wearing a thin gold chain that glinted in his open-neck shirt. He stood on the rug waiting for Mosquera's attention, which came late.

'He's sure he can do it this time?' Mosquera asked.

'Yes. He's been practicing.'

Mosquera stood up. 'Okay, let's see.'

Lock's drone fly shot through the narrowing gap of the closing door to follow the two men and the bodyguard down a wide hallway. The drone's sensors picked up the chemical composition of new paint, relaying the information to Lock's screen coupled with a warning of possible noxious gases that could impair its operating systems. The drone's power stuttered but it held its course and sailed through the entrance, following the men to a car. The car drove a couple of hundred metres to a large hut. Lock considered whether Mosquera was unable to walk far, given his clumsy gait. If so, when the assault took place Mosquera would be unlikely to sprint away and he'd be an easier target despite his bodyguards.

Mosquera entered the hut and four men stood up as a mark of respect. Lock took a look at the new place, turning the fly by the doorway. A single bare light bulb lit a windowless, almost empty room which had a map of Putumayo on one wall. An open laptop lay on a desk, the screen facing away from Lock. Mosquera stopped in front of a skinny native Indian and looked him up and down.

'You can do this, Miguel?'

'Si, senor.'

'Good.'

Mosquera sauntered to the doorway. Miguel stepped to the centre of the room like a condemned man, his hands clenched into fists and his bravado stripped away. Mosquera waved a hand at Miguel in a gesture that told him to carry on, and waited. Lock checked his glasses display and watched as a minute passed, and then two. Nothing happened, but Miguel's skin developed a yellow hue. That wasn't right. Lock had never seen a colour like that on a Shifter – or on any human being. Something was wrong. He wished Miguel would stop.

'Two thousand dollars,' Mosquera encouraged. Miguel straightened, the fear on his face replaced by resigned determination. His body wavered as though immersed in a desert heat wave and he disappeared.

Nobody in the hut said anything, but the Gold Chain Man held a phone to one ear and checked a digital stopwatch in his other hand. He said something into the phone, stopped recording the time and turned to Mosquera.

'He's there.' Mosquera nodded and the man reset the watch, still listening on the phone. 'He's returning now.'

They waited, and the minutes ticked on. Mosquera was impatient.

'How long?'

'Five minutes.'

'I thought you said he could do it.'

The man inclined his head, keeping his eyes on the stopwatch. Lock checked his own clock on the control display. He made it six and a half minutes. Nothing happened as the long seconds ticked on. Sweat poured off Gold Chain's forehead.

'How long?' Mosquera demanded.

'Six minutes. He did it okay this morning.'

Mosquera turned abruptly for the door.

'Let me know if he returns.'

Something emerged from the air and slumped on the concrete floor behind Mosquera. The men near the table recoiled in horror. One gasped and stepped backwards, falling over a chair with a crash. Two others crossed themselves. Lock moved the fly so he could see past Mosquera. His blood ran cold. The lumpy mass on the floor looked as though the Devil himself had grabbed Miguel, squashed and scrambled his skin, muscles and bones, and dropped the mess back on the concrete. Like everybody else in the room Lock was in shock, not wanting to believe what he saw. People didn't die in teleportation. He'd never seen anybody die, but the evidence was in front of him. What on earth had Mosquera used?

Mosquera flew into a rage. He shouted insults at the cringing Gold Chain man. He said he had wasted money. The money would come from his pay, and if he didn't pick the right man next time, being one of the family wouldn't save him. He would be the next volunteer. He had to clear up the mess, and he had to do it on his own, nobody else was to help. Mosquera stormed out of the hut. The Gold Chain man threw up. The drug lord's reaction to the horrific death of his bribed volunteer filled Lock with a surge of loathing and the desire to hit back.

He circled and filmed the remains, not wanting to be there, but unable to drag himself away. He couldn't make the leap from years of confident belief in the safety of Shifting, to the grim discovery that it had been founded on ignorance. Shaken to the core, a morbid fascination kept him circling and filming the clean-up until he realised he had been there too long. The insect drone shot out of the open door and he chased the car back up the hill. The drone arrived too late. The door he'd used previously was closed. The windows had mosquito netting over them.

It took twenty minutes to find a way in from the unfinished section at the back of the villa and another ten to negotiate new obstacles on his way back to the study, using a drone bee he put in a hover over the villa to direct the fly. The fly registered two warnings about noxious fumes before it reached the study door, where a statuesque woman waited to be let in. She looked annoyed. As soon as the door opened, the fly followed her inside. Lock headed for the bookcase behind Mosquera, but before the fly reached it, the display on the control glasses flashed warnings of system failures.

The world spun. Lock grabbed his tree branch and held on tight as the fly spiralled out of control. Something he didn't recognise filled his view. The blurry image moved, sharpened and defined itself into lines, and when the object moved away, he realised he had been looking at creases on Mosquera's shirt. The fly had fallen on his desk. It lay centimetres from Mosquera's hand, a finger's length from being squashed by the large, fleshy palm.

Mosquera hadn't noticed it. He and the woman, whom Lock realised must be his second wife, glared at each other across the desk, embroiled in a row about her being kept waiting outside like one of his whores. Lock had the impression of a longstanding argument, repeated many times. The quarrel moved on to the party. Mosquera complained that she was giving him a headache and he had already put the staff to work on sorting out details. She retorted that he'd forgotten the magician, with only a week to go. He hadn't given instructions to the staff about the magician. His grandson, Enrico – a name she emphasised as if he didn't know who his grandson was – should have what he wanted for his party. It was his party, after all. He was only five and wouldn't understand why his granddad broke his promise.

Lock made a mental note about the event being a young child's party. That meant other children would be there. Stringer's plan for an assault would surely have to wait for another day, regardless of the temptation presented to the SIS to hit Mosquera during a business meeting, possibly taking out his entire organisation. He listened to what Mosquera and his wife said and tried to breathe life into the fly. Enraged, Mosquera said he hadn't forgotten, he resented her implication that he hadn't considered Enrico, and if she wasn't the mother of his sons, he would have kicked her out long ago.

The argument might have gone on, each party taking perverse pleasure from it, had the fly not interrupted. The systems came back online, taking Lock by surprise. The fly went into a whirl that turned its vision into a blur of grey lines. The tiny motor rose in pitch and volume, sounding nothing like a fly. Lock accessed the control menu and cut it. The world slowed and the fly halted facing an upside down Mosquera, who stared at it. He dismissed his wife, instructing his bodyguard to escort her out of the room. Leaning over, he examined the fly. His upside down eyes, enormous and underscored by caterpillar eyebrows, resembled the less human parts of the mess in the hut.

'Rodrigo. Over here.' His bodyguard joined him. 'Have you ever seen a bug like that?'

Another pair of eyes peered at it. A banana-shaped upturned moustache parted as the bodyguard replied, revealing a set of bad teeth.

'No, Boss, can't say I have, but I ain't interested in bugs.'

'Take a closer look. This bug doesn't look real.'

The head bent closer.

'I dunno, Boss. I can't tell. There's something kind of sticky on the wings, though.'

Lock activated the legs and the faces sprang back.

'It's alive, whatever it is,' the bodyguard said.

'Call Big G. He's native, he should know about this kind of insect.'

Lock heard the guard on the radio. It dawned on him that the paint fumes the fly complained about had not come from newly whitewashed walls, as he assumed, but from the dabs of oil-based paint he put on the fly's wings earlier. Flying in hot and humid air had melted the paint. The control glasses display showed the flight capability as only thirty-eight per cent. He cursed his bad luck. He had to get the fly out before the Indian arrived. If Mosquera exposed the fly as fake, it would reveal the surveillance and the operation would be compromised.

That wouldn't be a bad thing as far as Lock was concerned, after his discovery about the boy's party. If Mosquera did another runner, the assault would not take place. The more he thought about it, the more attractive the idea seemed, until he considered his report. Stringer, and those above him, would never see losing the fly as an accident. Given Lock's hostility to the assault plan, they would assume he'd sabotaged the operation.

Mosquera armed himself with a biro and jabbed the fly. Lock activated the legs again, a reaction a real insect would have to being attacked. He willed Mosquera to push the fly and dislodge it or flip it over. That would at least stop it being stuck to the desk. Mosquera pushed it hard, releasing the wings from the desk. Lock flipped it the right way up. He tried to lift it off the desk. Mosquera responded by emptying a whisky tumbler, upending it and plonking it over the fly. Lock swore. There was nothing he could do. He watched as the door opened.

The Indian walked over and examined the drone. The tumbler muffled his softly-spoken words but Lock made out most of it.

'I've seen bugs similar but this one's smaller than most. It looks like it tangled with fresh paint. It's harmless enough.'

Mosquera wasn't convinced.

'Squash it. Rodrigo, find a magnifying glass. I want a better look. If I see guts I'll believe it's real.'

Lock panicked. The flight capability had gone up to forty per cent, which meant either the fumes weren't so bad, or the paint was drying, but it might not be enough to get out of trouble. The tumbler lifted and Lock zipped out backwards, a move he hoped would fool his captors by its unpredictability. The room jarred as the fly hit something.

'Get it. Don't let it get away,' Mosquera ordered. Using thought to control the fly, Lock shot forwards and upwards, away from faces that wobbled in and out of view. The fly responded sluggishly, the flight capability numbers counting down. Something, probably a hand, swiped at it. Lock headed for a large vase on the floor and crash-landed behind it.

'It went over there. Keep the door closed.' The shouts were accompanied by the sound of something heavy approaching. Lock saw a dark overhang and dashed for it.

'It's gone under the bookcase. Move the bookcase out of the way.'

He heard loud creaking noises and grunts from people heaving the bookcase. He switched to infra-red vision, which didn't help much, and scuttled forward until he hit something. He thought about climbing it. The fly responded by clambering vertically and Lock stopped when it hit something else. Shadows disappeared, horizons swayed and lit up, and then the darkness descended again. He must be clinging to the underneath of the bookcase.

'Where the fuck's it gone?' Mosquera demanded. Lock stayed put while the search went on, and all the time the flight capability numbers crept upwards to forty-two per cent, forty-five, forty-seven.

'It must be underneath. Take the books out. Turn the bookcase upside down. Call Pablo and Tony to help look.'

Lock heard books being thrown on the floor until Mosquera shouted at his men to be careful, the books were valuable. Light flooded in as people raised the end of the bookcase. The capability number was at fifty-two per cent when Lock flew for a gap between somebody's legs. The fly made it out of the other side, to curses from Mosquera. Lock circled the room, keeping out of reach of a fly swatter. The door buzzer sounded.

'No!' Mosquera shouted. The door opened a fraction and Lock hurtled through the gap over somebody's head and into the freedom of the hallway. Zipping back into the unfinished section of the villa, he was aware that his left arm hurt, and tuned in to his real surroundings in the jungle canopy. He gripped the branch so tightly, his muscles had gone into spasm.

An hour later, outside the training hut, he conferred with Bilton. They agreed to leave it until daybreak before telling the men about the way Mosquera's volunteer died. Lock gave Bilton details of the business meeting and party. He didn't tell Bilton that during the return journey he deliberated over whether to wipe the data transmitted to the recorder and say the fly had succumbed to electronic defences, but decided against it. Mosquera was into something to do with Starbirth and his operation needed to be shut down, especially because of his experiments with what Lock suspected was the toxic reverse-catalysed product.

Bilton's response to news of the party was predictable.

'Perfect. That's when we'll hit, when his whole organisation is there.'

'No, it can wait. Mosquera doesn't have AH-4. If he did he wouldn't be trying to reverse-catalyse.'

'But he has Starbirth. He's trying to create teleporters.'

Lock flicked at insects around his neck and checked again for the presence of other people spying on them. Lack of sleep made him irritable.

'It'll be slaughter at a party for kids, for fuck's sake. One day more or less won't make a difference.'

'Yes, it will, we'll lose the chance to get him. If we wait, he'll have strengthened his electronic defences. We go on the day.'

Lock's patience snapped.

'No, we don't. I'm overruling that decision.'

'As field commander I'm saying we go.'

'As field commander your responsibility is to your men and executive action. As operation commander, my job is to ensure the mission is intelligence-led. There'll be too many civilians involved and too many potential casualties. Not to mention the risk of publicity afterwards. Choose a different day.' He wheeled and levitated to the hut.

CHAPTER 9

Though he didn't put his feelings into the compartment labelled orgasmic, thinking the expression rather vulgar, that was Stringer's experience as he looked round the conference table in Cabinet Office Briefing Room A. Situated thirty-five metres underground and connected to the PINDAR bunkers under the Ministry of Defence, Cobra was a soundproof, windowless executive suite dedicated to one function: decision-making at the highest level in the land, and he had a seat at the ten metre-long, highly polished, burr walnut table.

A brightly-lit notice on the wall reminded everybody, 'Mobile phones must be switched off at all times.' In between video screens, decorative mustard velvet curtains softened the fortified concrete walls that lay behind them. The blast-proof steel door was shut. Two closed-circuit cameras recorded the meeting, adding an element of security to the notes of official minutes-takers who sat lower down the table. The room had the flat, toneless feel of being exempt from the realities of life in Whitehall, while above double-decker buses, cars and black taxis ferried in early morning workers, but the impression was false. It gave Stringer a kick to think millions of people overhead went about their daily lives unaware that below ground a very few, select individuals decided their fate.

Some of the twenty-two brown leather chairs at the rectangular table were empty, but the quality of the occupants was what counted, not quantity. The Prime Minister sat opposite Stringer. Going round the table from the PM's right side, Stringer saw C, the Director of the SIS, and then Stringer's boss, Palmer. A woman and a man from the Joint Intelligence Group sat next to the head of MI5. The Director of the SAS sat next to a good-looking woman from the Joint Terrorism Analysis Centre. There was a representative from the Defence Intelligence Staff and the Metropolitan Police Commissioner, lastly a bullet-headed member of Special Branch. On the left of the PM sat senior government ministers including the Minister for Defence – generally regarded as incompetent – the Secretary of State of the Foreign and Commonwealth Office, and the Home Secretary.

Given the nod by the Prime Minister, Stringer stood at the lectern by the side of an eight-panel video wall and delivered his presentation on Lock's biography and involvement with the intelligence and security services. The computer screen built into the lectern showed him what he relayed to the video screens around the room.

Stringer cast Lock in a positive light, starting with his background. He explained how Harford was a teleporter from the age thirteen, following accidental exposure to an unknown substance, later believed to be AH-4, while living in Brazil with his parents. His mother died shortly afterwards, the result of sudden illness. Harford's father, worried about the boy's developing ability, took him back to England and put him into the care of his uncle, an intelligence officer in the SIS who used his contacts to ensure Harford had the best care available. Harford's father visited the UK frequently to check on his son's progress and intended to settle permanently after completing his contract as a research biologist, but he died in a plane crash in Brazil. Harford had a difficult period of adjustment, after which his early contact with military and intelligence personnel developed into close collaboration.

He was instrumental, Stringer said, in saving many lives on operations due to use of his extraordinary abilities as a teleporter and neuro-sensor who could detect the presence of living organisms more effectively than radar or thermal imagery. He showed great courage while under fire and took part in many successful operations which owed most of their success to his ability to move troops, place them where they would be most effective and evacuate them safely. He had considerable experience as a result of working alongside Special Forces and had increased their capabilities by at least forty per cent. This was all before he reached the age of eighteen, when an unfortunate accident affected him badly. He lived overseas for two years but returned five years ago, renewed his links with Special Forces and resumed his work with them a year later.

Stringer looked at the Prime Minister, a heavy-set man with greying hair, and saw he was glazing over. The meeting took longer than expected, after dealing first with the terrorist attack on the British High Commission in Australia. A great deal of the subsequent debate centred on whether or not to have a team of enhanced-ability operatives. Several influential people voiced misgivings about the new team's position of power. Others were alarmed over Britain's lack of preparation against teleporter terrorism. Early in the meeting the PM put forward the idea of a team as if he had always approved of it. It irked Stringer to keep quiet about his role in proposing the plan, but tact dictated letting the Prime Minister take the credit, as it ensured it would be put into effect. The notion was not new – the US already had a team, the Eagles.

Stringer concluded by saying Harford's experience made him the ideal candidate to lead a team of enhanced-ability operatives, indeed the only candidate since the UK had no other teleporters, apart from a few Starbirth addicts. He left the lectern and resumed his seat at the table, knowing he wouldn't escape that easily – particularly if Raines, a deputy representing MI5, had anything to do with it. The thin, hawk-nosed man with a well-known dislike of the SIS was itching for a turf war and the chance to put forward his preferred candidate, a charismatic lieutenant-colonel in the Parachute Regiment with strong connections to MI5.

The PM cleared his throat, brushed his hair back, regained some life and asked for questions. Raines jumped in first and spoke directly to the Prime Minister.

'What is the assessment of Harford's continued loyalty to Britain?'

The PM looked to Stringer for a response.

'In my view it's unstinting. There's no doubt about his loyalty whatsoever.'

Raines picked up a sheet of paper and made eye contact with Stringer.

'The brief says he spent some years in other countries, didn't he? Some of them dubious with a high level of terrorist activity, according to this list.'

'Yes, Sir, that's true, but he only visited as a tourist when he was younger. It has proved to be an advantage because it's given him an insight into other cultures. However, this is his homeland and he identifies with this country more than any other. His loyalty and patriotism is never in doubt. His wife and son are here and there's no indication to suggest he wants to live anywhere else.'

'But he upped and left for two years when it suited him.'

'Mr Harford was eighteen and had been under considerable pressure.'

'So he snaps under pressure. That's hardly a recommendation for the leader of such an elite team, which will be a powerful position.' Raines knew how to press the PM's buttons regarding who would have control. Stringer was ready for him and had expected this.

'We're talking about somebody who developed abilities that had no parallels at the time. He can be forgiven for being confused by them and seeking answers elsewhere seven years ago. The truth is that we failed him, not the other way round. He was not offered sufficient support.'

'Who's to say he won't snap again when he's under a bit of pressure? If that happens when he's in charge of a unit of people like him, and he turns hostile, the results would be catastrophic.'

'I agree it would be, but the possibility of that happening is remote,' Stringer said, taking the wind out of the MI5 man's sails. 'I would go so far as to say it would be well-nigh impossible for Harford to change allegiance, given the precautions in place. He undergoes compulsory assessments of his mental state and there are regulations regarding his behaviour given the extraordinary nature of his abilities. We'd have early warning of anything amiss. Mr Harford has been in situations that have put him under pressure many times in the last four years since he's been working with Special Forces, and he has proved himself capable of handling stress. He is loyal, brave and has been at the forefront of danger many times for the sake of his colleagues. What better person to have in a position of protection for our country?'

Stringer saw the SAS colonel nodding agreement, but the Home Secretary had other thoughts.

'You're implying he's potentially so dangerous that we need to keep him on side. That doesn't inspire me with confidence.'

'If we were talking about anybody except Harford I might have my doubts, but he is not a natural killer. He's an idealist.'

'Idealists are dangerous,' Raines interrupted. 'You show me a disgruntled idealist and I'll show you a potential deadly enemy.'

'I think we should let Mr Stringer continue,' the Prime Minister interjected. He turned to Stringer, who revelled in the furious expression on Raines' face. Raines had to have the next word.

'He may not be a natural killer but you have admitted he's not a natural leader, either.'

'Yes, but that's not surprising since his unique abilities set him apart from other men. If he was in charge of a team with similar powers the result would be different. He scores highly for responsibility and his trait for team involvement means he would nurture other teleporters. He's the only person in the land who has years of experience in teleportation. He's an asset – not a liability.'

Attack and riposte continued until the PM, known for his liking of breakfast before ten o'clock, called a halt.

'I think it's obvious that Harford is the only person suitable to be leader of the proposed unit. Taking everything into account I see no reason to doubt either his sanity or his loyalty. How soon can we get this team up and running?'

Stringer's boss Palmer answered.

'With the right candidates, it could be a matter of weeks, although it depends on genetic screening for compatibility with the drug. With your agreement, we can draw up a list of people we think would be suitable.'

The MoD man interrupted.

'Harford is employed by the Ministry of Defence. The new team will be for defence purposes, therefore it makes sense if candidates are put forward by us.'

Raines put his foot down.

'Not necessarily. I suggest names are drawn from all the armed forces and intelligence services.'

'And the police,' interjected the Metropolitan Police Commissioner.

'Harford's employment alternates between the MoD and the SIS. When he does operations for us, which is often, he is on our payroll,' Palmer said.

The Prime Minister looked at his watch and then at C, who hadn't spoken.

'What's your opinion on this?'

'If it's speed you want, we have some people who have already been vetted. With your approval, we can set things in motion very quickly.'

Stringer thought the PM was going to go for it. The PM considered it, drumming his fingers on the table, but true to his nature he caved in under the pressure of his paranoia regarding the power wielded by the SIS.

'No, we need to cast our net wider. It will be kept within the armed forces, with input from the intelligence services. That works well enough for the SAS.' The PM swivelled his chair towards the door, indicating the end of the discussion. 'We have to work together on this. We face a grave threat, one which won't be taken lightly. Both Harford and the new team will be under the command of the MoD. I want screening of suitable candidates from the armed forces to take place immediately. I want each department to buy in the latest anti-teleporter systems and install them in every sensitive building in the UK, starting with Downing Street, Thames House, Vauxhall Cross, the MoD and the Houses of Parliament.'

There was no doubt, C said to Stringer and Palmer afterwards, when the PM was scared it got him off his arse. Though, he added, the MoD was misguided when it came to picking candidates, something which would have to be monitored. He hoped they caught his drift, he said, handing them a list of names.

~~~~~~~~

Unaware of the decisions being made about him thousands of kilometres away, if Lock had known he wouldn't have cared. He hung motionless in the centre of a vast living room like a set of limp clothes pegged out on a washing line, his secret invasion laid bare by bright diode lights overhead. A control panel flashed lights intermittently and an alarm siren shrilled in his ears. Flickering red laser lights glued to his chest over his pounding heart, and two more glinted near his forehead. On the other end of the laser targeting sights, laser weapon barrels stuck out from holes in the walls and made him think twice about attempting to teleport out, even if he could focus through the buzzing in his skull.

A door crashed open and a chunky figure, clad only in boxer shorts, crouched in combat pose by the doorway, pointing a pistol at him. Lock would have laughed at the sight if he could have moved more than just his eyes and wasn't mortally afraid of being shot. Behind the man's muscular, toned physique, an equally toned blonde woman in skimpy white T-shirt and knickers aimed another pistol towards the other side of the room. The
~~~~~~~~

straw-haired man glanced at a sensor panel, lowered his weapon and stood up.

'It's okay, he's a friendly. Switch the alarm off.'

The lithe woman tapped on the control panel keypad and the shrilling and buzzing stopped, leaving a hissing noise in Lock's ears. Lasers shut down and weapons slid back inside wall panels.

Mike Northwood, Lock's friend, sauntered over a stone-coloured carpet, stared up at Lock's face with piercing blue eyes and grinned. A mass of dishevelled hair fell in disorderly clumps to his neck, and the prematurely weathered skin on his face creased with laughter lines around his mouth and eyes. Northwood enjoyed the moment. Over the years there had been few opportunities for him to be in control of Lock, and he relished the chance that had been handed to him. Lock didn't like it. If he had been able to move, he would have given Northwood a good-natured kick, though his growing annoyance at being helpless might have put a bit more force behind it than would be good for either of them.

'Let him down?' the woman asked. Before she received a reply, somebody hammered on the front door of the apartment and she left to answer it.

'Should I let you down?' teased the twenty-eight year old leader of the Eagles team. 'What the hell kind of time is this to come calling? And in that state. You smell worse than a cesspit. You've been on a bender at the pub, haven't you? Don't look at me like that. You're the one who Shifted in here without so much as a by your leave. It's not my fault you got caught like a fly in a spider's web.'

Lock tried to say something rude but his mouth wouldn't form the words.

'Nah, I think we'll leave you there till breakfast, teach you a goddamn lesson for waking folks up in the middle of the night,' Northwood said.

Two men in tracksuits came in with weapons drawn, scanning the room. The blonde woman followed them, pulling on an oversized sweatshirt.

'Everything okay, Mr Northwood?' one man asked, staring at Lock and his dirty clothes in wrinkled nose disgust. Northwood waved a hand without turning round.

'Everything's fine, boys, but you'll have to be a damn sight faster than that.'

Lock was annoyed being suspended in mid-air, even if it was playful. He focused for teleportation but Northwood stopped him.

'Whoa, don't do that, you'll trip the alarms again. Kes, let him down. It's okay, boys, you can go.'

The men holstered their weapons, gave Lock a hard stare of disapproval and turned for the door. Kes tapped on the control panel and Lock tumbled in a heap on the soft, deep-pile carpet, his fall slowed by

Northwood's strong grip on his left arm. Kes called out,

'You can clean the carpet.' Northwood waved a hand in dismissal and said to Lock,

'You'll recover very soon. I'll be right back.' He walked out of Lock's sight, leaving him helpless on the floor. Tiny sparks pricked across Lock's skin like the needle-tipped feet of myriads of insects. The sensation wasn't painful, just unpleasant. His limbs felt as though they had been hit by multiple injections of local anaesthetic. The numbness began to wear off and he moved his arms and legs weakly to test them.

Northwood returned dressed in pants and a navy blue sweatshirt, without his pistol.

'Geez, man, what've you been doing to yourself?' he laughed, examining Lock's left cheek. He braced his feet and helped him up. Lock struggled to form the word 'Bastard,' followed by a weak grimace intended to be a smile.

'Tried to phone.'

'I was busy.' Northwood amended his statement. 'We were busy. I turned the phones off. We have to have privacy some time.'

Lock glanced at Kes, taking in her long legs. The man's sweatshirt swamped her skinny frame. He guessed her age as early twenties and assumed she was Northwood's latest conquest. Northwood always did like girls younger than himself, since it meant he didn't have to mature, or take on any commitment.

'Hey, Kes, how about fixing coffee?'

Kes gave Northwood a killer glance.

'It's four in the morning. I'm going back to bed.' She turned and swept out of the room, flicking her hair over her shoulders. Northwood looked at Lock and rolled his eyes at the ceiling.

'No stamina, these women.'

'I heard that, Mike Northwood.'

Northwood laughed and put his hand on Lock's shoulder. 'Kitchen.' He steered him down the hallway after Kes and raised his voice. 'We'll do it ourselves, don't you worry about it. You get your beauty sleep – you need it.'

Northwood and Lock passed a doorway and a pillow hurtled out of it. Northwood sidestepped and laughed.

'I need your help,' Lock said with greater clarity as the last effects of numbness wore off.

Northwood gave him a serious look and gripped his shoulder twice. Lock understood and nodded once in return. Northwood didn't present the world with anything less than full-blown cheerfulness, usually fuelled by drink. He was a genuinely sunny man and well-liked for it, but over the last year Lock had the impression Northwood's relaxed attitude hid an altered view of life that was not laboured, but weary.

The ultra-modern kitchen was as large as the living room. A maroon-topped oval breakfast bar filled the centre, contrasting with creamy wood veneer cupboards on the walls. Northwood's bare feet slapped on cream-flecked pale tiles sticky with drink splashes as he led the way past a cooking range that looked rarely used. Empty takeaway cartons were strewn over dirty surfaces. Pulling out a bar stool for Lock, he brushed crumbs from the red plastic cover.

'We had a party. Bit of a mess.'

Lock nodded and sat down. Northwood opened a tall refrigerator, rummaged around and brought out a carton of milk. 'Nice of you to volunteer for testing out our new equipment.' He grinned, found a couple of clean mugs in a cupboard and pushed dirty dishes aside to make room for them on the counter. 'How do you like it?' he asked as he picked up a wooden-handled teaspoon and an electric kettle.

'Impressive.'

Northwood laughed. 'No, I mean your coffee.' He took a jar out of another cupboard.

'Yeah, right, I knew that.' Lock grinned. 'White with one sugar.'

Northwood opened the jar, pressed something on the handle of the teaspoon and stuck it in the instant coffee granules. Lock stared as a holographic image of a keypad appeared on the side of the coffee jar.

Northwood touched a couple of numbers on the virtual keypad. Holographic figures of three and zero appeared above it, changing to twenty-nine. Northwood turned to Lock, suddenly serious.

'We can't talk here, it's not private. We have twenty-eight seconds before quiet time ends.' He pointed at the numbers counting down. 'Can your urgent matter wait for half an hour?'

'Yes, it's not desperate.'

'Good. Make as though you're going to stay in the guest room. Have a shower or whatever, get into bed fully clothed. I'll call you in half an hour.'

'Won't your minders notice we've gone?'

Northwood smiled. 'I have it fixed.'

The numbers reached zero. The holograms disappeared, and he removed the teaspoon with a spoonful of coffee. Thirty minutes later Lock did as instructed. Northwood appeared in the bedroom, put his finger to his lips, gestured for Lock to get up and teleported them both out of the apartment.

Lock enjoyed and envied the chaotic colours of Northwood's teleportation. It felt like being in somebody else's head during mind-blowing hallucinations, an electrifying dreamscape of extreme sensory stimulation. Nobody had been able to explain why Lock's teleportation was full of greys and mists, while Northwood's burst with colour. Lock stretched out his left hand and his fingertips stroked an undulating stream of scarlet, creating a shower of maroon sparks.

Nothing in Northwood's world followed rules of expectation. Instead of being velvety to the touch, scarlet felt gritty and smelled of bananas. The colour changed to rose pink, silky but with a perfume of pine forests. In quick succession pink changed to plum purple which brought with it a feathery ruffle and a pleasant odour of salt spray, followed by the oily touch of apple green with a tang of sawdust. Lock pulled his hand away from apricot orange, which looked like sunrise but stank of bad eggs. A burst of grass green sparks heralded the end of teleportation.

Lock was disappointed as they descended through darkness into a secluded spot by the edge of a forest, overlooking the calm waters of a river estuary. One day he'd have to get Northwood to take him on a longer journey than a couple of hundred kilometres. It had been a long time since they last went anywhere together.

'Remember this place?' Northwood asked.

'Yeah. It's years since we were here.'

Lock struggled to recall the name. It was something quaint. Tippity Wichity Island – that was it – a low-lying, small island at the tip of a long estuary in Virginia, surrounded by fertile farmland beyond the water.

'I'll never forget the look on their faces when you Shifted out of Washington. There were all those military and intel people waiting to see you – and suddenly you'd gone.'

Lock zipped up his borrowed jacket and smiled.

'It caused a stink, didn't it? Four helicopters full of Special Forces turned up here to collect me after I phoned you. Scared the shit out of me.' He shivered and pulled the collar up round his neck.

Northwood gave him a wry look.

'If you'd been older than fourteen, I think their response would have been a bit different than giving you a ride back. It scared the hell out of them too, having a foreign teleporter loose doing who knows what.'

Lock watched moonlit ripples and the dark shapes of trees on the other side of the river channel.

'I was sick of being prodded and treated like a freak. You coped with it better.' Though he admired many things about Northwood it wasn't the luxury lifestyle, or the abundance of advanced technology. What he would have liked most was Northwood's capacity to shrug off life's complications as nothing more than tiresome hiccups.

'I was seventeen. It gives you a different perspective on life, being that much older. Makes it easier.' Northwood paused. 'You know, I envy you.'

'Why? You have everything you want. Good home, nice car, girls. Everything, you get whatever you want. The Eagles, the aircraft – the lot.'

'But less freedom.' Northwood gave a brittle chuckle. 'It gets harder to take a piss without somebody holding a container.'

Teleporting from South America to the US, plus the teleporter trap, had taken it out of Lock, and he didn't reply. Northwood scraped up a handful of small stones and hurled one at the river.

'This last year things have gotten worse and it's not just because of being hogtied by lawyers saying we can't do this or that, or go there, shit like that. Just since November, there've been three lots of bugging and being followed. Three times in just over a month.' He threw another stone, savagely.

'Was it the Decons?'

'Maybe. Bunch of assholes. One time in early November might have been down to them, with their fingers in so many places. It's impossible to be sure who's doing it. We have around eighteen intel agencies here and you can bet your ass Decons have infiltrated most of them. It isn't hostiles from other countries we have to guard against; it's our own damn people. So far, we've had the protection of the Pentagon and the ones who find us useful. One day that won't be enough. We never know who we can trust, even on a basic level of wondering if they're thinking about killing us because of what we are. I'm pretty sure it isn't this bad where you are. Sometimes I think I should up sticks and move to little old England.'

The pine trees creaked in a cold breeze. Withered plants near the water's edge stirred with a papery rustle.

'England couldn't handle you, and anyway I doubt you'd find it so different.' Lock recalled the surveillance bugs in his house.

'Yeah? You got trouble too?'

Lock backed off. It was easy to forget that Northwood reported back to others who might find their conversations useful.

'It's not much, not really a problem,' he lied, and lapsed into silence. Northwood didn't press him. He changed the subject.

'Anyway, why the visit? What gives? It must be something special for you to wake us up in the middle of the night.'

'I need a good disguise. None of the latex stuff, it's got to pass close inspection.'

'Why're you asking me? There are hundreds of places that do good disguises.'

'They can't do it on a cellular level, or provide anything that will last a long time.' Lock realised he'd overstepped the mark by disclosing how much he knew about an Eagles team member. When Northwood spoke the steel doors slammed shut.

'Can't do it, Lock. Sorry.'

Lock backtracked but he'd already blown his chances.

'I wouldn't come all this way to ask if it wasn't vitally important–'

'I know. I'd like to help. If it was up to me I'd help, no problem. But my hands are tied.'

'There's a lot riding on it, a lot of innocent lives – including women and kids.'

'Don't. You can't persuade me by laying on a guilt trip.'

Lock stuck his hands in his pockets, disappointed. His overrule of Bilton about timing the assault on Mosquera's villa during a children's party day had been overruled by London, to his fury and Bilton's glee. Lock had to obey orders and he knew Mosquera's Starbirth production had to be stopped. He reasoned that the assault would go ahead with or without him, and his presence would save innocent lives, but he needed an impenetrable disguise for his role during the assault and ordinary disguises wouldn't do.

'Nobody has to know.'

'The answer's still the same.'

Lock knew better than to push it. He checked for other people in his radius. In the midst of whispering trees nobody else enjoyed the pleasure of being out in a forest at night. After a couple of minutes they spoke at the same time, and laughed. Northwood said,

'You'll have to start using a door when you come calling. I know it's easier our way, but you'll always get caught.'

'I didn't Shift in because it was easier. The 'Signal Friend or Foe' blocked me out. When I got closer to the apartment I couldn't sense you, the place was blurry. The phone gave a disconnected signal, and your Secure Link was disabled.'

'It's all being updated.'

'I didn't know. I thought–'

'You thought I was in trouble and came bursting in to the rescue,' Northwood chuckled.

'Well, when I saw those goons in the van further up the street and spotted the drone over the apartment block, I thought something was going on.'

'Whoa, back up. What van? And what drone?'

'A big black van. Not yours?'

'No. What did you see?'

'A van fifty metres up the road. Three auras. From their positions, and the way they didn't move around, it looked like surveillance vans, the type your Secret Service guys use. Big. And it was a small drone. I could hardly see it. I thought it was a bat but it wasn't flying right. That's what made me look closer.'

'It was flying over the apartments?'

'Yeah. It was circling.'

'Let's get back.' Northwood sounded worried. Lock waited for him to teleport, but Northwood said,

'Hang on. This isn't an early New Year's prank, is it?'

'No, I wouldn't play tricks with something like this.'

'That's what you said before, you lying bastard.'

'Not this time, Mike. It's real.'

'Okay. But I'd better not find any damn cardboard cut-outs of armed goons when we get back.'

Two minutes later they hung in the air thirty metres above Northwood's penthouse. Lock saw no sign of the van and no drone. He gave himself a headache trying to do a rapid sensory reconnaissance of the six-storey apartment block, past the roof, ceiling and the strange buzzing in his skull. It was like trying to punch holes through metres of rolled-up paper. As he probed deeper the buzzing increased until it lay like a weight in his head. He told Northwood about it and detected wariness. Northwood said to ignore it and hurry up. Lock assumed it was some kind of electronic security device aimed at keeping Shifters at bay. Intrigued and disturbed by the sensation, he wanted to know more but reined in the impulse to ask.

'There's only one person in your apartment, alive and not moving.'

'You're sure that's not a holograph?'

'I can't sense holos, remember?'

Reflected light from the city's street-lamps delineated Northwood's broad cheekbones as he gazed at the roof.

'Yeah, but the new ones imitate breathing and heart rate.'

Lock frowned. Resentment at the US being far more advanced than the UK bubbled close to the surface, a partner to envy, though he was unaware that one gave life to the other.

'I'm telling you, there's only one real person in there.'

'Nobody else?'

'Not in that apartment.'

'What about the guys below?'

Lock checked.

'They're still in the same place, they haven't moved.'

'And Kes, you're sure she's alive?'

'What the hell is this, Mike? You've known me all these years and suddenly you don't trust me? If you want me to test out some shit-hot equipment you've got in there, just ask. What're you trying to do, guard against me?'

Northwood put a hand on Lock's shoulder.

'It's not you. You're taking this too personal. It wasn't meant that way.'

'You know I can't sense dead bodies. You don't need me to tell you she's okay because you already know, right?'

'Yeah, you're right. I should've said. Wait, don't go off angry. It wasn't about you, believe me. There's all these folks developing powers and we're trying out new stuff against telepaths – not you.'

'I'm not a telepath.'

'Yeah, I know. It just seemed like a good opportunity. You're right, it was dumb. C'mon, let's go inside and have a drink while I give some folks grief over the van. I need you to tell me in detail what you saw.'

'That wasn't connected to you?'

Northwood shook his head. He took out a small device and tapped the keys.

Lock watched the apartment block. A lone SUV sped past, with speakers blaring bass notes that thudded up the road. They watched it until it turned the corner towards the highway.

'Doesn't a breach of security bother you? You don't seem too worried,' Lock said.

'I'm getting kinda weary of moving house. Sometimes it feels like you've just got to take a stand, you know?' Northwood looked at numbers on the phone screen. 'We're linked to the holos. When you go in, your hologram stays on until you replace it in bed. Do that first. If they hear us talking in another room while the holos are in the bedrooms, it'll attract attention.'

'Won't your guys in the apartment below know we're coming in?'

Northwood smiled, putting the piece of kit back in his pocket.

'The holos emit a signal that creates a concealed tunnel for us, electronically speaking. As long as we're linked to them, we can get in and out without anybody knowing.'

'Apart from the agency that supplied the kit.'

Northwood grinned.

'Yeah, well, let's just say there's some guys owe me a favour or two. Big ones. See, I'm trusting you with this stuff about the holos, man. Don't pass it on to your research guys for the next ten days. By then it will be out of the bag anyway.'

'I don't do that.'

'Yeah, you do. So do I. Ten days' grace, right?'

'Sure. Tell you what, if you get another piece of kit like that, throw it my way.'

Northwood laughed. Lock didn't seriously expect to get any kit like that at all.

CHAPTER 10

Three days after Lock's secret visit to Northwood, Jimmy crept forward with Vicar to relieve Mick and Nails at the Observation Post set up in the jungle overlooking Mosquera's new villa. He lifted his leg over a rotting branch and put his foot onto spongy ground on the other side, heel first, then the ball of his foot, pushing away any twigs or small branches that might snap. Around his feet, gnarled roots rose off the ground like fossilised arches of lumpy intestines sticking out of a stinking, mosquito-infested swamp. Condensation dripped. Glittery, green drops of water hung from leaf ends. The weight pulled the leaves down and they rebounded when the drops fell.

Everything around him stayed perpetually damp, including his clothes. Humidity made movement a challenge. Trouser fabric was sticky and stiff with mud, blood and salty sweat, and it chafed his legs. Leeches had a feast on various parts of his body and he was aware of all thirteen of them in a way that he had never been before, including the one attached to the inside of his mouth, but it was his elevated consciousness that gave him the creeps, not the parasites.

During his time in the OP, the sensitivity that started in his fingers spread to the rest of his body. Hearing, smell, sight and particularly touch – the senses that increased to allow him to attune to his environment – went far beyond being heightened. They reached realms so invasive he felt them as an experience he couldn't describe. Not pain but not a lack of pain either, and definitely not pleasure. Mentally it freaked him out. If he let his control slip, the jungle was a sentient being, slowly engulfing him, eating him under his clothes and choking the breath from his chest. He wanted to flee. He'd never felt that before. The jungle had always been comfortable in an uncomfortable way.

The buzz and chitter of millions of beetles, wasps and other things that flew or rustled created a heaving orchestra and chorus of insect voices. Far away the screeching of monkeys rose to a group crescendo as they argued and crashed through the canopy, breaking branches that fell noisily to the ground.

Something rustled, sending his adrenaline soaring. It could be one of Mosquera's random patrols coming down the animal track. Jimmy stopped and slowly raised his weapon, knowing behind him Vicar would freeze and cover the arc of fire on their left. Jimmy's gaze swept right, centre, left, and back again, and where he looked, the barrel of his weapon followed. Parakeets screeched overhead and his heart missed a beat. He opened his mouth under his camouflage face veil, a trick that allowed him to hear past the blood pulsating through his ears.

A familiar odour hit his nostrils, the stink of wild boar. The boar passed by and he relaxed into watchfulness. It hadn't noticed them. After four days in the OP the two scruffy, stubble-faced men had no human scent left, and they didn't look obviously human. Stems and leaves stuck out all over their chest webbing and bergens, giving them the appearance of walking shrubs. Face veils, soaked in gun oil and then rubbed in earth, hid any shape or shine of the features underneath. The gloom helped, too. Only six per cent of sunlight penetrated the forest to hit the ground in dim shafts of light.

Their twilight journey continued along a line of para-cord, skirting a hornets' nest. Moving from their resting camp, the Lying Up Place they had just left, to the Observation Post twenty metres away was the most dangerous part of surveillance. They took great care to step over the animal track without breaking any foliage or leaving sign of their passing. Jimmy bypassed a huge two-metre wide web, eyeing the eight-centimetre long body of the wolf spider dangling in the centre, recalling how he had walked into a similar web at night. The sticky strands had closed over his face, wrapping around his nose and ears. He'd panicked when the spider bit him, before he found out the painful bite wasn't fatal. Pete had laughed, of course.

Jimmy's heart jolted when a fuzzy movement caught his eye. He stopped dead, his right foot frozen off the ground in mid-stride, and watched in horror as a figure in profile emerged from thin air into a patch of lighter shade. A small woman aged about twenty-five stood less than three metres away, Creole from the look of her small nose and rounded face. His appraisal took in her inappropriate town dress and the way she stared at her empty hands, open-mouthed. He dared not breathe and willed her not to turn and see him. She looked as shocked as he was. Raising her hands to her head, she groaned and doubled over. The sound of her voice reverberated through the ferns, extraordinarily loud to Jimmy's acutely tuned hearing.

He put his right foot back where he had been and slid into deeper shade while she was preoccupied. He let out a quiet and steady stream of exhaled air, waiting, taking in slow, shallow breaths, and wondering if any more teleporters would follow. The woman straightened and looked around wildly as if she hadn't expected to find herself in the jungle. He prayed she wouldn't spot his eyes under the face veil and wouldn't feel the danger so close to her. His right hand balanced the Diemaco, while his left went to the knife in its inverted sheath on his chest. He'd never killed a woman before, but if she saw them the mission could go down the pan as the OP team would be compromised. They'd have to bug out fast before Mosquera's Lanceros and dog patrols found them.

The woman stumbled into a shaft of light and he realised that in her bewilderment and panic her only focus regarding her surroundings was to be terrified of them. He could put his hand over her mouth, pin her down, threaten her with the knife if she made a sound. It was better than killing her, but then what? They couldn't release her, and they couldn't take her with them.

She looked at her feet and gasped, whacking hysterically at the insects crawling up her legs. She danced around in her panic to get them off, her feet breaking dead branches with resounding cracks. Her voice grew louder with hysteria as she staggered in the undergrowth closer to Jimmy. He smelled her fear and his heart sank. Any second now she would fall into him and he would have to act. The knife slid out of its sheath, but before the woman took the fatal steps, she faded and disappeared.

Jimmy didn't move. He saw her reappear four metres further away in waist-high foliage, facing him. This time she raised her right arm as if she couldn't understand what was wrong, but Jimmy saw it. Her arm swung uselessly at the elbow, the forearm long and misshapen. Her eyes bulged as she stared at it in horror. A chill tingled down the back of Jimmy's neck. Her mouth opened and she gasped again, chest heaving, working up to a scream before she vanished. Jimmy and Vicar were frozen in the gloom. She didn't return. At a signal from Jimmy, they turned and crept on to the OP.

Nails and Mick heard the noise and wanted to know what happened. Nails compared notes with Jimmy using a digital waterproof pad, confirming that the woman's appearance in the jungle occurred less than a minute after another teleporter experiment involving a woman in Mosquera's hut. As patrol commander, Nails made the decision for all of them to stay in place, reasoning that since a teleporter could pop up anywhere, and the woman hadn't spotted them, there wasn't much point in moving. Besides, Harford would pick them up and take them back to Patuazon's training camp later on after a final test of Mosquera's electronic anti-teleporter defences. London identified the four flagpoles as relay transmitters and also described the anti-teleporter system as an invisible umbrella that was known to be temperamental. The OP team were about to test how temperamental.

Nails radioed an extra report about the teleporter to Bilton using a camouflaged radio smaller than a GPS. It sent reports as compacted packets of data by means of a burst of scrambled satellite transmission on the L-bandwidth, well above the frequency range used by most radios. The frequency was outside the scanning range of Mosquera's radio detection equipment. Mick and Nails handed over surveillance duty and took their turn to rest at the LUP, backing away from foliage covering the front and taking care to avoid moving leaves. Any sudden movement could be spotted by an alert perimeter guard, and Mosquera's men were vigilant.

Jimmy and Vicar took the camouflaged camera binoculars, the listening equipment and controls for two drones overhead as well as various sensors Harford had placed around the perimeter of the umbrella. They waited for Harford to appear just before last light. Jimmy couldn't concentrate. The image of the woman's arm tortured his mind, though relief that he hadn't been forced to kill her stayed uppermost in his thoughts.

Beetles warmed up for their whistling serenade at nightfall and crickets joined their tune-up. Water trickled down the central channel of a half-metre-wide dark green leaf and dripped off the end to add to the puddle forming by Jimmy's left elbow. He raised his arm to let the water run off the poncho underneath him. The gentle chugging of an electricity generator started at the back of the villa, preceding nightfall by half an hour. Jimmy panned right from the gang of men putting up tents for the party and saw perimeter security lights switch on two hundred metres away. Nobody had replaced a broken spotlight and he made a note of it in the logbook.

Steam rose from the river. The last of the cocaine shipments from Mosquera's laboratory began its journey downriver to an illegal landing strip and a small plane which would smuggle the drug to the coastal city of Buenaventura for a longer sea journey to the US. Drone surveillance revealed that some packages were marked and stored separately from the rest and Jimmy assumed they contained Starbirth. Three convoys of boats left during the day, escorted by men armed to the teeth. The first boat returned from the landing strip with weapons that went into the armoury near the guards' billets. Mosquera bought Rocket Propelled Grenades and shoulder-fired missiles, as well as some weird armaments the OP group didn't recognise. That caused a buzz of excitement, relieving the boredom associated with OPs.

Watching drug dealers in Colombia took the SAS into familiar territory. Over many years they penetrated the region, working to stop South American drug trade links to Irish terrorists. The terrorists bought cocaine, shipped it to Ireland and sold it on the UK mainland, thus financing their purchase of weapons for their fight against their fellow Irishmen and the British Army. The SAS had the task of conducting covert surveillance of the supply route and interrupting the passage of drugs whenever the opportunity arose. They played a small but vital role in the war against drugs, albeit an unconventional one made difficult by the drug dealers' habit of moving mobile cocaine processing laboratories from one area to another to avoid detection.

In an attempt to slow the flood of cocaine making its way north, American dollars and equipment such as crop-spraying aircraft boosted the Colombian government's coca eradication programme. Powerful defoliants killed off not just illegal cocaine-producing plants, but anything else growing alongside them. Sometimes ordinary crops were blitzed by mistake. Innocent farmers growing maize and cereal grains suffered alongside the guilty.

The spray allegedly caused illness and disease among farmers and their families and stripped them of their means of income. Harbouring a great deal of anti-government and anti-American sentiment, angry men and women were driven into joining bandit gangs. The prospect of a grassroots upheaval, and possibly millions of Colombians hostile to the US, sent a chill down the Pentagon's spine, so both the US and Colombian governments trod a delicate path between controlling drug production on one hand, and avoiding huge numbers of disaffected people on the other.

Despite their advanced technology, the Americans couldn't discover the source of the essential ingredient of Starbirth, AH-4, and they suspected the supplier used teleporters to deliver the goods. Nobody had produced a system or piece of kit that enabled people to track teleporters who didn't want to be tracked. To add another trouble to the pot of woes, Colombia's neighbours objected to increased US presence in any South American country, putting considerable pressure on the US to act quickly. As far as Jimmy was concerned, the politics of the situation didn't matter. He was out there to kick ass, and Mosquera presented the SAS with a legitimate target. Like Lock, Jimmy knew the assault had to happen soon.

He checked the clock on the handheld computer through its waterproof wrapping and let Vicar know by hand-signal that they had three minutes until the test time. Vicar acknowledged. Jimmy trained his binoculars on a section of the perimeter fence earmarked for the test while Vicar covered the area opposite. Harford wanted to use the natural roosting time of birds at nightfall as cover for the test, having watched the habits of a flock of parakeets over several days. Hopefully, Mosquera's men wouldn't attach any importance to a difference in the pattern of the birds' behaviour.

Fifteen seconds after the countdown time, Jimmy heard the sound of a flock of noisy parakeets near the perimeter fence. He couldn't see the birds and assumed they were the ones Harford had caught and kept in quick-release cages ready for the test. It was hoped they would fly over the villa to their normal roosting site, but the frightened birds scattered. Some flapped into the jungle above Jimmy's head. One fled into the fence and was electrocuted, causing changes to the numbers and graph lines on the OP group's instruments.

The remaining birds played ball and flew over the top of the fence into the twelve-metre high sensor field as intended. Graph lines and numbers danced crazily and two birds in Jimmy's field of view plummeted to the ground. The survivors wheeled away from the estate, reuniting to form a single flock. Instruments recorded data until the birds disappeared into the canopy. Jimmy looked at the numbers and wrote them in the logbook. They sent a message back to Harford and Bilton that the anti-teleporter net was fully functional, fast, did not distinguish well between humans and birds and included lethal lasers.

Darkness does not descend gradually in the jungle. One minute shafts of light relieved the gloom, and the next it seemed the team had gone blind. Jimmy and Vicar watched the daily lockdown at the villa. Armed men moved Mosquera's helicopters out of sight under a canopy of trees surrounding the small clearing. Kitchen staff prepared the evening meal and the swimming pool was covered over for the night. Guards walked around inspecting and locking outhouses and huts, and professional armed men – Jimmy identified them as Lanceros – took up positions by the armoury.

Day staff clustered noisily by worn-out coaches until a guard shouted at them. Cowed, they boarded quickly and the coaches groaned and creaked towards the newly-built road leading out of the estate. Jimmy debated whether any of the lower-ranking staff knew who they worked for. No photographs of Mosquera existed apart from a very grainy picture of him as a teenager and the titles to the land were held by a business which had no discernible ties to Mosquera or his family.

He glanced at the clock on the sensor control. Harford wouldn't return to extract them to the training camp for several hours and apart from guards and dog patrols wandering over the estate there wasn't much to see at night. It was a question of waiting for somebody to make a phone call and listening in using an automatic translation machine that occasionally made mistakes, giving them some laughs to break the monotony.

Jimmy lowered his binoculars and the hairs on the back of his neck rose. He turned his head and looked over his shoulder, but couldn't see anything. Vicar gestured at him questioningly. Jimmy shrugged and went back to his surveillance of the villa. Ever since the incident with the woman, he had an uneasy feeling they were watched, but he put it down to being spooked.

An hour later the instruments intercepted a cryptic call that promised to be interesting. The automatic language translator relayed it piecemeal to their headphones.

'Got him. We're ……. him in now.'

'Take him to the back.' The reply came from Mosquera. Further calls gave instructions to the guards at the checkpoint. Jimmy and Vicar switched drone coverage to view the estate's main entrance and the back of the villa. Twenty minutes later they saw car headlights approaching the entrance. Jimmy logged the time as nineteen-thirty. Two SUVs were waved through the checkpoint. The cars sped to the back of the villa.

The drone images from the rear were not good quality, but Vicar recognised the overweight man bundled out of the first SUV as Mosquera's brother, the informant known as Nightingale. For the first time Jimmy saw the go-between who had set up the disastrous deal at Bogota, the one that killed Snapper. He felt a surge of hatred towards the man who had sold them out to Patuazon. Nightingale headed for a sticky end as Mosquera's men pushed him into a bare, half-finished room. Jimmy didn't make any comment to Vicar about the botched Bogota deal. Only Bilton knew what went down a week previously, and Jimmy wanted to keep it that way.

Vicar tapped a computer control keypad and angled the camouflaged parabolic umbrella of a directional microphone towards the room. It was too far away to hear clearly above the noise of insects, but they caught snatches of Nightingale's crying and pleading with his brother to let him go. They didn't hear Mosquera's responses and it was quiet for fifteen minutes. Nightingale wailed louder and pleaded again, not for his life this time, but for a quick death. Mosquera left the room flanked by his bodyguards. He hadn't reached the back door of his quarters when the unmistakeable sounds of a beating reached Jimmy and Vicar. Jimmy took the headphones off after twenty minutes and left the task of listening to Vicar and the recording kit. He sent an update back to base to inform Bilton about Nightingale's capture and torture.

~~~~~~~~

At the training hut Lock made a last-ditch attempt to persuade Bilton to delay the assault by a couple of hours because a high number of children could be on site. It was certain that at some time, civilians would get caught in the crossfire. Bilton retorted that was Lock's area of responsibility. Lock said he needed to get all the women and children together in a tight group and he couldn't round them up like sheep. If he tried to teleport them out singly, or in small groups, half of them would be dead before he had time to get them clear.

Bilton shrugged it off, repeating that civilian safety was Lock's problem and when he had a solution, he'd be interested to hear it. In the meantime, could they please get back to planning the final details? Lock looked away from the pallid face he detested and stopped arguing, well aware that Bilton had the last word as field commander and they were overheard by PC and Ginge. Ginge would tell the other lads about the quarrel, even if he left out details of what they quarrelled about. The men were unsettled if the bosses bickered.

Bilton angled a virtual map on the wall and called Ginge and PC to join them.

'Okay, moving on, a review of what we've decided,' Bilton said. 'Given
~~~~~~~~

the restrictions of Patuazon's helis, our force is split into six separate teams, five in choppers, and one team on the ground. Kilo One, the Black Hawk on loan from a private military company, is Command and Control. PC, you're Archangel.'

Lock raised an eyebrow. They were lucky to have use of the Black Hawk gunship, a fearsome combat helicopter, but he thought Bilton would be in it, taking command. Airborne controllers were often nicknamed Archangel due to their aerial oversight role of the operation. Bilton giving up control to PC came as a surprise, but Bilton's next sentence explained why.

'You've got experience with Black Hawks. We're limited to four missiles and I want to make sure those missiles reach their targets. Make every one count.'

PC glowed with pride at being given such a prestigious task. Bilton pointed at a spot on the map two kilometres from Mosquera's estate.

'Kilo Two, the small Huey, will carry the attack force to hit Mosquera's cocaine lab. Mick will be in charge of that, with six men plus the door gunner.' He went back to the map of Mosquera's villa.

'That leaves the remaining three choppers. Kilo Three and Kilo Four will be our heavies for the main assault on the villa, carrying four fire teams, twenty-eight men total. I'll be in Kilo Three with Jimmy. We'll lead a fire team apiece. Vicar will be in Kilo Four with his fire team and we'll have one of the Colombians heading the last fire team. It looks good if we use one of Patuazon's men in an important position. Any suggestions about who would be best?'

PC spoke up first.

'Ramon. He's a clever tactical leader and he's led fire teams in practice.'

'Yeah, he's good,' Ginge agreed.

'He has a steady hand and he's capable,' Lock said.

'Okay, Ramon. That leaves Kilo Five.'

Bilton paused.

'There's no way I'm trusting that youngster, Patuazon's second cousin of a second cousin or whatever he is, to pilot an attack chopper on this operation. He's reckless.'

PC nodded and murmured agreement. Bilton said,

'He'll be in charge of Kilo Five, the old Huey, for casevac only. That leaves us a pilot short, but I have a replacement in mind, an ex-Blade who flew choppers out East. He lives in Cali.' He looked at Lock. 'When you go out tonight to retrieve the OP team, I'll go with you. I'll give him a call outside the perimeter and see if he's interested. If he is, we'll meet up.'

Bilton pointed at a spot south of Mosquera's estate.

'Ginge, you set up the mortar team, Kilo Six, here. Nails will be your Forward Air Controller. Obviously you can't be Shifted in because of the Colombians in your team. You'll be taken by chopper at first light tomorrow to this point here,' he indicated a spot two kilometres south of Mosquera's estate. 'You'll tab the rest of the way.'

Ginge nodded, unfazed by a Tactical Advance to Battle on foot. Bilton looked at Lock and continued,

'You'll be in charge of getting civilians out of any crossfire. Take them to the field hospital and clearing station in this village northwest of Mocoa. Medics will be waiting. They'll sort them out so you can go straight back to the villa to help with casualty evacuation. If your disguise is good, Patuazon's men won't recognise you.' He looked round the group. 'Everything clear so far?'

PC, who was frowning at the map, spoke.

'We're a bit short on heavy firepower, Boss. Mosquera's got RPGs and shoulder-fired missiles, plus the new weapons they've been talking about, the ones we haven't got sight of yet. From the sound of it, they've got a couple of plasma burners and something else. Plasma burners are bad news.'

Lock glanced at Bilton, knowing he and Jimmy had experienced plasma burners first-hand after their tangle with Bloater in Bogota, but he didn't comment. PC continued,

'All due respect to Ginge's mortar team, there's going to be too many targets, too much delay in taking out the watchtowers on the fence line as well as the guards' billet, the armoury and the bell towers on the villa. We need demolitions to take some of them out and we need to get something in place before the attack so we can blow up the armoury and the new weapons.'

'There's no way to neutralise the sensor field to get a team in,' Bilton said.

'Yeah, there is,' Lock interrupted. 'Whenever Mosquera's men have a teleporter experiment, they switch the field off, for up to twenty-five minutes sometimes. I can get a team in and out then.'

They waited for Bilton to respond.

'There's no guarantee they'll be doing an experiment on the night.'

'Then I can short out the circuit and make it look like a malfunction. They've had a few of them.'

'Okay. Get the charges made up. Go out after nightfall in two days' time. Anything else?'

'What about the Colombians on our side, what they'll see? It's going to look odd if things blow up the second we get there and they haven't set it up themselves. It's going to make them think we've got a Shifter,' Ginge said.

'They don't need to know about the demolitions,' Bilton replied. 'When the shit hits the fan there'll be so much happening, I doubt anybody will know who's taken out what, except us – but to be sure, I don't want a word of the demolitions operation to reach the Colombians. Understood?'

Everybody agreed.

Later that night, Lock and Bilton armed themselves with Browning pistols and left the camp to contact the ex-Blade pilot Bilton wanted to employ. Lock thought it a pity levi-flying was the quickest and quietest method of reaching the perimeter fence. Given the chance he would have led Bilton on foot, accidentally brushing into huge wolf spider webs on the way. When they reached the tunnel, which he negotiated without any discernible Shifting, he was forced into grudging admiration of Bilton's lack of complaint about being covered in slime.

Lock teleported them out, muck and all. They reached the lower level of a mountainside, overlooking the lights of Cali's highways and the city centre that drew roads to it as if siphoning lines of liquid honey. Bilton stood in the darkness. He didn't move and didn't answer when Lock asked if he was okay.

'Bilton?' Lock reached out a hand to Bilton's shoulder. Bilton shivered. 'Sit down,' Lock ordered. Bilton didn't react. 'Sit down,' Lock repeated, pushing on his shoulder.

Bilton's legs collapsed like a house of cards and he fell into a sitting position, swaying. Lock grabbed hold of his arm and overbalanced onto one knee. He squatted next to Bilton, pushed into the role of unwilling rescuer.

'What's up?'

Bilton mumbled something, his eyes glassy in the light from Lock's torch.

'Are you okay?' Lock realised the absurdity of the question when it was clear that Bilton wasn't. His teeth chattered. His condition baffled Lock. Bilton had teleported before, without any problem.

'It's all alive,' Bilton muttered, not to Lock but to the sky. Lock checked his pulse while the city roared and blinked its multi-coloured Christmas lights in the sweltering night. Bilton coughed and sat still, head down. He didn't respond to Lock's questions. After a minute he lifted his head and looked around, bewildered.

'I'm okay. Just a bit dizzy, that's all.'

'You said something about it being alive.'

'I didn't say anything.' Bilton insisted he felt fine. All he'd felt was tingly, hot, and everything had been misty. Nothing else. 'Must've just been a quirk.' He took out his phone from its waterproof container. 'Let's get on with it.'

Lock considered getting Bilton back without teleporting. Bilton spoke to somebody called Chris. Lock watched him and reflected that such a reaction had never happened to any of his passengers. He had seen panic attacks at the end of a journey, but nothing as marked as somebody being unresponsive and suffering temporary amnesia. Bilton ended his call.

'We meet at the Cassin nightclub on the east side.' He looked at a map of Cali on his phone screen and plucked at a smelly, wet sleeve. 'We can't go in like this, we'll need a change of clothes and a wash.'

'No problem, but I'm not happy about you teleporting.'

'I doubt I'll get dizzy again.'

'It wasn't dizziness. You were fully awake, but you were out of it. It was more like shock.'

'You're mistaken. It was dizziness, nothing else.'

'No, there was definitely…..'

'I said, you're mistaken. Leave it.'

Lock tried a different approach.

'It's happened once and it could happen again.'

'It's a risk I'll take. There's no other way. I can't do this unless we teleport and I don't have time to argue. The attack is in three days and there's still a lot to sort out, so let's go.'

Lock persuaded Bilton to do a couple of short trips across the field and back. He hoped the weird effects would happen again so that he could film it on Bilton's phone as proof, but mostly he worried about Bilton. Much as he hated to admit it, he was a capable commander, despite being prickly and distant, and at such a late stage of planning he was needed.

Colombian shops were different to other countries, Lock and Bilton discovered. Because of Starbirth crime, the larger stores employed extra armed security guards to watch over the premises at night, and the same appeared to be true of banks and businesses. Everywhere they went, they saw armed men who regarded them with suspicion and challenged them for walking down the street. Twice Lock had to teleport away from trouble. It took him a while to find a closed clothing store that didn't have sweaty, trigger-happy guards shooting at the slightest noise. Even the rats had a tough time in Cali.

He changed his trousers in the dark on an upper floor, glancing out of a cracked window. The street looked like a war zone with shop fronts boarded up and pavements glittering with broken glass. Some shop owners hadn't bothered protecting their empty premises and left windows shattered and jagged, with the goods inside looted or wrecked. The area had a forlorn, hopeless air.

Cali confronted Lock with what could happen in London, Birmingham or any other UK city. The burden of trying to prevent it weighed heavily. It felt horrible. The war zone had always been over there, somewhere else, a different continent, but in Cali it was right where it shouldn't be, in a place familiar to him. He couldn't reconcile the two, or accept the inevitable change facing him and the UK, the country he regarded as his home, his safe harbour.

Lock felt it was the honourable thing to leave dollars behind in payment for their clothes, though the amount he had in his pockets didn't equal the prices on the tickets. Bilton left nothing. They used a filthy kitchen area to wash their heads and hands before stuffing their dirty clothes in plastic bags and leaving for Cassin's, which definitely lived up to the description of being downmarket. Heavily guarded, it was popular judging by the heaving mass of bodies on the dance floor. People whipped up Christmas cheer on a Friday night. They had to shout into each other's ears to hear above the Latino-Western dance mix. Topless girls slithered up and down poles or arranged themselves erotically inside cages, pouting and sucking their fingers, playing with the top hem of skimpy thongs, giving punters who couldn't reach them the kind of lingering eye contact that signalled forbidden pleasure.

What the place lacked in the way of genuine sexual heat, it made up for in terms of real heat. The air conditioning couldn't cope. Cigarette smoke curled like fog in shafts of light. Deodorant, perfumes and aftershave mingled in a heady battle with natural body odours, altering from one person to another as Lock and Bilton pushed towards a door marked with a star, Chris's meeting point.

Bilton didn't want Lock too close when he spoke to Chris, who turned out to be a dishevelled, paunchy man in his forties who looked as though he hadn't shaved or washed for days. He looked familiar and Lock remembered seeing Chris in Bogota and recognised him as one of the men included in Bilton's team at the hotel. While Chris and Bilton were in conversation Lock waited, ready to Shift out at a moment's notice. He watched people nearest them for sign of weapons.

Before long he became aware he and Bilton were being watched in turn. Body language betrayed true intentions, even in a dense crowd. Each time the arm-waving, curving dancers parted they revealed a svelte figure, a dark-haired girl standing with a man who looked American. Their stillness gave them away, added to an apparent indifference to the atmosphere that should have captivated them and carried them with it. The dancers cavorted and whirled, but whenever Lock caught a glimpse of her face, it was turned in his direction.

Subtle signals gave him an intuitive awareness of danger, something he had learned to respect. He switched to sensory awareness. Auras wisped, swayed and glided without arms or legs in a feathery mix of blues, but the one he stared at held him spellbound. It was unique. It wasn't just blue, it blended hues of green and yellow in a shimmer around the edges.

Lock could hardly breathe. Out of all the millions of human auras he'd seen over the years he had never seen anything like this one. Perhaps it wasn't human. The blue auras closed in, obscuring it. Lock lurched to the side, catching a glimpse before bumping into other auras. Somebody shouted angrily and he switched mode, apologising for his clumsiness before anybody could pull a weapon on him. In sensory mode, he caught another glimpse of the strange aura, moving behind a cage near the exit. He followed but lost it when a hand gripped his arm, jolting him back to normal life in the club.

'I'm ready. Let's go,' Bilton shouted above the din.

Lock hurried towards the exit, frustrated by the crush of bodies. As soon as they were out of sight of Chris, he rushed outside with Bilton and scanned in all directions for the woman with the strange aura, catching a drift of greenish-yellow turning a corner close by.

'What's wrong?'

'I thought I saw something. This way.' Lock dashed to the corner. The aura vanished inside a doorway. Ignoring Bilton's questions, Lock chased her into a gloomy, packed bar. People gathered in groups around tables, descending into an alcohol-driven haze of loud voices, bad jokes and excessive goodwill. He lost her in the densely-packed auras.

'What the hell's going on?' Bilton demanded.

'A different kind of Shifter. Odd movements,' Lock lied, knowing she wasn't moving fast enough to be a teleporter. He strained to see over peoples' heads until the TV screen near the counter caught his eye. Somebody had left it on the news channel. The aerial view of Washington stopped him in his tracks. He knew that view. He'd seen Washington from the air enough times over the years and he'd seen that particular view days ago. The spot belching out a plume of black smoke was where Mike Northwood's apartment should be. Lock couldn't take his eyes off the screen. He moved forward, trying to see the words on the ticker-tape underneath the images, but Bilton pulled his attention.

'What d'you mean, a different kind of Shifter? Is this a threat to us?'

Lock ignored him. He pushed closer to the screen. A repeated loop showed first the aerial images as a chopper circled the smoke, then it changed to a ground backdrop behind a reporter. It was definitely Mike's street, though the reporter stood further up behind a cordon. A gaping hole existed where Mike's apartment would have been, and the block next to the blackened debris was on fire. The Breaking News tickertape at the bottom said, '34 dead, 50 casualties.'

Lock pushed his way to the door. Bilton followed, complaining about wasting time. Lock remembered the strange aura and stopped. Bilton bumped into him.

'What the fuck's wrong now?'

Lock scanned the room but couldn't see the woman.

'Nothing. I have to make a call.' He took out his mobile phone, trying not to let his agitation show. He couldn't tell Bilton about his friendship with Mike. Bilton's level of security clearance didn't allow it. Nor did he wish to tell him about the odd aura, sensing that it had great importance even if he didn't know why.

The Secure Link, the encrypted satellite phone link set up specifically for him and Mike, was disconnected. He couldn't get through on the public line. Somebody had possibly murdered Mike, one of the few people capable of stopping his country descending into the kind of chaos seen in Cali. It didn't make sense to murder him. Shocked, Lock teleported. He took Bilton to the Observation Post, where Mackenzie and his colleagues monitored Mosquera and his men. He barely registered what they were doing, because a thousand fears tormented him. Powerful people had got to Mike. Those same people could come after him next, or worse, his family.

The team left the sensors in place at the OP. Lock took them back to the perimeter of Patuazon's estate, still stunned by so many things happening at once – Bilton's reaction to Shifting, the strange aura, Mike's likely death. Stopping near the fence, he made an effort to get a grip on himself and control the grief that threatened to consume him. Anger replaced it. No fucker was going to get to him or his family, no matter how powerful the threat might be.

CHAPTER 11

The same night that Lock discovered a different kind of human aura, he perched in the tangled branches of a tree forty metres from the ground in the Colombian sub-tropics. He didn't choose the highest vantage point. He could have roosted in a Brazil nut tree nearby, seventy metres above ground, but it was too obvious. An airborne enemy might take up position there if they wanted to do surveillance on Mosquera's estate, and Mosquera's men would be aware of that.

He took care not to make any movement beyond leaning back against a large branch for better balance, letting his Diemaco Special Forces Weapon dangle in its chest harness. It didn't take much effort to set the tall trees swaying and plenty of eyes in Mosquera's watchtowers would be drawn to the canopy, just as they had scrutinised a large group of monkeys that passed through on the eastern perimeter fifteen minutes earlier.

Through the eyes of two insect drones Lock watched events at the unfinished back section of the villa. Antonio Mosquera's men took their time over the slow process of murdering Ramon Mosquera, Antonio's brother. Ramon was a paid informant of the British Government, code-named Nightingale. Antonio discovered his brother's treachery and was determined to exact his revenge in the most brutal fashion his men could devise. They only had a break because Nightingale passed out and they didn't want him to die too quickly. Lock turned one of the drones away from the room and scanned the relay transmitters of the anti-teleporter net, waiting for his opportunity to get in and rescue the victim.

It enraged Lock that the SIS could callously discard an informant, knowing it put him in danger of being tortured and killed. Bilton scoffed at Lock's concern, saying Nightingale was bloated from the spoils of drug running, actively helping the family business by taking on the role of weapons buyer. Mosquera bought weapons through Nightingale and sold them to bandits in exchange for allowing Mosquera's drug shipments safe passage through their territory.

Lock thought it morally indefensible to turn a blind eye and let Nightingale be tortured and killed. He resolved it would not happen, as long as he could prevent it. He told Bilton he needed to do another reconnaissance of the southern perimeter of Mosquera's estate. Bilton reminded him that any interference by way of an attempt to rescue Nightingale could lead to compromising the operation, let alone the assault plan.

Lock transferred thought control of the insect drones from his sunglasses to his helmet and visor and he arrived at the estate, going against the wishes of Bilton and the SIS. He wondered how the hell he could get Nightingale out of there. Getting in undetected posed no problem; it could be passed off as a glitch in the electrical network, similar to glitches that had sent the system haywire when birds flew into it. He wouldn't need long to get in, snatch Nightingale and leave, but he needed a trick or distraction to cover his tracks on the way out. It was imperative that it looked as though Nightingale had escaped by his own methods to avoid flak from both the Colombians, and Lock's chain of command.

He hoped Mosquera would conduct more teleporter experiments because his men switched off the anti-teleporter net when a teleporter was active, but Mosquera had already retired to bed. Even if the net was switched off, unless the men inflicting pain on Nightingale left him alone, Lock could not get in and out without being seen.

He was frustrated, limited to listening to what went on and observing through the eyes of a drone clinging to the outside of a window frame. He didn't want to watch the man being brutalised. He couldn't remain unaffected by it. Sadistic brutality appalled him, but he couldn't help seeing it as he observed the layout of the room and the positions of the occupants. The conversation between the men turned to discussing a new weapon. One had the idea of using it on Nightingale. Lock listened while they fiddled with it, trying to work out whether it was safe to use it inside a room.

He listened to the conversation and moved the drone on the window, trying to get a glimpse of what the men held as they strutted around, but they huddled over the weapon and he couldn't see it properly. They were unsure how to arm it, what the computer settings meant, and whether the darts would hit the target or go off and hit everybody else as well.

The more Lock heard, the more it intrigued him. One of the men was exasperated and said it was too complicated and dangerous. They needed a manual to operate it and they should get the burner instead. Another voice objected that the burner was even more dangerous. He'd been told they had to use it with extreme caution because it could blow up. Lock's ears pricked up. He held his breath and waited. The first voice said angrily, they'd been shown how to use the burner and he wasn't going to act like a frightened girl, so go and get the bloody thing. A short, stocky man left the room. As the door opened, it revealed a glimpse of Nightingale tied to a chair, broken and bloody. His head hung on his chest. Lock prayed he wouldn't die before the man returned – he looked as though he might.

He decided he couldn't wait. His entry would have to be a system malfunction. He wiped sweat from his face, took out a bee drone pre-programmed to disrupt anti-teleporter defences, and sent it on its way. It took a long time for the man to return from the armoury, struggling with a large weapon. Lock photographed it and his computer confirmed it was a plasma burner, a temperamental weapon unless handled with skill. Most military forces regarded the plasma burner as unrefined, unwieldy and too heavy to be carried by a foot soldier. The UK considered its use as a vehicle-mounted weapon but turned it down and it was sent back to the research and development technicians for modifications, but in the hands of somebody as sturdy as a bull, like Bloater, the weapon was lethal and the plasma beam had the capacity to blast people into particles and punch holes the size of dinner plates through titanium.

The weedy man lugging it up the slope was no Bloater. He cursed in between gasping for breath. He gave up, left the weapon on the ground and went for help. It took two men to carry it into the room. Lock pulled on fire-retardant clothing, a balaclava and gloves, and put his helmet and visor on. He abandoned the plan to stage an escape. Something else he hadn't considered hit him at that very inappropriate moment. He would have to kill the men in the room. If he left anybody alive, they would talk about Nightingale's rescue and Mosquera would know about it.

Lock's resolve wobbled. He had no problem with firing in combat, at people who tried their best to kill him. This was different, and akin to the assassinations the SIS would love him to do, and which he had always refused on the grounds that it made him a murderer rather than a fighter. Cold reasoning spoke to him. These men were engaged in murdering somebody else and in three days' time, they would be trying to kill his teammates. That last thought obliterated his qualms.

When the men went back into the room Lock acted. He took out a magnetised high-explosive grenade and set the timer to seven seconds. Taking a deep breath, he pressed the buttons to start the timer sequence and thought-propelled the bee into the net to short-circuit the controls. Waiting for one second, he teleported into the room. Shifting in and finding his bearings used up one second. The remaining four seconds felt like four minutes.

At first only one man saw him. The other two had their backs to him. The man didn't have time to move. Lock clapped the magnetic grenade on the fuel cartridge of the plasma burner and scooped up the other strange weapon. The torturer's mouth opened in a yell of terror. He dropped the plasma burner and turned for the door. Lock grabbed hold of the back of Nightingale's chair with his free arm across the top of his chest and teleported out, chair and all.

He came out of teleportation in time to see the room explode. White heat seared through the windows. The makeshift roof disappeared as plasma fuel expanded and erupted in a jet of fire that shot twelve metres above the walls. He alighted in foliage outside the estate, where he started from. Nightingale was alive but barely conscious. Lock left him in the chair, put down the new weapon and fumbled in his haste to check sensors monitoring the anti-teleporter system to see if it returned to normal as expected. His sensors registered the system as inert, which puzzled him.

Using his visor to zoom in on the estate, he looked at the raging fire in the partly-demolished room. Plasma fuel burned like puddles of white phosphorus across the courtyard. Frightened people emerged from doorways, looking at each other for leadership and finding none until armed Lanceros raced to the scene. One assumed charge, shouting orders and gesturing. Armed men took up positions, lights went on and then off, and although it appeared people knew what they were doing, the scene was chaotic.

Lock spotted the reason why the anti-teleporter net didn't work. One of the four flagpoles of the net transmission system leaned at an angle. A power cable had snapped. It would take time to repair it, maybe as long as three days. A back-up power source kicked in restoring the system, not to normal, but to a lesser degree of efficiency. Mosquera would find out from the men guarding the armoury how the plasma burner had been taken out and used in the wrecked room. Lock doubted Mosquera would think it amounted to anything other than a careless accident. More than likely it would put him off attempting to use another plasma burner and with a bit of luck, the absence of Nightingale's body would never be noticed.

Nightingale groaned. Lock picked up the weapon and teleported him away from the estate, stopping on the fringes of Cali. Attaching a torch to the side of his helmet, he pulled a survival sheet from a pouch on his belt kit, laying it on crushed plants. He turned the chair on its side so Nightingale lay on the ground, and cut the cords binding Nightingale's ankles to the chair legs. Moving to the back of the chair he released the bonds at Nightingale's wrists, noticing that two fingers on his captive's right hand were missing and his face had been badly beaten. He was a mess.

Lock pulled the chair away. Nightingale moaned as pain kicked in. He muttered through swollen lips, his voice gathering strength. Lock spoke in Spanish, reassuring him, and took out a syrette of morphine from his belt kit. Nightingale said hoarsely,

'I didn't know he was going to turn up. Please, don't hurt me any more. I didn't know Bloater was going to take the package; it wasn't me who told him. I didn't know about the deal with the gringos, or the money.'

Lock stopped with the syrette in his hand when he heard Bloater's name. The last time he heard it was when Bilton said it. He sat on his haunches. Perhaps Bilton's worry over Bloater was not just concern about the proposed assault on Mosquera.

'Where did Bloater turn up?'

Nightingale shuddered, moving an arm feebly.

'Please. I already told you.'

'Tell me again. From the beginning. No lies. Who had the money and who had the package?'

Nightingale was out of his mind with pain and shock, and seemed to be drugged. Lock discarded the syrette, thinking it wasn't a good idea to add morphine to the mix. Nightingale gasped out the whole story, with Lock filling in gaps about the deal Mosquera set up with some gringos. He heard how Bloater turned up and wrecked the deal. Wrapping Nightingale in the survival sheet as the story came out, he wondered why he hadn't put two and two together – the reported gunfight near Bogota along with the injuries he'd seen on Bilton and Mackenzie three days later. The clues were there and he'd missed them. He had blindly bought the tale of them being caught in the crossfire of a gang fight because such events happened regularly in Colombia. It was sheer luck none of Patuazon's men recognised them at the training camp.

The more Lock thought about how he had been fooled, the more his fury was as white-hot as the burning plasma. Stringer had deceived him, not with words but with the absence of words. The planned assault on Mosquera's estate was not for the sake of good relations with Patuazon, but an act of revenge over the lost money. Nightingale shuddered, his voice faltering as he pleaded to be spared. Lock regarded him with a mix of concern and revulsion. Even if Nightingale had not been involved with murders, kidnappings and extortion, he had turned a blind eye to it. It had all fallen on his head. Lock couldn't pity him, but the man had suffered enough. He tied the ends of the survival sheet around him.

'I'm not going to hurt you. I'm taking you to a hospital. I'm a friend.'

Nightingale didn't understand. Lock repeated it. Nightingale stirred, staring at Lock's covered face with the eye that could still see.

'A friend?'

'Yes.' Lock scanned a computer map of Cali for hospitals.

'No, no, my family. See to my family.' Lock told him he needed medical attention first, but Nightingale insisted. 'My family, they're not safe. You must help them. Please, my youngest daughter, she's only eight.'

Lock sighed. Nightingale mistook his sigh as a refusal and said,

'Wait. I can tell you about the demons.'

Lock thought Nightingale was going off his head and got ready to teleport to the Santa Marta hospital in Cali. Nightingale gripped his sleeve.

'The weapons. The Demon weapons. I know how many.'

Lock halted as the words sank in. He looked at the weapon he had taken from Mosquera's villa. Light from his torch glinted on the steel barrel. He picked it up and held it closer to Nightingale, tapping the side.

'This one?'

Nightingale opened his eye with difficulty and peered at it.

'Yes. That one.' He closed his eyes.

'What about it?'

'My family first.'

The moment they reached Nightingale's mansion in the affluent part of Cali, Lock knew something wasn't right. No guards watched the driveway or the front entrance. Some lights were on, but it was too quiet. Lock's neuro-sensory search found only one aura in the house, a small one, not moving. Leaving Nightingale fretting by the gate, Lock went inside cautiously, keeping watch for Shifters.

In the living room, the bodies of five guards and servants lay by one wall. They had been lined up and shot. Scattered among other rooms were more bodies, an elderly couple, two women, a teenage boy and two girls. The live aura upstairs belonged to a small girl, bleeding and unconscious from a gunshot wound to the head. She looked as though she had been dragged from under her bed and shot. The cruelty of that one act threatened to overwhelm Lock.

Nightingale was weeping when Lock returned. He knew they were too late. He collapsed when he saw his daughter and learned everybody else had died. Lock felt pity, and told him he would take him and his daughter to the Santa Marta hospital.

'Not the Santa Marta.' Nightingale gripped Lock's arm with his bloodied left hand. 'It's the hospital Tony uses.'

'Your brother? Tony Mosquera?'

'Yes. He has people there. They'll kill us.'

They agreed on a hospital in Bogota and Lock teleported. He left Nightingale hidden outside the hospital and put the girl down in the Emergency Room. Calling for the attention of the staff on duty, he left before they alerted security to the presence of an armed man wearing fatigues, helmet and balaclava. He returned to Nightingale's side on an empty road.

'Tell me about the Demons. Then I'll take you in there.'

After leaving Nightingale at the hospital, Lock stopped in darkness in a farmer's field outside Bogota to compose himself. The adrenaline ran wild. His hands shook and he felt jittery as though pumped with electricity. Wild thoughts flew through his mind. The cool air couldn't put out the fire of his fury or take away the rawness of flashbacks of the girl's head wound. He wanted to go back to the villa at Mocoa and kill Mosquera. Nothing less would do. He raged at Mosquera, and at the SIS, and Stringer. He was furious with Jimmy. He knew but said nothing when they had their chat by the lake. Lashing out at the thigh-high crop, he broke stems and flattened sharp-edged leaves. The crushed plants filled the air with a pungent, sweet aroma.

Long-dormant emotions stirred and tapped at the door of his conscious thoughts, adding to the unpleasant buzzing in his body. He enjoyed the thrill of going into that room to rescue Nightingale. Coming close to death and escaping intact exhilarated him in a way that nothing else did. At that moment, he felt more alive than he'd felt for years. That scared him. He tried to shut the exhilaration out of his mind, but once there it was as real as the ground beneath his feet.

The deaths of three men meant nothing. That discovery dismayed him, because his feelings when he was involved in the rescue differed from the person he wanted to be. It was a dark reminder of who he'd been at eighteen – an adrenaline junkie taking things to deadly excess in search of thrills. Had he not changed since then? He told himself that his wife and young son meant the world to him, more than any thrill. 'Should mean the world,' a devious voice said in his mind – he banished that with more ferocity and he twitched, tingled, buzzed, burned feverishly and tingled some more, until he realised the tingling came from a pouch on the left-hand side of his belt kit.

He pulled out the Secure Link phone and paused before hitting the connect button in case an official on the other end told him Mike Northwood's body had been found.

'Yes?' He expected the worst.

'Hey, man, how's things?'

'Mike.' Lock nearly shouted the name but caught himself in time. 'They didn't get you, then.'

He heard a dry chuckle from the other end of the line followed by a short wheeze.

'I'm hard to get rid of. We had a warning and got out just in time. I'm a bit knocked about but I'm okay.' Northwood didn't sound okay.

'I thought you were dead. Scared the shit out of me. Is Kes okay?'

'Fine, she's fine. She's a better rocket Shifter than I am. She didn't get caught in the shock wave. Listen, I don't have a lot of time here. D'you still want help?'

Lock grinned. Did he still want help? As if Northwood needed to ask.

'Yeah, if it's on offer and if you're up to it.'

'Sure it's on offer. You warned us about the truck. If you hadn't they'd have caught us with our pants well and truly down. What time d'you want to do this?'

Lock looked at the clock setting on his visor.

'Tonight? That's the twenty-first. Say at twenty-one hundred hours?'

'Fine. Meet me at Tippity Wichity on the opposite side of the river from where we were. See you then.'

'Wait. Um – do you have any of that new PixelRain stuff?'

'Geez, you really go for the sensitive items. What do you need?'

'Four suits, two large size men's, two medium.'

'I'll see what I can do.'

'No, I need to know now if you can or can't.'

'Okay, it's a definite yes.'

'Great. Thanks, Mike. See you later.'

Lock smiled when he put the phone back in the pouch. His elation was short-lived. Something fell in the plants, about fifteen metres away. A man's deep voice yelped the word 'Fuck' then stifled the sound. Lock froze and resisted the urge to move fast. He brought his Diemaco round, lowered himself into the plants and sank into the night shadow of trees by the edge of the field. He switched from the visor's night vision to neuro-sensory aura awareness. Two auras, different sizes, the smaller one a woman or a youngster. Two Shifters. They hadn't seen him. He scanned a complete circle with himself at the centre. He saw three faint human auras in the ranch house a hundred and fifty metres away, with a herd of plum-coloured cows nearby.

He went to the two humans. Using night vision, he peered past the foliage to see if either of them carried weapons, but he couldn't see much beyond the plants and didn't dare raise his head in case they had night vision as well. He alternated between aura mode and night vision. One of the auras moved from behind the other one. The smaller aura had a light green tinge. Lock blinked and looked again. Maybe his mind played tricks on him. He stared, mesmerised, at an aura that had patches of light jade green on the tendrils, just like the one he saw earlier. No, not like the other one. No yellow – only green.

What were the odds of finding two new auras on the same night? Too great, and the fact they had turned up beside him in a field miles outside Bogota could only mean they were tracking him. But that was impossible. Nobody could track a Shifter, and he'd checked all his clothes and equipment for electronic devices before he'd left. He needed to get closer and went for the oldest distraction trick in the book, counting on his calculation that neither of them had military training. He moved slowly, hoping they didn't have thermal imaging kit which would spot his heat even through the plants. Taking out a satphone he switched it on and lobbed it to his left, behind the auras. Levitating fast across the short distance, he landed in front of them, weapon at the aim. His trick worked; they faced away from him until he landed in the plants.

'Don't move,' he shouted. They appeared to be unarmed. They vanished, leaving behind rustling plant leaves.

Lock went into neuro-sensory mode but couldn't see them. He boxed the terrain for several kilometres outside the field, in much the same way as he did in Scotland when he searched for Mackenzie. He found blue auras, but on closer inspection none of them had jade tendrils. After twenty minutes he returned to the field, deflated and considering the implications as he retrieved the Demon weapon and used his mobile phone to ring the missing satphone. It took minutes for the satphone to react, probably due to trouble with satellite coverage, but it gave him time to think.

The couple's vanishing act told him they were rocket Shifters, people who could teleport fast at the outset. Generally rocket Shifters couldn't sustain their speed or distance, dropping out of teleportation within a few minutes. They needed time to rest before the next jump, unlike Lock and Northwood who set off slowly but maintained long periods of teleportation and covered huge distances. The retreat of the strangers told him they didn't want to get into a confrontation. The notion of being watched displeased him considering he spent a great deal of his time spying on others. He didn't like being a target. Who were they and what were their intentions?

Lock returned to Patuazon's training camp an hour after he left. PC let him through the camp's outer sensor defence system.

'Boss wants a word with you.' PC eyed the bulky weapon in Lock's hand. Lock didn't reply. He was prepared for Bilton, who rose from his bunk fully dressed.

'We need to talk. In private,' Lock said.

'Fine. The daily report is overdue.' Bilton picked up the bergen containing the radio kit and his laptop. He nodded at the weapon. 'What's that?'

'That's what we need to talk about.' Lock led the way out of the hut.

After they left the perimeter fence, Lock teleported to the other side of the Andes mountain range, on the lookout for sign of the mystery woman and her companion. He landed on an isolated hill, in a clearing created by a fallen tree amidst sub-tropical jungle. The clearing allowed a better satellite connection for sending the nightly report. He switched on his green low-light torch and squatted on the ground. Bilton dropped next to him and looked at him expectantly.

'This is a nasty piece of kit.' Lock turned the weapon over and pointed to the bottom of the stock. 'Chinese figures and the Western letters DMON, which stands for Dongxian Missile Operated Nanotechnology. A Demon weapon. I heard about this a year ago.' He pulled out a Demon magazine from a pouch on his belt kit. 'Each magazine has ten capsules which contain five laser-tipped darts, like tiny heat-seeking missiles. The weapon acquires a target and the capsule opens on firing. The darts disperse and each one locks on to the target, or multiple targets. They go for less protected areas like arms, legs and heads. The dart hits and injects nanomaterials into the bloodstream.'

He passed the weapon and magazine to Bilton.

'The Chinese invented the Demon as a means of track-and-trace, so they could inject trackable nanomaterials into protesters and rioters. The security services could locate people at their leisure later, after everybody thought they were safe. Then somebody had the bright idea to make the payload lethal. The nanomaterials in this magazine are programmed to go for the heart and destroy its nerve supply. Mosquera has these weapons.'

Bilton stared at the Demon in the green beam of the lowlight torch, turning the weapon over in his hands.

Lock continued, 'If all five darts hit the same soldier, he's dead within two or three minutes of being hit. Four darts, it's around five to ten minutes. Three darts, it's fifteen minutes, two darts thirty minutes max. Even if a soldier is hit by one dart he won't be alive after forty-five minutes. This is what the lads are up against. Mosquera has another nine of these.'

Lock did an aura check. Bats chattered and swooped in the canopy. A flowering shrub filled the air with a heavy perfume.

'Mosquera has another nine?'

'Yes. And each weapon is potentially capable of taking out fifty men.'

'How many magazines does Mosquera have?'

'I don't know. Nightingale couldn't tell me, he didn't recall. He wasn't making much sense by then.'

'Nightingale? What d'you mean? Nightingale's dead. Isn't he? What the fuck have you done?'

Bilton was speechless with either disbelief or rage or a mixture of the two as Lock described the rescue.

'I gave you a direct order not to attempt a rescue.'

'My remit is to use my own discretion. In this situation, Nightingale was more use alive than dead.'

'It wasn't your call to make! I don't care how you're used to operating, or what your civilian-equivalent rank is, as field commander I make the decisions of who goes where and why. You answer to me. Your actions have compromised the entire operation.'

'No, the Demons have compromised it. The assault should be aborted until we know more about the nanomaterials in this weapon and obtain an antidote.'

Bilton rubbed a hand over his receding hairline, an action Lock recognised as a subconscious signal of distress. Ever since the reaction to teleporting, he'd been acting weird, like the way he held the weapon by his side as if he had forgotten it was there and the tight, anxious sound in his voice. It was all new.

'That's why you did it, isn't it? You're trying to get the assault cancelled.'

'No, Bilton, it was because I couldn't sit on my arse with a mug of tea and pretend torture wasn't happening. If I hadn't got Nightingale out of there, we wouldn't know about the Demons.'

Bilton stared at Lock and dropped his gaze to the weapon. He pushed the Demon and magazine back at Lock.

'The assault is going ahead.'

'My advice is the assault should be delayed, or better still aborted altogether. The Demons are a problem.'

'The Demons are not a problem. They'll keep these in the armoury. We'll target the place with enough demolition charges to blow them into even smaller particles.' Bilton took off his bergen and unpacked his computer and the radio kit.

'There's no guarantee the weapons will be there. Even if they are we might not be able to destroy them all.'

'That's a chance we have to take. From what you've said it's obvious they don't know how to use them. The sooner we go in, the less time they have to sort that out.' He tapped on the laptop keyboard. 'We need to move on and get the report off to London.'

'There's something else to put in it.' Lock told him about the two Shifters, adding that he wasn't sure if the woman was a Shifter or a passenger.

'How can you be sure they were following you? There're hundreds of them in Cali. And in Bogota. It could've been any Shifters out for a stroll.'

Lock didn't want to reveal knowledge of the new aura, not to Bilton.

'It was different. In my view they were tracking me.'

'Different how? Unless you can give me more to go on than that, you're not going to stop or delay the assault. It's going ahead regardless. If you want to back out, do it now, so I can alter the plans and get on with it without having you undermining me and the operation.'

'I'm a professional. I don't do things for my own purposes, I'm telling you about real and credible threats.'

'There's no firm evidence about the Shifters. Unless you're not telling me something else, like where you went on the seventeenth. Where did you go, Harford? You left the camp at one in the morning and didn't get back until first light. Where were you for five hours?'

Bilton sat with his laptop on his knees. Lit from beneath by his laptop, his features took on an unearthly appearance. Infuriated, Lock recalled his visit to Northwood's flat in Washington, and Northwood's earlier refusal of help with a disguise for the day of the assault. He wasn't going to satisfy Bilton's demands by telling him about it.

'I told you, it's classified.'

'Classified. Right. So London knows about it and it won't matter if I put it in my report. I'm also putting in how you're endangering this operation by taking matters into your own hands.'

'Endangering? Don't talk to me about endangering the operation. I know about the deal in Bogota. Yes, that's right, the one that caused your injuries. You and Mackenzie. Nightingale told me. Did you consider how much you endangered my position here, let alone the operation of monitoring Patuazon? You tried to do a deal with the man he hates, got into a fight involving some of his men and turned up here three days later. If any of his men had ID'd you or Mackenzie the whole operation, months of work, would have gone down the toilet. Me and the lads could've been killed in revenge. So don't talk to me about not being open, or compromising the operation, or endangering it. If you'd told me about the deal when I saw you in Bogota, instead of being so secretive we could've worked something out, I could've helped make it safer.'

'What, you would have rushed in to save the day?'

Lock's hand clenched into a fist. He breathed hard, staring at the older and shorter man, as close as he had ever been to decking him. The only thing that stopped him was that Bilton remained squatting and made no eye contact, preferring to give his attention to his laptop.

'I might have made a difference.'

Lock recognised Bilton's demeanour as a deliberate tactic to avoid conflict by not making direct eye contact. Judging by the stillness in Bilton's pose, like a coiled spring, he was ready for a fight if Lock offered it, and that would go down in his report, too. Bilton was out to discredit him.

The moment passed. Bilton tapped on the keyboard, as if aware his provocation hadn't worked. Lock hadn't done a neuro-sensory aura check for over three minutes. When he finished, he moved away, sat cross-legged on the ground, pulled out his computer and typed out his own report. Bilton sent the main report in a burst transmission, took photos of the Demon and sent those, then handed the radio over to Lock for the second report to be sent. They waited for an acknowledgement and any orders, sitting apart without speaking.

~~~~~~~~

Five hours ahead of Colombian time, at nine-fifteen in the morning, other matters preoccupied Stringer. He sipped coffee from a thermal plastic cup and watched the news on the TV screen opposite his desk. A gang teleported into Selfridges the previous night and ransacked the store, making off with half a million pounds' worth of jewellery before the police were aware of the robbery. A square box flashed in the corner of the screen, notifying him of an incoming message from the team in Colombia. The printer sprang to life and chattered as it churned out the overdue report.

Stringer put his cup down and reached across his desk for it, still watching the news. He glanced at the report and lost interest in the rest of
~~~~~~~~

the world. The more he read, the more he frowned, his early morning good mood slipping away like the Thames water sliding under Vauxhall Bridge. He reached for his jacket on the back of his chair, knowing what was coming. The phone buzzed and the LED display lit up with the single word, Palmer.

'Have you seen the report?' Palmer asked.

'I haven't had a chance to read it.' Stringer lied to buy time. Lock had often been told that his questionable actions reflected on both of them, but he refused to take it seriously and his attitude had backfired.

'My office. Now.'

Stringer headed down the anonymous corridor, reading the report again on the way before confronting his boss.

Palmer's bald dome glowed like eggshell. It always gave Stringer some satisfaction seeing it, knowing that due to genetics he would keep his own thick head of hair for the rest of his life even if it did go grey. He suspected Palmer, who had been a vain man, added that to his list of grievances concerning Stringer, together with the discrepancy between their respective levels of fitness. Palmer used to be fit man, but since arriving at his mid-fifties he tired of the gym provided downstairs at Vauxhall Cross. Easy living claimed him as its victim and showed itself in the roll of flab developing around his middle.

The biggest grievance was Palmer's resentment of Stringer's blood relationship to Lock. Palmer made it clear as far as he was concerned Stringer had got his promotion not by virtue of hard work, but because of his good luck in being a cousin and mentor to the UK's sole legal teleporter.

Palmer sat in an expensive chair behind his antique, carved mahogany desk.

'You said he would toe the line.'

'He has. For a long time. This is out of character.'

'A return to previous form, you mean.'

'Sir, if Harford is bucking the reins it means he's unhappy. In my view it's because of the increasing restrictions being imposed on him and the implied lack of trust regarding his movements.'

'He can't go off doing whatever he damn well pleases.' Palmer jabbed a finger at the report on his desk. 'This comes straight after the Americans informing us he went to see Northwood. It's making us look silly. We don't know where our operative is, or what he's doing – and now he goes and rescues somebody without permission.'

'I'm sure Harford thought he had a good enough reason to save a man being tortured.'

'He's saving the wrong bloody people; they're on the other side! Not only that, he's acting like a schoolboy maverick.'

'Harford's friendship with Mike Northwood gives us a valuable informal contact. It's provided us with plenty of good intelligence about the Eagles, their equipment, systems of anti-teleporter defences and so on.'

'Don't change the subject. This isn't about his friendship with Northwood, it's about him taking matters into his own hands. He's your responsibility, Stringer. Do something about it.'

'I'll have a word with him and remind him about the chain of command when he's out in the field.'

'No, do a face-to-face before this goes any further. Get on a direct flight from Heathrow, today. Tell him, if he's not prepared to follow the rules he'll have to submit to a tracker implant injected into him, whether he likes it or not.'

'He knows we won't do that, Sir, it was discussed before. If he's tracked by hostiles it would compromise his safety. Considering all the knowledge he has, the breach of security would be extensive.'

'There are always other methods, Stringer. Put the fear of God into him. Make him believe that's what we'll do, because if he doesn't, it may be taken out of my hands.'

'Understood.'

Stringer's single word encompassed more than Palmer might have thought. It contained Stringer's own assessment of Palmer's moral cowardice in threatening an act sanctioned by Palmer, but passed off as being required of him by somebody else. Stringer would never give voice to that thought inside or outside Vauxhall Cross.

On the way back to his office his mood brightened. Maybe he'd have time to fit in a visit with Consuela in Bogota.

~~~~~~~~

'How long will it take?' Lock asked. The dark-haired girl Northwood introduced as Cheena didn't answer. She scrutinised his face with the intensity of a surgeon mapping out her first incision and leaned forward to pluck at the skin on his forehead. The open zipper on her close-fitting, leather-look jacket revealed a generous cleavage, way too close for comfort. Lock had an eyeful of the curve of her breasts. The fact that she wore nothing else under her jacket set off the same uncontrollable chain of raw hormonal instincts as had happened a week ago with Patuazon's probable mistress, Maria. Cheena brushed a hand lightly down his cheek and round his ear, sending visceral shivers through his abdomen. Something else stirred, lower down. If she noticed she didn't say anything. He shuffled self-consciously on bales of straw that acted as a reclining seat and pulled his jacket down to cover his groin. Bemused, he tried to figure out what was
~~~~~~~~

wrong and concluded it was a natural reaction to being away from home for weeks.

She pursed her lips, twisting his head this way and that. She looked part North American Indian, her fine features accentuated by the lamplight.

'It shouldn't take long. About twenty, thirty minutes,' she said in a mid-Western accent. 'When I start on your face, you have to stay real still for the first ten minutes.' She glanced at Mike Northwood. 'That means no asking questions or talking.'

'I can talk for both of us.' Northwood waved a hand in dismissal. He didn't look up from the equipment that monitored the electronic bubble surrounding them in the hay barn.

'Yeah, I know, but you can practice being quiet, Sir. Sit there looking pretty while I demonstrate what I'm going to do.'

Northwood smiled at Lock as though they were in a private men-only club and inclined his head towards her.

'See what happens when you let these upstarts in? Been in the Eagles less than five months and this is how she orders me around.'

Cheena ignored the remark and picked up Lock's right hand, applying cold gel to the back of it. The slitheriness of her touch sent tingles up his spine.

'I'll start here first so you know what it feels like. It's kinda weird but doesn't hurt.' She massaged the back of his hand. 'What I have to do is make the skin thinner so it loses its elasticity and wrinkles up like elderly skin.'

Lock glanced at Northwood. He couldn't see any outward sign on Northwood's face of the explosion the previous day. He looked unscathed, apart from being haggard and as though he hadn't eaten for a week. Maybe accelerated-healing factor made him look thin due to burning up calories, but he had a haunted air about him that Lock hadn't seen before. The gentle massage became more than that. It felt as if she kneaded dough with her fingers. She pulled his skin upwards and moulded it until he thought it would detach from his hand. Lock looked at it as she stopped kneading.

'Now I have to put the wrinkles in.'

Something passed from her fingertips, like a feathery net going from one side of his outstretched hand to the other. It became as fierce as thin wires generating prickles of electricity. As he watched, folds and fine lines appeared over the back of his hand forming deep circles over the knuckles.

'Now some blotches.' She looked as though she enjoyed her work. After another minute she stopped and pinched some of the liverish, brown-spotted skin on the back of his hand, heaping it into a ridge.

'See, it doesn't spring back like younger skin does.'

'Kinda like cosmetic surgery in reverse,' Northwood chuckled. Lock looked at his hand. He would have liked to admire the result, but he found it revolting. The distant headlights of a car flashed through cracks in the barn's corrugated iron walls, indicating somebody returning home to the farm.

'They can't see us, right?' Lock said.

'Not even if somebody walked right in here,' Northwood replied. 'All they'll see is the barn, even close up. They'd have to touch this thing to know it's here. We can see out, they can't see in.'

'What about the lamp?'

'Doesn't show up.'

'No talking now,' Cheena said. She put her hands on Lock's face. He flinched.

'Hold on. This is temporary, isn't it?'

'It can be permanent if you want,' she replied with a mischievous smile, adding, 'most of it is temporary, it reverts back over time. Transformations done this way are unnatural. Generally they don't last more than twenty-four hours because they don't have a solid basis in your own physiology. Sometimes they last more than a day, but that's rare. It's similar to the body rejecting an organ transplant. It recognises the changes as alien because tiny traces of my genetic make-up are transferred to you. Don't worry, it won't harm you. Your body rejects it. That's why, after a while, your hands and face might feel inflamed. It's the body rejecting the alterations and changing you back. Stay still, now.'

Northwood monitored the movements of the farmer. Lock wondered what gel could so magically transform his features. Nanomaterials, perhaps. He felt safe in Cheena's hands. She exuded confidence. Every movement breathed out self-reliance and composure as though she carried out a routine. He relaxed and enjoyed the massage interspersed with crackles of tiny electric shocks, which were pleasant once he'd got used to them. When she started on his earlobes and the areas behind them his pleasure turned guilty, and his awareness of the changes down below was more acute. He thought of Lianne, but that only made things worse. Northwood came to his rescue.

'The farmer's gone inside. You realise I'm being allowed to see you, right?'

'Maybe we should discuss that later.'

Northwood chuckled.

'If you're worried about Cheena, put it out of your head. She won't repeat anything she hears. Right, Cheena?'

Cheena stopped what she was doing.

'Yes, Sir, but you can't ask him questions, he can't answer right now.' She resumed the massage.

Northwood nodded, as though his mind hadn't engaged with what she said.

'Oh, yeah. Well, anyway, after what happened in Washington some people wanted to stick you on the terrorist watch list due to you coming into the country without stopping for a hello at passport control. I had a hard time persuading them not to. That's got to change. We can't do spontaneous any more. Ever since Starbirth and Shifters, my government's very nervous about us meeting. They're not happy to leave it up to our respective agencies to log the dates. Other government people are muscling in and trying to take over. My guys are resisting, of course, but there are more procedures to follow, more forms and restrictions. We're going to end up like any other travellers. You might even need a visa.'

He smiled, wryly.

Allan Defford, Lock's nominal boss at the MoD, had warned of similar security changes in the UK. The MoD wanted Lock to have a chip implant 'For your own protection, so if you get into trouble we can locate you easily by satellite.' Since it wasn't compulsory, Lock's answer had been an emphatic 'No'. He didn't like the thought of every move being tracked, and he didn't trust the MoD to stop the information falling into the wrong hands.

Cheena started on his left hand.

'It's okay to talk now.' Lock felt around his face and ears. She pulled his hand away. 'Don't touch until I say. It needs time to settle in.'

Lock and Northwood exchanged a glance and laughed.

'What? What did I say?' Cheena stopped.

'Nothing,' Northwood said, grinning.

'It wasn't nothing. What did I do wrong?'

Lock gave her a sharp look. Sometimes Northwood's leadership style was too laid-back when he let his subordinates talk to him in that manner. Northwood shook his head.

'You didn't do anything wrong.' He chuckled. 'When we were kids, my Mom said that. She used to bake cakes and bread at the mission in Brazil. That was her mantra, 'Don't touch until I say'. We didn't take any notice, though, did we?'

'Nope,' Lock agreed.

'One of us used to distract her and the other one would sneak in and lift a couple of small cakes. It worked for a while.'

Cheena was unimpressed.

'That's mean. If you did that to me I'd be annoyed.'

Northwood waved a hand dismissively.

'Aw, we were kids. Anyway, I found out a few months later, she used to bake extra for the purpose.'

Lock chipped in, 'It was an ongoing joke for a long time. She loved it, being teased. She teased us a couple of times by putting salt in some of the cakes instead of sugar.'

'Until one day they got mixed up with the mission batch.'

'Those nuns spitting them out.'

Lock and Northwood roared with laughter. Northwood sounded a little manic. Cheena resumed her work, shaking her head.

'By the way, man, it's your turn this year,' Northwood said, fidgeting.

'I thought it was yours.'

'Nah, I did the shoes, remember?'

Cheena glanced at Lock and Northwood.

'Is this another in-joke?' she asked.

'Yeah, I guess,' Northwood said, still grinning. He checked the bubble equipment.

Lock took over the story.

'It's a New Year's thing. We started off giving each other late Christmas presents on New Year's Eve, silly things like a used Christmas cracker or a piece of old turkey from dinner. It went from there. Y'know, like a live turkey in the sitting room.'

'Loads of sheep in the front yard, crapping everywhere.'

'A Sherman tank. I woke up one morning and there was a US tank on my driveway.'

'It was a museum piece, not a live one,' Northwood protested. 'Anyway, the object is to return the gifts to their proper place without anybody seeing, and best of all, without people noticing they'd gone in the first place.'

'It's going to be harder to do at our homes now. I don't fancy getting caught in your neural net again.'

'You'll find a way.'

Cheena stopped working on Lock's hand.

'It's finished. I haven't got a mirror but you look fine. I added some extra weight under your chin and jaw line by moving fat cells around. They're unnaturally bulked up so they'll shrink in a few hours. The skin will take longer.'

Lock puzzled over how the gel could move fat cells around. It was amazing what nanomaterials could do. He sat up and felt his double chin, wondering what Lianne's reaction would be if she could see him.

'I thought once fat was in place you couldn't get rid of it. You know, like collagen implants.'

'Even collagen gets broken down after a while. You'll lose the fat out of the cells. Active guys like you lose it fast. Yeah, your ear lobes and nose are bigger, too. That's what happens to guys when they get older. The scar's gone, the one on your cheek. I can put it back later if you want.'

'No, I don't want it back.' It made him too easily identifiable. Northwood prodded a kit bag with his foot.

'This here is the PixelRain stuff.'

He pulled out a shirt and handed it to Lock. The pinpoint pattern of the material altered as it picked up shapes and colours from the environment.

'Feel the fabric,' Northwood said, sounding like an over-enthusiastic tailor. 'It's thicker than what we're used to, going covert, but it's flexible, tough, thorn-proof, stab-proof and bullet-proof up to 5.56 rounds. Sensors on the outer layer react to an incoming round and the gel molecules inside it alter density at the point of impact. It can still stop a 7.62 but the pixels get damaged and the guy underneath has a whopping bruise. A 7.62 round takes out a section of the pixelated pattern about nine inches square and leaves a grey patch which is more visible. But the guy's alive.'

Lock held the shirt near the pile of straw. He couldn't see where the shirt ended and the straw began.

'Of course it's not entirely foolproof,' Northwood continued.

'Nothing ever is.' Lock grinned, admiring the way the shirt pattern changed as he moved it.

Northwood said, 'It won't stop a 9mm at close range and it won't stop lots of incoming at the same time since it can't react in too many places at once. The material can be sliced by a sharp knife but only if the blade goes slowly, so it's an advantage at close quarters. Nobody's going to stand around while somebody knifes them slowly.'

'Are you sure your people are okay with me having this?'

Northwood's face clouded.

'My agency is fine with it. The people I got these off, they don't even know they're missing. Fuck 'em. Whoever did the job on my apartment had inside knowledge. I can't prove who set it up, but I have a good idea, and the very least they can do is lose some of this shit. I got you five suits, not four. Some guys'll be shitting themselves tomorrow morning when they find out they're gone. They didn't even have a pop at me when I was on my own. They blew up the whole fucking apartment, thirty innocent people killed and my team guys below.'

He choked with emotion. Cheena turned and fiddled with the bubble equipment.

'It wasn't your fault, Mike,' Lock said.

'Wasn't it? I didn't have to live there among civilians. I could've protected the apartment better.'

'Sir, should I remove the bubble now?' Cheena asked. Northwood didn't appear to hear her.

'What hurts is being the target and others suffering because of it. We think one of my guards was working for the Decons. It explains how they got so close, though he couldn't have expected to be one of the victims.'

'Sir, the bubble,' Cheena said, anxious to get Northwood off the subject of the bombing. Northwood turned, taking a few seconds to register her presence.

'Yeah, take it down. And there's one other thing, Lock. The loan comes with a price.'

'Which is?'

'You share any info if you get close to the source of AH-4.'

'That's fine,' Lock said. He tucked the shirt in the kit bag and took his leave.

CHAPTER 12

The following morning – the day before the planned assault – Lock paid a visit to Bogota. The British Embassy, a square building resembling an upmarket mausoleum, sat among its low-rise neighbours near the financial district. A swathe of dusty barrios, laid out in a uniform grid pattern with no sign of trees or greenery to make life in them more pleasant, separated the British Embassy from its American cousin. The US Embassy sprawled near lush parks, its modern buildings set in sculpted grounds with a roof helipad in one section and a small runway nearby for light planes. It broadcast an air of overt power.

By comparison, the British Embassy was discreet, but it disguised an important presence in the politics of Colombia. Nobody except local intelligence agencies recognised the comings and goings around the entrance as anything other than tourists getting visas or businessmen making links, or staff going out for lunch. Those who did keep an eye on the place might have spotted British Special Forces among the visitors. Most Colombians were not aware of their existence let alone what they did in terms of reconnaissance and intelligence-gathering.

Lock didn't enter at the front. He Shifted straight into a teleporter-designated room on the eighth floor, in which desks and computers gave the impression of an office with a clear space in the middle. Armed guards from the security detail met him. He looked nothing like the photo in his passport and the guards held him at gunpoint while they checked DNA, retinal scans and fingerprints. They were equally thorough with his bergen. One of the guards radioed the all-clear and Stringer breezed into the room. He stopped short and burst out laughing when he saw Lock.

'Good grief. If that's how you're going to look when you're older I'd seriously think about some plastic surgery now.'

Lock passed a hand over the flaccid flesh on his face.

'I might keep it this way. It makes me look distinguished, like part of the Establishment.'

'It won't be a step up the ladder, not when you look about eighty.' Stringer chuckled and led the way out of the room. 'Are you sure you can manage to walk downstairs? Maybe I should open the door for you.'

Lock bent his knees, placed a hand on the small of his back and wobbled to the hallway.

'Now you mention it, maybe you can find me a walking frame.'

The Embassy had turned the basement into a bunker resembling a shabby version of the Cobra room under Whitehall. It had blank white walls and the table had no built-in microphones or computer consoles, or plush leather chairs around it. Four video conferencing screens hung on one wall, and two computer consoles with multiple screens sat on one side of a round wooden table. The bunker didn't look like a state-of-the-art war room. The bareness gave no hint that the walls, floor and ceiling were two metres thick, reinforced with steel and lined with copper mesh to deter radio signals. It was fitted with banks of equipment that made it impossible for electronic spyware to eavesdrop.

Stringer sat down and asked Lock about his temporary blindness, as if establishing a serious tone in which he could lay down the law. He didn't wait for Lock to finish his answer before launching into a speech about how Lock had to stay within his remit and not interfere with Bilton's decisions. Wrong-footed by Stringer's initial friendly greeting, Lock replied less forcefully than intended, restating his view that allowing a man to be tortured to death was very un-British. Stringer interrupted to ask if Lock knew Nightingale betrayed Mosquera's deal to Patuazon and indirectly caused the death of Snapper. He nearly got Bilton and Jimmy Mackenzie killed. How did Lock feel knowing he saved the life of somebody who did that? It would have been better not to interfere in something he didn't know anything about.

Lock said regardless of the circumstances he would do the same, and if Stringer had seen the state of Nightingale he would have rescued him too, had it been in his power. Hmm, replied Stringer, and neither agreed nor disagreed. The realisation that Stringer wouldn't have saved Nightingale disturbed Lock.

'Under all the rules and morals Westerners are supposed to abide by, we should not condone torture, even if it only involves us indirectly and even if it's being done to an enemy,' Lock said.

'Where is Nightingale now?' Stringer put the question mildly, as though the answer had no importance for him. Lock hesitated.

'He's in a safe place.' Stringer fixed him with a cold eye as Lock continued, 'He doesn't have the money. He doesn't know where it is. Mosquera set up the deal and didn't tell Nightingale anything.'

'I know.'

'And Nightingale's motive for betraying his brother wasn't about money, it was anger and revenge. Mosquera undermined Nightingale and a business venture went wrong. Nightingale and his family suffered, despite the fact he's Mosquera's brother. They beat him up over it and threatened them.'

'And you believe all this?' Stringer tapped on his computer keyboard.

'Is this conversation being recorded?'

Stringer stopped, piqued.

'No. I'm just making some notes.' When Lock didn't object he continued typing. Lock paused, eyeing his cousin. He wondered if he knew Stringer at all.

'Do you believe Nightingale?' Stringer asked.

'Yes, I believe him. He doesn't know who is behind the shipments of Starbirth. The way it works is that Mosquera sends out packages of cocaine to a rendezvous point using a teleporter. He gets a smaller amount of Starbirth in exchange. It confirms what we thought about him using Shifters. That's why we can't follow the supply of AH-4 back to the source. Mosquera needs teleporters. He lost his best Shifters during the botched deal here in Bogota. Why didn't you tell me about that deal, Steven? Don't you think I should be told more about what's going on if you want me to act effectively?'

Stringer didn't break mental stride as he outlined the reasons why Lock hadn't been told, and yes, he realised the implications for the safety of Lock and the SAS team, but considering Lock's closeness to Patuazon, and the need for Lock to act naturally, he thought it best to keep it from him. Lock interrupted, cut to the quick by the implication that he couldn't handle keeping a secret. He could have helped with the deal, he said. Stringer dismissed it.

'And Patuazon would notice your absence, there would have been reports of your activities in a fight and your position at his estate would have been compromised.'

'You didn't trust me.'

Stringer snorted.

'Come on, Lock, don't pretend to be that naïve. Trust didn't come into it. We made the decision based on the situation at the time – but if we're talking trust, you're not giving people reason to trust you. Look at what you've done. You've flouted agreements concerning your friendship with Mike Northwood and taken matters into your own hands regarding Nightingale. Surely you must see that, in today's climate, people are going to regard you as a loose cannon and therefore dangerous?'

He leaned forward, rested his forearms on the table and continued,

'Circumstances have changed since Starbirth. A lot of people are scared out of their wits and they're inclined towards knee-jerk reactions. Don't give them the opportunity to react like that. You have powerful friends, including some in the SIS, but if you carry on disregarding orders you'll lose them.'

'They gave me the flexibility to act on my own, as I see fit.'

'Times have changed. You have to adapt to the new rules.'

'And give up what I fought for? It took years to gain the kind of freedom I have. I'm not giving it up.'

Stringer spoke quietly but determinedly.

'Think about the alternatives. You have a good situation in England. You have employment doing a job you like. Your home is protected by the latest equipment and you have professional staff, people you can call on twenty-four-seven if there's a problem. It's all free and comes with the territory. Now think how it would be without that. You'll be dropped as leader of the new team of enhanced-ability operatives, and that's only the beginning. There'll be no more work with Special Forces. You would have reduced protection for your family and you can't be there every minute of the day to keep them safe from other teleporters. Even if you did get lucrative work, a great deal of your money would have to go on protecting Lianne and Thomas. If you decide to move to another country who would take you in if they think you're a rogue operative? Lianne wouldn't like living anywhere else, or moving from place to place.'

'She might.'

'I think you know she wouldn't. You have enemies, Lock. Over the years you can't help but create enemies due to your line of work, and some of them would have no hesitation in hunting you down, or your family, regardless of where you live. Being with us and the Regiment may not always be the ideal you would like, but in terms of countering threats it doesn't get much better than this. You'll lose that vital network. You won't have the edge in intelligence.'

Lock didn't need to be reminded of his position and vulnerabilities, but somebody else giving voice to his fears made them concrete, as real as the building he and Stringer sat in. He met Stringer's gaze while considering the other man's motives for applying pressure.

'I could always find a job in something else. There would be plenty of opportunities.'

'You tried doing other jobs. It didn't work, remember? You didn't like having to hide who you are and not using your abilities. It's not you. You have skills that need an outlet and you're using them in the right way. It's just the question of security regarding Northwood and your actions.'

'Look, I do understand all that, about security. And I'm aware, more than you think, of what I could lose, but it's a mistake to stop the meetings with Northwood. He's provided good intel over a number of years, and we've worked well together. You said yourself, it was good for US-UK relationships. So I don't see the need for changes.'

'Because we're at war. They're at war. In war, even friends come under suspicion, not necessarily because they would turn hostile, but because you don't know how good they are at keeping safe the important info you tell them. Don't you see, it's not about you – it's Northwood. That's who they're worried about. They're worried he'll tell you something he shouldn't. Didn't you say you thought he was developing a drink problem? So how far do you think they'll trust somebody who can't hold his liquor? Every time you turn up unannounced at his place, or even when it's arranged, somebody over there gets closer to a nervous breakdown.'

Nobody else but Northwood understood the opposite poles of experience in being a teleporter, the lows as well as the highs, the alienation from every other society and culture in the world as well as the thrill of what they could do. They shared the exhilaration of leaving everything behind in an instant, the amazing opportunities to travel the globe, and the guilt at not being able to fix every problem they saw. It had always been a bond of 'them and us,' two boys and the rest of the world, a shared heritage that lasted into adulthood. When Stringer put the case for lack of contact with Northwood it felt like the equivalent of Stringer cutting off an arm. Not only that, the friendship symbolised the front line regarding the freedom Lock didn't want to lose.

Stringer continued,

'I know this friendship is important to you, but the consequences are too high a price to pay.'

'Mike's the only person in the world who really understands what it's like. He's been there for me since we were kids, he's like a brother to me.'

'And your family? What about us?'

Lock felt trapped, consigned like a condemned man to the ordinary. He recognised the truth in Stringer's words and the truth hurt.

'You have to consider what you really want, Lock. Sometimes you have to let go of the past, even if it's painful. You have to see it from their point of view. In intelligence terms, there are no friends,' Stringer said as if he had read Lock's mind. He prodded, 'You have a wife and son, who need you. You're young, even if you don't look young right now. There's a whole world of opportunity opening up. There's the chance of a team of people like yourself, and be in no doubt, they'll need you too. They'll need your experience.'

'Until you replace me, first chance you get.'

Stringer shook his head.

'That's just you being cynical because you're hurting. Why get rid of somebody who is years ahead of everybody else? As far as I'm aware, nobody with enhanced abilities has your neuro-sensory skill in detecting people. There are lots of teleporters, but no other neuro-sensor. That's a gift. Use it wisely and that alone will keep you at the top.'

'So what do people at home want from me? I suppose they'll want a tracker implant next.'

'It's not such a big deal. All employees in sensitive positions have to have an ID implant, including me. It's a quick procedure and the implant is tiny and injectable.'

'It's not the procedure that bothers me.'

'I know. You're looking at it as a loss of freedom. So did I. But there are advantages to be considered, your safety being one of them. I know what you're going to say and I accept there's a small risk of the implant being used against you, but it's a very small risk.'

'I wouldn't trust the MoD with details of my favourite snack, let alone something like access to an implant. Look at how much sensitive information they left lying around on trains and in taxis.'

'Then let us do it. We're much better at keeping secrets. The greatest benefit to you is that if you're pursuing Shifters into sensitive buildings, the implant will identify you as a friend. With the technology being developed, believe me, that's going to make the difference between life and death.'

'What do you mean?'

Stringer paused, looking down at his computer, as if weighing up whether or not to reveal what was on his mind.

'There is a new laser system put in place in sensitive buildings. It uses lethal force against terrorist teleporters.'

Lock was aghast.

'But they already have neural nets that paralyse. People like Patuazon use killer nets. The British government doesn't have to use lethal force.'

'Let's just say you were lucky.' Stringer switched off his laptop. 'Let's get out of here. It's making me claustrophobic.'

Three days before Christmas, Bogota was heaving. Tree-lined roads were swollen with vehicles full of Christmas shoppers and office workers heading for the centre. Unseen, Lock and Stringer rose from the Embassy roof into hazy morning heat and a clear sky against which the mountains stood rigid and ancient, their hard-edged, tough peaks undisturbed by the ant-like bustling of the city at their feet.

They landed in a secluded place in a wooded park a couple of kilometres from the Embassy, where Lock had stashed the Demon weapon and the spare PixelRain suit. He had put them under a camouflage cover and installed a sonic disruptor to deter curious dogs. The scent of orange blossom wafted from a grove of ornamental trees, borne on a warm breeze. They were alone aside from birds flitting away at their arrival. Sunlight filtered through branches and where it touched the soft, woody ground, newly-minted seedlings pushed past brown leaves into the sunshine.

Lock's spirits rose with the sun. He pulled out the suit.

'I wouldn't have been able to give you this if it hadn't been for Mike,' he pointed out, but Stringer showed more interest in the Demon. He handled the weapon with undisguised elation before putting it back in its holdall.

'Good,' he said, though he didn't elaborate on what was good about it. 'Drop me off close to the American Embassy and take the suit back to ours. Think about what we discussed. Work on resolving your differences with Bilton.'

'He's making decisions that place a lot of people in unnecessary danger.'

'But they're his decisions to make.'

Stringer paused.

'You wanted to be privy to more intel, so let me tell you something about Bilton, just between us. Four months ago his younger sister died during a trip to New York, caught in a store robbery. The guy who shot her was a teleporter, so you can imagine how Bilton feels. She came from a close-knit family and he was very protective of her. Cut him some slack – back off for a while, give him time to get over it and get used to who you are.'

Lock felt resentful hearing that. He didn't want to be under obligation to feel sympathy for Bilton, and he didn't welcome news that Bilton nursed a grudge against teleporters.

'Where did you say Nightingale is?' Stringer asked.

'I didn't.'

'Let me have his location. He'll need protection, he knows too much.' Stringer took out his mobile phone. Lock's hesitation encompassed a whole range of thoughts and emotions, centred on Stringer's willingness to let Nightingale die.

'You're going to kill him.'

Stringer raised his eyebrows and studied Lock.

'Of course not. If I wanted him dead I'd just leave him in whichever hospital I assume he's in and let Mosquera or Patuazon do the job. We need to speak to him. He's not as ignorant as he claimed. Why are you bothered about a man who betrayed and endangered some of our lads? I can find out in other ways, but it would be quicker and easier if you just showed me on the map.' He held out his phone so Lock could see the map of Colombia on the screen.

Lock hesitated, but he made his decision, took the phone, zoomed in on Bogota and the hospital and handed it back.

'There. On the junction of those two roads.'

'Believe me, Lock, I'm not out to murder anybody.'

Lock didn't respond. They hardly spoke after that. The implication of their short exchange about Nightingale was not lost on either of them. Lock's level of trust in Stringer had declined and when they parted company near the American Embassy Lock had indigestion that didn't arise from what he'd eaten for breakfast. On the way back to the training camp he realised he'd forgotten to tell Stringer about the new aura, but it never occurred to him that he'd subconsciously blocked it because he didn't want to tell Stringer at all.

~~~~~~~~

Late that evening the demolitions team left for Mosquera's villa to put the first part of the assault plan in action. Jimmy sweated buckets inside his new PixelRain suit, which covered him from head to toe and included hood, face veil, poncho and coverings for boots and his weapon. It might be good at camouflaging people but it didn't allow sweat to evaporate. It made him itch. He couldn't see PC or Vicar, or even Harford crouching next to him, unless they activated built-in identification armbands on their left sleeves. The demolitions team waited for rain, which would increase the PixelRain's capability to disguise them once they entered Mosquera's compound. The suits wouldn't have to work so hard to compensate for differences of environment between back and front.

They waited near the perimeter fence for Harford to test the way in first, but nobody complained. Waiting played a vital role in getting it right. The SAS were well-trained in getting things right and not taking a step too soon. Most activity involved long hours of surveillance or reconnaissance in hostile territory. Years of gruelling training and combat missions prepared Jimmy for moments like this. The discomfort, and ignoring insects that found their way inside his poncho, paled into insignificance. He enjoyed knowing he had the ability, even without a pixelated camouflage suit, to be so close to an enemy he could reach out and touch him without the guy knowing he was there. One minute alive, the next minute dead. He had no fear of killing the bad guys, only fear of being killed – or worse, maimed for life. He felt exhilarated.

Parts of the compound were lit up. People wandered between the service areas and main wings of the villa where Mosquera and his family had their quarters. Guards stood in place on the watchtowers. Through the eyes of the night vision scope on his Diemaco Jimmy saw a watchtower guard yawn, lean back on his heels and stretch his arms. A General Purpose Machine Gun, a fearsome weapon whose rounds were the sort Harford had said would damage the suits or penetrate them, sat unattended in front of the guard. The man wasn't switched on. None of the guards were professionally alert. They looked unconcerned about the possibility of an infiltration or attack in the evening, as if it wouldn't happen because everybody was still up.

A drop of rain bounced off a leaf in front of Jimmy, joined by others until they beat like a snare drum on foliage around him and washed over the black surface of the river in rippling sheets. At last they had a downpour.

'Zero, all stations, acquire targets. Acknowledge,' Harford's voice said in Jimmy's left ear through his in-the-mouth receiver.

Jimmy already had the guard's head in the crosshairs of his night vision scope. He pressed a button near the trigger on the Diemaco to send a silent
~~~~~~~~

radio message indicating he was ready to cover for Harford in case the test went wrong. He waited.

'Zero, all stations, I'm going in now.'

Jimmy had the scope clock in the corner of his peripheral vision. The guard leaned forward to take out a cigarette and light it. Jimmy's crosshairs followed. His finger sat on the trigger and he waited. At one minute fifty seconds Harford returned and said,

'Zero, all stations, breach undetected. Take up landing positions. Moving to first target.'

By the time Harford repeated the message, Jimmy slid the barrel of his weapon back from behind a plant and adopted the stance of somebody landing from a parachute drop, knees bent, weapon into his shoulder. Harford said, 'Stand by,' and then, 'Go'. The compound wavered, faded and Jimmy stood inside the grounds facing a couple of armed guards less than fifteen metres away. His heart leapfrogged and he froze, every nerve screaming at him to pull the trigger. They were bound to see him at that range. They didn't. They carried on chatting and laughing and getting wet as they moved. Jimmy's crosshairs followed them while Harford disabled the electronic alarm system on the armoury – their first target – designated Tango One.

'Moving inside Tango One,' Harford said.

Inside the windowless, warehouse storage building they stood still for ten seconds, waiting for the sound of an alarm, or shouts, or the approach of heavy feet. Nothing happened. Nothing moved from behind shelves groaning with light weaponry and mortar shells, or from the heavier weapons piled against a long wall.

'All clear. Activate armbands,' Harford whispered. He was their eyes and ears from inside the hut, standing still, hood down around his shoulders. Jimmy lowered his weapon and squeezed his left sleeve three times to activate the armband material. It glowed a dull blue. He switched on the green low-light torch on his headband, removed packages of plastic explosive from his bergen, set radio controlled detonators and hid the packages among crates of ammunition. PC did the same on the other side of the warehouse. They finished and looked for the Demon weapons. Each one had an individual box, and Jimmy pulled a Demon out to disable it by removing the firing pin.

During the short time he handled it his expert eye noted details. It came from the same batch as the one he touched when Harford passed it round at the training camp. The sleek, composite material of the shoulder-fired rifle weighed lighter than his Diemaco but the magazine of ampoules was heavy. The user would have to compensate his aim for the extra weight when they fired the weapon. An inexperienced person might be wide of his mark, although given the target-acquiring nature of the darts it wouldn't make much difference. The thick weapon barrel resembled an underslung grenade launcher. He measured the diameter as the width of two of his fingers. He had wide, stubby fingers, so it made the barrel very wide. The box included a laser sight and the weapon had computer controls near the breech mechanism. The trigger had three settings – safety on and off, single shot and double tap.

'Three of the Demons are missing,' PC whispered as they finished removing firing pins from the six they found.

'Search again. Make it fast,' Harford said. Jimmy glanced at Harford's disembodied head, finding it strange to see his face transformed into an old man. The team scrambled among mortar rounds, Rocket Propelled Grenade launchers, boxes of ammunition, M-16s and AK47s until Harford called a halt. Jimmy thought it likely the missing Demon weapons had been taken by the Lanceros and were in the guards' billets, or in the villa. It wasn't good news. Though the Lanceros were not as highly-trained or disciplined as the SAS they ranked as the equivalent of Tier Two US Special Forces, which made them extremely dangerous even without Demon weapons in their hands.

'Close up. Deactivate armbands. Moving to Tango Two.' Harford pulled his hood and face veil over his head.

The next targets were the control centre relays for the anti-teleporter system, poles that resembled flagpoles. Set in a rectangle around the villa, they were the most exposed and dangerous targets to get at. Jimmy guessed Harford and PC were working according to plan, since he couldn't see either of them. Harford took PC up and held them in mid-air at the top of each pole while PC attached small packets of plastic explosive just under the antennae.

It took nerves of steel for Jimmy to crouch in the rain, by a wall, in full view of guards in the bell domes, trusting that his new suit would camouflage him. He heard a noise. A woman appeared from one of the doors. He stayed as still as a statue. She hummed to herself as she walked briskly towards him. She would bump into him. He had to move. He stood up and flattened his back against the wall, his heart thumping. She didn't miss a step and passed by less than two metres away without seeing the weapon barrel pointing straight at her from under a fold of the poncho. Jimmy exhaled slowly. The PixelRain kit was good.

Harford and PC finished and the four men split up for the next targets. Harford and PC went to deal with Mosquera's three helicopters by fixing explosives in the tail rotors. Jimmy and Vicar ran forward to Tango Three, the guards' billets, to conceal explosive packages under the eaves by the window frames. When they finished, Jimmy sent a radio bleep to Harford to let him know.

'Zero, acknowledged,' Harford said. 'All stations move to Tango Five.'

Jimmy and Vicar moved to the left-hand side of the U-shaped villa before going six hundred metres across the compound to the boathouse near the perimeter fence. Outside it, Jimmy kept watch with Harford while PC and Vicar set charges on the boats. The rain shower eased off.

The team split into pairs to deal with two watchtowers apiece. Jimmy and Vicar went for Tango Seven, the one closest to the boathouse. Vicar laid explosives by the feet of the watchtower. The guard didn't react. When Vicar finished Jimmy sent a silent signal to Harford, indicating their move to the next watchtower.

'Zero, all stations, go firm, go firm, go firm,' Harford hissed. Jimmy and Vicar didn't move. Jimmy couldn't see any threat. 'Dog approaching, one hundred metres from Green. Stay firm.'

Jimmy peered at a ridge line. A dog shot into view over the rise in front of him, less than thirty metres away.

'Stay firm, stay firm,' Harford said. 'We've got you covered.'

Jimmy didn't find that thought comforting, given what he knew about Harford's skill with weapons. He hoped PC did the covering for him. The dog kept on coming, stopping every now and then to prowl over the ground, sniffing. Jimmy couldn't see any human patrol behind it and the dog didn't look like a guard dog, more like somebody's pet. It stopped sniffing and bounded towards them from about ten metres away, white patches on its fur standing out as brilliant flashes against the ground in the night vision light. It caught their scent and stopped four metres away, pacing and looking in their direction. The dog couldn't see them, but it knew something was there in the darkness.

'Stay firm, stay firm,' Harford whispered. Jimmy had the dog in his sights.

The dog's ears pricked up. It turned its head to listen and raced away. Just when Jimmy thought the danger had passed, Vicar slipped on some mud. Jimmy heard him fall over. So did the dog. It halted and turned, barking furiously. A watchtower searchlight switched on at Tango Eight above the heads of Jimmy and Vicar. Another one lit up at Tango Seven behind them. Sharp beams of light raked the scrubland between the towers, sweeping over the dog. Harford told them not to move.

Jimmy watched the animal getting closer and trained his weapon on the searchlight at Tango Eight. His throat tensed. The beam was coming dangerously near – and so was the dog. Blinded by the searchlight, it stopped barking, sniffed the ground less than four metres away, raised its head and barked louder. The guard at Tango Eight shouted and something metallic hit the ground near the dog with a tinny crash, frightening it into running away. The guard yelled again then laughed. The searchlight switched off, and so did the one from Tango Seven.

'Stay firm, approaching you for evac,' Harford said.

A short ride later, the demolitions team tumbled into all-round defence in a clearing a minute away, waiting for Harford to give the all-clear. They were on a grassy knoll overlooking a big town, judging by lights on a hill opposite and in the valley. They moved into shadow, removing their hoods so they could see each other.

'Vicar, Jimmy, on stag,' Harford ordered. PC had an urgent conversation with Harford about the feasibility of going back. They decided against it because of the dog on the loose.

'The helos will have to take out the remaining two watchtowers. We'll go for the cocaine lab now,' Harford said. 'We've still got hours before first light.'

Something flailed in the foliage close by Jimmy. He saw a man wearing night vision goggles stumble forward in long grass and spotted the sharp outline of a weapon in the man's hands. The newcomer raised his weapon. Jimmy threw out his arm, pushed Harford aside, screamed, 'Contact!' and fired, all in the space of a second.

The man fell backwards into the grass. The crack of weapons fire reverberated off the hills. Vicar leapt forward to cover the fallen man, kicking his weapon away. Jimmy and PC took up defensive positions with Harford. Jimmy scanned his arc of responsibility, expecting more men.

'All clear,' Harford whispered. 'Must've been a Shifter. He wasn't here when we landed.'

'He's dead,' Vicar said.

'Search him for ID.' Harford waited, going into his listening pose.

'There's nothing on him.'

'I want a look at him.'

Harford squatted by the dead man, examining him with a low-light torch.

'We should get the hell out of here before any more turn up,' PC said.

'Take him with us?' Vicar asked, pointing at the dead man with the barrel of his weapon.

'Leave him,' Harford said as he straightened up. 'He might have a transmitter implant. We should get out of this PixelRain kit in case it's got trackers embedded in it.'

'If there'd been anything in the clothes we'd have known,' PC countered.

'Unless it's newer technology than ours. It came from the States. Somebody could've put something in it.'

'You think he was tracking us?'

'I don't know.' Harford sounded shaky, rattled by the contact. He took out a camera and a torch. 'I'm going to take some photos. Jimmy, cover me.'

Jimmy peered at the dead man as he took up a position by Harford. The man looked about thirty and was too fleshed-out to be a Starbirth addict. He was of Western appearance, carrying an AK47, and dressed in dark jeans and camouflage shirt. Not an average Colombian.

'We could set a booby trap if you think we're being followed,' Jimmy suggested. Harford finished taking photos.

'No. We're too close to the town. He might be found by some kids or a farmer. There's no point in going to the cocaine lab now in case he was following us. We'll Shift to another spot and change out of the PixelRain kit just in case.'

Back at the training camp the discussion between Harford and Bilton turned into a Chinese Parliament with everybody involved. Harford thought the teleporter had shadowed them. He might have compromised the assault plan and the team didn't know who he was working for, what he saw, or who he told. Harford thought it might be the same Shifter, one of a pair who landed near him two days earlier.

'Might be,' Bilton interrupted. 'You're not sure?'

'No, I'm not sure, but it seems like more than coincidence.'

Bilton made his points as if talking to a wayward child. The two events could not be linked and the fact they occurred near a city and a town increased the likelihood of a chance encounter, and there were other factors. He pointed out Harford's face had been changed between the first encounter and the second. If anybody was following him they would have to know about that and it was unlikely, especially since only Northwood and his colleague knew about it, besides the troopers. Teleporters couldn't be tracked unless they had an electronic transmitter on them. Harford interrupted.

'Yes, but who knows what abilities people are developing.'

Bilton continued as if Harford hadn't spoken.

'The first man was unarmed. The second was armed with an AK47, a weapon you can find anywhere in most parts of the world, Colombia included. Surveillance on Mosquera's villa doesn't indicate any panic or preparation for an assault. Everything has settled down following the explosion in the unfinished wing. If you have nothing more to go on than a gut feeling, it isn't a good enough reason to affect the assault plan which is only hours away. The guys need to rest, not get involved in a last-minute argument.'

Bilton put it to a vote and the rest of the team wanted to go ahead with the assault. Even Jimmy thought it should go ahead as planned. Despite their decision, the men took extra security precautions. Harford picked up a large, empty bag and said he would retrieve the suits so the lads could use them, if the suits didn't have any trackers on them. And if he did find trackers, maybe Bilton would change his mind.

~~~~~~~~

At the place where he stashed the PixelRain kit, Lock called Northwood on the Secure Link line. He listened very carefully to Northwood's tone of voice when he replied to the query about whether the package could have been bugged with tracking devices.

'No way, man. It was brand new. That came straight from the manufacturers and nobody would have had a chance – you know what I'm saying? Between the package being made and you acquiring it, no chance.'

Northwood hinted that he had stolen the suits but didn't want to say so openly. Lock had his suspicions about how secure the Secure Link was.

'There's nothing fitted as routine by our less friendly acquaintances?' Lock asked, using code for the Decons.

'I can't say for sure, you know? But it's unlikely. How would they know in advance which package was going where? I don't think it's an issue. But if you think there's a problem, my advice is, don't use the package.'

'Okay. Yeah, okay. Thanks, Mike.'

'Sure. You stay safe now, hear?'

'Yeah. See you.'

Lock looked at the bag of PixelRain suits at his feet. He hadn't found any trackers. The suits would be invaluable for the lads during the assault. He mulled it over and decided Northwood was right, the scenario of the suits being fitted with new technology didn't add up. The motives were wrong. He doubted Northwood would have done it, he didn't need to. If Northwood wanted to find out what was going on, he'd use drones, satellites, or any item from a vast store of US military technology.

Lock levi-flew to the body. Switching on his low-light torch he knelt, took out a sensor and scanned it for tracking devices. He recoiled in shock when he found one. It was located at the back of the man's head. Lock went into sensory mode, detecting nothing, but a body with a transmitter meant somebody would be picking up signals on a receiver. He was about to retreat to consider his next move when something about the man's face made him stop. The flesh looked odd, as though it was melting away from the bone structure underneath. It wasn't natural. He recalled what Cheena had said about the change in his own face when the alteration wore off and how it would be inflamed and swollen. His knees went weak. The man's face had been altered. Lock knew only one person who could do that. Cheena. He might be looking at one of the Eagles, a member of Northwood's crew.

The hairs on the back of his neck prickled. He was being watched. He spun round but saw no human auras, only wild pigs and small carnivores some way off. The tall, dark grasses crowded in on him like hostile witnesses. He subdued his nerves and began the grim task of taking DNA,
~~~~~~~~

which had to be done if he wanted London to identify the body. That done, he took a look at the dead man, hoping he and the demolitions team were not responsible for the death of one of Northwood's colleagues.

CHAPTER 13

During his time as a medic Jimmy had been called upon to treat many ailments, from snake bites and gunshot wounds to migraines and ingrown toenails. His current task, just before first light on the day of the assault, presented a more unusual problem.

'You'll have to spread 'em more, mate, and relax your muscles. Mick, hold the light closer. Relax, I said.'

'I'd like to see you fucking relax,' Nails said.

'It'll hurt more if you don't.' Jimmy pulled on latex gloves.

'Oh, great.'

Mick's grin widened as he said in his Tyneside twang,

'If you don't relax he won't be able to pull the bugger out.'

'Stop winding me up, wanker. There's no damn wotsit up there.'

'Candiru acu,' Mick said.

'Kangaroo what?'

'Not kangaroo, muppet. Can-de-roo ass-oo. Parasite fish.'

'Great, a kangaroo with a cold. Oh, for fuck's sake. What're you doing, digging your way to Australia? Mick, stop laughing, you cunt.'

Jimmy looked up.

'Hold the light still, Mick.' His finger touched a bulging mass, an abscess. 'Yep, I can feel its tail.' He winked at Mick, who smothered a laugh. Jimmy finished his examination and reached for his medical kit.

'Is it out?' Nails said, looking over his shoulder.

'Not yet. You have to keep still; this is going to hurt a bit.'

'Going to? What d'you mean, going to? I've got tears in me eyes already.'

'Stop being such a wimp.' Jimmy put a retractable lancet and a syringe on a piece of sterile paper. 'It'll be very quick. Think how much better you'll feel afterwards.'

'It's not the afterwards that bothers me, it's the before. What happens if it doesn't want to come out?'

Mick chipped in, interrupting Jimmy's reply.

'It'll eat its way up to your liver. That's what they do. I told you not to sit in that pool. Did you listen to me, you know-it-all Southerner? Did you fuck. Just be grateful it didn't go up your dick. They follow the scent of urine. You must've been pissing out your arse.'

Nails collapsed forward over the table, holding his head in his hands and groaning as Jimmy got the lancet in place. Mick nearly doubled up guffawing and the light wobbled. Jimmy kept his face deadpan and concentrated, sympathetic considering the site of the abscess.

'Hold that light still. Nearly done, mate.' He opened the lancet and pushed the blade hard into the obstruction.

Nails was still cursing when PC stuck his head round the door.

'Boss wants to know what's going on.'

'Fucking murdering me,' Nails said.

'Nails is having medical treatment.' Jimmy squirted antibiotic solution into the affected area to wash it out. PC relayed the information and listened.

'He wants to know if Nails is okay to take part in the assault.'

'Yeah, he'll be fine.'

Nails looked round over his shoulder.

'Course I'll be able to. How about some privacy here. I've got everybody in the bloody camp having a look up my arse.'

'Drama queen,' Mick said.

'You just wait, you bastard.'

A couple of minutes later Jimmy dispensed some antibiotic tablets and reassured Nails that the fish was well and truly gone before telling him it hadn't existed in the first place. He made a quick getaway from Nails' boot.

Bilton informed them by radio that Patuazon intended visiting at first light. Jimmy dismissed Nails.

'Walk around for five minutes, let the infection drain.' He checked his watch. 'You've got forty minutes to get to the tunnel.'

'I'd rather go in by chopper. It's better than going with Lewis.'

Jimmy grinned.

'Too late. It's the Puke Express or you walk. You soft Londoners, you don't know when you're well off. You don't even have to sit on your sore arse to get there. Forward Air Controller? Bloody doddle. All you have to do is lie down and tell the choppers and mortar team where to fire.'

Nails picked up his kit, gave Jimmy a good-natured one-finger salute and limped off as if he still had the lancet inside him.

Jimmy turned his attention to his own body. A bull leech, a large creature with a white stripe, had attached itself to the inside of his left thigh. Leeches often went undetected until they grew larger, but Jimmy had been aware of the bull leech. They used a natural anaesthetic when they attached themselves to their hosts and an anticoagulant in their saliva to keep the blood flowing. Jimmy lit a cigarette and applied the burning end to the back of the leech. It bucked, let go of his leg and fell on the floor, where Jimmy had the satisfaction of crushing it with the heel of his boot.

He dosed the wound with enhanced healing factor to stop the copious bleeding, put a clean dressing on the red patch left behind and pulled his fatigues back on, scrutinising a scale model of Mosquera's villa and photos of the buildings. The mission had new emphasis with the discovery of the Demons. It wasn't Patuazon attacking Mosquera, but a search-and-destroy operation to eliminate the Demons and find out how Mosquera obtained them.

The Colombian government turned a blind eye to the operation. Allowing Patuazon to mount the assault meant the government reaped the benefit of removing Mosquera while having plausible deniability. If the raid went wrong they didn't know anything about it and the assault forces were nothing to do with them.

For ease of reference the U-shaped villa had been colour coded into four areas – Black, White, Red and Blue. The back of the villa, gutted by fire, was coded Black. The front, the glamorous, but tacky, section with fake Doric columns and an inappropriate grand entrance, was coded White. On the right side of the U, Red wing housed the extended family's main living quarters. Blue wing on the left hand side contained the meeting room where Mosquera and his men would gather, and it was the assault team's priority. They had eight high-value targets to capture in Blue wing, including Mosquera and his inner circle.

Bilton gave the six helicopters the code name of Kilo. Each fire team had a code name using the military phonetic alphabet from Alpha to Delta. Jimmy led the fire team called Bravo Three. If rehearsals were anything to go by, Jimmy's fire team would be first on the ground. During the short time Jimmy worked with the seven Colombians in his fire team, they'd bonded as well as could be expected. The Colombians comprised the usual mix of mercenaries found in private armies, motivated by money rather than any high-flown idealism. Most of them were combat-hardened ex-military, or ex-members of gangs who tended to be over-confident, morally deficient and tactically nowhere near as good as the SAS. Only the Lanceros came close to being professional, once they had been knocked into shape. Each of the four fire teams taking part in the villa assault contained two Lanceros. Jimmy had no problem with the two attached to his team. They followed orders well, learned fast, did their best and weren't lippy.

Bilton's team contained one of the more unpredictable Lanceros, a small man named Gonz. He had an inferiority complex that was mostly under control, but it could take over in attempts at proving himself tougher, faster and more ferocious. He was bad at judging when his attitude turned into recklessness. If it had been up to Jimmy he would have put Gonz in a less prominent position, but it wasn't his decision. Bilton thought training had curbed Gonz's tendencies though nobody could predict how a man would react when live rounds whistled past his head.

Bilton decided not to tell them about the Demon weapons, because of not knowing how the Colombians would respond. If they knew about the weapons a third of them might pack their kit and leave. The figure would be likely to increase to three-quarters if they found out the nanomaterials mutated like real viruses, rendering any antidote ineffective. Even the Regiment troopers were daunted when Bilton told them the nanomaterials withstood extremes of heat and cold, which meant they would not deteriorate in storage or transportation. Each man dealt with the threat by thinking that if the darts hit somebody, it wouldn't be him. Anybody caught carrying a Demon would meet his Armageddon. There wouldn't be any notion of taking the man prisoner.

Bilton decided not to use the new pixelated suits for the assault. Nails took one for his undercover role in the tropical jungle as Forward Air Controller, which left three suits among thirty-two men. Bilton said it set the wearers apart from the rest of the men and thought it would lead to dissension among the Colombians about the British soldiers being better protected than they were. Resentment could lead to under-performance or even desertion. Mick and Jimmy tried wearing the new suits under their ordinary fatigues for extra protection, but the bulk was too cumbersome and hot so they abandoned the idea.

Just after first light, at ten past six, the sensor equipment on the table bleeped. The screens showed the approach of two helicopters, which the equipment identified as Patuazon's choppers. PC keyed in an acknowledgement and the lights went back to green.

'Guess we'll go out to meet and greet,' PC said, putting his Sig Sauer back in place on his thigh. 'Jimmy, stay here on stag.'

Jimmy nodded as the helicopters roared in from around the hillside. PC and the other men left the hut and Fred the lizard rushed for cover in a crack near the window. The first chopper landed and the rotor blades whined down. Jimmy closed the hut door and watched the sensor and camera input on the laptop screen. The usual entourage of bodyguards landed in the first chopper. They jumped down first and made sure everything was safe before the second chopper landed. Patuazon got out with his granddaughter Rosi and the woman Maria, who was the teenager's chaperone and bodyguard. Maria was armed with an M-16 assault rifle and a pistol in a thigh holster.

Patuazon used Rosi's presence as a statement of intent, a signal that he came in peace. If he arrived alone, it was a heads-up. Sixteen-year-old Rosi enjoyed trips to the camp because she was infatuated with one of the Lanceros, Ramon, which was the subject of a lot of leg-pulling by the other Colombians and an embarrassment to Ramon. Patuazon doted on his granddaughter. Only a brave or drug-addled man made a play for her.

Jimmy switched to another camera and watched the men gather round

Patuazon for a pep talk. In the background, Cocaine Chris ambled out of the Colombians' hut. For security reasons, the Regiment lads wouldn't have him staying with them in case he overheard something and repeated it. It pleased Jimmy that Chris wasn't piloting any of the villa assault choppers. Bilton had confiscated Chris's stash of cocaine and assigned him to the smaller helicopter, the one hitting the cocaine lab. Everybody appreciated the irony of that, even Chris. He wandered at the edge of the group, heading towards Rosi. Jimmy couldn't blame him. Rosi was maturing into a fine-looking girl. Maria stepped forward, her aggressive stance creating a barrier. Chris stopped, scratched his head as if he remembered something he'd left behind and ambled back towards the hut.

Maria caught Jimmy's eye. She would have done so anyway, as a beautiful and well-endowed woman. Her head turned and she stared at the Regiment hut. Actions like that always stood out in a crowd. She said something to Rosi, waited until the girl moved to Patuazon's side, and walked towards the hut. Jimmy watched her getting closer and didn't like the way she moved. The pouches on her belt kit might contain more than spare magazines for her assault rifle. She could be carrying scanners to spy on the team's equipment. When she closed to within three metres he intercepted. He opened the door and greeted her as if he was surprised to see her.

'Hello. Can I help you?'

He smiled. Her expression altered to one of relaxed friendliness, but she didn't fool Jimmy.

'Is Senor Lewis here? He wasn't well and I haven't seen him for a few days.' She stepped closer and glanced past him at the closed door.

'He's okay as far as I know.' He shrugged, wondering what she wanted with Harford.

She carried on walking towards him. Her perfume was intoxicating.

'Are you sure? Sometimes people say they are well when they aren't.'

Jimmy stepped in front of the door to block her path. He checked for anybody else trying to get to the hut.

'He isn't here.'

'That's a pity.' She reached into a pouch. Jimmy tensed but she took out a wrapped snack bar. 'I brought him this to help him recover,' she said, holding it out. Jimmy took the bar and her fingers brushed against his.

He said, 'I can give him a message, if you–'

He choked. A tidal wave of something overpowering engulfed him, racing through his veins, catching the words in his throat and firing him into a frenzy. He wanted sex, right there and then. He wanted to take her in the hut, grab hold of her breasts, grasp and grind and suck, ripping off those stupid tight jeans guaranteed to drive any man insane, he'd screw her on the table – no, not in the hut, in the ferns, for a long time. He'd screw her hard and then do it again. She looked up for it.

He trembled like a teenage novice. His balls hurt. His breathing was ragged. He wondered what the hell was happening to him. It made him dizzy and if he didn't do something soon he'd lose control. She smiled.

'No. No message.' She smiled again, coyly, as though they shared a secret nobody would ever know. She turned to leave. He wanted to reach out and grab her to stop her going, and only just managed to control the urge. She ambled a couple of steps away then glanced back over her shoulder.

'There is a message.'

'Yes?' He would have done anything for her.

'If you're sure he's not here, I can tell you instead.'

'He isn't.' He wanted to yell, I'm here, I am, come and fuck, with me.

'Just tell him I'm glad he's feeling better.'

He watched her saunter away and went into the hut, perplexed and drained, his body sweating and limp except for one part of his anatomy that throbbed and ached in a way he hadn't experienced for years.

~~~~~~~~

Seven hours later that day, at thirteen-forty-five hours, twenty-five minutes before the attack, Lock put the second phase of the assault in place. Drink in hand, he stood in the sprawling grounds of Mosquera's villa holding a conversation with a talking corpse. Repelled by the image that darted into his mind, he glanced at other party guests. They spilled down stone steps, a colourful human waterfall heading towards open-sided marquees. He saw them all as potential corpses, like the unknown Shifter who died in the field. They pulled his attention because they placed a burden on his shoulders just by being there. Greedy, cowardly courtiers in thrall of a corrupt king. Ridiculous people dressed in the latest expensive trends, ignoring the danger they had exposed themselves to. Some behaved like addicts in the process of warming up, though most didn't need it. Judging by their wild behaviour they had already powdered their noses with Colombia's finest.

If Lock hadn't taken on the task of ensuring their safety, he wouldn't care what happened to them, but he felt responsible for the children. Small girls fluttered past like bright butterflies. Boys dressed as mini-adults scampered around the grounds between a bouncy castle and a carousel. They played too close to the explosives hidden by the guards' billets. Seeing them as figurative corpses made Lock's nerves do a more urgent salsa than the older kids warming up on the wooden dance floor.

Lock's swarthy companion, a retired third-rate gangster if anybody believed his stories, plucked at Lock's sleeve and rambled on drunkenly about men who were dead – men he claimed to have murdered.
~~~~~~~~

'So that bastard, he got slotted because one of the dead guys near him farted and gave away their position.' The man grinned and lurched against Lock, steadying himself with a podgy hand on Lock's shoulder. 'Can you imagine that? Getting yourself killed because of a fart.'

He bellowed. Lock smiled politely. The image of this man as a corpse didn't bother him. He took a sip from his glass of Aguardiente and calculated the distance between the play areas and the entertainment marquee, but no matter how many times he looked at it he knew they were too far apart for him to cover the gap successfully. The old man took his hand away. Lock hadn't been sufficiently sycophantic in his response.

'I see I'm boring you.'

'No, senor, not at all. This humidity affects me.' Lock saw his chance for a courteous exit. He gestured at thick jungle beyond the tall perimeter fence, and its accompanying strip of slash and burn. His heart missed a beat as he caught sight of a dog patrol nearing a watchtower that had explosives by its base. He watched the dog's progress and continued, 'I'm not so used to the heat any more. The drink just goes through me these days.'

He pulled out a handkerchief and mopped his face. He wondered if the gesture was too theatrical, but he needn't have worried about his acting, or the dog patrol which carried on safely past the watchtower.

'Ah, yes.' The man laughed with a camaraderie Lock didn't share. 'Not so good for us older ones, eh?'

'No. Excuse me, I need a piss.'

'That way.' His companion pointed towards the toilet block.

Passing an ornamental tree, planted for the party but already wilting, Lock put his glass down on a wall, helped himself to a mangostino fruit drink from a waiter's tray and checked the time. Thirteen-fifty, twenty minutes to the assault deadline at fourteen-ten. A forlorn entertainment marquee stayed empty. He needed the women and children close together inside it, fast. He glanced up at birds wheeling lazily on thermals in a steamy sky. The rain promised by the weather report had not arrived to drive everybody under shelter. People were scattered over the villa's grounds.

He scanned the crowd for the vital ingredient of the afternoon's entertainment, the magician, but instead caught the gaze of an attractive young woman standing by one of the wilting trees. Although she appeared to be listening to one of several admirers, she stared past his shoulder at Lock, who had the impression she recognised him. He looked away, disconcerted. Maybe his acting wasn't as good as his disguise after all. Behaving like an old man of eighty, rather than his real age of twenty-five, was harder than expected. Either that or she was one of the pair who had been tracking him.

He moved, but kept her in his peripheral vision. He slipped into neuro-sensory mode when somebody knocked his elbow, spilling his drink. A short, snub-nosed man in his twenties looked at Lock as he brushed past.

'Sorry, man. My fault.' The man spoke Spanish with an American accent. The apology seemed genuine, which wasn't unusual since it didn't pay to be impolite in Colombian drug society. Rude people frequently ended up dead. Lock waved him away.

'No problem.'

Brushing fruit juice from his trouser leg he watched the American hurry towards the attractive woman. They greeted each other with expansive gestures and a welcome on her part that seemed forced, and awkwardness on his part as though he'd done something wrong and knew she hid her anger behind a smile. She flicked back long, dark hair. Sunlight shimmered on auburn highlights. She took his arm. Her admirers melted away, disappointed. The woman and the snub-nosed man turned and sauntered away, deep in conversation, and Lock relaxed. She wasn't checking him out after all. She'd been looking for the man on her arm.

He spotted the magician with a couple of girls by the end of a set of food stalls and hurried past dishes piled with corn tamales and chilli burgers.

'Excuse me senor, a word with you,' Lock said. Annoyance swept across the magician's face at the intrusion on his efforts to get laid after his act. 'Excuse me, ladies.' Lock smiled at the girls, who looked like young hookers. They laughed at his quaint figure of speech. He took the magician's arm and steered him away. From the corner of his eye he saw the same young woman, but this time he didn't give her another thought.

'Senor, you do understand why you're here?' Lock nodded towards Mosquera.

'Yes, of course.'

'No, I don't think you appreciate the situation. You're here to entertain Senor Mosquera's grandson, the birthday boy. You're due on stage to start at fourteen hundred, yes? That's less than ten minutes away. It would be a great shame if your act played out to only a handful of children and the little boy went away disappointed. Now do you understand me?'

The magician nodded. The implied threat sank in as his gaze flicked between Mosquera, the empty marquee and the carousel full of kids.

'Not many people like magic acts these days.'

'That's your problem, senor. If you're half as good as you say you are I'm sure you'll think of something to pique their curiosity.' Lock paused as if thinking, but not for too long in case he lost the magician's attention. 'Maybe you can promise them something they haven't seen before. Like making somebody rise off the ground and disappear, for example.'

The magician gazed at the carousel as if it were a deadly enemy. He shook his head.

'I can't do anything like that.'

'I can. I used to be in the business. I can help, if you want.'

The magician frowned, weighing up whether to walk off and ignore Lock or grasp a last-ditch opportunity, in spite of his suspicions.

'Only Starbirth freaks can do that sort of thing.'

'Do I look like a Starbirth addict?'

The man hesitated then shook his head.

'My apologies. But it still wouldn't work. We haven't rehearsed it, there isn't time.'

Lock looked at him with a combination of pity and disdain.

'Your funeral.'

Lock strolled away, sending a silent prayer that the magician would take the bait. He reached the end of the path and thought he had misjudged the strength of the opportunistic side to the magician's character, when he heard a shout from behind.

'Senor, wait.'

Lock stopped and raised his eyes to the sky in thanks before turning round.

'Why do you want to help?' the magician asked. Lock carried on strolling towards the entertainment marquee, forcing the magician to accompany him.

'As an old family friend, I'd like to see the boy happy. The entertainment is partly my responsibility, so your failure is my failure. I'm not going to fail, you understand? Besides, I've seen too many people end up with lead in their chests instead of money in their pockets. D'you want my help or not?'

The reference to being shot clinched the argument for the magician.

'How do we do it?'

'Call me on stage five minutes into your act. Introduce me as Jungle Spirit. Got that? Good. I'll take it from there. Not all of us have lost the art of magic, eh?'

'Okay, but Starbirth or no Starbirth, make sure it's a good trick.'

Lock winked.

'It will be.'

The magician set about persuading his audience into the marquee so vigorously that he turned red in the face and was drenched in sweat. The process was agonising despite his efforts and the help of the excitable warm-up DJ on the sound stage advertising the magic act. Twelve minutes before the assault was due to take place, hyperactive, excited children, accompanied by matronly childminders and a scattering of well-dressed mothers, filled half the seats in the marquee. The rest were still outside.

Important men in Mosquera's hierarchy left the bars, heading towards the villa for the business meeting, starting at the same time as the magic act at fourteen hundred. Mosquera lingered at the side of the entertainment marquee, flirting in a covetous manner with the attractive woman Lock had seen earlier. A compere introduced the magician with a Latino flourish, shouting too loudly into the microphone, but to Lock's relief the frenzy drew more children to join Mosquera's enthusiastic five-year-old grandson. Only a couple were still on the bouncy castle. Lock would have to deal with them after he cleared the marquee.

Adults gathered in clumps at the back of the tent, chatting in low voices and laughing at the compere's clowning. A movement in the front row caught Lock's eye. Mosquera's grandson raced across the lawn to catch hold of Mosquera's hand, dragging him towards the marquee. To Lock's dismay the amused drug lord allowed himself to be bullied. Mosquera was supposed to be in the villa. Lock hoped the spotters, watching through the eyes of small surveillance drones, had seen the development and would inform PC so that last-minute adjustments could be put into effect.

~~~~~~~~

At fourteen hundred hours, the Bell Huey helicopter carrying Jimmy, Bilton and their fire teams, banked around the side of a hill and swooped low and fast over the tops of trees and wax palms. Jimmy swayed against his seat belt and looked out of the open door at mist rising from a churning river. White froth tumbled over waterfalls and rapids, rushing downhill ahead of the helicopters. Flocks of parrots and macaws scattered at the approach of the noisy metal monsters, their scarlet and yellow plumage dropping into the endless green canopy like jewels falling from a broken necklace. He looked at the hazy blue sky of the oncoming dry season. It was perfect weather for an attack, as good as you could get in the Colombian tropics. There were no low clouds to obscure the pilot's vision and send him on a collision course with a hill. The Huey twisted to the other side and the roar of the engine filled his ears under his fire retardant black balaclava.

They were armed to the teeth. Each man wore thigh pistols and carried semi-automatic assault rifles – M-16s for the Colombians, Diemacos for the Blades. One man in each team carried a shotgun for Explosive Method of Entry techniques, to blow the hinges off doors. A couple of them had Rocket Propelled Grenade launchers. Three men in Ramon's team, Delta Four, carried Light Machine Guns – belt-fed, heavier weapons to be used for putting down suppressing fire when Ramon secured the quadrangle.

Besides spare ammunition for their personal weapons and extra rounds for the shotgun man, they had stun grenades which contained a mix of explosives and CS gas, and popper canisters of an odourless, non-lethal nerve gas called KLX. It was the most important weapon in their arsenal. The KLX canisters contained a propellant which dispersed the non-lethal gas and disabled anybody inside the room within seconds. It was perfect for capture missions.
~~~~~~~~

Gazing down the narrow valley Jimmy glimpsed the Black Hawk gunship leading the way and skimming tree tops as the pilot kept under the radar of the Colombian military. The cylindrical shapes of the Hawk's Hellfire missiles stood out against the green backdrop. Kilo Two, piloted by Cocaine Chris and with Mick and his team of six, followed. PC, in his role as the commander in the sky, would use the military designation of Zero on the radio. Everybody tuned in for the 'Go' signal from Zero.

The operation must have cost Patuazon a fortune. Missiles and helicopters weren't cheap. The two modern military-style Hueys were probably hired or borrowed from the Colombian army. The last chopper, a lightly-armed old Huey unsuitable for combat, would not be joining the battle. Kilo Five's role, with Patuazon's careless young relative at the controls, was to ferry out captives and casualties at the end of the operation and hopefully not break down in the process.

The slim man sitting opposite Jimmy adjusted and re-adjusted thick leather gloves that would stop his hands burning when the men fast-roped from Kilo Three and Kilo Four, at a speed of fifteen metres per second. Gonz sat next to him nursing a Rocket Propelled Grenade launcher by his knees. The first man caught Jimmy's eye, stopped twisting his hands and gave him a clumsy thumbs up instead, accompanied by a grin that disappeared under his balaclava.

Jimmy nodded to his fire team member and turned his head away, zoning and feeling calm but fired up at the same time in a juxtaposition of emotions. Chris's voice over the radio common channel broke into his thoughts, roaring a wordless version of 'Ride of the Valkyries' and though rough, it was easily recognisable. The Colombians laughed. It broke the tension, but meant that Chris might be as high as a kite, not something that would go down well with Mick in the back of Chris's chopper. The helicopter peeled away to follow a separate valley to the drugs laboratory, leaving the other four on course for the villa.

PC's voice crackled over Jimmy's in-the-mouth receiver.

'Zero, all stations, four minutes. Respirators on. RPGs in position.'

Jimmy fixed his respirator in place. The familiar smell of surgical wipes combined with old sweat filled his nostrils, bringing with it the associations of combat. He adjusted his throat microphone on its neck band. The rest of his men checked boom microphones at their necks.

The teams unfastened their seat belts. Gonz moved to the door to fire the RPG at one of the sniper bell domes. Jimmy eyed the rappel ropes coiled on the floor of the chopper, the ends ready to be thrown out of the side doors. Adrenaline pumped hard, sharpening his senses, making him feel alert and alive. Colours were brighter, and sound clearer. All he wanted was to get out, get on with it and make sure his fire team did what they were supposed to. He looked at the other lads. One or two made the sign of the cross on their chests for divine protection, but they all had the same air of taut, single-minded aggression. Their blood was up, and nothing would stop them.

CHAPTER 14

Mosquera grinned as his grandson pulled him to the front of the marquee. Three bodyguards followed at a discreet distance, weapons tucked under loose-fitting shirts. A fourth heavy guard, perspiring in the heat, carried a Demon weapon. That posed a problem. When Lock teleported, he couldn't separate people in a crowd, which meant his passengers would include Mosquera and his bodyguard – and the Demon. Lock licked his dry lips and glanced at his watch. Three minutes before the first missile slammed home.

Mosquera sat in the front row. Distracted by the man with the Demon, Lock hardly noticed a light touch on his bare forearm, thinking it was somebody moving past. The touch turned to pressure which tingled up his arm and into his neck. He turned and came face to face with the woman who made him feel uneasy earlier. A hint of a smile played about her mouth, but her expression was hard. He moved his arm but she didn't let go.

'It's a good day for a party, Mr Harford,' she said in English.

A chill struck hard from his abdomen, coursed through his body like ice and froze in his face. He was compromised. Those few words peeled away his disguise. Needing time to react appropriately he tried to bluff it out by replying in Spanish,

'Pardon, senorita? I don't understand you.'

He smiled, a gesture intended to convey innocence. He noted her empty right hand and looked for sign of a concealed weapon under the slinky dress. She smiled back, her teeth white against burnished skin. Her left hand stayed on his arm.

'You have a strong heart, Mr Harford, but you won't need it.'

Searing pain lanced his chest. His heart fluttered wildly. He gasped and tried to push himself away. His muscles went into spasm and it felt as though her hand was welded to his flesh. He looked to see what she was using and what he had missed. She laughed at him. He wanted to yell a warning to the incoming assault teams but his tongue felt thick, as though it wasn't his. Something squeezed his throat, choking back the garbled words and strangling the blood flow to his head.

She reached forward with her other hand to grip the back of his neck and fire surged down his spine. It flowed like lava inside his ribcage while the rest of his body slipped into a deep freeze. The world wobbled and the spasms stopped. Muscles gave way like wisps of grass and his useless arms couldn't save him from falling. His head smacked hard ground and a wave of pain jarred his face as though his brain tried to get out through his nose. He lay on the ground, paralysed and fading. He heard the woman say in Spanish,

'I think he's having a heart attack. Somebody fetch a medic.'

Lock couldn't breathe. She put a hand on his forehead. It felt as though liquid nitrogen poured into his skull from her fingers. Bending over him, close to his ear, she whispered,

'Time to pay for what you did. You'll be dead before your friends get here.' She knew about the assault. Lock floated into a blizzard of stars. In his earpiece he heard Bilton's tinny voice break radio silence to say,

'Zero, all stations, stand by, stand by.' Lock heard without attaching any meaning to it. He barely noticed when the faint voice said, 'Go – Go – Go.'

His eyes closed and he went obediently, dissolving into a place where colour greyed and he was aware of a distant thudding in his ears. He felt shock waves through the ground but his mind didn't register the cause as explosive charges going off simultaneously. He didn't recognise the sound of a mortar shell as it demolished the closest watchtower, or feel the massive explosion from the armoury as the weapons cache hurtled skywards in a fireball. He didn't notice people stumbling over him.

What he did feel was the release of the woman's hands. His heart beat once, a rolling jolt that convulsed his body and kicked his lungs into life. He sucked air through his mouth and it surged into his chest, washing away the heat. Stronger heartbeats powered blood through weak limbs. The buzzing in his skull evaporated and he remembered where he was. He heard people screaming in between mortars pounding the ground and helicopter rotor blades thudding overhead.

He felt heavy pressure on his stomach. He pushed weakly at the obese man squashing the breath out of him and turned his head to find the woman. She lay on the ground, knocked down by people trying to escape and was pinned under women and chairs. Her fingers clawed across the grass to a hair's breadth of his right wrist as she struggled to free herself. Lock's heart rate pounded with a rush of adrenaline. He gathered his strength and lashed out with his fist, landing a heavy blow on her forearm.

Her hand went limp. He rose off the ground horizontally, rolled the man off his ribcage and stood up. Dizziness hit him; he swayed and almost fell back to the grassy floor of the marquee. The woman was free. She moved with speed and agility, like a cat. Striking a martial arts blow on a man blocking her way she knocked him to the ground and lunged at Lock. Levitating fast, he rose into the air and she missed. He kicked and his boot landed on her breastbone, sending her somersaulting backwards into a row of chairs.

Lock didn't wait to see what effect it had. Before she recovered her footing, he was on her, putting all his strength behind a blow to her jaw that snapped her head back. She crashed into some chairs and didn't get up. Breathing hard he stared at her face for sign of life, unwilling to get close. Dismayed by the chaos, the deafening gunfire and the terrified screams of children who would have been safely out of the marquee if it hadn't been for her interference, he kicked her hand. She didn't move.

He looked around the marquee. People trampled over chairs and each other in panic. Some people lay unmoving. Smoke clogged his nostrils. Voices were lost in the barrage of explosions. He couldn't see Mosquera, or his men. Bilton and his fire teams would be up the slope at the villa. Anybody close to the marquee, or running out of it, was likely to be a civilian. He changed into sensory mode.

He saw another aura by the attacker. He tensed for an assault, but their auras left the marquee in levitation. Ignoring their escape, he tagged the auras of fleeing women and children, rose into the air and hovered out of the marquee and into the grounds. He picked up more auras as he went as if scooping up fallen leaves. When he reached his limit he teleported them out of the estate.

~~~~~~~~

PC's Black Hawk gunship led the attack with the two assault team helicopters following on either side. They closed on the front of the villa in arrowhead formation. The last helicopter, Kilo Five, followed behind. A Hellfire missile streaked from the Hawk, exploding in the main bell dome and blowing a hole in the roof. It pulverised bricks and mortar into debris that rained on the front of the villa. The missile took out the men in the dome before they had a chance to use their shoulder-fired missiles.

Rounds from machine guns whistled past the Hueys from the smaller domes and from men on the ground. The Hawk was already closing in on the quadrangle at the back, circling like an angry wasp over a sniper bell dome. The Gatling gun on the Cobra's nose raked it with bursts of fire at a speed of three thousand rounds per minute.

'Incoming!'

The shout came from the pilot of Jimmy's helicopter, Kilo Three. The helicopter rose into the air to avoid an RPG streaking their way from the only standing watchtower. The rocket-propelled grenade missed and exploded in empty air. Gonz fired an RPG at the tower but missed by metres. A second one, fired from the back of the helicopter, hit the top of the watchtower and it disappeared in a cloud of dirty smoke.
~~~~~~~~

The Hawk moved to the corner of Blue wing, launching a hail of rounds outside the meeting room to keep Mosquera and his men from escaping through the patio doors. Another missile demolished a sniper dome. The roof caved, sending tiles and debris tumbling down the side of the wing. The two Hueys flared out fifteen metres above the quadrangle. Under cover of smoke bombs they fired rounds at armed men taking cover.

Jimmy heard a burst of return fire from heavy weapons. The co-pilot screamed at the men to go. The first two kicked out the weighted rappel ropes and launched into the air. Jimmy's team members were still on the rope when he grasped it. He was halfway down the rope. The helicopter bucked to avoid a hail of rounds that just missed the rotor blades.

Friction heat scorched through his gloves. He clung to the rope as the helicopter twisted and rose. PC yelled at the pilot in another chopper to stop firing, he almost hit Kilo Three. Kilo Three's pilot fought to stabilise the aircraft. Jimmy slid to safety. On the other rope, Bilton dropped from seven metres up. Jimmy rolled with his awkward landing and pressed the quick release fastener to bring his Diemaco into the aim.

The men on the ground deployed in combat pose and fired on hostiles. In the midst of smoke, and the spitting rattle of small-arms fire, two men hauled Bilton to cover. Jimmy ran to his target and a glance at Bilton was enough to see the Alpha team leader couldn't carry on. Bilton's right shoulder was dislocated and his forearm bent at an unnatural angle. Jimmy was glad the casualty was somebody else's problem and ran on. He heard Gonz tell PC he would take over as Alpha team leader and they needed casualty evacuation.

Jimmy's team hit the ground fast in a well-rehearsed drill. Throughout their training in clearing buildings the emphasis had been on speed. They knew the layout of the two-storey circular tower with its small shrine at the bottom and circular balcony on the first floor. Previous surveillance provided detailed information about the interior, from the flowery wrought iron railings on the balcony, to locked doors on both levels leading to buildings on either side. They knew they would find a guard on the upper floor, training his weapon on the entrance.

The first two men in Jimmy's team fired stun grenades from their underslung grenade launchers into the top floor, straight through slatted windows, creating a burst of deafening explosions and strobe-like flashes of light. At the bottom, another man used a shotgun to blow the door open, one shot to the lock, two to the hinges. The door keeled over at an angle and fell inside the room.

'Go – Go – Go,' Jimmy yelled.

The man in front of him jumped past the door, covered left and moved sideways out of the way with Jimmy entering on his heels. White smoke from CS gas billowed around stone columns on the ground floor and the balcony. Jimmy covered his arc of fire on the right looking at both floors, moving aside for the next man to follow in. One of Mosquera's men emerged from smoke on the balcony and reeled towards the railings, holding a bandanna over his nose and mouth. In his right hand an AK47 wavered as he fired, but his eyes streamed so much he couldn't see what he aimed at. Jimmy fired. The man collapsed backwards and the AK47 fell out of his hand, clattered past the railings and landed in front of a plaster statuette of the Virgin Mary. Two of Jimmy's team pounded up stone steps and checked him. He was dead, but not one of the eight high-value targets.

The team searched the guards' quarters for hostiles while Jimmy and one of his men covered the ground floor.

'Clear,' the lead man on the upper floor said. Jimmy headed for the next entry point. He switched his radio setting to call PC on the common channel.

'Bravo Three, Zero, Blue Two secure. One times X-Ray dead. Negative Yankee casualties. Leaving one Yankee at primary, moving to secondary.'

'Zero, Bravo Three, Roger that.'

Jimmy held a radar scope against the wall. The screen showed him a 3D image of a dining room on the other side of the wall, with a table and chairs in the centre. He saw a gunman crouched at a doorway and covering the corridor, expecting the assault force to come in from that direction. Jimmy adjusted the controls on the scope and its range extended into the corridor. He saw another figure but the scope range couldn't see beyond that. Jimmy showed his men the positions of the enemy and indicated what he wanted to do.

One of his Lanceros took out a shaped charge from his bergen and fixed the explosive on the wall while Jimmy attached a detonator. A new voice came over the common channel.

'Alpha Three, Zero, Gonz hit, Pedro hit.'

PC answered from the Cobra circling overhead.

'Zero, Alpha Three, acknowledged. Luis, take over. Regroup. Charlie Four, position.'

PC sounded calm but Jimmy knew it was bad news. Gonz's team were in the shit, no doubt victims of Gonz's recklessness. Vicar, leading Charlie Four, told PC he had captured one of the eight high-value targets and was taking fire at White, the front of the villa. PC ordered Vicar to reinforce Gonz's team when he had secured White.

Jimmy switched his radio to his team channel and took cover. The explosives blew some of the wall into the room and the team sped through the large hole. A jumble of shattered glass, broken table, overturned plastic chairs and bits of plates and cutlery covered the room. The man by the doorway had been blown off his feet. He sat up groggily and aimed his weapon, but like the guard in the tower he was dead in a second. Jimmy took the lead, ran across the room to the doorway and fired stun grenades into the corridor. He acted before the sequence of explosions and flashes of light finished.

'Go – Go – Go!' Two men went left, firing at a gunman. Jimmy and two soldiers turned to the right. Through CS gas mist Jimmy saw a disorientated gunman at the end of the corridor, trying to retreat while firing. Jimmy and his team fired back. The man screamed and slumped against the wall of the storage room, clutching his stomach, and a second man on the left fell into a doorway. A third man stumbled into another room on the left.

'X-Ray into Blue Five.' Jimmy left one man to disarm the injured hostile and put plasticuffs on him, while two more checked the storage room. He and two men raced down the corridor, their weapons into their shoulders. When they reached the doorway to the room designated Blue Five, a hail of gunfire hurtled out of it, and rounds smacked into plaster walls in the corridor. The men by Jimmy recoiled.

'Use the flashbangs.' Jimmy fired one into the room. He took the lead and rounded the doorway into a kitchen. A plump, middle-aged woman, one of Mosquera's unarmed servants, cowered on the floor by kitchen cupboards, coughing. The man in the kitchen was also unarmed, having dropped a heavy General Purpose Machine Gun. He staggered to the top of some stairs leading to a small utility area, a dead end, and held his arms up in surrender, shouting in Spanish.

'Get down,' Jimmy shouted. The man threw himself on the floor and the second soldier into the room plasticuffed him and the woman. Jimmy sped down a couple of steps into the utility area and searched it. It was empty. He turned and ran past the captives. They weren't high value targets, and he hadn't seen any of the three missing Demons. He followed his men back to the corridor. His team were switched on and working well, settling into the flow without needing to be pushed.

The first man into a room was the last one out of it, so Jimmy brought up the rear behind them as they went into the corridor, moving fast but tactically in an all-round defence pattern. On their left, a staircase led up to bedrooms. Jimmy's equipment told him they were empty, but he stopped in the corridor and checked again. Somewhere in the distance, a high explosive grenade went off. He led his men on, telling PC,

'Bravo Three to Zero, Blue Five secure. Moving to Blue Four.'

PC didn't reply. Jimmy assumed the radio had hit a comms dead spot.

Blue Four was Mosquera's study, inaccessible from the corridor, but it lay between the meeting room on one side and a storage room on the other. The team would have to blow their way in from the storage room next door. He left one man guarding the corridor and glanced around the room as he entered it. Building supplies, spare parts for machinery and metal tools hanging by hooks on the walls filled two-thirds of it. Old furniture was piled up at the other end.

He crouched by the wall with his radar scope, panting. Trying to breathe through a respirator in heat was like sucking in air through a straw. He wasn't getting enough oxygen. He ripped off the respirator, and at his signal his men did the same, their faces pink and red like boiled lobsters. Jimmy looked through his scope and counted six men in the study. They were barricading the connecting door to the meeting room.

He whispered to his men and as he did the radio receiver in his mouth crackled back to life. Vicar told PC that one of his team was down and one of Delta Four, Ramon's team, yelled that Ramon had been hit. Jimmy was fixing an explosive charge against the wall when he heard PC's message loud and clear.

'Zero, all stations, Shifter with package vicinity Blue One.' PC repeated the message.

Jimmy saw fear in the eyes of those who understood English. They would have been more scared if they knew the package was a Demon weapon. They faced the worst possible scenario – somebody on the rampage who could pop up anywhere, even in rooms they had already cleared. It explained why the other teams were taking so many hits.

He had to get in and capture the high-value targets before the Shifter could do any more damage. On his signal his men put their respirators back on and the blast blew part of the wall into the study. Jimmy leapt in first, firing at a gunman who was attempting to take up a position against them by the far doorway. The man crashed forward across the threshold and didn't move. The team swept into the study.

'Down! Down!'

Two of the five hostiles had sufficient understanding to do as ordered. One man slumped on the floor by a broken computer console, blood pouring from a head wound, and didn't respond. Jimmy recognised him as Mosquera's number two. Another one crawled around the floor on all fours until one of Jimmy's team pushed him face down and plasticuffed him. Jimmy identified two of the other captives as high value targets. He spotted a Demon weapon in the debris and disabled it.

'Bravo Three, Zero, Blue Four secure. Three target X-Rays detained. One package eliminated,' Jimmy told PC.

The other Regiment lads would hear the news and be encouraged that a Demon had been taken out of action. Jimmy called Vicar on the team channel for Charlie Four.

'Have you got eyeball on X-Rays in Blue One?'

Vicar's reply was terse.

'Negative. Busy over here.'

Outside the room gunfire erupted in bursts and the radio crackled with reports of the Shifter. In the study, fake books on shelves concealed cupboards. The doors lay open and empty boxes spilled over the floor, some Jimmy recognised as supplies for the Demons. Two of his team cuffed the captives and two more guarded the study while he crouched beside a wall and used his radar scope.

The rectangular room was like a hall. A huge home cinema screen covered the far wall opposite the study. Jimmy identified some of Charlie Four tucked behind a doorway next to it. On Jimmy's right the radar scope saw a drinks bar set into one side of the room with its back to the outer extra-thick brick wall. It faced the reinforced Alpha Three team, led by Luis, at patio doors on Jimmy's left. In the meeting room five figures lay scattered over the floor. The scope told him none were breathing. He relayed the information back to PC.

Jimmy couldn't see the bar very well on the radar scope. Adjusting the intensity to maximum, which blurred out some of the peripheral details, he discovered why. Something solid enveloped the bar area. He keyed in a query about its substance and the radar's sensors told him to wait. Ten seconds later the machine identified the material as a tough polycarbonate, five centimetres thick, able to withstand grenades and heavy calibre rounds, and it was fixed to the walls and ceiling. The solid cage had not been there hours earlier when insect drones checked the meeting room, so it must have slid into place from concealed slots. It was hidden well. Jimmy adjusted the scope settings and saw four fuzzy figures in the bar bunker.

He didn't know why they stayed when they had a Shifter who could get them out to safety. A Shifter should be able to go in and take them out one by one, or in a group like Harford. Maybe he couldn't. Harford told PC that not all Shifters could transport passengers. Why was the Shifter sticking around? He wouldn't risk his neck unless somebody in the room was important to him. The realisation struck Jimmy at the same time he thought about breathable air in the bar bunker, and air vents, and exits. Surely Mosquera wouldn't construct a fortified area without a way out? Jimmy got on the radio to PC and told him and the other teams what he had seen.

'Can you see a way out at the back?' Jimmy asked.

'Negative. There's a lot of debris from the roof. It might have blocked an exit.'

'What about air vents? There has to be an air intake pipe somewhere.'

'Negative.' PC spoke to all the teams. 'Zero, all stations, six minutes.'

'Under the ground?' Jimmy persisted.

He checked his watch, waiting for PC's reply, and looked round. Besides the captives, only one of his team was in the study instead of the four he expected. He gestured to his man to follow him and rushed to the cramped storage room. Two men stood on guard in there. He was missing two.

PC came back on the radio.

'There's a mass of pipes, but two small ones go out to the garden and there's an active heat spot that wasn't there before.'

'Show me.' Jimmy got his handheld computer and waited for PC to upload the images. He took off his respirator and turned to his men.

'Respirators off. Where's Juan and Mika?'

The men looked at him and shrugged, unwilling to admit their colleagues had run off.

Jimmy was livid but he had to get on with it. He picked the two Lanceros in his team. 'Felipe, Raul, with me.' He pointed at the remaining man. 'You get in the study and guard that door. Don't fucking move until I tell you. Got that?'

The man nodded and moved out.

Jimmy used the torch on the end of his Diemaco and scanned the storage room, pouncing on the metal head of a broken pickaxe.

'With me.' While PC kept watch on their route, he and his Lanceros hurtled to the outer wall of the meeting room. Jimmy called Vicar on the radio.

'Vic, you got your scope on the bar bunker?'

'Yeah. No movement. Shifter's still around.'

'Okay. When I give the word, move in, respirators on, blow a hole in it.'

The Hawk's equipment, and Jimmy's radar scope, located an air conditioning condenser hidden in bushes, and followed an intake pipe to the wall where it disappeared into the bar area.

'Zero, all stations, three minutes.'

Jimmy told Felipe and Raul to stay on guard and get popper canisters of KLX gas ready. He loosened mortar around bricks with the pickaxe head, thankful that Mosquera's builders had not been the best workmen, and levered two bricks out exposing the pipe. He told Vicar to get ready and turned to his men.

'Respirators on. Give me the poppers.'

He struck the plastic pipe with the pickaxe, trying not to smash it. The pipe dented. Jimmy struck it again, harder, making a hole in it. Taking one of the canisters, he pulled the pin and stuck the end over the hole, closing the gap with his hand.

'One in,' he told Vicar.

'Zero, all stations, two minutes. Get moving,' PC said.

'Nearly there.' Jimmy was unwilling to give up when he was so close. As soon as the canister was empty he put another one on, waited for that to empty and told Vicar,

'Two in. Go – Go – Go.'

He stuck a third one on for good measure.

Through the wall he heard the dull thud of an explosion. Vicar said,

'Charlie Four, Blue One secure. One X-ray dead. Coming out with three X-Ray prisoners. One Yankee casualty.'

'Zero, Charlie Four, acknowledged. All stations, phase two,' PC said, giving the signal to get out of the villa with whatever documents, hard drives, phones and other information they could carry. The Hawk lifted into a hover and Jimmy heard the two Hueys, Kilo Three and Kilo Four, coming in to pick them up before any more Shifters arrived. Switching to his own team channel he ordered the three men still inside the Blue area to get the captives and wounded outside while he took off for Kilo Three with Felipe and Raul on his heels.

A movement on Jimmy's left caught his eye. If he had been one step further on he wouldn't have seen it. He turned to look over his shoulder and saw a Shifter with a Demon weapon less than four metres away. Jimmy dropped to one knee, brought his weapon round and they fired at the same time. Their eyes met. The Shifter was one of Mosquera's three sons, crazy with bloodlust and fury. The man fell with two rounds in his forehead. Jimmy jumped to his feet and put another two rounds into him to make sure he was dead, kicking the Demon weapon away.

'Zero, Bravo Three, report,' PC said.

'Bravo Three, Shifter's dead,' Jimmy replied, picking up the Demon.

'Jimmy.'

The voice behind him made him whirl round. Felipe's eyes bulged as he gaped at darts sticking out of his body. Jimmy and Raul grabbed him and Jimmy pulled out the darts, but Felipe collapsed.

'It's okay, pal, we'll get you out and casevac'd. You'll be fine. Raul, help carry him.' Jimmy told PC he had a casualty. He lifted Felipe and pushed him towards the quadrangle, more as a gesture of friendship than real hope. Felipe was as good as dead. They couldn't help him run any further than the back of the tower. Felipe collapsed. Jimmy put him on Raul's back and they ran, with Felipe's feet dragging on the ground and his head lolling. He frothed at the mouth and his body contorted with convulsions. Jimmy saw the light leave Felipe's eyes.

They reached Kilo Three and hands pulled the lifeless body inside. Other bodies lay on the floor, men who looked as though they were asleep except for the froth at their mouths. Vicar, his balaclava off and still hopped up on adrenaline, followed his team from the broken mess that used to be Mosquera's meeting room. He saw Jimmy and called his name over the radio, the sound coming through despite the maelstrom around them and the throbbing of the rotor blades.

Whatever it was could wait, Jimmy thought. Vicar looked scared and worried.

'What?' Jimmy said.

'Stay still, mate.' He reached a hand to Jimmy's left shoulder. Jimmy looked over his shoulder and his knees gave way. Vicar held up a dart.

'Maybe it didn't go all the way in. Did it go through? It might've just got caught on your webbing.'

Vicar was gabbling. Jimmy didn't hear him. He was mesmerised by the dart, aware for the first time of a pain behind his shoulder that he had ignored and a growing, burning pain in his chest that he had put down to CS gas.

'Fuck,' he said.

~~~~~~~~

Lock headed for a village fifteen kilometres outside Mosquera's territory where clandestine medics waited for casualties, courtesy of a shady set-up engineered by people who went by first names only. He had assurances some impartial 'advisers' would be on hand to ensure nobody murdered the prisoners and he guessed the advisers would be American, possibly CIA. They had as much vested interest in locating the source of AH-4 as the British troopers. Everything relied on his getting them to the makeshift field hospital. He struggled to maintain a mental grip on such a scattered group of auras, the largest group he had ever teleported.

Thirty seconds into the Shift he made a discovery. One of the auras at the edge of the group glowed with shades of grass green and lemon yellow. He hadn't done an aura check on the woman who attacked him at the party. He had been interrupted. The mesmerising, unique aura probably belonged to her. Distraction tipped him over the edge. He came out of the Shift and plummeted. Focusing his mind, he struggled to hold on to everybody. He managed to slow the group's descent but lost control, dropped and blacked out.

Lock woke, without remembering he had lost consciousness. He didn't know where he was, or why so many sounds surrounded him. Dazed, he heard a wailing that rose in pitch like a faraway siren. Another one joined it and he recognised the sound as the voices of children howling. Somebody screamed, a full-blooded adult cry of pain and terror. People were screaming and shouting for help. He felt his chest rise and fall and as he became aware of his limbs, he knew he was definitely not dead. The knobbly, hard ground underneath his back creaked, cracked and broke. It brought him to his senses. Opening his eyes he grabbed a tree branch. It halted his downward crash.

Twigs and broken boughs scratched his neck and head and poked him in the back, but the branch held. The mental fog cleared and he saw other people in the same state as himself, caught in the canopy and clinging to anything they could grab hold of. He gathered his strength and went into neuro-sensory mode. One of the auras fell. He sped to the child's side, holding the aura steady and plucking terrified people from tree tops, lowering them into rainforest mist.
~~~~~~~~

Lock put them on soggy ground at a deadfall spot, a cleared area where an old, rotten tree had keeled over taking other trees with it. People hung in the canopy above him. Lock went up for them. He knew the woman posed a danger, not just to the civilians but to himself, yet the compulsion to save others was so ingrained, he operated on automatic pilot.

Lowering the second group of civilians to the ground he told them to stay put and keep quiet. It was pointless. People searched for loved ones, calling out names and trying to fight their way through the undergrowth. They made enough racket to frighten away large animals and birds, but it would have no effect on poisonous insects or venomous snakes. The noise would attract the woman with the unique aura. Lock told them either they could stay where they were and keep quiet, or they could risk death by ignoring him. Some of the group of thirty people quietened down, and some didn't.

He scanned for the strange aura but didn't see the woman until he lifted off, finding her at ground level near a few normal auras in another deadfall spot. He snapped out of neuro-sensory mode. A line of untouched trees, creepers and ferns obscured her from the people he had rescued. Lock went back to the canopy for people stuck at the tops of trees. He discovered two of them were truly stuck and couldn't be moved by teleportation no matter how hard he tried. He left them, took a third group of scared passengers down and returned to the tree tops to see what he could do. 'Stuck' had not been accurate. They were impaled. The swarthy gangster Lock spoke to at the party was dead. The end of a branch stuck out of his chest. The second victim was Mosquera, conscious but in deep shock. He hung grotesquely in a nest of branches. A broken shard of thick wood entered the back of his right thigh and emerged near his groin.

'I'll get you down.'

Lock wondered how he was going to do that considering the tangle surrounding Mosquera and the severity of the wound. He glimpsed something coming at him. He turned his head and ducked. A blinding light struck the tree, so close it caught Lock's body in teeth-rattling shockwaves. It punched a hole through half the trunk and several branches. Part of the tree disintegrated and the rest of it swayed like a blade of grass, crashing into adjacent trees. Branches cracked and fell. Mosquera slid and dangled at a more precarious slant. The pain of being moved overcame his shock and he screamed, a raw sound that drowned out the children crying below.

Lock couldn't help him. He levitated upwards, feeling naked without a weapon. High above the rainforest, he looked down and saw Bloater, the man who fought the Eagles and ambushed Bilton and Jimmy. Bloater searched the canopy, holding a weapon linked by a thick cable to a canister on his back. Lock hoped Bloater would go for Mosquera rather than himself or the civilians. Bloater roared something, hovered in the air and twisted without a glance at Mosquera hanging helplessly in the tree. A wave of dizziness engulfed Lock. His vision blurred, the world tipped, and Bloater spotted him. Lock sped out of the way as another beam of light sizzled through the air, missing him by centimetres. He couldn't teleport, had barely enough strength to levitate, and knew he was in deep trouble.

He headed for the safety of the rainforest and the mist, drawing Bloater away from clusters of auras huddled on the ground. He had the advantage of his aura skills, something that outweighed Bloater's weaponry. A forest tangle of creepers, hanging lianas and giant spider webs made it difficult for Bloater to navigate a way through, especially in the gloom. Lock heard the huge man thrashing and cursing. He evaded Bloater and had time to outflank him, reaching a point on the ground which brought him closer to the largest group of civilians. Every second allowed him to regain strength so he could lift everybody out of danger at the same time, leaving Bloater and the woman behind.

A beam of light seared through the undergrowth. People screamed and pleaded for help. Bloater was too close to them. The powerful beam would catch them in its range even if he aimed it at Lock. Bloater bellowed like a bull.

'You hurt my friend. I'm coming for you. I'm gonna tear your limbs off, you Brit bastard.'

The woman's voice cut him short. Lock didn't hear her words. He was taking in the fact that Bloater called her his friend. Bloater roared again.

'Come out or I'll kill the kids.'

The human noise level in the forest dropped. People snatched their children and scattered. Some hugged their kids and were frozen, not knowing what to do. Bloater shouted at people to stay still or he'd fry them.

'Don't hurt anybody. I'm coming out.' Lock cursed. He'd looked at it from the wrong perspective. Instead of taking the civilians away, he should have removed Bloater and the woman. Bloater could levi-fly, but he couldn't teleport. That would have given Lock an advantage.

'Don't hurt them. Let them go.' He expected the weapon beam to hit him, though he hoped that the woman wanted to get her hands on him again. It would buy him a few seconds to think about what to do. He pushed through foliage to reach the edge of the clearing. Bloater's weapon, held hip-high, pointed at a group of four terrified children. The oldest looked about ten. A woman and a man cowered at the tree line near the kids. The woman cried pitifully, covering her mouth with her hands and staring at the four children. Bloater yelled at Lock.

'Keep your hands where I can see 'em. Walk towards me. No sudden moves or they die.'

Lock walked forward, his heart thumping, but he used the time to mark the positions of hostiles. A man knelt awkwardly in combat pose, covering

Lock with a machine pistol. Lock drew closer and recognised him as the woman's companion at the party. The snub-nosed man supported the woman under her head and shoulders. He was injured, bleeding from a head wound, but she was worse. Her arms were limp and she didn't move, but she fixed Lock with a stare that would have melted him to a puddle if her thoughts had been weapons.

'Stop, that's close enough.' Bloater inclined his head in the woman's direction without taking his eyes off Lock. 'You wanna fry him? Let me fry him.'

'No,' she wheezed. Her chest heaved. She was having trouble breathing. She didn't raise her hand, and it dawned on Lock that she couldn't. He might have broken her neck and paralysed her when he kicked her at the marquee. 'She knows what it feels like now,' he thought, and he was glad her hands were useless.

'Come here,' she rasped.

He would rather be killed than allow her to touch him again, but he stumbled forward in the long grass, sweating, afraid, hot and damp. He needed to be closer to Bloater.

'Get rid of the kids,' she ordered Bloater.

Bloater pushed the children with his foot.

'Git.' They didn't move. 'Get outta here!' Bloater roared. Two of the younger children screamed and shook with fear. Lock wanted to kill Bloater. The oldest boy pulled a small girl to her feet, grabbed another youngster by the hand and they fled into the long grass, towards the terrified adults who hovered at the tree line.

'I meant kill them, idiot,' the woman wheezed. 'No, don't bother now.'

'Why are you doing this?' Lock asked, pulling her attention away from the children and taking two steps closer.

'Don't move,' the snub-nosed man ordered.

Lock stopped. She laughed and coughed weakly.

'He's forgotten. Did you hear that? It was only last night, but he doesn't remember.' The smile vanished. She hissed, 'Outside Popayan. The man you murdered, less than fifteen hours ago, he's not even cold – ah, now you remember.'

Lock did remember as he pretended to stumble and took another step closer to Bloater. She meant the Shifter who surprised the demolitions team, the one shot and killed by Jimmy and Vicar. Movement on his left caught his eye. One of Mosquera's bodyguards, a Lancero, pointed a Demon weapon in their direction. The snub-nosed man saw the Lancero at the same time, shouted and fired. Lock had already latched on to Bloater's aura and Shifted them out of the rainforest towards the Andes peaks.

Bloater must have teleported before. Teleportation stunned people the first time and they hardly reacted. Even if forewarned about teleportation, it was still a shock. Bloater showed no sign of being stunned, and was oblivious to anything but his attempt to shoot Lock. Lock watched Bloater trying to aim his weapon. Had Bloater known a bit more about the difference between the skills of levitating and teleporting, he would have realised his weapon was useless in teleportation, like the Demon darts suspended in the air perilously close to his right side and his exposed neck.

Lock had time to speculate whether Bloater's toughened suit would withstand the darts, but didn't particularly care if it did or not as he went into the Pacific Ocean. He wanted Bloater's weapon to continue being useless due to exposure to tons of sea water. Hopefully the darts would be rendered impotent, because in the air they were likely to change course and hit him if they missed Bloater. He plunged deep and came out of Shifting into the middle of a shoal of silvery fish, which fled from the intrusion into their dimly-lit world. The darts drifted, their momentum exhausted.

Bloater's eyes widened when he realised he was under water and, unlike Lock, hadn't taken a deep breath. He let go of the weapon, gulped and started thrashing. Lock gave Bloater a kick to his ear for good measure before teleporting out of the sea, his strength waning. He had been running on adrenaline and suddenly it dissolved. Levitating a few metres above the sea swell he barely made it to land and flopped onto a beach, so feeble he couldn't lift his head. He lay on his back and breathed, visualising strength returning to his muscles and sucking air into his lungs.

A child giggled, a melodious, joyful sound set against the mournful cries of seagulls and waves washing the shoreline. Lock struggled to sit up and scanned the sea for Bloater but saw only people splashing in the waves. Lots of people. He looked at the long stretch of golden sand and started at the sight of hundreds of bodies in swimsuits and bikinis. He was the only fully-clothed person on the beach. A group of children stared, open-mouthed. One of the girls giggled and glanced at her mother, who called her away, scared. A couple of men ambled towards him, ready for trouble. Lock got to his feet, wondering if they would recognise him as a Shifter who had dropped in. He remembered his old man face. Nobody would recognise him for another sixty years.

Adrenaline came back to help him as he thought about what was happening to the children in the jungle. Mustering his energy, he teleported back the way he had come, though he bypassed the plunge in the ocean. He homed in on his previous location like a migrating bird returning to its birthplace. He hoped he would outdistance Bloater. People who could levitate had not shown any homing instinct and were slower than Shifters, but Lock couldn't assume he would get there first. He wasn't in a good enough shape to face Bloater again.

When he dropped to the jungle he scrutinised auras, a whirl of thoughts bombarding him. Maybe Bloater drifted dead at the bottom of the ocean.

Even if the huge man levitated, it would take him so long to figure out where he was and which way to go, he might not arrive for hours. Lock didn't trust his hopes. Searching for the unique aura, he widened his circle to encompass a menagerie of animals, birds and insects, but he didn't find her. He went to the clearing where he'd left her. She wasn't there, and neither was the snub-nosed man.

Mosquera was dead. The bodyguard who fired the Demon lay dead in the undergrowth, executed with shots in his back and to the back of his head. Lock couldn't find the Demon. Looking at the scene, he guessed either her companion was a Shifter or there was another Shifter around. There was no other explanation for the disappearance of the woman. How else could somebody get behind the bodyguard to shoot him, or move a paralysed woman in the space of a few minutes? Whatever had happened, he had other problems, like fifty-odd victims who needed medical attention and a way out. Parents worried about their children, wives fretted about their husbands and men were aggressive about leaving the jungle.

Lock gathered them into one place, reassuring them and keeping the situation calm. He ignored episodes of dizziness and tingling pains in his neck and arm where the woman had touched him. He didn't want to take the survivors to the field hospital at the village. Some were too badly injured and needed proper hospital care. When Lock was sure he had all the auras he could find, he teleported them to the biggest, most expensive hospital in Bogota. He didn't explain to the medical staff what had happened apart from saying they had been caught in a gun battle in the jungle. His company would foot the bill for medical care, he said, and he gave the secretary a secure number intended only for his personal needs in an emergency.

A few of the dishevelled refugees didn't need hospital treatment. They clamoured at him for his attention. One said they would have been better off at the villa rather than being dumped in the middle of nowhere, getting bitten and stung to death or threatened by maniacs with space weapons, not to mention being stranded in the tops of trees suspended over a drop of a hundred metres. Others wanted to know where they were, how they were supposed to get home, and could he find a handbag that was too expensive to lose. What about my wallet said another man, how do you expect us to get home with no shoes and no money?

Lock levitated a metre in the air, raised his voice and bellowed at them to shut up. Everybody stopped and gawped at him, even the medical staff, including one nurse on the phone to security. Security guards were on their way. Lock looked at the sea of upturned faces and spoke through gritted teeth.

'Anybody who wants help to get home, come with me. Into this room. Now.' People didn't move. 'Nobody? Okay, then, stay here.'

'I'm going.' A man stepped forward into the office Lock had indicated.

Some of the others followed. Lock took the group of eighteen out of the hospital to a park and asked if anybody had a phone. A man did. Lock called the Embassy. Stringer answered and gave the green light for Lock to enter the teleporter-designated room.

'Meet me there.'

Lock explained to his group that a very nice man at the British Embassy would help them get back home from Bogota, and they were safe. Somebody protested he didn't want to go to the British Embassy and he'd rather go to the American Embassy.

'Tough shit.' Lock teleported into the room where Stringer waited with a security detail. Stringer was aghast.

'What the hell is this? Who are these people?' he shouted against the shrilling of alarm sirens.

'They're the end result of your decision to go to war on Mosquera. They're your responsibility. There's thirty more in hospital, you'll be hearing about them, too.'

Lock needed another few moments to regain his strength. He handed the phone to Stringer, who stared at the people being held by armed guards.

'You can't leave them here. For fuck's sake, Lock, what're you playing at? This is a breach of security.'

'Yeah, you'll want to destroy that civilian's phone, it has a sensitive number on it. I have to get back to the guys. Tell PC there's a woman, a hostile, a very dangerous one. Possibly with another Shifter. She's small, dark haired, early twenties, thin, has a neck injury. Her neck may be broken, but she can kill by touch. Tell them not to let her touch them. And Bloater is around. Tell the lads to keep their eyes open.'

Lock teleported, the fury on Stringer's face fresh in his mind. He nearly dropped from the Shift with laughing.

CHAPTER 15

The village field hospital was a place nobody wanted to be unless they were too far gone to care. Cockroaches scuttled in dark corners, even during daylight. Two surgeons and three paramedics worked at full stretch, dealing with soldiers, enemy prisoners and captive civilians alike. The long hut full of casualties reeked of blood and urine, attracting swarms of flies and biting insects in greater numbers than normal for the sub-tropical jungle.

It was the kind of place where medics patched up gunshot wounds without any questions asked, but Jimmy had no gunshot wounds. He received no treatment as nothing could be done apart from giving him a saline drip in his arm. He tried not to dwell on the way Felipe died and avoided looking at Ramon in the next bunk. Ramon had been hit by two darts and would not be reassured. He had seen the way others had died from the lethal darts. A bond sprang up between Jimmy and Ramon, knowing they were doomed, though neither of them said so out loud.

Jimmy resigned himself to imminent death and was determined not to make a fuss. His mates didn't know how to deal with him. The way they trod on tiptoes drove him nuts. He didn't recognise his aggressive instincts as a defence mechanism against something so horrible he couldn't even think about it.

Vicar presented him with two bottles of tequila he had liberated from Mosquera's villa on the way out. He stood by the dirty camp bed with a silly grin on his face as though he had appointed himself as Jimmy's personal guardian angel. Jimmy passed a bottle to Ramon and eyed the bottle of whisky Vicar kept for himself.

'What d'you want me to say? You don't bloody like tequila.'

'Give us it back then, you ungrateful bastard.'

That was more like it, black humour banter in a dire situation.

'No, I'll drink myself stupid before I take the one-bullet salute.' Jimmy unscrewed the top and gulped some down.

'I heard you told Bilton to fuck off,' Vicar said, and chuckled. 'Did you really call him a one-armed wanker who couldn't tell the difference between his dick and a piece of rope and he'd pulled on the wrong one?'

Jimmy smiled but didn't reply.

'You'll be eating your words when you get out.' Vicar broke off, staring down the hut where PC, Ginge and Nails interrogated prisoners, trying to find out if a store of antidote existed. Two American advisers observed the proceedings.

'No, I won't,' Jimmy said, saving Vicar from further embarrassment. 'I don't want to see that ugly bastard again.'

He eyed the door where an elderly Harford fidgeted, looking into the hut every now and then.

'If Lewis doesn't stop flapping I'll tell him to fuck off, too. He should be getting us out of here,' Jimmy said.

'We can't go until Mick's patched up. He took one in the gut.'

'How's he doing?'

Vicar grimaced.

'He's being operated on. Doesn't look good. I don't think he's going to make it.'

'Shit. He's a top bloke.'

'Yeah.'

The sound of an approaching chopper drowned out further conversation. The hut rattled and the downdraft threatened to blow the corrugated roof away, but it held. Jimmy swigged the tequila and got tipsy. It took the edge off the changes going on in his body. Sometimes he felt on fire, as though he'd been dropped into a cauldron of boiling tar, and horrible sensations flashed through his limbs. First one arm hurt like hell then the other and the agonising pain shot to his legs and back to his arms. He recognised the experience as something affecting his sympathetic nervous system, and sending out contradictory messages. He wasn't being prodded with red-hot pokers and his fingers weren't being cut off with pliers. Nobody stabbed needles or knives into his thighs and his feet weren't dangling over a fire – but it hurt like hell.

What he couldn't keep up with were the voices of millions of cells talking to each other in a massive battle. It involved every organ and when he closed his eyes and concentrated, he had the best seat in the house. He sensed his liver sending distress signals to his kidneys to tell them they'd better get rid of the enemy. The kidneys responded by sending a message back saying they had problems of their own and would get to it when they could. As long as millions of invaders were being pumped out by the heart, the liver would be better off telling the defence system to screen the things out. In a hazy state of drunkenness, Jimmy tried to do it himself, instructing white blood cells to get up and at 'em. He got the message back they were already dog-tired and tipping alcohol into his system didn't help.

The chopper took off. A few seconds later another one landed. Jimmy raised the bottle to swill another mouthful of tequila, but spat it out and allowed his bleary thoughts to roam where they would. He had no regrets about what he'd done with his life and if a God existed, he wasn't afraid to meet him. Sure, he'd killed people, but he and his teams captured more than they killed. He was a soldier and that's what soldiers do – they take captives or kill bad guys who would have killed him given half the chance to fire first. He had no problem with that. It didn't keep him awake at night, unlike the memories of dead friends' faces, of the mates he'd seen blown up. He made an effort to put it out of his mind. Soldiers in Special Forces developed a sixth sense about the way other men would react. They were attuned to each other and over time those bonds were closer than family bonds. It hurt like hell to lose mates.

The chopper's rotor blades subsided and wound down. He nearly got up to assess the situation outside then remembered he didn't have to do that any more. Vicar got up instead and Jimmy followed his progress to the door in a mental fog and closed his eyes. Vicar was a good bloke, too. The SAS and the regular army gave them a camaraderie that nobody outside the services understood. He couldn't leave the Regiment for civvy street any more than he could consider early retirement to live in an old peoples' home. Now he might not have that choice. Vicar returned and Jimmy sensed him squatting by the bunk. He opened his eyes. The distraught expression on Vicar's face disappeared but the forced cheerfulness came too late. Jimmy knew it was fake.

'Vic, there's something I want you to do when you get back. Some people I want you to see. I want you to give them a message.'

'Fuck off, you can tell them yourself.'

Jimmy's anger welled up and overflowed.

'Stop it, Vic. Fucking shut up and listen. Stop all this bloody pretence.'

'Okay, okay. What is it?'

'I want you to see my parents in Fort William. No matter what happens here, you're to tell them I didn't suffer. You got that? It's really important they know that. Okay?'

At the thought of his mother, the patient lady who had put up with four wayward sons, Jimmy choked, turning it into a coughing fit.

'Okay.'

'And I want you to see Angie, my ex-wife. Tell her–' Jimmy paused, a hundred messages going through his head and not all of them kind. 'Just tell her I'm sorry.'

'I didn't know you were married.'

'Yeah. It didn't work out. The usual thing, long times apart, the Regiment, that kind of stuff.' He paused. 'Still, maybe it's just as well. If she'd turned out like her Mam I'd have been married to somebody with a face like a painter's radio.'

They laughed, and Jimmy had a wild thought that if he put more effort into it, if he tuned in to his body, maybe he had a chance. It was worth a go, especially as he could still hear cells talking.

'Okay, Vic, fuck off now, I want some kip. Go and yap with him.' Jimmy nodded at Ramon, and for the first time noticed how many flies buzzed around Ramon, yet none buzzed around himself. Something was different.

Vicar said something uncomplimentary and turned to Ramon. Jimmy closed his eyes and slipped into a state of partial trance, trying to understand the cellular communications in his body. A flurry of excitement by the door distracted him. Rosi, Patuazon's granddaughter, burst across the hut and flung herself, sobbing, on Ramon's shoulder. Jimmy shook his head. Patuazon followed her in, looked at the soldiers crowding every camp bed and chair, shuffled awkwardly and went out again. PC and an American rushed from the other end of the hut and went after him. Jimmy yanked the tape off his arm and pulled out the cannula. Vicar noticed.

'What are you doing? Best leave that in.'

'I'm not staying in here with women crying.'

Vicar tried to remonstrate, but Jimmy wouldn't listen, lapsing into his Scottish accent.

'It's no doing me any good, this shite.' He threw the drip feed aside. 'I'm better off out there. Help me find a quiet spot.'

He swung his legs over the side of the camp bed, stood up and fell back. He'd never felt so weak in his life, and millions of cells warned him not to move. For the first time since being hit by the Demon dart the situation frightened him. He found it easier to be philosophical about the end of his life when he didn't suffer the effects so much, but imminent death stared him in the face, he was getting worse and it was another matter altogether. He sat on the bunk and glanced at Ramon. Until then he hadn't noticed Ramon's jerky movements. His muscles were going into lockdown. Ramon's eyes were sunken. Jimmy pushed himself off the bunk. Vicar steadied him.

'Look, pal, just sit down.'

'I'm going out.' Jimmy left the hut as Patuazon returned with his bodyguards to drag Rosi away from Ramon.

~~~~~~~~

Lock squatted at the back of the hospital hut among ferns, pulling equipment out of the bergen he had retrieved. The items included a respirator, a remote scanner capable of downloading an entire computer hard drive in less than three minutes, two insect drones and plasticuffs. He wanted to travel light, relying on his belt kit with PixelRain clothing for protection, rather than his helmet. The PixelRain suit, with its extra coverings, was stashed inside the bergen for later when nobody could see him putting it on. PC, the big Yorkshireman, stood guard although only a
~~~~~~~~

gaggle of native Indian children hung around. They peeped round the end of the hut. Lock spoke fast to PC as he worked.

'Command said Nightingale didn't know about any other antidote except for the small amount stored in Mosquera's villa, and it was kept in the side destroyed by fire. Any antidote was lost when it went up. What about the prisoners, do they know anything?'

PC shook his head.

'Nope. None of them knows owt. The only one that might is Mosquera's number two, the one with the head wound, and he's out of it.'

Lock stuffed sensor equipment in his pockets, together with the most important piece of kit, the insect drones, among them a specially-programmed drone bee that would disrupt the anti-teleporter system at Patuazon's estate. He pushed the control sunglasses alongside the box before speaking.

'You know how Mosquera got the Demons? How he got them on the cheap?' He didn't wait for PC to reply. 'They were discarded because the Chinese were worried about their status on human rights. Having biological weapons didn't look good. The darts don't discriminate between friend and foe. They lost more men from their own side than they killed. What's more, when the nanomaterials mutated they became unstable and acted like real viruses. The Chinese couldn't predict what they'd do.'

He paused, turning on an explosives detector to check the battery level. Satisfied, he switched it off and shoved it into a pocket next to his ruggedised computer.

'They thought the Demons might unleash a full-scale plague on their borders. So they sold them as a job lot, darts and everything, to Nightingale. They didn't care what happened on another continent.'

'Bastards.'

Lock put a Sig Sauer pistol in his thigh holster and reloaded a Diemaco assault rifle. He pushed spare magazines into his combat trouser pockets and his jacket, making sure nothing clinked when he moved. The children by the end of the hut giggled and one imitated Lock's movements. Lock double-checked the pouches holding the stun grenades secure. PC handed him a radio kit of throat microphone and its in-the-mouth receiver.

'Take these. Mick won't be needing them.' He paused. 'It's okay, I've washed the mouthpiece.'

Lock looked at the receiver. The hygiene aspect didn't bother him as much as the fact that Mick might never need the kit again. He put it on.

'Maybe I should stick around a bit longer,' Lock said.

PC looked at Lock with a hint of amusement. It was as if Lock was a student asking an eminent professor if he knew his subject.

'No. There's nowt you can do here until Mick's been seen to. Like you said, it's the last chance to have a crack at Patuazon's and see if he's supplying AH-4. We'll keep Patuazon here as long as we can. Chris is on standby with the chopper for evac if we get stuck.'

Lock put the receiver in his mouth, pushed it over his teeth on his upper jaw and reminded himself that even with three men down, the remaining four highly-skilled troopers were more than capable of holding off what remained of Patuazon's army if they had to. He looked at an altimeter reading on his computer screen.

'The drone's up at three thousand metres. We should have a clear signal. It's low on battery but we should have comms open for about an hour.'

Lock and PC checked their radio channels to each other as well as the common channel to Stringer in the Command and Control room at the British Embassy in Bogota. When they finished Lock picked up his bergen with the suit inside and teleported to Patuazon's estate.

PC met Ginge on his way out of the hut.

'I was just coming to call you,' Ginge said. 'Mosquera's number two is conscious. He's ready to talk. He's scared shitless at being left with this lot. He keeps drifting but I think we can push it, and get more out of him about an antidote.'

PC nodded and went to Nails, who stood guard over the frightened prisoner.

~~~~~~~~

Lock stopped before Patuazon's perimeter fence to put on the PixelRain suit before Shifting in. The estate sprawled over several kilometres and lay three hundred kilometres further north than Mosquera's villa, located in a strip of green between the Andes and the coast. Foliage surrounded it, a sub-tropical jungle that wasn't as dense or aggressively fertile as the dark undergrowth near Mocoa. Lock didn't rise into the range of Patuazon's radar. He put on the control sunglasses and sent an insect drone above the canopy to get a satellite fix on his position. The GPS confirmed his position as where he expected to be, west of the estate and out of range of Patuazon's electronic defences. He keyed the radio channel for Stringer, reported in and added,

'I'll contact you when I can.'

'Understood.'

Lock teleported nearer to the entrance, too far away for his neuro-sensory skill to detect people, apart from guards at the checkpoint tower.

'Going in now. Comms off.'

Stringer and PC acknowledged and Lock shut down the connection. He had reached the point of no return. His next move would make him Patuazon's enemy, the opponent of a man much more intelligent than Mosquera, more cunning, and with considerable resources at his disposal.
~~~~~~~~

Lock wasn't frightened. He had waited for this for weeks. He was determined to get in and find the information, escape safely and send the package by radio to Stringer. Patuazon's men would know somebody had penetrated their defences. He had to make sure he left before they realised who it was. He double-checked the position of the guards, sent the drone bee in to disrupt the anti-teleporter net and teleported to the side of the servants' cookhouse.

Lock expected to be hit by a hidden laser. When that didn't happen in the first five seconds he went into neuro-sensory aura mode, watching for any movement of auras towards him. The extractor fan behind him hummed and rattled and a smell of fried onions drifted on the air. He retrieved the disruptor bee drone.

The next phase would test the suit to the limit and he had to trust it would keep him camouflaged on a walk of forty metres over a wide expanse of dusty ground. Teleporting within the estate would trip alarms. Slowing his breathing, he stepped from behind the building, weapon into his shoulder under the poncho with the end of the barrel poking out. He crept towards the western side of the villa, keeping his steps quiet and steady and watching for other people. Neuro-sensory checks were not possible unless he stopped walking, and he didn't want to stop. Exposure in the sunlight with no chance of rain made him vulnerable to guards in the towers.

Heat rose in his face and his skin felt tight. He recalled what Cheena said about his hands and face feeling inflamed. Maybe the process of transformation to his real age had begun. Sweat drenched his clothes. Every step took him closer to the villa, away from an imaginary weapon trained on the back of his head.

A truck screeched to a halt, out of sight. Lock's heart thumped, and a twinge of pain shot through his chest. He stopped and checked auras, listened to shouts coming from the truck and turned his Diemaco in their direction. The auras made no quick movements and stayed near the truck instead of fanning out. A man laughed and shouted in rapid-fire Spanish. Lock continued his journey faster. Men at the truck complained about unloading it, and somebody else not pulling his weight.

Without warning two swarthy men in jeans and T-shirts with pistols in waist holsters, appeared on Lock's left, carrying heavy sacks. They walked towards him, engrossed in their complaints. The short man did the grumbling. The taller and older man marched on as though he'd heard it all before. Lock increased his pace to get out of their way. The tall man looked up, frowned and stared at him. Lock stopped. His finger twitched on the trigger. Any second now. The man slowed, staring. He halted, squinting in Lock's direction.

The shorter man carried on then stopped and looked back.

'What's up?' he said, staring alternately between the tall man and what the tall man was looking at. The man took a step to one side and cocked his head as though it would improve his sight.

'I thought I saw something.'

'Where?'

'Over there.' The tall man nodded with his chin towards Lock, who froze, sweating, his finger taut on the trigger, measuring the distance and deciding which target to go for first. The small man peered in the wrong direction.

'Over where?'

'There, about five metres away. Something moved.'

The older man side-stepped like a marionette. The short man shook his head impatiently.

'There's nothing there, Miguel. You're hung over. Heat crazy. Come on, they're waiting for this stuff.'

'There was something, I tell you, Juan. Something moved. Like a demon, a spirit.'

'There's nothing. You loco, old man. Come on.'

He walked on faster, spooked. Miguel followed, looking ahead and muttering prayers to the Virgin Mary. They hurried past Lock six metres away. Lock hadn't moved anything except his eyes. He watched until he couldn't see them then kept a close aura eye on them until he heard the creaky cookhouse door open. The clatter of cooking utensils was louder. The door slammed and the noise subsided. He continued his walk to the relative safety of the villa and squatted by the brick wall, trembling at how close he came to being discovered.

Scanning inside the villa, he detected a few fuzzy auras in that part of the complex. Guards on the rooftops didn't see him creeping round the outside walls. Standing in deep shadow, he removed his hood and the sunglasses, put on the respirator and replaced the hood. Slipping inside the doorway he moved cautiously along tiled floors to the eastern wing, which contained Patuazon's locked rooms. He passed underneath closed-circuit cameras. If they picked up his movements along corridors they didn't raise any audible alarm.

Voices interrupted his progress and he dodged into a room close to the secure area. A man and woman walked past, engrossed in conversation. Lock recognised Patuazon's eldest daughter and her lover. He waited until they had gone and checked auras again. Two auras were unmoving in a room on his left, and he saw another one ahead of him in a corridor, a guard. Beyond the guard he glimpsed two other humans, their auras dimmed by something that might be steel or concrete. They moved and he saw three auras, not two. He thought he saw another one further off, but they were all lower down than the level he was on.

It wasn't just a locked wing, he realised. Patuazon had a bunker. The discovery excited him. The bunker meant Patuazon must have something to hide in it. Lock considered his next move. He could overpower the guard and force him to open the door, or he could use the drone disruptor and teleport in. Either way, his presence would be detected and he'd have little time to find information and get out. There was a third option, a slim chance he could make the guard do what he wanted without arousing suspicion or setting off alarms. He crept forward, within metres of the man.

The guard stood by the door with the glazed air of boredom, but snapped out of it. He pressed a button on the radio by his lapel, brought his weapon up, put on a pair of thermal imaging goggles and stared down the corridor away from Lock. Something was wrong. Suspecting compromise, Lock pulled out a CS gas stun grenade.

'Where? Nothing. What am I looking for? Camouflage?' The guard turned, stared at Lock and his eyes narrowed. 'Shit.'

Lock had already activated the disruptor drone. He teleported into the bunker, leaving behind explosions and CS gas mist.

His hood was tangled with the respirator and he could only see out of one eyepiece. He ripped off the hood, dropped it and disabled the steel door from inside, shouting at two men and a woman and ordering them to get down and stay still. Lock glimpsed his reflection in the shiny door – a disembodied head in a respirator. He looked more like a bug than a human. It gave him a psychological edge, as it was obvious the men and woman were unarmed technicians and not military personnel. Lock's appearance and aggression terrified them. None of the three were willing to die for Patuazon's sake and they didn't put up any fight. He made them lie face down and bound their wrists with plasticuffs.

Lock faced an array of six computer terminals. He plugged his scanner into a laptop and while it downloaded data, he looked around. The bunker was five metres long by three wide, with another steel door at the far end and a lot of fuzziness behind it. On his left he saw an ordinary door.

'What's in there?' He realised the man he shouted at couldn't see his suited arm pointing at the ordinary door. Lock pulled off his poncho and unhooked his sweat-drenched respirator. The remote scanner beeped to say it had finished. He bellowed his question again, picking up the scanner.

'Bathroom,' a man said. Lock pointed at the steel door.

'Where does that lead?'

The man quavered,

'It doesn't go…I don't know. Nobody does. Nobody is allowed in there, only Senor Patuazon.'

'Get up. All of you. Move.'

Lock plugged the scanner into a second computer, leaving it to do its work while he pushed the prisoners into the toilet area – a small, basic room with two toilets, a washbasin, paper hand towels and a bin.

He checked the computer room for auras. It was empty, as was the corridor where the guard had been, so he turned his attention to the steel door. Trying to see past the fuzziness, he perceived the area behind it leading into a hollow space. Although he concentrated, he couldn't probe any further. The only way to find out what was on the other side of the door was by teleporting into the hollow. Patuazon must have used a trusted Shifter to get him inside. He collected the scanner, but stopped. Patuazon would have set traps for teleporters. Or was claustrophobia holding him back? He pushed the scanner into a pocket, pushed his fear into an imaginary pouch, took out the drone disruptor and switched it on. Anti-teleporter systems were new and not always reliable. The disruptor covered most of the bases. He teleported.

A spine-tingling jolt struck him as he emerged into the capsule, confirming he had been right about Patuazon's defences. Lights flashed on the door and an alarm shrilled, but the disruptor worked well enough to keep him alive. The tiny room had another door at the far end. Lock retrieved the disruptor and teleported forwards. Something threw him back and sent him sprawling inside the capsule. Aura sense told him the door butted against solid rock. It didn't lead anywhere. He stood in front of it, bewildered. There must be something – why go to all the trouble of setting up such a place when it didn't go anywhere? Maybe Patuazon hadn't finished it. He checked his watch. He'd been in the bunker seven minutes, too long. Patuazon would be in his helicopter and on his way back. Time to leave, but Lock lingered. He had a gut feeling the computers he'd already hacked into would not reveal anything useful.

Patuazon, the crafty fox, must have something else in place. Lock scanned the wall on his left and discovered a space within the dense rock formation, like a tunnel, barely discernible in aura mode. The door was a bluff, constructed to fool ordinary Shifters into believing they had reached a dead end. Patuazon had created the anteroom as a mouse trap and the tunnel beyond was nothing more than a natural cavity in the rocks. He could follow a fissure; he'd done it before, but fear of tunnels and caves squeezed his chest and gave him a sharp pain. He slowed his breathing, relaxed, and the pain passed.

Holding his weapon at the aim, he went for the tunnel beyond the wall before he had time to change his mind. The Shift felt like being squeezed through the tight neck of a glass bottle but he carried on, following his instincts and mentally feeling for changes in rock density. He hit a space and stopped. Gasping for air, he emerged into a windowless, door-less chamber six metres square. Low lights on the walls glowed green, giving the impression of being in a bowl of pea soup. Something hummed.

Patuazon had built a series of chambers within his bunker complex. There was the main computer room under the villa, the anteroom, and now this – the guy was good. The cold, musty chamber carried the odour of bare concrete. A wide, rectangular stone pillar bisected the room into separate areas. On Lock's side of the pillar an easy chair with deep cushions had a control panel set into the right arm. A large, wall-mounted television screen had home cinema equipment underneath. Boxes of DVDs and a few memory sticks lay in untidy piles on a black rug. Lock knew the cavern was empty, but he checked for people on the other side of the pillar before lowering his weapon.

He found what he had been looking for – a desk with a switched-off desktop computer and an array of monitor screens above it on the wall. Cables hung against the concrete. Adjacent to the desk, a small electrical generator kept a closed air conditioning unit working and the green low-level lights alive. Near it were two metal tables, one covered by an electric kettle, battered cups and a jar of coffee. On the floor a plastic container of water sat next to empty whisky bottles, jars of coffee and powdered milk. A switched-off radio transmitter filled the other table. Discarded wrappers from packets of biscuits and snacks were strewn underneath. Patuazon might be crafty, but he wasn't tidy.

Lock switched on the computer and in neuro-sensory mode penetrated deep outside the room while he waited for the computer to boot up. Solid rock hemmed in two walls and a third concealed the tunnel he'd used to enter. On the opposite side to the tunnel he detected another space. It felt the same as those he had wormed through while searching underground for Jimmy in Scotland. It was like another tunnel covered by another wall, extending further than his neuro-sensory skill could follow. The computer jingled to let him know it was ready. He set the scanner and looked at the memory sticks.

Between the chair and the television screen a low wooden coffee table was at an angle, as if pushed aside by a foot. Somebody had thrown magazines over it. The top one was open and the centrefold showed a naked woman in an erotic pose. Next to the magazines, a three-quarters full bottle of whisky and a dirty, part-filled glass told their own story. Three DVD cases of pornographic films were left on the corner of the table. Patuazon had made his lair comfortable, even going so far as to hang a painting on one side of the pillar. It showed a languid, naked woman exposing her genitals. His den revealed a side of his character Lock had suspected, the antithesis to his religious conversion and the tidy, rigidly proper décor of his villa. It uncovered his unrestrained pleasure in worldly things and delights of the flesh. It was a lonely place.

Lock wasn't interested in the contradictory nature of Patuazon's character. He pocketed the memory sticks. They might not have anything on them other than more porn, but it was worth a look. The room baffled him. Why would Patuazon build such inaccessible, intensely private chambers? The implication of where he was hit him like being felled by a tree. He hadn't paid attention to what mattered. He'd made a mistake. The only way in or out of the room was by teleportation, and the only person who used the room was Patuazon. Which meant Patuazon didn't need a personal Shifter, he was a Shifter. He would know about trouble at his villa, and didn't need a helicopter to get back. He could return any second.

Lock went into aura mode. He saw nobody in the tunnel leading to the cupboard-like anteroom. The scanner beeped, making him jump. He grabbed it, stuffed it in his pocket, looked to his left and froze. Patuazon was in front of him, pointing an MP7 weapon at him. Lock's heart missed a beat. He didn't see what hit the back of his head, but the shock travelling through his body thundered in his skull like an express train just before he fell.

~~~~~~~~

Lock didn't lose consciousness. He lay face down on the concrete floor, stunned. Grit and dust clogged his nostrils, and he couldn't move. The thought of ending his life in a dark hole, thousands of kilometres from home, terrified him. He thought of Lianne and Thomas. She'd never know what happened. Thomas would grow up without a father. He had to get out. The need to sneeze aggravated his nose, but he couldn't sneeze because of the paralysis.

'Don't kill him. Search him,' Patuazon ordered. He covered Lock with his machine pistol as an unseen man groped at the poncho. A thought made Lock break out in a cold sweat. Patuazon was going to torture him. He liked torturing people. He would be dinner for his tigers.

'Keep hold of him.' The man tugged at Lock's belt kit. 'I can only see his head. That stuff he's wearing makes my eyes go funny.'

Fingernails dug into Lock's neck and specks of light whirled in front of his eyes. He went into aura mode. The person with a hand on his neck had the unique aura. She was supposed to be paralysed, not him. The man pulled off Lock's pixelated gloves and started on the poncho, revealing the belt kit underneath. Lock was helpless and he hated it. Frustration and dismay consumed him but he pushed it away. He was overpowered and held captive for the second time that day, but they knew his position in the chamber before teleporting in. Patuazon must have used hidden cameras, which Lock's sensors hadn't detected. He couldn't have prevented their attack.

Patuazon put his MP7 machine pistol in its shoulder sling and touched a keypad in the wall, the control for the generator and air conditioning unit next to it. The hinged panel opened, revealing a second control keypad behind it. Patuazon pressed buttons and the bilious atmosphere in the
~~~~~~~~

underground chamber disappeared. Lock blinked in blinding white light. Patuazon left the panel open.

The man took all Lock's weapons and equipment and stacked them in a pile well out of Lock's reach.

'He's clean. He had this on him.'

The gunman strode towards Patuazon and Lock saw a Demon weapon strapped to his back. It was the woman's companion. He must have taken the Demon while Lock was busy with Bloater. He handed over all the sensors, including the scanner with the computer information, then covered Lock with his MP7 machine pistol. He still had an ugly head wound, an open gash on his forehead just below the hairline, sticky with dried blood. Injury made him vulnerable.

While Patuazon examined the equipment, the woman sent a spasm screaming around Lock's body. All his muscles cramped until they felt as hard as stone. It was agony. His chest tightened. He wanted to get his hands on her and stop her. She inflicted pain for the hell of it. The sadistic bitch. She didn't kill him but she enjoyed taking him to the edge. Lock tried to detach his mind from the excruciating pain and thought about his options. He was entombed in the deepest part of Patuazon's chain of underground chambers, a long way from the villa. Nobody could come to his aid because they didn't know about the chambers. He was on his own and getting weaker. He thought about the escape route along the long tunnel to the other three rooms, but had no strength to teleport. She stopped the spasm, leaving him gasping. His heart hammered out of rhythm. If she took her hand away for long enough he would have one chance, a slim one at that, against three armed Shifters.

Patuazon ambled towards Lock, frowning at the scanner in his hand. Lock tingled when he realised Patuazon didn't know what he held. It didn't surprise him because the scanner was a British invention, way ahead of anything the rest of the world had, and secret. It was a seriously expensive piece of kit, packed with electronics inside a smooth, matt titanium outer case. The scanner resembled a large cigarette box, fifteen centimetres long by ten wide and two deep. It had no keypad. Sensitive microphones were embedded and concealed in the outer casing, with nothing visible on the surface. It could only be activated by Lock's voice coupled with a coded command. It took force to smash it open, which triggered automatic destruction of the contents. Patuazon couldn't get in and Lock could use that to his advantage.

Patuazon looked at Lock as if weighing up a prize specimen in his zoo.

'Are you sure it's him?'

'Quite sure.' The voice was cold, as it had been at the party. Patuazon peered at Lock.

'Doesn't look like him.'

'It's him. He's been changed by a transmute and made to look older.'

Startled, Lock wondered how she knew. Patuazon leaned closer. Hooded eyes studied Lock from under heavy brows, and the bright light exaggerated acne scars on his cheeks and chin. His gold teeth glinted. He held the scanner near Lock's face.

'Lewis, or Harford, or whatever your true name is, I need to know about this. She's going to take her hand away and you will tell me. It's no good trying to teleport, the system is back on line. It's set on lethal and you'll be dead before you fade.'

He paused, while Lock's heart sank. His sole escape route had been cut off and Patuazon knew all about him, including his teleportation technique.

'You fell right into my trap, like so many others before you. You were under surveillance the minute you arrived. I know all about your attempts at penetrating my villa with your miniature drones. I know you killed one of my best Shifters, and Maria knows it too. She's very angry with you.' He looked up. 'Isn't that right, Maria?'

She responded with another jolt of agony for Lock, adding more sparks and flashes to the specks of light obscuring his vision. His mind reeled, not so much due to her torture, but because of the revelation that the woman with the unique aura was Maria, Patuazon's mistress. She was in disguise at the party. It was a very good disguise. Impossibly good. She couldn't have recovered so rapidly from being crippled – unless she was a shape-shifter, a transmute. That's why she had a different aura.

His head whirled as she starved him of oxygen. He felt as if he split into three personas. The terrified part of him wanted to run in a blind panic. Another part was disengaged, almost clinical, dissecting information about whether she was a transmute. The third part struggled to hold it together and focus on the threat to his life.

'Let him speak,' Patuazon ordered. Maria released her nerve hold and transferred her grip to his forearm. His head cleared. He choked and shuddered but still couldn't move. His limbs felt disconnected, like useless lumps of meat hanging from his torso.

'Get him over there.'

The gunman grabbed Lock's right arm and dragged him across the rug, grunting with the effort. He pulled him into a sitting position against cold stone, next to the radio table. Lock had his first look at Maria. She was mostly like the Maria he met, although on closer inspection he could see differences – the face was rounder and the nose larger. He checked auras again, but there was no mistake. Maria's aura was identical to that of the woman at the party, cobalt with tendrils of jade green and an occasional hue of lemon yellow.

'Is this a transmitter?' Patuazon demanded, holding up the scanner. Lock guessed Patuazon was worried about something on the computer that

Lock had downloaded and sent to base. The specks of light flashing in front of Lock's eyes dwindled. He felt sick. Patuazon raised his voice and asked a second time. Lock didn't bother replying. Whatever he said, Patuazon would kill him so he might as well play sick for a few precious seconds and regain strength.

'Damn it, you've hit him too hard,' Patuazon said.

'He's stalling.' She sent a surge of pain up Lock's forearm. His back arched, his limbs stiffened and his feet scuffed the edge of the rug away from the stone floor. A groan escaped through his clenched teeth.

'Take your hand away,' Patuazon ordered.

Her action enraged Patuazon, but Maria seemed defensive, as if she detested the way he spoke to her. Patuazon liked to be obeyed and he didn't like the way her hand lingered. It was defiance and insubordination. Lock saw his chance. He knew Patuazon and his weaknesses.

She withdrew her hand.

'He's dangerous.'

Lock slumped against the wall. Patuazon ignored her, effectively putting her in her place.

'Tell me what I want to know and you'll live – you and your men.'

It was such a cliché Lock couldn't help a snort of derision.

'Answer or I'll let her have her fun. Is this a transmitter?' Lock didn't answer. He needed to be stronger. Patuazon nodded at the gunman, who operated the radio equipment on the table.

'No, it isn't a transmitter,' Lock croaked. He'd take the risk. Patuazon looked relieved, which confirmed the importance of the information downloaded from the computer.

'What is it?'

'It's a weapon.'

'You're lying.' Patuazon turned to the gunman. 'Whittaker, tell the men to kill the British soldiers.'

'No, wait,' Lock gasped, but Whittaker pressed a button on the radio and gave the order.

'Tell me what it is and I'll countermand the order,' Patuazon said.

Lock didn't answer Patuazon. He turned to Maria, forcing the words out.

'Where's your pal, Bloater? The big guy who trashed one of your own choppers when Mosquera's deal with the gringos went down in Bogota. Killed a lot of Senor Patuazon's men. Stole the money. You know, the guy who looks like a maggot.'

Maria was surprised, and it made Lock feel good. Patuazon saw the fear on Maria's face and knew he'd been betrayed.

'What's this about?'

'He's lying. He's trying to set us against each other.'

Lock kept the pressure on. Every second that passed he grew stronger.

'What did you do with your share of the blood money? Did you give Bloater half, or did you keep it all? You were the one who set up the ambush, he was just the muscle who trashed the chopper and killed your boss's men, how many was it? Three, four or five?'

'Five.' Patuazon's voice was cold. His weapon was holstered but he moved his hand towards it. Lock kept his gaze on Maria but he could see Patuazon out of the corner of his eye. Maria's mask of indifference dropped into place.

'I don't know what he's talking about. I don't know this Bloater.'

Lock's stressed heart leapt at the opportunity presented by the lie.

'Yeah, you do. He's the guy who got you out when we attacked Mosquera's villa. Handy having somebody like that around, especially when he's got a plasma burner that can take out a chopper.'

'Shut up.' She lurched forward, aiming for Lock's neck to strangle the words in his throat. It was a mistake.

Lock launched himself, feet-first, levitating like a bullet at Whittaker, the person he judged as the one in a position to do the most damage. Lock's feet smashed into his chest with enough force to break ribs. They flew past the pillar and cannoned into the table with Lock sprawling on top of him. The table broke under their weight, scattering DVD cases and shattering the whisky glass.

At the same time there was a burst of gunfire. Patuazon, or Maria – or both of them – fired and moved. Rounds whistled and ricocheted off the walls and roof in the confined space. It would be a miracle if any of them came out alive. Whittaker was winded, too slow to stop Lock yanking the MP7 out of his grasp. Using the butt of the machine pistol Lock clouted him hard on his open head wound. Whittaker slumped with a groan, clutching his head. Lock dropped to one knee and fired a sustained burst into the control panel by the generator to disable the anti-teleporter device. The lights went out and seconds later the firing stopped. Everybody knew muzzle flash would give away their position and act like a bullet magnet.

Lock wasn't sure the anti-teleporter system was offline and didn't want to take the chance of trying to escape just to be killed. He kept his knee on Whittaker's chest, his hand on his neck and the MP7 jammed against his temple. Either Whittaker had the sense to keep still and quiet, or he was too dazed to do anything else. Lock switched to neuro-sensory mode and levitated himself and his prisoner above the television screen. Somebody panted in the pitch-black darkness, moving fast. Lock entered his grey world of shapeless forms, dark blocks of objects in front of each other, and auras. He saw Maria's aura moving round the pillar. The lights flickered back on.

They were all in different places. Patuazon slumped against a wall by one side of the easy chair, his arms hanging by his side, his MP7 machine pistol still in his right hand.

'Whittaker, get me out!' Terror filled Maria's shriek. Lock turned his head to her voice. As if in a still frame from a movie, he glimpsed her crouching by the pillar, her shirt drenched in blood. The lights went out. In a frozen moment Lock realised she wasn't a Shifter after all. Whittaker disappeared from under his fingers, reappeared by Maria and they vanished together. It caught Lock by surprise. No Shifter could teleport alone if somebody else had hold of him – until now.

In the silence Lock changed position to hover in the air and put the stone pillar between himself and Patuazon. Maria and Whittaker were hit. He didn't know how badly, but didn't think they'd be back soon. At least he knew the anti-teleporter system was knocked out. He heard Patuazon's rasping, curdling breaths and saw half of his aura, behind something blocking it. Patuazon didn't move. Lock guessed he had a chest injury, a bad one or Patuazon would have teleported as well. Lock needed him alive.

Lowering himself by the television, he felt around and picked up a DVD case. He threw the case across the room towards the thick mass he could see in aura mode. The case clattered. Patuazon fired into the darkness at the sound. Lock flew at him, hitting his right side. Patuazon yelled hoarsely then choked. Lock grappled for the weapon. Patuazon was weak. Lock took the pistol out of his hand as if taking it from a child. It was slippery with blood. The smell of it permeated the air, mixing with the acrid odour of cordite.

'Don't fucking move,' Lock shouted.

In the middle of searching Patuazon for weapons he heard a metallic click from Patuazon's left hand. And then everything was white.

Chapter 16

At the field hospital Jimmy wasn't in the mood to be reasonable.

'Mackenzie, back off.' Bilton nursed his shattered right arm, his face creased by pain despite a heavy dose of painkillers.

'Get the fuck away from me.' Jimmy pointed his Sig Sauer at Bilton's chest before shoving the pistol barrel up at the end of his prisoner's nose. Bilton wilted and sat on the end of the next man's bed, barely able to sit upright. Pinned against the hut wall by Jimmy, Mosquera's number two was pale. His eyes were bloodshot under the bandage covering his forehead and he gabbled in Spanish. The SAS patrol's automatic translator couldn't keep up, pouring out a stream of tinny nonsense. Jimmy lost patience. He looked at the knot of Patuazon's men, who had come into the hut to see what was going on. They were faced off by PC, Ginge, Nails and Vicar, who wouldn't let them interfere.

Jimmy saw one of the doctors.

'C'mere. You speak English. Translate.' The doctor stepped forward. 'Ask him where the antidote is. Tell him if he lies I'll fucking kill him.' The doctor feigned ignorance. 'Do it, now. Translate or you're dead.'

Hesitantly the doctor asked Mosquera's number two the question, stumbling over the words. The man shook his head, gabbled and trembled.

'What's he saying?'

'He does not know.'

Jimmy fired the Sig Sauer near the prisoner's leg. The round punched a hole through the wooden floor. He flinched, shook his head in fear and words poured out of him.

'Jimmy, easy, mate.' Vicar took a step towards him. Jimmy ignored him. Vicar wasn't serious about intervening.

'That'll be your brains next time. Where is it?'

The doctor translated, though the prisoner already had a non-verbal understanding of Jimmy's intentions.

'He does not know, only that it went to a laboratory for tests.'

'Which one?'

The man shook his head and rattled off quick-fire Spanish, and Jimmy didn't need to recognise more than, 'Por favor,' to know the man pleaded for his life.

'Which. Laboratory.' Jimmy emphasised his words by pushing the barrel harder against the prisoner's nose.

'He doesn't know which one. It could be anywhere in Colombia.'

PC conferred with Bilton and Nails. Jimmy's lifeblood drained away. His mates couldn't cover the whole of Colombia unless Harford was around.

'Take over, Vic.' Jimmy pushed the doctor aside. He swayed and his pistol arm dropped. 'Damn Demon stuff's making me feel weird.'

Jimmy turned and met PC's eyes. In the flicker that passed between them he saw anxiety on PC's grimy face and felt the fire growing in his belly. He wobbled outside into less stifling air, made it to his sheltered spot and sat down heavily, turning his thoughts inwards to re-join the battle against the nanomaterials. Vicar stayed by his side, chivvying him into staying awake although Jimmy didn't have the strength to answer him. He alternated between moments of lucidity and times when he was either swirling into the ground or surging into the sky. During his non-lucid moments he resented the nanomaterials' partying in his vital organs. In clearer moments he saw the damage they did, the death of parts of his liver, kidneys and pancreas, and it terrified him. They burned his insides, melting them. He could protect his heart, but if other organs failed he would die anyway.

He opened his eyes and asked Vicar to fix up a drip feed of saline. Pulling it out of his arm had been a mistake, taking a crucial element away from his side of the battle. Vicar pointed at Jimmy's left arm. The line was already in place and Jimmy hadn't noticed Vicar putting it in.

'Want me to add some whisky, mate?' Vicar asked. Jimmy smiled without humour, coughed and lay back.

A village girl of about nine years old sat close by and stared at him solemnly. The other kids kept their distance. Even when he growled at her to go away and waved a hand in a gesture of dismissal, she didn't move. She carried on staring at him with big, luminous eyes. Jimmy tried to ignore her but she unnerved him with her sickly, thin face and lank hair. She looked ill, as though waiting for the inevitable. For death. Her own or his?

'Vic, mate, tell her to go.'

'Who?'

'The kid. The girl, sitting on the log. Tell her to fuck off.'

Vicar looked again.

'There's nobody there, Jimmy.'

Jimmy stared at her, having trouble focusing.

'She's right there, you blind git. Two metres away.'

Vicar glanced round then smiled.

'So she is. Okay, pal.' He got up, walked straight past her and told somebody invisible to sod off. He returned to Jimmy's side. 'Okay now?'

Jimmy peered at the girl with the deathly face. She hadn't moved. Her sad eyes stayed fixed on him.

'Yeah, Vic. Thanks.'

Hallucinations. The next step down the road to the end of his life. He closed his eyes, shivered despite the heat and concentrated on firing his white blood cells to attack the marauders in his liver. He heard PC talking to Vicar.

'All this from one Shifter with a Demon,' PC said. 'Know how many lads the Colombians lost? Ten. And Ramon just died, that makes it eleven.'

News of Ramon's death hit Jimmy like a kick from a horse. He was next in line. It wouldn't be long now.

'Their attitude's changing. Like I said, keep your eyes open. I think they're turning on us,' PC said.

'I'm picking up some hostility out here, too,' Vicar said. 'I overheard one guy moaning they'd not been warned about the Demons. He said we tricked them. That sort of thing. And they want to get past us and lynch Mosquera's man. They want somebody to blame and we make an easy target. The sooner we get out the better.'

'Mick's nearly ready. Nails and Ginge will take care of him. You get Jimmy ready for when I give the word. Take the drip out.'

Jimmy heard PC speak to somebody else though he couldn't hear what was said; he was stuck in a cement mixer chugging round in a deep hole. He opened his eyes and saw the black shape of a chopper's underbelly loom over the village. He looked at the girl, but she wasn't there. His friend Pete stood there instead, his hands bandaged after the incident somewhere in Scotland, though Jimmy couldn't recall where.

'You're doing this wrong. If you don't get it right soon, it'll be too late,' Pete said in a Scottish accent.

'What? What am I doing wrong?'

'You're not doing anything wrong,' Vicar said, gripping Jimmy's arm and fiddling with the cannula. Jimmy tried to pull his arm away but Vicar's grip was too tight.

'Fuck off, I'm no talkin' to you.'

'He's delirious,' Vicar said to PC. 'We might have trouble getting him on the chopper.'

'So what is it I'm doing wrong?' Jimmy asked.

Pete replied, but PC drowned him out.

'Ginge and Nails are coming up with Mick. Where's Patuazon?' PC frowned and looked around.

'Shut the fuck up. I cannae hear him,' Jimmy said.

'You're using those cells the wrong way, you're wasting time.' Pete unwrapped the bandages on his hands with a third hand. Jimmy thought it unfair Pete had three hands to his two.

'I'm going to get Bilton. Get him up,' PC said.

'What am I supposed to do, for fuck's sake?' Jimmy said to Pete.

'Get on your feet, that's what. We're going for a walk,' Vicar said cheerfully, tugging at Jimmy's arm.

'I didnae ask you. Stop jabbering and let me listen.' Jimmy refused to budge. Vicar swore at him.

Pete said, 'You haven't learned about your enemy. You've been too busy setting up a defence in one place. And you forgot the first rule – if they fire at you, turn and become the aggressor, advance on them.'

'How can I attack? I don't know what to do.'

Vicar replied roughly. 'Jimmy, get with it. We're not attacking, we're bugging out. Get on your feet, soldier.'

'Look closely at your enemy. Look for the weak spot.' Pete pointed at a sea of cuboid nanomaterials. 'Hurry up, before it's time for the one bullet salute. See, there?' Pete pointed at a single cube. 'That side. The pattern. The yellow.'

'What about it?'

'Don't you see – it's the insides of your white cells you need, not the outside. The strands in your white cell fit right on there. Infiltration.'

'Aye, aye, I see it.'

'Get a move on, then, for fuck's sake, or you'll die here in this god-forsaken shithole.'

'But how do I get the stuff out?'

'Just fucking order them to do it. Get with it.'

'Jimmy. Jimmy,' Vicar tugged at him. PC grabbed his other arm and they hauled him upright.

'But my cells have to die,' Jimmy said, perplexed.

'Nobody has to die. Come on,' PC urged, forcing Jimmy onto his feet under a thudding black cloud lowering ahead of them. Pete said,

'That's right. You've got it. Now do it.'

Jimmy ordered his white cells to open up and commit suicide. Cubes piled high but new ones took their place, faster than Jimmy's cells replenished their ranks.

'I need reinforcements,' Jimmy said, as something dragged him through several metres of stickiness that clung to his legs. He couldn't see the bottom of the hole, or an end to the cubes. They were everywhere, led by green and brown shapes with weapons.

'Shifters!' somebody yelled. PC and Vicar dropped him. When the sky stopped surging, Jimmy lifted his head and saw shapes he recognised among the cubes, men in fatigues with weapons raised, and he heard a lot of shouting in between the thudding. They all had weapons pointed at each other.

'I'll show you how to get reinforcements,' Pete said, but the girl was back.

'Time's up,' she whispered, laying a thin hand on Jimmy's arm.

'Fuck off. I'm not done yet.' Jimmy couldn't hear his words above the sound of people shouting and the black cloud roaring.

~~~~~~~~

Lock's consciousness returned in a rush with the realisation that Patuazon had detonated explosives in part of the chamber. He lay on his back and stared at flickering shapes and shadows dancing over a flat surface. He puzzled for a couple of seconds until he realised something was burning. The light came from flames, but he couldn't hear the sound of fire crackling. He couldn't hear anything. Both ears were ringing. The explosion must have ruptured his eardrums.

He tasted blood and struggled to move. Murky, acrid smoke from the burning generator curled across the upper part of the room. The fire sucked oxygen out of the air. If he didn't get out he'd die. He choked and coughed, and it hurt. Everything hurt except the lower part of his torso, which was protected by the tough, pixelated trouser fabric. Blood poured from his nose. His eyes stung and watered and the right side of his face felt as though it had been peppered with shrapnel. Rolling onto his side, he tried to get up on his knees but when he moved his thigh an agonising pain shot through it. Movement brought a wave of dizziness, and he threw up. Levitating face down he sucked in the last remnants of clean air and remembered Patuazon. There was no sign of an aura or a body, and judging by bits of plastic on the floor Patuazon had detonated an explosive in the computer before he died. Lock would have died too if the stone pillar hadn't shielded him.

The light dimmed as flames dwindled. He spotted some of his equipment scattered in a corner, partially covered by PixelRain kit. Floating to it he searched for a torch to find the scanner with the secret information from Patuazon's computer. Every fibre of his body screamed at him to get out, but he needed the scanner. The dizziness increased and he went down with a bump and lay on the floor as shock kicked in. He scrabbled in the debris for the first-aid tin containing a syrette of anti-shock drug, a substance based on accelerated-healing factor. He found the tin dented but intact. Opening it with shaky fingers he took out the syrette and jabbed it into his arm, gasping for air. Staying low, he found the torch and hit the switch. A beam of steady light dispelled some of the darkness. The drug worked and the dizziness subsided.

Every second that passed felt like an hour. He made a bag out of the poncho, shoved his kit inside and quickened his search for the scanner among the shards on the floor. Something lay by the broken television. His spirits lifted but sank again when it turned out to be part of the computer.
~~~~~~~~

Breathing was harder. The need to stop searching and save himself was urgent, but he was spurred on by the thought that Whittaker might return and get the scanner. He found his Diemaco, and when he picked it up he spotted the scanner among shards of glass from the coffee table. Grabbing it he found the wall with the space behind it and teleported.

It took three seconds to discover that in his confusion he'd chosen the wrong way. The fissure was too tight and too dense. He was heading deeper into the bowels of the mountain. He didn't know how far he'd gone and baulked at the thought of being trapped inside the rocks. He stopped and emerged in a flat space with rocks above and below like a corset around his chest, squeezing the life out of him. The Diemaco in his hands jammed into his abdomen and only his feet and head were free.

Panicking, he lost his grip on the torch. He teleported and hurtled backwards until he rocketed into the smoke-filled room and hit a wall with his left shoulder. Disorientated, frantically he looked in neuro-sensory mode for the space that led to the anteroom and the villa beyond. He found a tunnel behind a wall. Was it the one he'd just come out of? He scanned again and located another tunnel behind an adjacent wall. Unsure which to choose he went with his gut feeling into the one that felt right. It was like going through the glass bottle neck in reverse. The dense masses gave way to a lighter grey and he collapsed in the anteroom, gulping air and coughing, overjoyed he had made it out alive.

The ringing in his ears changed tone. He worked out the new sound came from the alarm, which shrilled like a demented bird. Looking down at his leg injury, he saw the end of a piece of metal sticking out through a tear in the pixelated fabric. Gritting his teeth he attempted to pull it out, but the pain intensified and his hands were slippery with sweat. He left it. A rush of horror hit him when he remembered Patuazon's order to kill the Regiment team. They might be dead by now. He couldn't receive messages because he had lost the in-the-mouth radio receiver, probably when he was sick, and he couldn't call anybody because Whittaker had removed his throat microphone.

Three auras were in the toilet area, where he'd left them. He teleported into the computer room and remembered he had no drone to disrupt the anti-teleporter system that covered the outside of the bunker system. He couldn't be sure of getting out of the bunker alive. He cursed as minutes ticked by and he returned to the toilets. Teleporting one of the computer operators out he uncuffed him and shouted at him to disarm the system. His voice vibrated, as though muffled by several layers of blankets.

The scared man did as he was told. Lock was in so much pain that he would have shot him if he'd refused. When the man finished, Lock cuffed his hands, took him back to join the others and returned to the computer room, still in aura mode. He paused. Levitating closer to the exit, he saw fuzzy auras in the rooms leading off the corridor – Shifters. Though he couldn't hear anything, there was a running battle going on.

He had to get back to PC and the other guys, but a new thought stopped him Shifting. Maybe PC had reached the villa to look for him and got into a fight with Shifters. He should check. Unwrapping the poncho he put his belt kit on and stuffed equipment into pouches. If he wanted to avoid further injury, he needed the PixelRain hood he had thrown down, as well as the poncho. He searched for the hood, found it and put it back on, looking out through the face veil. As long as he kept his hands covered by the poncho, the damaged material would be good enough to disguise him while he had a look in the villa. Choosing a light grey space that marked the centre of an empty room, he teleported.

The room was bigger than expected and expensively furnished in the modern style favoured by Patuazon. A fierce battle had taken place. Bullets had punched through abstract paintings on walls and smashed glass cabinets leaving them full of broken china. Strong sunlight streamed in through shattered windows, and he levitated past an overturned chair towards a hole that used to be a window. His heart jumped when he discovered he wasn't alone. A body lay on the floor. He went into sensory mode, but there was no aura. The man was dead.

He heard the faint sound of gunfire and turned his head. Another aura appeared by the doorway. Lock aimed his Diemaco under the poncho, his hands slipping on the metal. He switched to normal vision to see the target better and stopped, finger tight on the trigger. There was nobody there. He slipped back into aura mode and saw a small, cobalt blue human aura. Whoever it was, they hadn't seen him. The small aura crossed the room to the dead body. Lock returned to normal vision, squinting and blinking away tears under his face veil.

He covered the area and switched twice between normal vision and aura mode, detecting a tiny shimmer in normal vision. The woman or youngster wore a pixelated suit. Lock very nearly spoke but caught himself just in time and stayed rooted to the spot. Even if the person was not a hostile, they could turn and fire before he had time to identify himself. A metal shape emerged out of thin air and drifted over the body, emitting a green light that turned red. Lock recognised a sensor.

The box disappeared and the body on the floor buckled and flopped. The camouflaged person tried to turn it over, and Lock saw why. The weapon barrel poking out was thicker than normal. A Demon weapon. The attack on Mosquera's villa hadn't accounted for all the Demons. The body on the floor stopped moving. Above it, the lower part of a face appeared in mid-air, followed by a nose, a forehead and long, blonde hair pinned up as the person pushed back a hood revealing a young woman whose lips moved, although Lock couldn't hear any words. He had seen her before, at

Mike Northwood's place – Kes, one of the Eagles team. He couldn't fathom why the Eagles had been drawn into a fight with Patuazon, but he should go. It was getting harder to stay focused.

A second Shifter materialised, a man in combat fatigues. Kes had her back to him and she didn't hear him. The Colombian saw her, though. He swung his AK47 round to shoot her in the back and Lock fired. As the man went down Kes spun round like lightning, firing in the Shifter's direction. She disappeared under her hood and at the same time Lock levitated out of the window hole and teleported. Kes could look after herself judging by the way she reacted, and he felt ill. Even though he flew in clear air he had difficulty breathing. He wanted to get to the lads while he still could.

~~~~~~~~

Stringer sat at the Command and Control Centre at the Embassy in Bogota, waiting to hear from Lock. An urgent message called him away to let him know the SAS team's situation at the field hospital had become untenable. It meant a halt in trying to locate the last supply of Demon weapon antidote, and the delay jeopardised the life of trooper Jimmy Mackenzie. The search hit a wall apart from one slim hope: the informant, Nightingale. He denied knowing anything about an antidote, but he might be persuaded to reveal useful information.

Stringer wanted to see Nightingale's interrogation. He left orders for Command and Control to contact him immediately when they heard from Lock and went to the hospital with Max, the SIS station chief. They stepped inside a training room, over cables running across the floor from electronic equipment stacked on top of a battered table. Television screens on a wall showed live feed from hidden cameras inside Nightingale's room. A Colombian sitting at a desk near the door took off his headphones, stood up and offered his hand to Stringer.

'Colombian police colonel Miguel,' Max said. 'He's our liaison here. He helped set this up for us.'

The colonel shook hands and sat down. The people manning the equipment didn't look up. One of them spoke into a microphone, translating from Spanish to English. The screens showed views of Nightingale lying on his hospital bed in a reclining position with drips attached to his arms and a nasal air-mix tube on his nose.

Max said, 'He's got kidney damage, a ruptured spleen, two cracked ribs and they cut off two of his fingers. They killed his wife and three of his children. Only his eight-year-old daughter survived.'

A man in his thirties sat on a chair close to Nightingale. He leaned forward earnestly, keeping intense eye contact with him while speaking although Stringer couldn't hear what was being said. Behind the
~~~~~~~~

interrogator a Colombian in his mid-forties sat by a bedside trolley making notes.

'What do we have so far?' Stringer eyed Nightingale's bruised face.

'He says he doesn't know anything about an antidote going to a lab,' the police colonel said without looking up, 'but he's lying.'

'Can we hear it?'

At the colonel's nod a radio operator passed two hands-free headsets to Max and Stringer. They put them on and heard the middle of what Nightingale said hoarsely to the interrogator.

'You don't understand. You're a gringo, all respect to you. Not a Colombian. There's a code you don't break. Tony, he broke it. Twice. That's more than I could stand, you know? Yes, I sold out my brother to Patuazon, but only after he betrayed me, over and over. She was my wife, not some second-rate hooker, but he, you know, he had to have her. He laughed in my face. He could have had anybody he wanted, but it had to be her. Just to show how much power he had, how he controlled me. Well, he didn't control me, I showed him he didn't.'

'I understand, my friend. It must have been humiliating. A stain on your honour.' The interrogator had a British accent.

'That's Ed,' Max said in an aside. 'One of our best guys.'

Ed sounded sincere. Nightingale grimaced. Ed didn't take his eyes off Nightingale's face and asked a direct interrogation question.

'Tell me, who went to meet the Chinese to buy the Demons and the antidote?'

Nightingale's face stayed impassive.

'I told you, me and Emilio, the Shifter. The one who's dead.'

'You said you were going to tell the truth.'

'I am telling you the truth. I'm not lying.'

A flicker of movement in Nightingale's left hand betrayed his unease. Ed sat back, frustrated.

'Look, we are friends now. We have already helped you. We saved you and Anna from your brother. You said you would help us in return, but your story isn't credible.'

'I swear, I'm telling you everything, I'm trying to help.'

Stringer was frustrated. He wanted to put some aggression into the interrogation, but he knew that even a hardened gangster like Nightingale responded better to a patient, persuasive approach. Ed tried a different tack, asking Nightingale about his relationship with his brother, and his brother's affair with Nightingale's wife. Ed used Nightingale's anger to get under the prisoner's defences and persuade him to cooperate, but Nightingale resisted. Ed tried a new tack.

'I want to show you something.'

Ed took a folder from the Colombian behind him and pulled out photographs, holding them in front of Nightingale one at a time.

'Your brother's villa was hit this afternoon.'

Nightingale squinted with his good eye, his attention riveted. Stringer looked at the screen focusing on the photos. He saw aerial shots of the wrecked villa, close ups of prisoners and dead bodies. Nightingale scrutinised all of them without saying a word or giving any hint of emotion, but the skilled team picked up from his retinal scan that he was searching for something. He came to the last photo, a drone close-up of Mosquera's corpse hanging in the tree, and gasped. The tension in his body gave way, his head dropped back on the pillow and a tear formed in his good eye. He closed it and Ed waited to see if his gamble had paid off. It was impossible to be sure if the tear signified release or grief. Perhaps both. Nightingale opened his eye.

'Tony did the deal with the Chinese.'

'So you told me a lie when you said it was just you and Emilio?'

'Yes, but I'm telling you the truth now.'

'Where did the antidote go?'

Nightingale was anxious again.

'I told you, I keep telling you, I don't know.'

Stringer took off his headset, disappointed, and spoke in a low voice to Max.

'We're wasting time. I don't think he knows.'

'But he's holding something back.'

'It might be nothing to do with the antidote.'

Max had one ear to the headset. 'Wait, you might want to hear this. They're talking about the Demons deal.'

Stringer put his headset back on.

'How was the deal set up?' Ed asked.

'The Chinese wanted some of the drug. They got hold of Tony to do the deal, the Demons for the drug.'

'Demons for Starbirth?'

Nightingale shook his head.

'No, the real stuff. Tony didn't have much of it. That's why we didn't get many Demons.'

'How many did you get?'

Another hand flicker. Something wasn't right. Nightingale displayed more than fear of his dead brother.

'Ten. We had ten.'

'That's not what you told us before.'

That held Stringer's attention. Both the British and the Americans wanted to know how many Demon weapons were dispersed throughout Colombia. They needed to be found before they ended up in the hands of people worse than Colombian gangsters.

Nightingale was flustered and looked up and to the right. He was going to lie. Eye movement to the right indicated the subject accessed the creative side of his brain, the part he needed to spin a story. Stringer knew it and so did Ed. Nightingale said,

'I was confused. The pain, the medication, it confused me.'

'But you aren't confused now. How many?'

Nightingale looked at the Colombian.

Ed said sharply, 'Don't look at him. I asked you the question.'

'We bought ten.'

Nightingale looked away. He was a bad liar. Ed stared at him. Beads of sweat broke out on Nightingale's brow. Ed changed course again.

'Did you tell Senor Patuazon about the Demons?'

Nightingale's mask dropped and for the first time outright fear danced across his features. The merest mention of Patuazon had him rattled.

'No.'

'Yet you told him about Tony's deal with the gringos.'

'Yes. It was important.'

'And the Demons weren't? Tony had his hands on lethal weapons, and it wasn't important enough to tell Senor Patuazon?'

Nightingale didn't reply.

'Do you know what the penalty is for murder?'

'Yes.'

'What is it?'

'Life in prison.'

'And do you know what the penalty is for murder in Texas?'

'Death.'

'That's right. You are facing a murder charge there and the Colombian authorities will extradite you to the US.'

'I didn't kill that guy.'

'Perhaps you didn't, but the US will want you in a court of law to prove it one way or the other. And if they find you guilty, you will face the death penalty. But it doesn't have to be like that. Help me to help you.'

'I want to help. I am telling you everything.'

Ed shook his head.

'No, you're lying. Don't you want to help yourself?'

Nightingale gripped the bed sheet.

'You have a bright star in your life, one spark of purity. Your little girl, Anna. She's a lovely girl, a real gem, and she's making a good recovery. But how long will her sweetness and innocence last without either of her parents looking out for her? You've lost your wife, but she's lost her mother. She's crying. She needs you. Wouldn't you like to be there for her? You love her, don't you?'

Nightingale didn't reply, but the muscles in his face worked to disguise the emotion that touched him. Ed pressed him.

'I can help you. I can arrange for you to see her, now, but I need you to be truthful otherwise I can't make it happen. If you co-operate, you can be protected under the witness protection programme. I can ask the US to be lenient, and to give you special status because you co-operated. You could start a new life with Anna. With a new identity, a new home away from here. You'll both be safe.'

Nightingale wiped a tear away with his good hand. Everybody in the viewing room waited, spellbound. Ed continued,

'Think about your choices. You don't have many options. Think of Anna's future. I want to help you, but I have to know I can trust you. Don't disrespect me by lying.'

A tear trickled down Nightingale's face. He muttered something that ended in a strangled choke.

'What? What did you say?'

'Thirty-five Demons. Ten for Tony, twenty-five for Senor Patuazon.' Nightingale's voice dropped to a whisper.

In the viewing room Stringer gasped. Colombia had nearly thirty Demon weapons on the loose, not four. That changed the situation.

'Did you help Senor Patuazon buy the Demons?'

'Yes. Tony didn't have the real drug, but Senor Patuazon did.'

A chill of excitement shivered through Stringer's abdomen. Patuazon had AH-4. That news outweighed any consideration of Mackenzie's plight, or even the Demons. Finding the antidote was less important. Ed queried,

'You saw him give them the drug?'

'Yes. They tested it and they were happy. It was the real thing.' Nightingale paused. 'He will kill me and my girl for telling you this.'

Stringer's phone buzzed. He took off his headset, pulled out his mobile and gestured at Max to accompany him to the corridor. Lock's gut instinct was right. Patuazon was the source of the AH-4 after all, but he had twenty-five Demon weapons. That put the SAS team in critical danger, going up against more Demons. They could all be killed.

'We need to get our guys out of there,' Stringer said. He walked so fast Max had to work hard to keep up. The woman on the other end of the phone informed Stringer they had received a radio call from PC saying the troopers were under attack. Stringer paled.

'I think we might be too late.'

~~~~~~~~

Lock's homing instinct took him behind the field hospital hut, to the place where he spoke with PC before leaving for Patuazon's villa. No smiling village children peeped round the corner of the hut, and inside there were
~~~~~~~~

only a few auras. Glancing in through a window he saw the doctor and his assistants tending to three wounded men. He couldn't see PC or the rest of the SAS unit, or the prisoner. Resorting to aura mode he detected a large group of people in the jungle to the southeast of the village, auras of different sizes moving slowly. He had found the villagers moving away from trouble. He teleported forty metres to the landing zone. It seemed normal at first glance, but when Lock looked closer he saw beyond the deceptive outward appearance.

Scattered auras trickled through foliage to the west, thirty metres away, but he didn't know who they were, or if they fired weapons because he had no comms and couldn't hear anything. The chopper piloted by Cocaine Chris was in the clearing, unnaturally idle. The rotor blades drooped and the engine was lifeless. Lock hovered nearer the front. Chris was slumped forward in his seat, shot dead. An empty stretcher lay twisted on the ground a few metres from the chopper. A silver survival sheet was next to it as though hurriedly discarded, but an arm protruded from underneath.

Lock alighted by the body, dreading what he would find. He pulled the sheet away from the head and his stomach knotted up at the sight of Mick's grey face with his eyes half-open. Lock put a hand on Mick's neck. No pulse, no breathing, no aura. Anguish and rage overcame him. He'd been away too long. He checked his watch. Fifteen thirty-five, he'd been gone forty minutes, twice as long as expected. The guys were forced to ditch Mick.

He lifted off the ground and pursued the auras scattered in the jungle. How long had the troopers been trying to fight their way out of trouble? If he hadn't gone to Patuazon's bunker there would have been no order to kill them. If he'd been back earlier for casevac, Mick might still be alive. They couldn't have gone far, not with two casualties and a prisoner. A wave of dizziness swept through his head. He fell out of levitation onto the ground, stumbled forward and fell over, putting a hand to his ear as if he could ward off the pain. He stretched out his other hand to push himself off the ground and pulled it away, recoiling from a leg in the undergrowth. Stumbling to his feet he suppressed the pain and stepped forward to look at the dead soldier. He relaxed when he didn't recognise the man. Another soldier lay nearby, one he did recognise as a member of Patuazon's army.

Rising a couple of metres off the ground, he scanned the jungle, detecting several auras. A small group crept along, either stalking somebody or working their way out of danger in a flanking movement away from two larger groups of auras, one near the village and one further in the jungle. The small group might be the troopers, though he saw only four auras. Two more faint auras hovered above, well over a hundred metres in the air, in the middle of something denser than the air around them. It was a helicopter. Switching to normal vision Lock saw one of Patuazon's choppers overhead, more than likely using sensors and thermal imagers to find their prey.

Landing quickly, he moved under cover, teleporting as close as he dared to the four auras on the ground. The SAS team would be switched-on to the slightest sign of teleporters and would be twitchy, so he levitated just above the ground when he drew within thirty-six metres of them. It was impossible to levitate past heavy, sodden undergrowth without making a noise as the poncho brushed slippery leaves. He inched forward. The humidity made it more difficult to breathe. He mulled over picking up the auras and spiriting them away, but decided against it because he wanted to be certain of their identities. He didn't want to waste his dwindling mental and physical energy on teleporting some of Patuazon's men.

When Lock got close enough for a glimpse, he recognised one of them as another of Patuazon's men. Two stood guard while one huddled over a small laptop. The fourth man spoke into a radio. Angry with them for wasting his time, Lock was about to slip away when another figure appeared abruptly by their side. Lock froze when he recognised a Demon weapon in the hands of the Shifter. The clinical side of his nature rose took precedence. They were using nanomaterials against his colleagues, men who had trained them and lived and worked alongside them. They might have already given his team-mates a death sentence. He switched the Diemaco setting to single shot, took aim and fired.

The Shifter dropped. The other men dived for cover, but Lock was already fading, locating other auras and teleporting towards them. He picked a larger group on the western side because they were at the leading edge of those going away from the village whereas some of the others were turning back. There were seven auras. He tracked them, creeping stealthily and switching between normal vision and aura mode. He detected other auras not much further than fifteen metres from the group he shadowed, close enough to be dangerous despite the foliage in between. That wasn't the only problem. He had no way of telling the guys he was coming. They were certain to hear him before he could identify himself.

He pressed on, approaching from the left side. He was on top of them. Peering through the gloom, he couldn't see anybody, yet aura mode told him two people moved in front of him with the others either side of them. He stood still, watching the auras. Spotting a tiny movement among leaves he levitated off the ground for a better look. He didn't recognise the person in the lead. The second man should have been directly behind the first, yet in normal vision he saw nobody. Two auras, but only one man was visible. It had to be PixelRain. The second one, part of the SAS team, was in a pixelated suit.

In his eagerness to move forward Lock brushed a leaf with his arm. Something slammed into his chest, knocking him backwards into the undergrowth. He'd been shot. They'd shot him. Disbelief turned to panic and he yelled at them, frantic in his effort to stop them killing him. He could barely hear his own voice, but he could see the barrels of two weapons pointing at him, one in front and one on his right. He pulled off his hood and face veil and kept on yelling at them not to shoot. Ginge's head appeared out of nowhere and an invisible hand clamped itself over Lock's mouth. PC, not wearing a suit, appeared from his right with a man Lock recognised as Mosquera's deputy.

Using sign language, Lock indicated he couldn't hear. Ginge nodded, lifted his hand away, finger-probed Lock's chest under the poncho for wounds and gave a thumbs up to say he was okay. He gestured for Lock to move fast, pulling him to his feet. They'd attracted attention. Hostile auras were homing in on them. Lock indicated where the enemy were and PC and Ginge took up positions. Lock trembled so hard he could barely stand, but he whispered to PC he would teleport them out to Bogota. PC signalled they would wait one minute for four more men. Lock nodded. He wasn't sure he could take everybody if they were more than half a metre apart, though he didn't tell PC that. He took a couple of slow, deep breaths. His heart thudded. He could hardly believe he'd been shot after everything he'd been through, but the poncho had held. No rounds penetrated, though grey patches showed where the camouflage effect of the pixels was destroyed.

The rest of the group appeared. Lock looked round, taken aback when he saw Jimmy, gagged and with his hands bound, pushed ahead by Vicar. He didn't query it. They must have their reasons for trussing Jimmy up. He was amazed Jimmy was alive considering the time lapse since he'd been infected with the nanomaterials. Nails appeared, followed by another shimmering poncho. The aura under that had to be Bilton. Seven auras formed a circle around Lock and he gestured at them to close in tighter and teleported, still shaking.

Lock planned to go straight to the Embassy in Bogota, but trouble hit seconds into the Shift. The battering his heart took during the events of the day caught up with him. His chest felt as though a band tightened around it, stopping him breathing. Stabbing pains shot up his neck and lower jaw, and down the inside of his left arm. He knew enough about heart attacks to recognise the symptoms.

He stopped teleporting, came out into levitation and dropped like a stone. At the last second he angled his descent towards a field. Cows scattered when the group landed in the midst of the herd. Lock pulled out the scanner with information from Patuazon's secret bunker and gave it to PC.

'Make sure this gets back to the SIS. Nobody else. Only the SIS.' He collapsed.

CHAPTER 17

Floating in a state of detachment Lock was aware of a sequence of sounds. First a roaring, throbbing, hard sound that vibrated. It receded quickly, replaced by a buzzing that rasped before it descended into hissing, like steam escaping. Then a voice. Definitely a voice. It gave him a focus and awakened his instinct that something else existed besides himself. The length of his body rested on something, which brought recognition that he had a body.

'He's coming round.'

The voice sounded dull and blanketed, competing with a clattering of metal on metal. His body was tugged and pulled.

'Lock. Lock, can you hear me?' He felt hands on his bare chest, and more on his legs, pulling his boots off. Many pairs of hands. Friendly forces. His chest tightened, the voices disappeared to a whisper and he sank back into oblivion.

When consciousness returned it was accompanied by confusion and an automatic mental check to see what hurt. In the middle of that, he remembered the explosion, the flight from the village, his collapse and all the injuries he had sustained. Bewildered, he registered the fact he could hear when he shouldn't be able to, and nothing on his body hurt, not even his ears.

Thinking he might be dead, he opened his eyes and saw a man in blue medical clothing by a bank of machines. The hissing continued, from an air mix outlet attached to a plastic mask over his mouth and nose. He saw a solid-walled cubicle in which he was hooked to a heart monitor and a drip. Outside the open door, busy medics moved purposefully. Lock heard voices that carried no hint of urgency. People spoke normally. He saw an armed man in American combat fatigues by the doorway. The medic by the machines turned round. He walked over, removed the mask, turned off the air mix and called out,

'He's awake, Sir.'

Northwood walked into the room. Lock tried to ask a question but his dry throat just managed a hoarse gasp.

'You're okay.' Northwood anticipated his thoughts. 'You're in a US Navy hospital in Cuba. You've been out for hours.'

Lock shook his head. That wasn't what he wanted to know, he wanted news of his guys.

'How's Jimmy? The others?'

'Oh, right, your team. Don't worry about them, they're being looked after. We went back for your two fatalities. They're in the morgue.'

A pain like a knife pierced Lock's spine as he remembered that Mick and Cocaine Chris had died. He didn't pursue that line of thought, preferring to focus on the living.

'Jimmy's alive?'

'Jimmy? Which one's Jimmy?' Northwood's face cleared. 'You mean the first guy that got hit by a dart? He's down the corridor. Our team's working on him. He's a real fighter. The guy's amazing, he oughtta be dead by now. And you. You took a hammering. You had two heart attacks. You nearly died twice.'

'What?' Lock stared at Northwood.

'Don't fret – we took care of it. Not me personally, but – anyway, it's okay. Your heart's as good as new. Probably better than you were before Scary Mary damn near killed you.'

'Scary Mary?'

'That's what your boys called her.'

Lock paused, trying to take in things that didn't make sense without the benefit of background knowledge. Warmth and strength coursed through his limbs. He had no chest pain and felt fine. He was sure he didn't need the drip in his left arm. It felt as though he had just woken from a really good sleep on a bright summer's day and he was hungry. He could demolish two American breakfasts. Maybe three.

'Hang on – what do you mean, 'The first one that got hit by a dart'? Who else got hit? How come I can hear? What happened, what's going on? What happened at Patuazon's after I left? Did you get into his secret room?'

He pushed himself up but Northwood put a restraining hand on his arm.

'Okay, relax, I'll bring you up to speed. We heard about Patuazon's attack on your team and you were in trouble so we went to the coordinates your guy PC called in.'

'Wait, before that. What happened at Patuazon's? You were there before I got the guys out of the field hospital.'

'No, we went to Patuazon's after we brought you and your team here. You got as far as Florencia before you passed out. We arrived just in time, after you'd had your first heart attack.'

Lock frowned, confused.

'But you were at Patuazon's before I left. I saw Kes there–'

'No, we weren't there. You're mistaken.'

He was evasive. Lock always knew when Northwood was hiding

something because his eyes narrowed and he raised his shoulders slightly, as if taking a mental step back.

'But I saw her, when I came out of the bunker. She was looking at a body in the villa. A guy with a Demon weapon.'

Northwood chuckled as he strolled to the doorway.

'Maybe it's a false memory. Y'know, a hallucination.' He looked in the corridor, searching for somebody, or trying to get away from an awkward question.

'Mike, it wasn't a dream.'

Lock stopped. Either Northwood lied or it had really been a hallucination. It couldn't have been a hallucination, it was too real. Northwood was lying. For some reason he didn't want anybody to know the Eagles had been at Patuazon's at that time. He let it go. The guy had just saved the whole team.

'So, when you went there afterwards, what happened? Did you find Patuazon's body?'

Northwood shook his head and strolled back.

'We didn't see him.'

'In the secret room. You got to the secret room, right?'

'Which one are you talking about? The computer room, or the bathroom with the prisoners?'

Lock hesitated about giving Northwood information that should be for Stringer, but reasoned Northwood was the only one with the resources and ability to go to Patuazon's lair and it was important to find out if Patuazon died. He related what he'd seen. Although Northwood listened Lock had the impression he knew already. He reacted wrongly, as if the news about Patuazon's lair wasn't news at all. Northwood feigned surprise and got on the radio to somebody Lock assumed was one of the Eagles. Northwood's face and voice didn't have a note of excitement when he told Lock they would check it out. Lock wanted to get back there himself. He didn't tell Northwood about the second tunnel that went into the mountain from the blind-walled room. Northwood changed the subject.

'We got to your position just in time. Cheena saved your life. She stabilised you, we got you here and you had another heart attack. She pulled you out of that and repaired everything else, including your burst ear drums.'

Lock remembered his right thigh where the shrapnel hit, and felt for the sharp end sticking out.

'Yeah, it's gone, and the shrapnel in your face, too. You're back to normal.' He had a glint in his eye. 'We discussed making you handsome, but in the end we didn't want to give you another heart attack when you looked in the mirror.'

'You said 'The first guy that got hit by a dart' – you mean they got more than one of the boys?'

'Yeah, one of the others. I'm sorry, I thought you knew. What's his name, it's odd.'

'Vicar?'

Northwood shook his head.

'Nope, something else.'

'Ginge? Nails?'

'Nails. That's it. He got hit by two, but we're working on it, he's doing okay. Hey, you're not supposed to get up yet.'

'I need to see them and get in touch with our HQ.'

'Your HQ already knows you're here.'

A young nurse in blue scrubs poked her head round the door.

'Sir, we can't find him.' She stopped when she saw Lock. 'Wait, we're not done yet. I need to check you out before you go anywhere.'

'I'm fine. Take this out, I'm leaving.' Lock pointed at the cannula in his arm and pulled off the heart monitor sensors on his chest. She marched across the linoleum floor. Putting warm hands around the biceps on his right arm, she gripped him firmly and gazed at him with blue eyes that glittered like pieces of glass.

'If you Shift you'll be taking me with you. Now behave yourself, Harford, and let me do my job.'

Startled, Lock glanced at Northwood, who was amused.

'This here is Cheena.' He nodded at the nurse, who looked nothing like the Cheena that Lock met at Tippity Wichity Island. The girl had light auburn hair and more Caucasian features than the part-North American Indian that had been Cheena.

'I didn't know. I mean, thank you.' Embarrassed, Lock sat down. 'Thanks for saving my life.'

'No problem. Keep still and lie back. I have to do a final check to make sure everything's okay.'

'Yeah, of course.'

He flinched involuntarily at her touch. It reminded him of Maria.

'Relax.'

She didn't use any gel when she touched his neck. Lock wasn't surprised. Having experienced Maria's ability to harm his body through her fingers, he saw how mistaken he had been to assume a transmute needed gel or nanomaterials.

Cheena's new disguise was just as attractive as the one he had seen earlier. It was having a disturbing effect on the lower part of his anatomy, just as it had when she turned him into an old man, and this time he had no handy jacket to put in a strategic position. He fidgeted and self-consciously brought his arm across his groin. Cheena was professional and pretended not to notice, but Northwood couldn't keep a straight face. Lock distracted himself by switching to aura mode. What he saw made his heart jump and go into overdrive. Cheena took her hand away.

'Relax. I'm not your enemy, I'm not going to hurt you.'

Lock muttered something and fidgeted again. Cheena's aura wasn't just cobalt. It was the same as Maria's – cobalt with translucent tendrils of jade green and light yellow. Electrified, Lock switched out and back again with the same result. For a moment he thought she might be lying and could be Maria in disguise. When he met Cheena her face looked North American Indian and her aura was no different to the millions of other ordinary human auras, yet now it glowed more than blue. He remembered when he met Maria, her aura was blue as well. After she disguised herself as the woman tracking him, and at the party, her aura altered. The import of the discovery sank in. Transmutes in their natural forms had normal auras, but when they changed themselves, their auras changed too. He was probably the only person in the world who could detect a transmute in disguise.

Excited by his discovery he watched the aura, lost in his world of greys, blues and tendrils that floated green-yellow. He forgot about the throbbing down below.

'Harford?' Cheena repeated. He noticed the silence and snapped out of aura mode.

'Sorry, I didn't hear what you said.'

'You're fine, all clear.' She removed the cannula, pressing cotton wool on the puncture wound. 'You had extensive damage to your heart. It looks good now and it should be fine, but all the same, no strenuous activity for a few days. Just to be sure.'

Lock nodded.

'Okay, fine. Thanks. It's great, what you've done.'

Inarticulate and floundering, he was unable to thank her sufficiently for his life. She removed the heart sensors and Lock got off the trolley.

'Where's my kit?' He disguised his lack of eloquence and his rigid member by crouching to look under the trolley.

'Your clothes were trashed so we got you some new ones and an ID card,' she said. 'Your guys have your belt kit.' She bent over the end of the trolley, making Lock's heart beat faster, and pulled out some combat fatigues in US military camouflage pattern. 'These are for you.' She turned to Northwood. 'Sir, I need to speak with you about the special case.'

Her words implied urgency.

'I'll be right out.'

Cheena hurried out of the room with Lock's gaze glued to her shapely rear. Northwood chuckled.

'Don't worry about it, man.'

'Don't worry about what?' Lock said innocently as he put the pants on, with difficulty doing up the zip. Northwood leaned closer and lowered his voice. His breath reeked of mouthwash.

'It happens to everybody, man. It's the pheromones. That's why she has that effect on you.'

'What are you talking about?'

Northwood laughed.

'Pheromones, man. The natural chemicals that attract people to each other. We all have them, we all give off pheromones but we can't consciously smell some of the most powerful hormones.'

'Yeah, I know that. I know what pheromones are. Are you saying hers are different?'

'Different? You bet. Ten times more of them than normal. That's why you got a hard-on. All I'm saying is, it's not you – it's her.'

Pheromones. The same thing happened when he met Maria, uncontrollable sexual arousal. It explained a lot.

'Are you saying she's doing it deliberately?'

'No. It just happens. She can control it to some extent, but when she's busy and concentrating on something else she gets distracted.'

'So how come it doesn't affect you?'

'Trade secret.' Northwood grinned. Lock assumed he meant Cheena had altered him physiologically to enable him to overcome it. Northwood chuckled and said,

'You should see the problems we have sometimes in meetings with guys. It's hilarious. Especially when it's a colonel, or a general. Guys go red-faced and rush off to the bathroom.'

'How good is a transmute at recovering from serious injury?'

'Excuse me?'

Northwood's mood altered and he was serious. Lock told him about Maria's wounds. Judging by the way Northwood's tension eased it occurred to Lock that Northwood thought he was making a threat against Cheena, rather than asking about Maria.

'I dunno, to be honest. Cheena's never been hurt that bad – but I wouldn't bet on Maria Zamora being dead.'

His radio squawked and he turned away to take a message. Lock reflected that if Maria was still alive, and he had another run-in with her, he had some knowledge on his side to detect her presence – aura and pheromones. He buttoned his crisp, new shirt, attached the identity card over his breast pocket and pulled on the new boots. As he laced them Northwood finished his call.

'They've found the underground room, where you said it would be. It's empty, no body.'

Lock looked up from tying the final knot in his laces.

'That can't be right. Tell them to look again, in the part where the armchair is.'

'They did that. They found patches of blood, but nothing else.'

'That's impossible. He couldn't Shift, he was too weak. He had to be dead.'

'If there's no body, there's no body. Maybe he wasn't as badly injured as you thought.'

'Or he had help.'

It wasn't a direct challenge, but Lock's suspicion grew. Northwood's joviality could be due to drink. It wasn't the first time he disguised the smell of whisky with mouthwash. Lock had seen Northwood drunk many times, but his manner was more like smugness, and being cock-a-hoop.

'Yeah, I guess it's possible.' Northwood was distracted by his phone. 'He had Shifters. We know that. One could've gotten through from the computer room.' Northwood stopped, absorbed by a text message. 'I have to go. The Marine outside will take you to your guys. Take care, buddy.'

He hurried into the corridor. Lock followed him out. Northwood spoke to armed Marines and loped up the corridor. Something agitated him. Lock would have liked to be in the loop.

The Marine escorted Lock in the opposite direction. Medical staff hurried along side wards that were guarded by more armed Marines. The number of armed guards was excessive. Maybe they expected an attack. The conversation with Northwood played through his mind. Northwood hadn't asked what he saw in the lair. Lock had told him about the vital computer and normally Northwood would have been keen to find out what Lock had seen. As he followed the Marine Lock thought about Northwood's reaction and Patuazon's disappearance. Maybe Patuazon didn't disappear. Northwood's lack of interest might be because he had a better source of information. Perhaps the source was Patuazon himself. The Eagles might have him in custody, the special case Cheena referred to. No matter how badly Patuazon had been injured, she could have pulled him round.

Lock was incensed. The more he thought about it, the more he was convinced. If he'd read Northwood's body language accurately, they had Patuazon. They would find out the origins of AH-4. Despite everything Lock had done over the months at Patuazon's estate, it looked as though the Americans had walked in and taken the prize from under his nose. Something else struck him like a kick in the guts. If the Eagles rescued Patuazon from the underground lair, they left their friend behind. Northwood put the capture of Patuazon above the rescue of one of his closest friends. Northwood wouldn't do that to him. Would he? Lock hoped he wasn't correct, but logic about Northwood's priorities told him otherwise.

Halfway along the corridor Lock remembered Mick and how he died alone next to the chopper. He might have made it if he'd been evacuated from the field hospital. Chris might still be alive, too. Guilt and apprehension slowed Lock down. He hadn't seen any of the troopers since then and he didn't know how they would react. They might blame him, as other soldiers had blamed him for the accident that killed their comrades when he was eighteen.

By the time he reached the small ward his mood changed to black, but the mood among the troopers was anything but downcast. They greeted him heartily. Even Bilton was less frosty than usual, and in reply to Lock's query said Cheena had healed his shoulder. The rest were in good spirits apart from Mick's death; they did their best to blot it out as their way of coping. Jimmy was the only one who reacted in sombre fashion, nodding a hello and staring into space.

'Don't mind him, he's communing with his spirit guide,' Nails said.

'Spirit guide?'

Nails grinned. 'Yeah, from a vision quest. He says years ago he had a pow-wow with some North American Indian tribe. He took a hallucinogenic drug and found his spirit guide.'

'Beaver, was it, Jimmy?' Lock asked.

Ginge and Vicar fell about laughing. Jimmy gave them a one-finger salute without looking round.

'What type of beaver, Jimmy, blonde or brunette?' Nails teased. Ginge chimed in,

'Hey, what goes blonde, brunette, blonde, brunette?' he asked, and before anybody could come up with a suitable reply said, 'A naked blonde doing cartwheels.'

Amidst the laughter Vicar scoffed, 'You got that off the internet.'

Jimmy didn't react. Bilton beckoned Lock towards the corridor, but when they reached the sliding glass door an armed Marine blocked their way.

'Sir, you can't leave the ward.'

The conversation behind Lock died.

'What d'you mean, we can't leave? We're not prisoners.'

'Sir, those are my orders, Sir.'

'Whose orders?'

'My commanding officer, Sir.'

Bilton eyeballed the Marine, who stood his ground.

'Get on the radio, tell your CO I want to speak to him.'

'Sir, he's unavailable. Those are my orders.'

The Marine's courteous speech belied his belligerent body language. Lock stepped in before Bilton blew a fuse.

'Sergeant, even majors and colonels have to use the bathroom some time. One of your men can escort us.'

The Marine hesitated, rock-solid, as if weighing up whether or not the Brits were really a major and a colonel. He glanced at the other men behind

Lock and Bilton, two in medical gowns and the others in combat fatigues of different camouflage patterns, all with their eyes fixed on him, most carrying arms. It must have been daunting, especially if he thought all of them were highly trained Special Forces including Lock, who wasn't.

A second Marine, sensing trouble, joined the first one. After a few seconds of being stared down by Bilton and Lock, the Marine in charge nodded curtly at his colleague and stepped aside.

'Escort them to the bathroom.'

Bilton and Lock followed the Marine up the corridor, slowing their pace to put distance between him and themselves. Bilton muttered,

'Don't be fooled by the high spirits in there. Those two guys don't know it yet, but they won't survive.'

'What?'

Shocked, Lock stared at Bilton's grim face.

'We've been told it's inevitable. The transmute, Cheena, she's done the best she can. She's worked hard. She keeps trying. The thing is, it's only delaying the end.'

'How come?'

'The nanomaterials, they're too invasive. They've eaten right through their bodies. She can't contain them. It's just a matter of time.'

Lock stared at the floor and thought how cruel fate was to present a hope – and then take it away again.

'There must be something we can do.'

Bilton shook his head.

'We've gone over it. There isn't anything. There was an antidote but it went up with the villa. Command said a small amount went to a research lab somewhere, but it looks like a rumour. We've drawn a blank. The transmute said she's only able to do a holding job, and eventually she'll be called elsewhere.'

The Marine stopped outside the toilets, eyeing Lock and Bilton.

'I'm sure we can manage from here,' Bilton said.

'Yes, sir.' The Marine waited.

The toilet area was as spotlessly clean as the corridor and the ward, and smelled of disinfectant. A soldier stood at the urinals and a man in a dressing gown hobbled away from the sinks.

'How much time do Nails and Jimmy have?' Lock asked, keeping his voice low.

'With continuous intervention, she said it was likely to be less than four hours. Without it, as it stands now, maybe an hour before they have major organ failure. Nails first. She said he was in worse shape than Jimmy.'

'Shit.'

Lock paused, going over options. The soldier at the urinals gave them a funny look and left without washing his hands. Bilton continued,

'They've taken blood samples. They've got people in the labs here, working on trying to come up with something, but they say it's impossible to create a fresh batch of antidote in that space of time. Without it, there's nothing that can be done.'

'Hang on a minute. Research labs. You said some antidote went to a research lab.'

Bilton nodded.

'That's what our prisoner said.'

'Hospitals have research labs.'

Lock's excitement rose as he recalled his conversation with the informant Nightingale, Mosquera's brother. He turned on his heel and led the way out of the toilets, anxious to get back to the ward. The Marine increased his pace to keep up with them along the corridor. Bilton said,

'Command looked at all the places in Colombia. Including hospital research labs. We looked, the Colombians looked.'

'He said 'Not the Santa Marta.'

'What are you talking about?'

'Nightingale. After he was wounded, I said I'd take him to the Santa Marta in Cali.'

An alarm shrilled. Lock and Bilton exchanged a look and listened as the Marine took a radio message.

'You need to get back to the ward, Sir,' the Marine said. He brought his weapon round into a combat position and herded them down the corridor. Marines came at a run from around the corner and took up combat poses. One yelled at the Marine escorting Lock and Bilton,

'Get those guys outta here.'

'What's going on?' Bilton asked.

'Stay inside, Sir. This is not a drill.'

The Marine closed the ward door and took up a position outside it, his body visible through the glass.

'I know where the antidote is,' Lock said.

'What's going on?' PC asked.

'Lockdown,' Bilton replied. 'Get ready in case we have to bug out.'

Jimmy and Nails put belt kits on and picked up their weapons. Lock spoke in measured tones.

'Bilton, listen to me. I know where the antidote is. The Santa Marta in Cali. Nightingale was terrified of being taken there. He said Mosquera had people there. If Mosquera had a lab to manufacture an antidote, it would be at the Santa Marta.'

Lock had their attention. His revelation was greeted by silence. He looked around the ward.

'Where's my kit? I'll call Northwood direct.'

'Here.' PC pulled Lock's bergen and belt kit from a space by Jimmy's bed.

Bilton said, 'So get us there, then. Shift us out.'

'No, we can't just Shift out. Northwood wouldn't have brought us here unless the place had anti-teleporter measures.' He rummaged in his belt kit and brought out the Secure Link phone, his line to Northwood, and switched it on. The set lit up but there was no connection. 'I'll have to try another way.'

The Marine at the door refused to contact Northwood. The ward door slid shut. Lock swore, turned and caught a worried expression on Nails' face. He looked away.

'I have to get hold of Northwood. We need to get out of this ward.'

'Okay,' Bilton said. 'Vic, you stay here with Jimmy and Nails. Create a diversion at the door just long enough for us to get out.'

'No, boss.' PC shook his head. 'Not you. You stay here, we'll go.'

Startled by the uncharacteristic interruption from his second-in-command, Bilton stuttered,

'What the hell – what are you saying?'

'When we Shifted here with Northwood, you had a funny reaction after. You didn't come out of it for fifteen minutes. If you do that again you'll be no fucking use to anybody.'

Lock thought Bilton would explode. PC stood firmly in place, feet planted apart. Unlike the Marine, he wasn't going to be stared down by Bilton. It would have been funny to see them in a stand-off had the situation been less urgent, but Bilton had the good sense not to argue with the most experienced, longest-serving member of his team. If PC put himself in the firing line like that, Bilton knew he had a good reason. He turned to Lock.

'You go. PC, Ginge, Vicar, you're with him.'

Nails couldn't contain himself.

'Boss, how come we need the antidote? I mean, the girl's sorting it, isn't she?' Bilton didn't reply. Nails turned his gaze to Lock and then his mates, who couldn't bear to look at him. 'Shit,' he said in a small voice.

'We'll get it for you,' Lock said. 'Is there any of that PixelRain kit left?'

PC shook his head. 'No, the Yanks took it back.'

'Not all of it,' Ginge said. He pulled something from under a bed. 'I've got mine.' He handed it to Lock. The poncho, hood and face veil were intact.

PC rummaged in a pouch on his belt kit.

'Your scanner, boss.' He handed it over with a meaningful glance and without saying anything about Lock's instruction to give it to the SIS. 'How do you want to play this?'

Two minutes later Bilton demanded to speak to the Marine officer in charge, saying one of his men was getting worse. The guard at the door refused and ordered Bilton to stay inside the ward or risk getting shot. Bilton conferred with Lock, having achieved the objective of a reconnaissance of the corridor.

'Eight Marines. Two at each end of the corridor, two in the middle, two outside our door.'

Lock nodded, taking his Diemaco.

'Get in position to cover me. PC, Ginge, Vicar, be ready to leave when I get back.'

PC and Ginge stood strategically by Jimmy's trolley, shielding Lock's movements. Out of sight of the Marine guard, Lock donned his chest sling, clipped the Diemaco in place, tugged on his bergen and the poncho, hood and face veil.

'Okay, I'm ready.' He drew his legs underneath the poncho and levitated, close to the ceiling.

Jimmy wailed, clutching his stomach and writhing on the trolley. Ginge and Vicar made a show of holding him down. Bilton shouted at the Marine, who said something into the boom microphone in front of his mouth and entered the ward. As the doors slid open Lock levitated past the Marine and into the corridor, his heart thumping. He made it safely past the two Marines in the middle, levitating fast, and entered a second corridor following Northwood's path. Further down Marines engaged in a room-by-room sweep of the building.

Lock went into aura mode. If he could find Cheena's altered aura Northwood might be nearby, but brick walls and a multitude of desks, chairs, filing cabinets and medical equipment got in the way. He persevered but found nothing. He tried the next floor down and thought he saw her in one of the corridors. There was only one way to find out if she was on that floor. Negotiating a path past a few Marines and some medical staff, Lock drifted down two flights in a stairwell and entered the next floor, setting off a flurry of activity due to tripping more alarms. He moved fast, before anybody thought of PixelRain kit.

Rounding a corner he saw Cheena, Northwood, a Marine commander and another man he didn't recognise. The stranger was a tall, muscular man with a brutally short haircut and a military stance. Northwood stood with his hands on his hips bellowing at everybody. He tore into the Marine commander.

'I'm telling you it's a waste of my fucking time doing a room-by-room sweep. Don't you understand what a Shifter is? It's someone who can re-enter a room after you've cleared it. You understand what a teleporter is, right?'

'Yes, Sir.' The commander eyed Northwood as though he would like to use him for target practice.

'Then for fuck's sake concentrate on getting the anti-teleporter measures up and running. Get your men on that, do it now. Go.'

The Marine commander turned away and barked orders into his radio. Northwood jabbed a finger at the unknown man.

'As for you, I'm holding you responsible for this mess. He's escaped on your watch. You took your eye off the ball and let him get away. Now we've got to get out there and find him again, thanks to you.'

'He can't have got far, he was injured.'

'Yes. He was injured, for Chrissakes. That's why he was here. That's why Cheena spent all that time on him, and she didn't do it just so you could screw up. I told you. I fucking told you, don't think Patuazon is less dangerous just because he's injured. But you knew best, didn't you? You think because your Daddy's rich you can get away with whatever the hell you want.'

Lock had heard enough. He Shifted straight back to Bilton and PC, anxious to get out before the Marines installed the anti-teleporter measures Lock had assumed were already in place, and before his rage at being left for dead by Northwood got the better of him.

~~~~~~~~

After he left the hospital with PC, Ginge and Vicar, Lock didn't go straight to Cali. The route passed Bogota, and the scanner with its information from Patuazon's computer acquired a significance it didn't have prior to Patuazon's escape. Using PC's radio, Lock gave the Embassy the password and pin code for entry and teleported with PC, Ginge and Vicar into the teleporter-designated office. Their arrival set off a loud alarm. Four armed guards entered at a run. One of them checked their identities while the others kept the group under guard. Two security personnel arrived and scanned Lock's team and their equipment to discover what had set off the alarms. The sensor covering Lock beeped.

'You'll have to remove your clothes.'

Lock took off his bergen and his American shirt, which were scanned again and pronounced clear, as were his boots and socks. Nobody else had to remove clothing. Security pronounced the rest of the team clear. They unpacked pouches on their belt kit for equipment to be scanned. Lock had just removed his belt and new combat trousers when Stringer walked in. To Lock's surprise the sensor's beeping reached a crescendo over his trousers, which were bagged and taken away to be searched for electronic trackers. On the way out the guard spoke to Stringer and showed him Lock's clothes and the sensor readings. Stringer glanced at them and nodded.

'Get him some new clothes.'

Feeling self-conscious wearing nothing but a T-shirt that barely covered
~~~~~~~~

essential bits, Lock gave Stringer a brief report on what happened, including what he found in the bunkers, his subsequent heart attacks, the rescue by Northwood and the urgent need to resupply equipment so they could find the antidote in Cali. He asked for more insect drones and control sunglasses, though his helmet visor could act as a method of controlling the drones. Stringer made a call on his phone. Without switching it off, he said,

'I've authorised it. The guys downstairs are working on intel about the Santa Marta research lab. Anything else you need?'

'Have you got an anti-teleporter system disruptor?'

Stringer spoke into his phone, waited and nodded.

'It's on its way up.'

'The trousers were bugged, then?'

'Yes. The same as the ones we found in your shirt and belt in Scotland.'

Dumbfounded, Lock stared at Stringer's grave face. Stringer continued,

'It's a sophisticated design. Technologically advanced, which is why we didn't pick up on these new pieces of kit months earlier. US, according to the boffins. But I suppose you expected that. It looks like your friend Northwood has been bugging your clothes.'

'No, Mike wouldn't do that.' Lock trailed off. He couldn't say anything to defend his friend and be certain it was true. Northwood lied about the timing of the Eagles' presence at Patuazon's villa, and then kept quiet about the capture of Patuazon. Lock couldn't say with certainty his friend was unlikely to stoop to planting bugs, since Northwood had displayed a side of his character Lock hadn't known existed. The belt he received before the trip to Scotland arrived as a personal gift from Northwood. Under standard operating procedures it had been scanned but nothing showed up at the time.

'Where did you get the combats? They're US issue,' Stringer asked.

'From the hospital. The US Navy hospital.'

'That's your answer, then. Sorry to be the one to tell you if you hadn't guessed. We only found the trackers this time because we recalibrated our sensors after discovering the first lot in Scotland when we checked everybody's clothes.'

'That time in Scotland – it's a month since then.' Lock paused, going back over the events of the SAS team being overdosed with Starbirth and the bug that Lianne found at home in the bedroom light. His head whirled. The revelations and discoveries came so fast he could barely keep up.

'If that's how they found the guys in Scotland, it doesn't make sense. The Eagles saved our lives today. They wouldn't target a Regiment patrol in Scotland. Why would they?'

'Your guys weren't the target. You were.'

Lock shivered.

'How do you know?'

'The confession from the barman who spiked the drinks. You were supposed to be at the pub, as you would be normally after a training stint. He had instructions to overdose you with all the Starbirth, but you weren't there. He got jealous over his girlfriend and decided to use it on the other men instead. It was his revenge for them having a good time with his girl.'

He paused, glancing at a guard who brought a new set of clothes for Lock. Behind him a second guard distributed equipment among the troopers. Most of it was standard-issue quality, rather than special forces quality, including helmets, but it would do. After the guard walked away Stringer continued,

'If the barman had succeeded in drugging you, it would've sent you crazy before you died. Massively good publicity for the anti-Shifter movement. They'd have had a field day. A high-level operative goes rogue when he's hopped up on Starbirth. We'd never be given permission for a covert team of AH-4 enhanced operatives. No way.'

Lock put on loose grey chino trousers. Checks on the rest of the group had finished and they re-packed their kit and checked new bergens and equipment, putting on radios and sorting out ammunition.

'Where's the scanner?' Stringer asked. He took out his smartphone. Lock didn't answer, still occupied by thinking over what Stringer told him. More questions than answers went round in his head. Stringer was wrong about Northwood, he was sure of that. He had to be wrong.

'The scanner,' Stringer prompted.

'Yes.' Lock picked it up from his pile of equipment on the floor.

'Maybe you should let the Colombians do this. They can get to the Santa Marta.'

'There's not enough time. They'd get caught in all kinds of red tape. This needs to be done fast, no fuss.'

'Okay. D'you have your computer?'

Lock nodded. Stringer continued,

'Good. You and the guys wait here, switch it on and I can send you floor plans for the Santa Marta and any other Intel we have.' He looked at Lock like a disapproving uncle. 'Let them do the heavy stuff. Save your energy. By the sound of it you shouldn't be doing this so soon.'

'What are you saying, that you've known about this for a month and you haven't told me until now? My family have been at extra risk and you didn't tell me?'

'Your family were never in any more danger than usual. You have many enemies. We had it under control.'

'But you didn't think to tell me about this threat, like I'm some fucking kid.'

Stringer glanced significantly at the rest of the men and the security staff still in place, who were no doubt listening to the exchange.

'They're safe, they're being well looked after. Let's talk about this later, when the pressure's off.' He stalked off towards PC.

'You should've told me,' Lock said to Stringer's retreating back. He left the Embassy with his team a short time later.

Intelligence gleaned by Stringer showed where to find the research laboratory. Lock, PC, Vicar and Ginge, their faces covered by balaclavas or scarves, descended in force on a two-storey outbuilding attached to the Santa Marta hospital. The building was undefended and had no anti-teleporter measures. Getting in turned out to be the easy part. The laboratory director said he knew nothing and the frightened lab assistants, four men and two women, gave Lock blank looks when he demanded to be shown where they stored Mosquera's antidote. They shrank from PC and glanced at Ginge, who kept the director cornered in his office while Vicar stood guard at the main door.

Lock searched the refrigerator and freezer units, but the task was impossible because he didn't know what he was looking for or where it would be stored. Ginge questioned the lab director using the translating machine. He pushed him out of the office and into the lab.

'He knows more than he's saying, I'm sure of it.'

Lock took the director aside.

'Mosquera is dead. You don't have to worry about him. We know he gave you something to work with here, a liquid. Where is it?'

The thirty-something director shook his head and pleaded ignorance. His dishevelled suit stretched tight creases over heavy thighs and a bulging stomach. Wet patches of sweat darkened the material under each armpit. Lock didn't see that. A picture of Nails' worried face and Jimmy's resigned posture flicked into his mind. He wasn't going to let them die too. His patience snapped. He spoke to PC.

'Stay here. Move only if you have to. I'm going to sort this moron.'

He grabbed the director by his arm and teleported with him into the air about eight hundred metres. Lock dangled the man by his wrists.

'For the last time, tell me where you put the substance you got from Mosquera.'

The man's eyes bulged. He looked down in terror and his legs flailed as he tried to wrap them around Lock, who avoided him easily. The director yelled once, a strangled sound cut short by fear. It turned into a huffing sound coming from his gaping mouth.

'Where is it?'

Lock heard no comprehensible answer from the man, so he dropped him. The director plummeted with Lock just behind. After a couple of seconds Lock grabbed the man's arms and levitated, holding them both in mid-air.

'Where is it? Where's the antidote?'

The director's mouth worked, but only gibberish came out, so Lock dropped him again. He would keep on doing it until the bastard talked.

Lock stopped as the awful truth seeped into his awareness. His actions had nothing to do with the wretch slipping from his grasp. The man was only a civilian. Lock could not use his pent-up anger and sense of betrayal on a civilian. The hospital director might not be innocent but he didn't deserve to be terrified to the point of pissing himself, as he had done. It had been many years since Lock acted like that. Despite the rawness of recent experiences he shouldn't be going down this path. Shame overcame him and he tightened his grip on the director's arm, grasped him by the back of his trouser belt and hovered, holding him steady. He wasn't that person who went crazy in his late teens. This was different. He couldn't forget his resolve to keep his emotions in check.

The director sobbed, shouting something between gulps and gasps.

'I can show you. Please, don't kill me. I can show you, please, it's in the lab.'

He knew something after all. Did the end justify the means? Considering how little time Lock had to save Jimmy and Nails, he thought it was worth the risk of giving the director a heart attack. In the future he would hold back. Sometimes extreme physical duress produced results in the short term, but long-term it was inhumane and counter-productive. Lock teleported back to the laboratory. The director couldn't stand up due to a state of shock. He indicated the refrigerated unit storing the antidote and through chattering teeth whispered the number on the glass container to Lock, who relayed it to Vicar. Lock felt PC's eyes on him and turned away, embarrassed.

Vicar came back holding a glass vial with a tiny amount of clear substance in the bottom. It contained hardly enough for one person, let alone two.

'Is there any more?' Lock asked the director, gently this time. The director shook his head and shivered. Lock patted him on the shoulder, a gesture intended as reassuring though it was ineffectual under the circumstances. The man recoiled.

'Let's go.' Lock motioned the others closer, and teleported back to the outer perimeter fence at the US Naval hospital in Cuba. 'I can't stay, I have to check out something at Patuazon's villa.'

'You're not going on your own. Me and Ginge will go with you to watch your back,' PC said. 'There's nowt to do here. Vic can sort it.'

Lock hesitated then nodded.

'Okay. Get ready. Vicar, go in by the main gate. Ask for Colonel Northwood. When you get to Bilton tell him where we've gone.'

Lock used his new phone and got through to Northwood on an encrypted line and informed him about Vicar's return with the Demon weapon antidote and where to pick him up. He cut the connection before Northwood finished asking what the hell was going on. Lock left with PC and Ginge, before Northwood Shifted out and picked him up as well. He had a tunnel to explore at Patuazon's bunker.

CHAPTER 18

The long, sweltering day switched abruptly to a humid night. PC and Ginge put on night vision goggles and watched activity in Patuazon's estate from a safe distance. Lock got ready to explore the mysterious tunnel leading into the mountain from Patuazon's bunker. He took off all his equipment leaving only two pouches on the belt kit, put on his helmet and visor and covered himself with the PixelRain kit they had between them. Patuazon's villa was normally a quiet reflection of the country-club atmosphere to which the drug lord aspired. Now it lay bare with its secrets exposed, just as Patuazon had been exposed after hiding behind a façade of respectability and religious conversion.

Lock couldn't make sense of the chaotic scenes in the darkness. He discerned many auras on the estate and around the villa, some of them firing weapons. The Eagles did not appear to be among them, though Lock's visor could not detect PixelRain kit. He spotted a familiar movement near a group of women huddled by a helicopter waiting on the helipad.

'Shifter, two o'clock, eight hundred metres.'

Ginge swung his sniper rifle round.

'Targeted.'

'Hold your fire.'

The Shifter passed a bag to one of the women and disappeared.

'Looters,' PC commented. 'The hired help get really pissed off when there's no more pay packets.'

The helicopter pilot gestured to the women. They climbed aboard and the aircraft took off, heading west. Lock put on a respirator and pulled down his hood and face veil.

'Going in now.'

He didn't need the net disruptor. Anti-teleporter measures were down, perhaps destroyed by the Eagles or switched off by Patuazon's staff and soldiers. Lock avoided the computer room and the lair, suspecting the Eagles had removed anything of intelligence value. They might have left a surveillance trap in place to see who turned up after they left. Patuazon was too smart to show up, but Lock couldn't be certain of that. A man might do anything when his entire fortune was in danger. He concentrated on differentiating dense masses among grey and black mists, and headed for the bathroom and the tunnel beyond it.

He came out of teleportation a short distance in the tunnel, inside a space just large enough for him to kneel bent forward with the weight of the mountain pressing on his back. He tugged at the poncho. It had creased over his right side trapping his arm. Freeing his hand he took out a torch. By its light he pulled out the last two insect drone bees from a pouch on his belt kit. Grid lines on the lenses gave him something to focus on, but his hand shook as he held the bees in front of him and confronted his fear of cramped caves.

Accessing a command code to orientate them he set them free and the bees sped into the darkness. They flew on automatic sensor pilot without real-time instructions from Lock, feeling their way through the darkness using infra-red vision and sonar, similar to bat sonar. Lock had pre-programmed them to find the largest spaces and move from west to east recording everything they saw. He hurtled out of the tunnel into the night, crash-landed by PC and Ginge before he had time to tell them he was coming, and found himself on the end of a tense unwelcoming committee.

Near the mountain's peak Lock retrieved his bergen and put PC on one side of the mountain and Ginge on the other to wait for the burst of radio signal that would announce the arrival of one or both bees. They didn't know which side would reveal the tunnel exit, or even if an exit could be found, so it made sense to cover both sides. It would take a while. There might be many blind tunnels and dead ends, with reverses and navigation of new routes.

Near the peak of the mountain, mist rose wraith-like from the tree line, a frothy sea sliding upwards. Lock stood in shadow, pondering over a confusing mass of motives and counter-motives. Who should he believe about US involvement, Northwood or Stringer, given the contradictory facts and assumptions? He wondered whether Northwood's lie about Kes's presence at the villa meant he was capable of leaving Lock unconscious, but it didn't make sense in light of Northwood's rescue of the team, unless he wanted to control how much information about Patuazon's lair got back to the Brits. If he contained Lock, the only other friendly to have seen the lair, he could keep a lid on anything to do with AH-4.

Lock was not naïve enough to believe Northwood always told the truth, or even told the truth most of the time, or that he put somebody else's welfare above his duty to his country's interests, but it horrified him to think Northwood was capable of leaving him to die. Perhaps guilt drove Northwood to rescue the team, or he did it because Command requested it and he couldn't refuse. If Stringer had not contacted the Americans, would Northwood have intervened? Lock's anger rose and created a sea of indignation fierce enough to drive away any threat from Maria, or Whittaker, or Bloater.

That last name sparked a jolt of nerves and sent him into another aura scan. He didn't know what happened to Bloater. If both Bloater and Maria lived, as he suspected, it wouldn't be long before Bloater was doing her bidding. The fool didn't even know she manipulated him by her use of pheromones. He was ready for Bloater, and for her.

'One out,' PC's terse message said. Lock lifted Ginge from his hiding place and they settled by PC on his side of the mountain. The grid lines on Lock's visor lit up and the bee transmitted exact coordinates of the tunnel exit. The discovery of a long way out of Patuazon's lair excited Lock. The second bee did not emerge for another ten minutes. Lock ran through footage from the first bee. It was disappointing. No other chambers, just a long tunnel system and three reversals from dead ends.

While the recording absorbed Lock's attention the hairs on the back of his neck tingled. He did another sensory check but found nothing at close range. The uneasy feeling persisted, so when he retrieved the second bee he took PC and Ginge to a new spot in a valley on the other side of the mountain from the tunnel entrance. It was closer to Cali in a sloping farmer's field near some forty-metre high, swaying wax palm trees. PC and Ginge squatted and took up defensive positions among tall crop plants while Lock scrutinised footage from the second bee to see if he needed to send the insect drones back into the tunnel system to have another look.

The centre of Cali, two kilometres away, lit up the horizon like a dull sun. Cars droned on a highway a quarter of a kilometre away on Lock's right, some heading for the north, others going towards Cali. Crickets chattered, beetles flew clumsily and collided with his poncho. The air was still and heavy over the lower levels of the hill.

Something thwapped on Lock's left and PC fell on his side. Lock recognised the familiar, ugly sound.

'Sniper!' He dropped the insect drone and brought his Diemaco round, but even as he yelled, and before he could see where the shot had come from, a second round thwapped on his right.

'I'm hit,' Ginge shouted. PC made no sound. Lock moved to cover Ginge, fastening onto his aura to get them out of the sniper's range. PC had no aura. Lock groped for PC's arm. Ginge groaned and writhed.

Another aura appeared on Lock's left, twelve metres away. Muzzle flash lit up the night as the stranger fired. Lock had his hand on PC's weapon. He raised it and found the trigger on the underslung grenade launcher. The round streaked out and hit the aura. Releasing his grip on PC's weapon Lock levitated. He switched his Diemaco setting from single shot to automatic and fired as he hurtled forwards. He came out of aura mode still firing, saw nothing, went back in and kept firing. He didn't stop until he hovered over the aura. Cobalt tendrils faded and disappeared as if blown away by an invisible breeze.

Breathing heavily, his heart thumping and aching, Lock switched on the torch attached to the Diemaco and still saw no body, only the barrel of a long sniper rifle unattached to anything else. Keeping the empty space covered, he kicked out and his boot touched something solid. The person wore a pixelated camouflage suit.

Lock could barely breathe for horror that he would find Northwood. He knelt and felt his way up the body under the torchlight, keeping his senses tuned in case other auras appeared. He found a camouflaged semi-automatic pistol in the dead man's gloved hand and a massive greyed-out area on the chest where the grenade hit home. Rounds had penetrated the fabric over the chest and the face veil, but as he lifted the veil he saw the face was intact, a round having hit his neck just below the chin. Lock recognised the muscular young man Northwood shouted at in the hospital. Relieved it wasn't Northwood, at the same time his spirits sank. Unlike earlier, when he thought his team had shot one of the Eagles but they hadn't, this time he had shot, and killed, one of Northwood's Eagles.

Lock's bewilderment over the man's motives for shooting at them disappeared when Ginge groaned. Lock levitated back to him. Ginge tried to hold a pressure dressing on a leg wound. His left thigh had been hit.

'It's an in and out,' he gasped. Lock removed his poncho hood, switched on a torch and peered at the injury, exploring it with his fingers. He found an entry wound on the top of Ginge's thigh and a larger exit wound near the groin. Ginge had already lost a lot of blood and was going into shock. Lock pressed down on the wound to stop the blood flow and get the dressing fastened in place before moving him. He glanced at PC, felled by a head shot through his helmet, and scooped up the drone and the case.

Four auras appeared in a crescent shape around them.

'Get down. Get down!' The shouts came from all sides, Northwood's voice among them. Lock's head was exposed. He had no time to Shift out.

'Don't shoot.' He raised his free hand. Had Northwood had really sent his sniper to kill them? If Northwood had wanted them dead they'd be dead by now, so maybe Northwood didn't send the sniper. Ginge took his bloody hand away from his weapon and sank back on the damp ground. Several people shouted at the same time, including Lock. One voice belonged to a woman. He couldn't see anybody, only auras, two large, two smaller. The shouts stopped once they moved closer, leaving the voices of Northwood and Lock.

'Two men down. Your man shot them, he killed PC. This man needs attention, now.' Lock repeated the message over and over.

'Let me see your hands. Lock, let me see your hands,' Northwood said.

Lock raised his hand away from the pressure dressing and let his Diemaco dangle in its chest sling.

'He'll bleed to death unless you get him out of here. Mike, do what you want with me but help him.'

One second of silence prevailed while cars droned in the background, oblivious to the drama unfolding less than four hundred metres away.

'Hand over your weapons. Kes, get them. Cheena, see to the casualty. Orca, check Robert.' Northwood said. A small aura swept forward to Ginge's side and removed his Diemaco along with Lock's weapons. Another one moved to the fallen Eagle. Kes placed the weapons by Northwood's feet. Cheena threw her hood and face veil back before tending to Ginge.

'Robert's dead,' a voice said to Northwood as the other aura returned.

Lock stood up, fists clenched, facing the spot where Northwood's voice had come from.

'Did you send that guy out here? What the fuck is going on, Mike? Why did he shoot us?'

The familiar silhouette of Northwood's head appeared against the Cali glow. He didn't reply to Lock.

'Orca, get Robert. Kes, take this guy here.' He nodded at PC's body.

'This guy? This guy – his name is Paul Copper. He's a good soldier, first class, not some piece of meat.' Lock's voice carried across the field. 'What the fuck happened? You know why, Mike. You tell me why I just lost a good man. You owe me an explanation. Why, Mike?' Lock had fought with Northwood, drunk with him and loved him like a brother, but at that moment he'd never wanted to kill somebody so badly in his life.

'Not here. We've lost one of ours, too.' Northwood looked around. 'Get ready for casevac.'

In a shorter time than it had taken for Lock to get there, Northwood teleported them back to the US Naval hospital in Cuba. Medics surrounded Ginge and wheeled him away with Cheena by his side. Lock removed his helmet and visor and gazed after them as they disappeared through the doors of a surgical unit. Support workers arrived, put the bodies of PC and Northwood's team member on trolleys and covered them. The short, blond man Northwood had called Orca examined the sniper rifle and exchanged a significant glance with Northwood before walking out of the emergency ward with it.

'Your man will be fine, he's in good hands.' Northwood stared at the body of the sniper. He seemed more resigned than sad.

'I had no choice, Mike. He'd just killed PC. He was coming for us. I had no choice.'

'I know.' Northwood's voice was flat. 'Man, this is so fucked up. Come with me, we need to talk.'

'I have to tell the other lads what's happened, first.'

PC's death, so sudden and unexpected, was a huge blow to D Squadron, not just to Lock who felt the usual guilt pangs over being alive while PC was dead. PC had a wife and three kids. He was a committed family man, not one of the guys who had sex with every woman he met. He was popular. Lock's only consolation was that Nails and Jimmy appeared to be much better, in good health, if not in good spirits. Lock left PC's friends and colleagues in dismay, collected his weapons, equipment, bergen and belt kit and accompanied Northwood.

Northwood teleported Lock to an inaccessible beach overlooking the bay. On the far shore, four kilometres away, docks lit up for the night shift. Lock's shock gave way to sorrow and anger. Northwood informed Lock that the recovery of Jimmy and Nails owed everything to Cheena's intervention. She increased the amount of antidote, creating more from the basic template Lock and the team found. It made it harder for Lock to confront his friend in a state of anger, so rather than fire off difficult questions he waited for Northwood to take the lead once they finished setting up electronic security measures to deter eavesdroppers.

Northwood seemed diminished, his manner withdrawn and melancholy. Or perhaps it was shadows hollowing his face as the moon struggled to be seen from behind thin clouds. Lock's eyes adjusted to the lower light. Northwood didn't speak. He squatted on his haunches, looked across the bay and picked up a handful of dry sand, letting it run through his fingers while he stared at glittering spray thrown up on rocks. He stayed like that, brooding, while waves roared and thundered in the distance by a headland. A light breeze from the sea brought with it a whiff of seaweed and a sharp hint of salt. Northwood stood up and scrubbed his hand clean on the back of his pants as if he had come to a decision.

'I'm sorry about PC.'

Lock's tension subsided. A tear trickled down his cheek. He wiped it away savagely.

'Yeah. He was a good bloke.'

'There'll have to be an inquiry.'

'There always is.'

'Let's walk.' Northwood led the way towards the water line where dry sand became firm enough to stroll on without effort. The beach curved under a forbidding, dark cliff that towered over them, a black edifice leaning forward to catch Northwood's words.

'He wasn't somebody I had a high regard for. Robert, I mean, the guy who shot and killed your man. He joined us from the Green Berets as a sniper, very quick, smart, extremely skilled with weapons but not so good at relating to people. Not likeable. He wasn't my first choice for the Eagles.' He paused and kicked at the sand, sending a scoop of wet grit in front of his boot. It landed in a soft heap and his next step squashed it down.

'His family are wealthy. Well-connected, right up there with the politicians, the military and intel people. You name it, they're dug in.'

It confirmed what Northwood referred to in the argument Lock overheard, the mention of Robert's rich Daddy. At least Northwood was being straight about that.

Northwood continued,

'The Eagles needed funding, so the head honchos overruled me. But I always thought he was an asshole. I just never thought he might be rogue. I didn't find anything in his background to give any hint he would go bad.' He paused. 'Just before he shot your men we discovered he'd been using onboard equipment on our aircraft to track your movements. As soon as we found out we were on it. But not in time to stop him.'

'How did he track us?'

'It's pretty sophisticated technology. I'm not at liberty to say.'

'You mean like the tracker you put in the combats you gave me?'

Northwood's surprise seemed genuine.

'No, I didn't do that. We didn't bug your clothes.'

'Somebody did. We found it. It was the same as one in the belt you gave me three months ago. My men and I were attacked because of it, in Scotland.'

Lock couldn't suppress his anger. He glanced at Northwood, gauging his reaction. This time Northwood was shocked. He stopped then said firmly,

'I didn't do that. Look, I can't prove it, but we didn't bug your clothes. We don't need to. I'm not lying to you.'

'Like you didn't lie about Kes being at Patuazon's villa?'

Northwood walked on, clearly annoyed.

'I'm not lying about the bugs, take it or leave it. The combats we gave you, maybe Robert put them there. He had access. He was interested in keeping tabs on you for his own purposes, but I don't know why he wanted you dead–'

'And you weren't interested in keeping us monitored, and getting us out of the picture? The way it looks to me, you didn't want me anywhere near Patuazon's villa once you knew he was involved in supplying AH-4. After you got your hands on him, you had what you wanted, we were just–'

'We don't have Patuazon.'

'No, you don't have him now. But you did. You had him and he escaped.'

Northwood shook his head and said nothing.

'Don't fucking pretend any more, Mike. I heard you. You gave Robert a bollocking for letting him escape. I was right there.'

'What are you talking about? Right where?'

'I was in the corridor, in camouflage. You were there with Cheena and Robert and a Marine officer.'

Northwood didn't attempt to deny Patuazon's capture.

'And you're giving me grief? You're snooping on me and you have the gall to give me hell for lying? There are things I can't tell you because the authorities would haul my ass into court if I did. They'd shove me in a jail surrounded by an anti-teleporter system, keep me paralysed and throw away the key. Of all people, you should understand that.'

'Keeping something secret because of 'need to know' is a lot different than lying to somebody who's taking you on trust.'

Lock felt confused. Northwood was playing double bluff with him, swapping truth and lies like changing jackets. It was impossible for Lock to know whether he could ever trust Northwood. Northwood shook his head, exasperated.

'We all lie. I do it, you do it. It's part of the game, man. Why're you being so stupid about it?'

'No, there's a difference, the reason for lying. We've kept secrets from each other on grounds of national security but we don't lie about the serious stuff, or do things to compromise each other.'

'I have never, ever, done anything to harm you or compromise you. If I didn't care about that, why would I have answered the call to rescue you? Cheena just saved your life, man, doesn't that count for anything?'

Lock stepped in front of Northwood, forcing him to stop.

'You left me for dead. You took Patuazon from his underground room and you fucking left me there.'

Northwood shook his head.

'See, that's where you're wrong. Wait, let me speak before you go off with your paranoia. Patuazon wasn't in the underground room when we found him. We didn't know about it. We don't have that strange sense of yours, the weird radar you have. He was in the room with the computers, the command area, practically dead when Cheena got hold of him. A minute later and he would've been. We hauled him out and that's when his Shifters turned up looking for a fight. We had our hands full and there wasn't time to go exploring. They're fucking maniacs, fight to the death types. I don't know where he got them from but they sure wanted to kill Americans or die trying. The first I knew about you being there was when you saved Kes's life. That's why I was real happy to help you and your guys out when we got the call. C'mon, man, we've been friends for what, how long? How could you think I'd do that? If I wanted you out of the way I wouldn't have saved your ass by letting Cheena work on you, would I? Where's your common sense?'

Lock stood ankle deep in seawater with sand sucking at his feet. He puddled his feet out and moved to firmer ground. His anger dissipated. The contradictions made sense. Northwood's lies about Patuazon had their basis in security secrecy. Lock was right about it being a question of the Eagles getting there first and wanting to keep their discoveries to themselves. He had a lot to think about. Keeping sections of his own life in compartments was easy compared to dealing with Northwood.

Nothing presented itself as clear-cut. He could not differentiate any right or wrong attitude regarding issues of trust or lying, or an obvious path for future friendship, when state secrecy made things complicated. Something fundamental had changed within the friendship. Whether that was down to Northwood or himself he couldn't say. He needed time to reflect, he thought as they resumed their stroll on the beach.

A hip flask was thrust in front of Lock's downturned head, proffered by Northwood's outstretched hand.

'Thanks.' A burning liquid slipped down his throat. It went straight to his head. He choked, gasped and wiped his lips with the back of his hand.

'Bloody hell, what is that?'

Northwood chuckled. 'Some good ol' home brew.'

'Pure alcohol, you mean,' Lock scoffed. His feet floated over the sand. He drifted in a pleasant state of nonchalance, letting his mind wander while Northwood took another swig. Lock frowned as something occurred to him.

'How come Robert used the equipment on your aircraft without you knowing? Wouldn't it take a lot of computer savvy to pull it off without tripping alarms?'

He glanced at Northwood, who arched his back and flexed the tension out of his shoulders.

'Yeah, that's where I think he had help. A lot of help. With hindsight, I think he's had connections to the Decons. That bomb at my apartment, for starters. It had to be partly an inside job. I reckon if we dig deep enough we'll find he's been involved.' He sighed. 'The thing is, you've made a powerful enemy today. That's what I wanted to warn you about. The guy was connected. People will have you in their firing line.'

'Yeah, well, that's not new.'

'It'll be both of us, me as well. His Daddy, Robert Kempton senior, will hold me responsible for his death. I doubt he'll believe his son went bad, even with all the proof we can give him. He'll want revenge.'

'You've got powerful friends, too.'

'Not as many as you might think. It looks like we're not going to find Patuazon any time soon, and without Patuazon we can't deliver on the AH-4, so I'll have even less. That's before you even get to the mess with Robert junior.'

Lock considered the debt he owed Northwood for saving his life and the lives of the Blades, weighing it against Northwood's dilemma. He recalled his promise to share information with Northwood, yet he had concealed his exploration of the long tunnel leading from Patuazon's lair. As if reading his mind Northwood put the flask down and said,

'What were you guys doing out near Cali anyway? Or is that something you can't tell me?'

Lock thought about state secrets, about Stringer, and obligations. Fuck it. He'd explain his disclosure as improving US-UK relations.

'We were checking out the tunnel that runs from Patuazon's bunker, the one that goes under the mountain.'

'What tunnel?'

Lock told him what they had found. 'I lost the first drone, but I haven't seen all the footage from the second one yet.' He pulled the drone from his belt kit, shrugged off his bergen and took out his helmet and visor. Northwood was puzzled.

'We went over the underground room. We didn't find anything – holy shit. It was Robert who checked it out with the sensors. Damn. That's why he went after you. He must've found something. He didn't want you guys spilling the beans.' He trailed off. 'You weren't going to tell me about the tunnel, were you?'

Lock put on his helmet and visor. He shrugged.

'You weren't going to tell me you had Patuazon. Need to know, right?'

'Okay, fair enough. What've you got?'

It took twenty minutes for Lock to go over the footage in detail, during which time Northwood collected weapons from the Naval hospital and returned, removing the electronic security sensors from the beach. When he finished he teleported himself and Lock to the mouth of the tunnel.

They settled into lush undergrowth in a valley on the other side of the mountain separating them from Cali. Northwood set up the defensive sensor system and informed his crew of his new position without going into detail. He said he continued to assist Ghost with an investigation. Lock squatted on one knee on damp ground, flicking away insects. Sweat poured off him due to the abrupt change from cool sea air to low-altitude humidity. It was a minor irritant compared to his growing excitement at what Robert must have seen.

He reached the end of the recording and sat back on his heels, deflated.

'I can't find anything. I'll have to run through it again, and what we got from the first insect drone. I've missed something.'

'Take your time. We got both sides of the tunnel covered.'

'What d'you mean, 'we'?'

Northwood pointed upwards.

'My guys.'

'Oh, right.' Lock assumed Northwood had a stockpile of systems and equipment he could call on at any time, including specialised aircraft, and felt envious. The Eagles' stealth aircraft must be remarkably fast to get from Cuba to western Colombia in less than four minutes.

He transferred footage to his computer so they could both see it. Together they scrutinised it methodically, using all the computer tricks at

Lock's disposal. Northwood's more experienced eye picked out areas of interest, looked at them and dismissed them despite the fact he was still drinking from his hip flask and getting loud. When they reviewed the film from the first drone, which Lock had only seen on the visor, he spotted something.

'That's it.' He pointed at an oblong object the camera had picked up in one of the dead ends and zoomed in. The computer adjusted the angle and definition until it was clearer; it showed plastic drums beside the rectangular object. Lock glanced at Northwood and grinned.

'Are you thinking what I'm thinking?'

'Sure doesn't look like just wads of dollars to me,' Northwood got to his feet unsteadily. 'Looks like I better check it out.'

'No, I'll go.'

'You don't like caves.' Northwood swayed.

'You're pissed. I'll go. You can't even shoot straight.'

'Why would I need to shoot inside a tunnel?'

'We don't know where Patuazon is, or if anybody else knows about the store.'

Northwood snorted and took another swig from his hip flask.

'Patuazon's not in there, I know that. He's not near any tunnels, or caves. He's hiding out somewhere in Amazon country.'

'How do you know that? And hadn't you better lay off that stuff?'

Northwood turned the flask upside down.

'Empty. Happy now?' He attempted to squat by Lock, lost his balance and fell over. 'We know Patuazon isn't in there, because we can see.'

'Maybe you should go back to the aircraft.' Lock did a sensory sweep to see if the noise had attracted any attention.

'It's not nearby. No, we have a viewer. A remote viewer.'

'Oh yeah?'

Lock considered taking Northwood back and regretted not intervening earlier to stop him drinking. The computer created a spatial map of the system complete with dead ends, pinpointing the cache.

'You don't believe me. Well, man, we do have one. He's good. Damn good.'

Lock paid attention after the revelation that the remote viewer was a person rather than a piece of kit. Northwood continued,

'That's how we found Patuazon in the first place. That's how we knew what Robert was up to. Gil can see everything once he's focused. It's amazing; he can give a clear picture. He hooks up to a computer and we can see what he's seeing, and he ain't even down there, he's on the aircraft looking at what somebody else is looking at. Through their eyes. That's how we know that right now Patuazon's in the middle of the jungle. Clever bastard. He's hiding out where there's no point of reference, just trees and water for miles and miles.'

He stopped, aware of Lock's interest in what he was saying.

'Too much pop. I think I've said enough.'

Lock thought he had, too. He wondered if Northwood wanted him to know about Gil, using the cover of alcohol loosening his tongue, or if it was a genuine mistake. Whatever Northwood's motive, it explained things, like his casual remark that the Eagles didn't need to plant tracking devices on Lock. Of course they didn't, if they could get some guy to focus his mind and tell them what he was doing. He didn't ask about that.

'If your remote viewer could see Robert, why didn't you guys stop him before he opened fire?'

Northwood wagged a finger at him.

'No, Gil's not a telepath. It's different. Remote viewers and telepaths, it's different. He wasn't looking at Robert then. He was looking for Patuazon. He can't look in more than one direction at a time. So he didn't know there was a problem. And he can't read minds. It's not the same thing.'

Northwood squinted at the computer screen. 'Hey, that's less than a click into the mountain. Easy.'

'I'm going to send a drone back in and check things out a bit more. We might need some specialised sensors, biohazard clothing, that kind of stuff.'

'Screw that.' Northwood disappeared.

Lock swore. He pushed his equipment back into pouches and fumbled in his haste, cursing as straps got tangled in the Diemaco chest sling. He disentangled it, removed his bergen and put it on the ground, activating a tracking device for later retrieval. Pulling out a small sensor, he connected it by cables to his belt kit and helmet and teleported into the tunnel.

Teleporting into tunnels wasn't an exact science. Northwood could do it with relative panache, but dense rock buffeted Lock back, forcing him to crawl on his hands and knees in places where twists and dips in rock surfaces prevented an easy way forward. The computer used the motion sensor on his belt kit to tell him his location on the map of the tunnel system. He Shifted all over the place, sometimes emerging at dead ends. Sometimes he travelled forward too fast and was thrown back nearly to the tunnel mouth. It felt like a horizontal version of snakes and ladders. A couple of times he thought he heard Northwood laugh.

He ended up doing things mostly the conventional way, as he had when searching for Jimmy in Scotland. A bit of levitation here, a quick Shift there, interspersed with a lot of scrabbling about. The difference lay in the fact that he knew where he was heading, due to reconnaissance by the drones. When he reached the tiny, egg-shaped space with the oblong package and drums, Northwood was already there, holding a torch and sensor over one of the drums. He had prised the lid off the three-litre container, which looked like a plastic paint pot. He turned and grinned over his shoulder as Lock squeezed in beside him.

'This is cosy.'

'Fucking hell, Mike, you idiot.' Lock stared aghast at the open drum. 'That could be anything. It could be a bio-weapon.'

He pushed his computer into a pocket and tried to squash past Northwood to put the lid back on.

'No way, man, this gadget recognises all the components of AH-4 bar one.' He gave Lock a dig in the ribs. 'We've hit the jackpot, man.'

'Okay, well, let's get the fuck out of here.' Claustrophobia was biting – and it had sharp teeth. There were four drums. 'Let me through. I'll check they're not wired to anything nasty.'

'I already checked. They're clean.'

'Yeah, I'm going to double-check.' Lock couldn't get further past Northwood's body. Northwood thumped the lid back on the container, nearly giving Lock a heart attack, then pulled it towards himself.

'Mike, you fucking maniac, stop. You'll get us killed.'

Northwood pushed it towards Lock.

'Share and share alike, yeah? One for you.' He reached forward for the next one and pulled that out of position. Lock nearly fainted.

'Mike, if you don't stop fucking moving them, I swear I'll slot you right here.' He jammed the barrel of his Diemaco in Northwood's ribs even though he couldn't get his finger on the trigger.

'One for me.' A small red light blinked on something attached to the two remaining containers and a whining noise rose in pitch.

'Oops,' Northwood said.

Lock knew he wasn't the one teleporting. He sped in a heady mix of rainbow colours, bouncing around and shaken like a ball in a bucket. Northwood stopped. They were squashed inside a fissure in the rocks. Before Lock could open his mouth they were off again. Four more stops, four more uncomfortable places, and Lock was convinced he would die inside the mountain in a never-ending display of Northwood's exuberant teleportation. He regretted ever thinking he would like more of the experience. It was only one degree short of terminal insanity. When they popped out of the mountain like a champagne cork from a bottle, they hit the ground so hard Lock felt as though he'd been slammed into a brick wall.

He crawled onto his knees, shaking, and switched on the torch on his Diemaco. Northwood lay on his back a couple of metres away, drunkenly struggling to turn over onto his side.

'Mike, you mad bastard.' Lock laughed, then remembered to do a sensory sweep around their area. A puff of air came from the tunnel mouth, bringing with it a faint odour of cordite.

'Whooo! Massive, man.' Northwood grinned, pulling one of the two containers into his grasp. 'We made it.'

'No thanks to you.' Lock picked up the second container and noted that it was intact.

'Time to go home, don't you think? Break out the beers, have ourselves a party,' Northwood rose to his feet unsteadily.

'I'll make my own way back.' The thought of more of Northwood's Shifting all the way to Cuba made his stomach churn. Besides, he had to make a detour to drop off his paint pot at the British Embassy in Bogota.

CHAPTER 19

It took Jimmy a while to work out that the state of his groin area, which changed whenever Cheena walked onto the ward, had less to do with his unbridled libido and more to do with her. He guessed something wasn't natural judging by the way Bilton reacted. He'd never thought of cold, remote Bilton having any sexual feeling about anything, except possibly other men, and to see him go scarlet and try his level best to avoid Cheena gave Jimmy some sly amusement. He enjoyed seeing the confusion Cheena's appearances caused Nails and Vicar.

He found the solution by accident when he visualised sipping an iced whisky. He imagined the cold liquid pouring over the hottest part of his body and how that would feel. As if by magic the throbbing stopped and his bothersome member shrank like a burst balloon. In fright he peeked a look at it to make sure it hadn't disappeared altogether. During Cheena's next visit he allowed it to reach its normal dimensions when in a state of excitement before trying the iced whisky effect again. He felt gratified when he achieved the same result even if he didn't know how he had achieved it.

He had difficulty making sense of the myriad voices of his body except for those of the larger organs. Blood cells, hormones, neurons, all chattered at an incomprehensible rate that resembled an audio recording played at twenty times the normal speed. When Cheena put her hands on him, the voices tripled in volume and intensity. She lingered over him as if she knew there was something different about him compared to Nails. Even the latest casualty, Ginge, didn't occupy her time so much. Jimmy indulged in a fantasy that Cheena fancied him, but she wouldn't engage in conversation and he had to rein the thoughts in when they brought back his erection.

The fantasy passed the time between interminable blood tests. It kept his wrist supple and kept away any sad thoughts connected to the loss of Mick and PC. He hadn't known them for long, but he respected PC for his calm manner and professionalism and saw the devastation suffered by Nails, Ginge and Vicar. Like the other lads, Jimmy postponed his strongest feelings for when they were back in the UK and could hold a proper wake in honour of fallen comrades, raising some money for the bereaved families at the same time. As for Cocaine Chris, Jimmy felt a detached nod towards somebody who had been a liability, until he recalled that Chris got him and

Bilton out of the shit in Bogota.

Cheena came back and Bilton made an excuse to leave. She looked frayed by lack of sleep. Ginge gazed at her adoringly, fidgeted while she laid hands on his neck and arm, broke out in a sweat and the second she pronounced him all clear he excused himself from the ward and from her. Sniggers from Vicar and Nails followed him to the glass sliding doors.

'Don't take too long in there, mate, you'll go blind,' Nails called out. Ginge gave him the finger and disappeared.

Cheena took longer over Nails, who went scarlet when she told him the abscess had cleared, much to Jimmy's amusement when he remembered the joke they'd played on Nails by telling him he had a parasitic fish up his arse. When it came to Jimmy's turn he gazed at her smooth-skinned face and her beautiful and unusual eyes that were different colours, the blue one like a piece of sky trapped in human form and the brown one like deep chestnut. He kept his gaze away from her body. It worked for a few seconds and then he struggled.

While she concentrated, he took a swig of cold water with the intention of seeing if that helped with the visualisation process. As he swallowed, instant cooling turned into something else. Electrical charges zapped between nerve fibres, and crossed synaptic junctions like bolts of lightning. Cells squeezed and altered shape. The upper sphincter of his oesophagus relaxed. A smooth wave swept the water down his throat, with microscopic sparks telling cells to clear the way. Jimmy heard it all. He felt as though he was plunging down a water chute in an electrical storm accompanied by a thousand voices. When the liquid hit his stomach like a tidal wave, he gasped. The intensity of it left him amazed by voices that amplified and issued orders. He felt as though he sat in the hub of a control room.

'What's wrong?' she asked, taking her hands away. 'Are you okay?'

Jimmy paused while the cells in his stomach and other organs did a Highland fling in his abdomen, but the experience was dwindling.

'Put your hand back.' He raised the glass. She shook her head.

'No, I've seen enough.'

Jimmy tried not to let his disappointment show. Anxious to keep her there and to persuade her to lay hands on again, he said,

'How's it looking?'

'You're doing good. You and Nails.' The reassuring smile on her face was not echoed in her eyes.

'Bullshit.' The word tumbled out before he'd considered what to say. She sharpened up. Nails stopped talking to Vicar and listened without looking at her. She said,

'No, really. You're okay. It's just that there's a slight abnormality that shows up in your blood tests.' She smiled, turning away to leave. 'It's nothing to worry about.'

'What kind of abnormality?'

She hesitated.

'Look, if there's something wrong we should know.'

She turned back. 'He's okay.' She nodded at Nails. 'There's no evidence of any nanomaterials. The antidote did the trick, it's wiped them out.' She lowered her voice and turned her back on Nails to avoid being overheard. 'You don't have nanomaterials in you as they first appeared. That's the good news. But in you, for some reason we can't explain yet, they've altered. They're still there, just in a different form. They don't seem to be doing anything harmful, but we're not sure what they're doing. We don't know why the antidote didn't wipe them out.'

'So, what, they're just lurking there?'

She nodded.

'Dormant, maybe. Perhaps dead. We need more blood work to be sure.'

The door opened and Bilton came in, followed by Harford.

'Rise and shine, lads, we're going,' Bilton said. 'Get your kit together, we're out of here in ten.'

Cheena moved to leave. Jimmy grabbed her forearm, a move that startled both of them. A frisson of something more than sexual desire passed between them through their eyes and through the intimate physical contact. Cheena looked shocked but she didn't pull her arm away.

Jimmy said, 'You're saying those things could become active again? They might kill me?'

She put her other hand on his, sending shivers down his spine. The move didn't go unnoticed by the others, including Northwood who entered the room after Lock, though everybody pretended they hadn't seen it.

'No, I don't think they have that nature any more. We just don't know what's going on. I can't tell you any more than that.' She smiled, and Jimmy wanted to kiss her and take her somewhere quiet where they wouldn't be seen. She continued,

'Don't worry about it. If you're concerned, or if anything changes – ' She took her hands away and whipped out a biro from her sleeve pocket. 'Get yourself some of these tablets.' She wrote on his bare forearm. 'Call your commander, go through the channels, and we'll get back to you if we need to.'

Jimmy looked at his arm. It was a phone number. He pulled his sleeve down to cover it.

'Okay, thanks.'

'I'll get the medical records,' she said to Bilton, and walked out of the ward. Hot and cold chills ran through Jimmy's body. He couldn't look at anybody else. He trembled and his balls ached, but what he felt for Cheena was more than physical. His being ached for her.

~~~~~~~~

'Well, it wasn't a complete cock-up.'

Stringer assessed the operation in his concise and understated manner. He got up from his seat in the Command and Control room at the Embassy and stretched his thin legs. It had been a long debrief of accounts covering what each man had done, with less information coming from Stringer.

Lock stopped playing with his biro and tapped it hard on the table.

'It isn't a cock-up. We got some AH-4. We stopped Patuazon and made a significant dent in the supply line of Starbirth. For all we know, we may have stopped Starbirth for good.'

Stringer conceded the points but Lock felt that Stringer wasn't concentrating on what had been said or done but was thinking hard, absorbed in the task of sifting the intelligence into mental files, and looking for the best way to present it to his superiors.

'Are we going to search for Patuazon?' Lock asked.

'No. The US and the Colombians will follow up. We're out of the picture.'

He made a loose fist, a gesture that Lock recognised as suppressed anger. Stringer brightened and revealed that the US Embassy had made overtures about acquiring part or all of the British supply of AH-4 and he allowed himself a little smug smile that creased the corners of his eyes. Lock imagined him enjoying the moment of gaining a rare upper hand over his counterparts in the CIA. As for leaving South America, Lock had no regrets. Everything had changed since his previous visits and the place held too many sad memories. Patuazon and Maria Zamora joined a long list of enemies and he doubted he would cross paths with either of them again.

Throughout the debrief Lock took the role of quiet observer. He hadn't revealed his knowledge of the Eagles' remote viewer. He'd been considering his position regarding the Ministry of Defence and the Secret Intelligence Service. There was a lot he wasn't happy about. His relationship with Stringer and being kept in the dark over matters that were vitally important were uppermost in his mind, and he came to some conclusions. He hesitated, reluctant to tell Stringer about the remote viewer, thinking it betrayed a confidence from Northwood. He weighed that against what Northwood would do had he been in Lock's position, and with insight into Northwood's personality, Lock had no doubt Northwood would feel obliged to tell his superiors, without any hesitation. He might even relish it.

A security concern influenced Lock's decision. The SIS would be furious to discover their most secret actions were wide open to the remote viewer, should he choose to look in on them at an inappropriate moment. They would be even more upset to find out that Lock knew about him and even
~~~~~~~~

knew his name, but hadn't informed them. Lock saw how the knowledge would make the remote viewer a target for agencies world-wide. Stringer would turn it to the advantage of the SIS, bargaining to be privy to what the remote viewer saw, perhaps even using some of the AH-4 as leverage in return for information.

When Lock did tell him, leaving out that Northwood had been drunk, he imagined gears moving, wheels turning and the sharp mind already at work. Stringer's glee was evident.

'That's very indiscreet of Northwood. It's quite frightening how unreliable the man is.'

That sentence, though Stringer didn't realise it until later, heralded the sound of a closing door. Lock saw the truth in it but regarded the assessment as another example of Stringer's attempts to undermine the friendship between himself and Northwood, and he resented it. Stringer went on to the subject of the new team and assured Lock he would be leading it. Lock's mind was made up. He knew which direction he would take regarding his allegiances.

'No.'

Stringer gave him a blank look as though he couldn't believe the response.

'What do you mean, no?'

Lock sat back in his office-style chair and crossed his legs languidly under the table.

'I mean it. No. I'm not doing it.'

'You're not serious, surely? It's a joke, right?'

'It isn't a joke. I don't want it.'

Stringer's eyes narrowed. He wasn't used to people saying no to him, especially Lock.

'What's brought this about?' The question was quiet, with the undertone of a snake about to strike. Lock decided not to tell Stringer the whole truth.

'Because you said yourself, Patuazon has sent Demon weapons and AH-4 to the war zone in the Middle East. You found evidence in his computer files that he's trained militants as Shifters, armed them with Demons and sent them to fight there. He's sent them to kill Americans and British because of his hatred of the CIA and us. To me that's more important than leading a team in the UK.'

'Okay, but if you had a team with more people like you, you could be effective. It's better than just one.'

'Too much time will be wasted training them. You've seen what the Demons can do. We could lose hundreds before the team is ready. The MoD will send me out straight away, and I want to go. I want to help stop the Shifters.'

Stringer looked at Lock as though he was his worst enemy. He argued the case for not going, and fought for the new team. Lock argued vehemently for the opposite. They went round in circles until Stringer realised it was impossible to dissuade a determined man. He gathered his papers and said,

'You realise what this will mean? You recall our last conversation about your situation, and the security surrounding your family?'

'Is this a threat?'

'Of course not.' He tapped his papers into a neat pile. 'Take some time, and think it over. You've been through a lot, you're due some time off. Don't make any final decision yet.'

He brought the meeting to a close and left the room. Lock headed off to meet Jimmy, who wanted a private chat. He would let Stringer stew for a while and see what he came up with. Stringer's need to be in command of Lock far outweighed Lock's need to be allied to Stringer. Lock knew how to play their game to his own advantage. He would work with the SIS through Stringer on matters other than a new team because he needed access to their databases of intelligence, but it would be with eyes open. He called his own shots.

He took Jimmy to the roof of the Embassy, where they wouldn't be disturbed. Other stately government buildings baked in the sun, punctuated by trees. The distant buildings slouched away into low-rise tenements and the trees disappeared. Lock stood with Jimmy in the shade of a brick maintenance tower and listened.

'I'm not a bloody taxi service, mate,' he said in answer to Jimmy's query about being ferried back to Cuba before they had to leave for the UK. 'You don't look ill to me.'

'Well, there's something going on. Every time I eat or drink there's this shouting match inside me, especially if it's anything from the canteen, processed food, that kind of stuff.'

Lock was unsympathetic.

'Don't eat it, then.' Seeing the exasperated look on Jimmy's heavy-browed face he said bluntly,

'Look, mate, I'm not trivialising what you're experiencing but I'm not stupid enough to be played. You're wasting your time with Cheena. If the Eagles operate like the CIA, she won't be able to have any kind of liaison with you. Even if both of you are keen to get together, she won't be allowed. If she did, she could get kicked out.'

Jimmy leaned against the shaded wall and stared at the rooftops. Lock knew Jimmy's stubbornness made him determined to get his own way. He thought about his conversation with Stringer and the futility of trying to dissuade somebody hell-bent on making his own destiny, and he changed the subject and asked about Jimmy's strange body sensations, listening with interest to the tale of the hallucinations and the flight from the village field hospital.

'Not that I can remember much,' Jimmy said. 'The lads told me it was a right fuck-up. They reckon Chris was high as a kite, took too long to land and made himself a nice big target.'

Lock winced at mention of the failed casualty evacuation.

Jimmy continued, 'They wouldn't have needed the chopper if it hadn't been for taking Mick's body out. They would've bugged out into the jungle.'

'Yeah, it's a tough outcome.' Lock paused. 'Hang on. You said, Mick's body?'

'Yeah. He was already dead. Died just after being stitched up, poor bastard. If he'd been alive it would've been different.'

'He was dead before the casevac?'

Jimmy looked at Lock as though he was the kind of slow-witted boss he had to endure rather than get along with.

'Yeah, that's what I said.'

A weight lifted from Lock's shoulders. He wasn't responsible for Mick's death. Lock listened until Jimmy reached the end of his account. He looked at his watch and said they should get back, ready to Shift out. Jimmy frowned.

'Is Bilton going with us?'

'Yes. Why?'

'He was strange after we were taken to Cuba by that Eagles guy.'

'So I heard. What happened?'

'He said a lot of things that didn't make sense, he was out of it. A lot of religious stuff, mumbo-jumbo. Things like how we were all spirits, how everything was alive. We couldn't get anything out of him except that. He thought he was some kind of god.' Jimmy chuckled. 'Even when PC slapped him, he didn't come out of it. He doesn't even remember being slapped. He remembered me calling him a one-armed wanker, though.'

He stopped as if he'd gone too far, but Lock was laughing. It was odd that both Bilton and Patuazon had a religious conversion. There might be a link between Starbirth and delusions of grandeur. Jimmy asked,

'When we Shift, do our cells get scrambled? Y'know, like in those science fiction films? I was thinking maybe that's why Bilton went psychotic.'

Lock shook his head and chuckled.

'No, that's not it at all. We don't lose mass in that way. The scientists think there's another dimension besides this one and we Shift between them. That's where the name Shifter comes from. I suppose now there are so many people doing it, it will help with research, because it's amazing how each person's experience of Shifting is different. Yours won't be the same as mine, though there are some things that are similar, like when we brush through things or around them in this dimension.'

'Like buildings and things?'

'Everything. Clouds, rain, storms, insects, all those things.'

'What are those little ones that kind of suck at your energy and feel crackly?'

'Insects and birds, mostly. Bats, too. The bigger the animal, the more you feel it.'

'D'you think they ever feel it?'

'No, not as far as we know. Years ago the boffins had me teleporting through areas where they placed soldiers they'd 'volunteered' for the experiments. The soldiers didn't know what it was for, of course. They weren't aware of anything at all.'

'It must be fucking odd Shifting through a plane full of people.'

'It's more likely that we go around them. You know what trees feel like to me? Tissue paper. They feel soft and feathery. Bricks are crunchy, like layers of crisp lettuce leaves. Rocks are different, though. You feel them more.' His face darkened and he gave a shrug as if throwing off memories. 'You never get stuck in rocks or anything else, though. When you come out of teleportation you get shoved away, because your body can't occupy the space that something else has taken.'

'That's a relief. I'd hate to get stuck in a hill.'

Lock's phone beeped. He took the message while Jimmy waited. Lock smiled as he closed the phone.

'We're wanted downstairs.'

The message was an urgent one from the MoD asking when he'd be back and could he sort out somebody called Barfing Brad. The man was causing havoc in the UK, making people sick while stealing from them. He had made the Prime Minister very ill during a burglary at the PM's country retreat. Cheeky bastard, that Brad guy, Lock thought as he followed Jimmy down from the roof, though on reflection he could just picture the private smiles on the faces of many people at news of the PM's discomfiture.

EPILOGUE

A fortnight later, in mid-January, Maria Zamora sat in the grand lobby of an upmarket office block in New York, pretending not to notice as another young man took up position by a marble effect column. They tried to look innocent, but they always failed. She could spot them a mile off, even when the cut of their suits hid shoulder holsters. Her gaze swept across metal coffee tables and emerald green easy chairs and stopped at a woman by the water stand who chatted to a man in his early forties.

Kempton was pulling all the stops out in a show of strength, using women operatives as well as men and covering a broad range of age and appearance. Maria wondered how many more he'd send out of the side entrance to cover the front. Would it take seven or eight before he felt safe enough to see her? He had three security cameras trained on her, and those were just the ones she could see. She kept her hands in view. It wouldn't do to catch a bullet from somebody twitchy enough to make a move.

A confident young man in his early thirties appeared from the elevators. He walked towards the receptionist, leaned over and whispered something while pointing at the visitors' book. She responded with a smile and a brief nod. He sauntered across the marble floor to Maria and spoke courteously.

'Miss Zamora? Mr Kempton will see you now. This way, please.'

Maria followed him to the elevator. The receptionist gave her a sidelong glance and pressed a button on her desk. Maria felt other eyes watching her every step, and wasn't surprised when a man and a woman entered the elevator before her. Kempton used good people: not too close and positioned so they wouldn't shoot each other in crossfire. The surveillance pair chatted all the way up, pretending to ignore her.

The doors opened on the thirty-sixth floor. She stepped onto plush blue carpets in front of a set of glass doors. The letters, Kempton and Company, were written in gold. Her escort smiled at her as he held the door open. The second it clicked shut she heard the sounds of weapons being drawn. She looked round at hands holding machine pistols aimed at her head and chest, and sighed as she raised her hands.

'Really, folks, is this any way to greet a lady?'

'What do you want?'

Her escort's smile disappeared, revealing the steeliness that was there all the time.

'What makes you think I'll tell you instead of Mr Kempton?'

'Where's your teleporter? Where's Whittaker?'

'He won't be coming. He doesn't know I'm here. This is a private matter.' She smiled in a show of bravado. 'If I wanted to attack, do you think I'd be so brazen as to come here alone, using my own name and wearing these heels? I want to talk to your boss. I have a proposal to put to him.'

The escort stared at her. She was puzzled: her pheromones didn't work on him. He turned his head and nodded, listening to what she assumed was a hidden radio receiver. A woman with a smart business figure walked over. She wore gloves and held a scanner.

'Assume the position and keep your hands on the wall.' She scanned Maria, keeping her own hands well out of reach.

'She's clean.' She threw a pair of thick gloves on a counter top. 'Put these on.' She said, and gave Maria a contemptuous look as if dismissing a tramp. 'This way.'

Two men kept their weapons trained on Maria's back as she followed the woman down the corridor. The woman ushered Maria into an executive office. Maria's swift visual reconnaissance took in wooden wall panelling and a sumptuous Oriental carpet. Behind a carved oak desk a grey-haired man with keen eyes studied a computer screen. He rose to his feet, motioning her to a large easy chair.

'Have a seat. I'm sure you'll understand if we don't shake hands.'

'Quite.'

Kempton's men took up positions by the door, keeping their weapons on her. She eased into the chair, smoothed her short skirt over her thighs, crossed her legs and regarded him steadily, guessing his age at around fifty. He looked every inch the ex-military type Paul, her late partner, had described. Kempton sat down.

'Please stay seated for your own safety, Miss Zamora. There are laser weapons in this room locked on to your bio-signature. I wouldn't want an accident should you make any sudden movements.'

'I wouldn't have assumed otherwise, Mr Kempton. I'll come straight to the point. I'm sure you've heard of the British Shifter, Lock Harford. Five days ago, he killed one of your employees by the name of Paul Armstrong.'

Kempton tried to hide it, but she caught the briefest muscle tension in his cheeks as he clenched his jaw in surprise.

'I don't know who you're talking about.'

'Cut the crap. We're talking about my boyfriend. He worked for you.' She paused. 'You didn't know he told me? He told me everything, Mister Kempton. I know the names of every whore you ever bedded, and your home address.'

Kempton inclined his head with the chess player's hint of a smile. She was making her opening gambit and he would have his chance to respond or block. His demeanour and recovery impressed her.

'I'm here to offer my services in his place,' she said.

'What makes you think I'd employ a Starbirth addict, Miss Zamora? In fact, what makes you think you'll leave here alive?'

Maria didn't hesitate.

'I believe you're too astute to pass up an offer before you've heard it. I'm sure Paul told you all you need to know about my abilities. I didn't use Starbirth, I used AH-4. There's no problem with addiction. But I didn't come here to argue about that. I have a proposal for you.'

'Go on,' Kempton's burgundy leather office chair creaked as it tipped back to a comfortable angle.

'You and your organisation have a long reach in the US, but you don't have anybody taking care of business in Britain.'

'There's no need.'

'You're willing to let Harford get away with killing one of your employees?'

Kempton stared at her. She tried to read beyond the cultivated mask, but it gave no clues to his thoughts. She wished he would stop covering his mouth with his fingers because it disguised his facial language.

'Why would you help us?'

She caught the curiosity in his voice and played her ace, appealing to his vanity.

'Protection. Your organisation is gaining strength by the day and these are difficult times. I want a guarantee of my safety in return for my services.'

Kempton took his hand from his lips. His non-committal gaze didn't stray from her face or eyes.

'You're hurting. It's never a good idea to mix personal with business. People make mistakes. I don't employ people who are careless.'

'I can assure you, my personal aim in avenging Paul's death won't compromise any operations of yours. The two overlap. Sooner or later you'll want Harford out of the way as part of your programme of cleansing. It serves both our interests to take him out.'

He laughed derisively.

'You want me to finance an operation so you can get revenge on your boyfriend's killer? Ain't gonna happen.'

'There are other ways I can be useful. I can infiltrate any organisation and get rid of anybody creating problems for you, – all totally deniable. Give me a chance to show you my professional abilities by getting rid of Harford. As for finance, I'm not greedy. The amount you paid Paul will suffice. Personal transport won't cost you a cent, I have Whittaker for that. He gets paid out of my salary.'

'I'll let you know.' He stood up to indicate the discussion was over. 'Please keep the gloves on until you leave the building, Miss Zamora. For security purposes.' He tensed as she leaned forward and reached across his desk for pen and paper. She scribbled something down.

'My number, Mr Kempton. For the next twenty minutes only. Let me know what you decide.'

When the door closed behind Maria, an adjacent one opened and a short man entered briskly.

'Why didn't you just kill her while you had the chance?'

'She's a transmute, for Chrissakes. A rarity. She could be a useful asset.'

'No way. She's too dangerous, she knows too much. Get rid of her.'

'Harford killed my son. Remember him? One of the Eagles. Our undercover operator. An eye for an eye, Nathan. Besides my son, Paul was one of our best operatives, the only guy I knew who could track Shifters without using machines.'

'And he had a big mouth.'

'They were both killed by Harford.'

'Look, I'm sorry about your loss. I know it grieves you. But you said it wasn't a good idea to mix personal stuff with business. The board will never accept it. We'll lose our backers if we take her on.'

'This is good business. I think you'll find they'll come around when they realise what they're getting for their money. Cheap at the rate too. The time is right. Now is the time to hit Harford, while he and the rest of the Brits are unprepared for the different kind of warfare they're facing. The man owes me, and I intend to see he pays.' Kempton picked up his phone and dialled the number Maria had given him.

Glossary

.50 cal – heavy automatic weapon usually helicopter or vehicle mounted

5.56mm – standard size calibre bullets as used mostly by Western forces

7.62mm – calibre of rounds used in AK-47 rifles

A&E – Accident and Emergency

AK 47 – assault rifle

Bergen – military rucksack, often very heavy, sometimes weighing over 45 kilograms

Blades – unofficial name applied to SAS troopers, a reference to the winged dagger cap badge

Boss – unofficial SAS name for the commanding officer

Bug – covert surveillance device

Bugging out – tactical retreat, usually under fire

Burst transmission – sending a radio message by means of a burst of radio signal

Call sign – designation given to team member over the radio, using military phonetic alphabet

Casevac – casualty evacuation

CAC – Command and Control

CIA – Central Intelligence Agency, United States

COBRA – Cabinet Briefing Room A, also the people who meet in the room

CO – Commanding Officer

Comms – communications

Credenhill – headquarters of the SAS in Herefordshire

CS – gas used to disable opponents, tear gas

Decons – decontaminators

Diemaco SFW – Special Forces Weapon semi-automatic assault rifle, uses 5.56 bullets

DPM – Disruptive Pattern Material, military combat camouflage clothes

Eagles – US team of enhanced-ability operatives

Evac – evacuation

ERV – Emergency Rendezvous

Explorer – four wheel drive Sports Utility Vehicle

FAC – Forward Air/Artillery Controller

Fire Team – assault team

Firm – unofficial name for the Secret Intelligence Service, also known as MI-6, Military Intelligence 6

FOB – Forward Operating Base

Gas station – petrol station

GPMG – General Purpose Machine Gun

GPS – Global Positioning System

Go firm – stay put

Grunts – unofficial name for infantry soldiers, US terminology

Head Shed – unofficial name for SAS headquarters

Holo – hologram/holographic image

ID – identification

Leatherman – multi purpose tool

Lancero – South American Special Forces man

Levitate – ability to move using the power of thought, flying

LED – Light Emitting Diode

LUP – Lying Up Place

Maglite – torch

MI5 – Military Intelligence 5, officially called the UK Secret Service

M-16 Colt Commando – military semi-automatic assault rifle, used mostly by Western forces

MP5K – small semi-automatic assault rifle used by SAS

MoD – Ministry of Defence, United Kingdom

MTP – Multi-Terrain Pattern camouflage combat clothes

NAV – Nano Aerial Vehicle, a very small unmanned aerial vehicle used for surveillance

NVG – Night Vision Goggles

Op – operation, military mission

OP – Observation Post

OSA – Official Secrets Act

Oxbridge – Oxford and Cambridge Universities

Pindar – tunnel and bunker system under the Ministry of Defence

PM – Prime Minister

Ranger – US Special Forces soldier

RAF – Royal Air Force

Recon – reconnaissance

Regiment – SAS

RPG – Rocket Propelled Grenade

Round – bullet

SAR – Search And Rescue

SAS – Special Air Service, also known as 'the Regiment'

Selection – arduous process of selecting men to serve in the SAS

Sig Sauer – pistol using 9mm rounds

SIS – Secret Intelligence Service, UK, also known as MI-6 and The Firm/Office

Shifter – teleporter

SF – Special Forces

Stan – nickname for Afghanistan

Squadron – name of the troop sections of the SAS – A, B, D, G squadrons

SUV – Sports Utility Vehicle

Telekinesis – ability to move objects through the power of the mind

Telepathy – ability to read the thoughts of other people

Teleporter – person who can move through space/dimension through mind power

Thermal imager – equipment that can detect people or animals using body heat detection

Tooled up – armed with weapons

Transmutation – ability to alter own physiology and that of others through mind power

Trooper – soldier serving with the SAS

UAV – Unmanned Aerial Vehicle

UK – United Kingdom, Britain

US – United States

Vauxhall Cross – headquarters of the Secret Intelligence Service in London

Walther PPK – pistol using 9mm rounds

Zero – radio designation of military commander

ABOUT THE AUTHOR

J M (Jackie) Johnson is a freelance writer and e-book author based in the United Kingdom (Britain) and is a member of several online writing groups. She has published four books in the Starbirth science fiction and fantasy series and is writing the fifth and final book in the Starbirth series:

The Starbirth Assignment Part One (2011, revised, edited and updated 2016)

The Starbirth Assignment Part Two (2011, revised, edited and updated 2016)

The Shifter Dimension (2012)

Shadow Team GB (2015).

J M previously worked in a professional capacity as a podiatrist in the National Health Service and currently lives in Shrewsbury.

She belonged to a spiritual group for eight years, following a particular spiritual lifestyle and making three pilgrimage trips to India. Her involvement fostered a lifelong fascination with powers of the mind. Two decades later she had the opportunity to join a group run by British ex-Special Forces and was a civilian member for six years. During that time she did extensive research into the military and intelligence worlds. These background experiences helped in the creation of her books.

J M Johnson comes from a family of artists and authors.

Website and Twitter

Websites:
www.starbirthseries.co.uk
www.starbirthassignment.com

Twitter: @lockharford

62503290R00169

Made in the USA
Lexington, KY
09 April 2017